THE TAMING OF THE ROSE

The
TAMING
of the
ROSE

RJ CIVILE

RJ Civile
rjcivilewrites.com

Print ISBN: 978-1-7367562-3-2
eBook ISBN: 978-1-7367562-1-8

Printed in the United States of America

Cover design by Andrea Ho
Book design by Meighan Cavanaugh

First Edition

Author's note: This is a work of fiction. Names, characters, businesses, places,
events and incidents are either the products of the author's imagination or
used in a fictitious manner. Any resemblance to actual persons,
living or dead, or actual events is purely coincidental.

To my rose, M, my Love,

though we are separated in this world

you still live inside of me, always in my heart,

no matter your own heart's indifference—

you remain my only regret.

That kind of hurt—who could endure such heartbreak?

Such was your love for me at one time...

I am at last tamed.

ACKNOWLEDGMENTS

The author wishes to thank the following individuals for their contributions, encouragement, insights, support, and time: Jacqueline Rush, Brenda Milley-Wintrode, Eileen Gorman, Julia Nalpathamkalam, Denny Massilli, Maureen Rooney, Andrea Ho (Cover), Meighan Cavanaugh (Interior Design), Brooks Becker (Editor), Jeffrey Tisman (Jeff Tisman Photography), Alicia and Lucia Civile at LACE Photo Media,

—and M: *The Taming of the Rose* would never have been written without you. Your presence gives it beauty, class, dignity and grace. It is much more than my book—it is your book as well. It is our story book love—alas, without the story book ending...

And he went back to meet the fox.

"Goodbye," he said.

"Goodbye," said the fox. "And now here is my secret, a very simple secret: It is only with the heart that one can rightly see; what is essential is invisible to the eye."

"What is essential is invisible to the eye," the little prince repeated, so that he would be sure to remember.

"It is the time you have wasted for your rose that makes your rose so important."

"It is the time I have wasted for my rose—" said the little prince, so that he would be sure to remember.

"Men have forgotten this truth," said the fox. "But you must not forget it. You become responsible, forever, for what you have tamed. You are responsible for your rose..."

"I am responsible for my rose," the little prince repeated, so that he would be sure to remember.

—ANTOINE DE SAINT-EXUPERY, *The Little Prince*

CONTENTS

PART TWO

MOIRA, HIS PRECIOUS ROSE

PREFACE

How would I describe what kind of novel *The Taming of the Rose* is? It is a novel that takes place in the decade of the 1970s, purposely structured in two parts. Part One is written in an anecdotal style to present glimpses of people, places and events as a broad backdrop to connections and influences that set the stage for the second part of the novel. Part Two narrows the focus to four main characters whose inner thoughts and feelings are revealed to the reader in a deliberate shift of the narrative.

With that understanding in mind, I would describe the novel in the following way. It is a coming-of-age story that commemorates growing up in a small town with families that treasured common, traditional values and shared aspirations and dreams for their children and their community. A significant portion of this community had at its center a church, grammar school and two high schools that provided a firm foundation built on promoting faith and family. This novel is a homage to small town life, simple and majestic in its resiliency to rise up against the turbulence and tribulation that is a part of our daily existence by remembering what really matters in life: God, family and friendships. This novel is a recognition of the men and women, whether parents, teachers, clergy, coaches, scout leaders, family members, and friends— the spiritual brick and mortar that comprised those church and school buildings—who helped to shape that community and forge memories worth remembering. It is a novel that celebrates the sanctity of first love's beauty, innocence, and purity; and is a tribute to the character of Moira, who is the true hero of the novel.

As is the reality of life's experiences, there is some bad that is inevitably mixed in with the majority of what is good. It is a story that includes betrayal of trust by those so entrusted; disappointment in those who failed to protect when they had a duty to do so; and the violation of sacred truths and ideals by those who looked at truth and idealism through a prism of cynicism. Ultimately, it is a story of survival and forgiveness, and the never-ending power of faith, hope and love. It is my hope and desire that those in our lives who proved themselves untrustworthy, who forsook their duty, and who harbored cynicism, have found redemption in embracing fidelity, duty, truth and the ideal.

What it definitively is not, is a novel written in anger or vindication. As its author, I can clearly state that accusation, bitterness and resentment are not a lasting part of the story nor should it be construed as such; though there may always be a certain hurt, or sadness perhaps, that remains in remembering some of the past events in our lives…but that is the price one pays for being tamed.

It is my wish that the reader finds *The Taming of the Rose* an endearing, enthralling, funny, inspiring, touching, thought provoking, and worthwhile experience.

RJ Civile
The Taming of the Rose—1/14/2021

LISTENING IN

The other boys turned on the road that led to the swimming hole. Dominic watched until he lost sight of them. He caught the familiar scent of the grown-ups' cigarettes as the smoke drifted on the breeze. He quietly made his way unnoticed over to where they were sitting around the table engaged in serious grown-up conversation on the back deck. He sat down on the top step, leaned his back against the iron hand-rail to listen and observe.

The dynamic of the conversations was fairly straightforward. One of the grown-ups would start by making a comment and the others would opine. Or one could ask a question of someone, and then the person asked would respond and the others would agree, disagree or relate it their own personal tale. The topics ranged from people to politics to events to ideas. There was beer, wine and scotch for those who drank, and soft drinks for those who didn't. All the men smoked, either cigarettes or cigars, and most of the women smoked cigarettes but not all of them. Some of the grown-ups didn't really say much but Dominic could see in their facial expressions, especially in their eyes, the feelings and thoughts that spoke louder than words. He observed the stolen glances exchanged between certain grown-ups at the table while listening to someone express their view or narrate a story. From what Dominic could tell, these exchanged glances betrayed the fact that the person talking was either full of shit or was a dumb-ass. It was usually when Uncle Marty was talking. He spoke slow and monotone, kind of how he walked as well. He worked in a plant in Jersey City and Dominic's father, Salvatore, referred to him as lazy, and it was the brother-in-law that Uncle Tino called a cheapskate. His wife, Lena, Salvatore's sister, was a loud and obnoxious woman who brow-beat her husband and contradicted everything he said.

Uncle Phil was the quiet uncle. He didn't say much, usually just sipped a can of beer and smoked his Pall Mall Red cigarettes while offering the occasional chuckle in support of someone's posit or an "aw com'on with that" as a form of challenge to another view. He was married to Aunt Giovanna, who was the aunt most like Aunt Clara. Giovanna and Clara, like Aunt Lena, were sisters of Dominic's father. These were all traditional Italian women, with gigantic wet-nurse breasts, who went to the coiffeur once a week to have their hair set and whose husbands would drop them off at church on Sunday mornings and then circle back forty-five minutes later and wait for them with the car running. They bore the children, cooked the meals, cleaned the house, performed in bed, prayed the rosary, smoked their cigarettes, and avoided scandal. Dominic's father, Salvatore was one of nine children: he and his two brothers (Gerry and Louie) were the only living brothers. A younger brother—Angelo, had died at age twelve of leukemia. All five sisters were still alive. Aunt Clara's was the usual meeting place as she was the most gracious and accommodating of hosts, and her house was somewhat central to everyone else. At these gatherings, Uncle Tino usually chimed in with the perfectly timed sarcastic comment that tickled the funny bone or broke up the occasional momentary tension. He would sometimes slip in a risqué or off-color joke that would provoke a verbal reprimand from Aunt Clara. Friends of Aunt Clara who lived nearby or cousins of the grown-ups would make appearances as well, and that would spark more robust discussion with differences of opinions.

It was 1970. Nixon and Kissinger, the war in Vietnam, taxes, the economy, jobs, the unions, race riots, the college protests, the feminists, who was gay, who was a leftie, who was a patriot, drugs, the state of the education and schools, pornography, abortion, the coloreds, the Puerto Ricans, who was going to win the Super Bowl, who was the greatest Yankee of all time, the liberalization of the Church, what this kid or that kid was doing or not doing, food costs, the price of gasoline, coffee, cigarettes, and booze—all were discussed from a purely working middle class perspective. This was the WW II generation, the fighting spirit of the Great Depression who bore the scars and military tattoos and memories of sacrifice, loss and resiliency like badges, not of honor or pride, but of defiant survival. They lived for today and paycheck to paycheck not out of frivolous spending habits but because they knew that tomorrow wasn't guaranteed—nothing was for that matter. They fought to put food on the table, roofs over their heads, and clothes on their kids' back. They were beholden to the government, to their employers, to the Church and to their conscience. They didn't have the luxury of idleness or temptation—not if they were going to live their lives with dignity and respect and most of all, make ends' meet.

"A man who can work with his hands—he and his family will never go hungry."

Dominic recognized his father's voice. His father was a thinking man—never had the opportunity for a real formal education but of everyone sitting at that table, he was the only one who managed to get through high school, before joining the US Navy and serving in the Pacific. His father would listen to the others present their personal views and then he would offer a pearl of wisdom based on his own experience. His father disdained laziness. He also knew his father was a man more than familiar with disappointment, heart break and unrealized dreams. His father was a man's man—not a smidgeon of femininity in his whole being. His hands were like calloused paws made of hickory wood and covered with sandpaper skin. He also knew his father was an insecure man who felt his lack of formal education made him less than others. As a matter of fact, all of them sitting at that table admired—no, were in awe of—anyone with an education, especially a professional degree. Doctor, lawyer, engineer, professor, even politicians who they all mistrusted—one of these roles and you were a success in their eyes and given great deference. From Dominic's perspective, there was formal education and there was life experience education. For example, his Uncle Tino was shrewder than any college man—and a helluva lot tougher with a jab-hook—and-cross combination. You didn't mess with Tino. Nor Phil, Sal or even Uncle Marty who served in the Marines in WW II. They were all cut from the same fabric of the streets, of the rough and tough tumble of scrappy neighborhood life. Most of them ended up working in one of the manufacturing plants, either on assembly production lines or driving trucks. Some of them, like Aunt Clara, managed to save money and take advantage of company-sponsored thrift savings plans, and vested in pension plans that combined with modest living, afforded them some security in later years.

"FOR CHRIST SAKES, can you get to the point already, Marty!" snapped Uncle Tino. He rubbed out a Camel cigarette and grabbed another out of his pack. Dominic could see Uncle Phil's slight smile and amusement in his eyes through the cloud of cigarette smoke.

"I'm getting there, I'm getting there, Tino. You can't rush a good story," answered Uncle Marty. Dominic had to say the man was unfazed by any criticism. He sure had thick skin.

"Oh, is that what this is? Jesus, I already forgot what the hell you're even talking about!" Uncle Tino was relentless.

"Alright, Tino, let him finish already," Lena came to her husband's defense. "But hurry, Marty, before we have to beat the ending out of you." She was brutal too.

"Ok, I will. So, then I deliver the load to the airport cargo terminal. I give the terminal manager the transport paperwork. He's a real grease ball, starts busting my chops about…"

Dominic's eyes darted around the table. Uncle Tino was shaking his head in disgust as he brought his hand up to his mouth, his cigarette tucked between his middle and ring fingers, he drew the tobacco in and then blew it out his nose, looking at Uncle Marty. Aunt Clara was having a side bar with his father while the others all just waited for Marty to finish.

"....and that's when I said, screw that. Climbed back into the truck and told the guy to take it up with the dispatcher, I'm outta here." Uncle Marty picked up his glass of Dewar's and soda and took a big gulp.

"That's it?" asked Uncle Tino incredulously.

"What? Yeah, that's it, Tino. That's a true story. That's how it happened."

"What the...I'm not saying it's not true or not...I'm saying who gives a fig—Marty, I swear if you're ever waste our time with a story like that again, I'll ban you from here for life, you understand me?" Uncle Tino's exasperation cracked the others up.

"Lay off him, will ya, Tino!" shouted Lena.

"Aw, com'on," Uncle Phil managed through his half coughing, half chuckling.

"Hey Sal, you remember Eddie Gigante from the neighborhood?" asked Uncle Louie.

"Yeah, Eddie the Giant. He was a big guy even when we were kids. We all used to hate playing marbles against him. He wouldn't let the game end until he won. And nobody said no to Eddie." Sal clipped the end of an El Producto cigar and started to light it. He shot a look at Uncle Tino and then at Aunt Clara.

"Did you hear he died?" Uncle Louie continued.

From everyone's reaction, Dominic realized this bit of news and the story behind it was going to more than make up for Uncle Marty's tedious tale. The name had caught Dominic's attention as he recognized the name from having heard the grown-ups talk about Eddie the Giant from other conversations.

"So how did he die?" asked Uncle Tino.

"He was a bad man," commented Uncle Phil, which for Dominic was significant since this uncle was a man given to few words, especially ones that were judgmental.

"Nah, he wasn't so bad," countered Dominic's father. "He was a tough guy, no doubt about it. But he was fair."

"He was a hoodlum!" snapped Lena, "I never understood what Daisy saw in that man."

"She saw six and a half feet of one hunk of a man. A big hunk. I'm sure everything was big on Eddie," added Aunt Giovanna. The others laughed.

"He had a massive heart attack," Louie answered.

"Really? Figured he'd go out a different way," mused Tino.

Phil nodded in agreement. "Yeah, seems too serene an end for his kind."

"You knew him pretty well, didn't you Tino?" Marty figured it was safe to speak again.

Tino shot Marty a look to assure him it wasn't. "Ah, I was a member at the Italian Social Club as was he. I ran into him now and then back in the day. But I wouldn't say we ran in the same circles or were friends. But Sal is right, Eddie wasn't all that bad. There were games, and those games had rules, and if you wanted to play the games, you had to follow the rules. Eddie just enforced the rules." Uncle Tino stamped out a butt and lit another.

"I never liked him," insisted Uncle Phil, "and he wasn't so big. Not really. All in all, he was weak when it counted most." He looked at Sal. "Right, Sal?"

Dominic looked over at his father, who was staring down at his feet, lost in momentary thought. His father reached for the cigar in his mouth and tapped the grey ashes into the ashtray stand next to him.

"You know what I'm referring to, Sal." Phil sat back in his chair, keeping his eyes on Sal, anticipating a response.

"What's Phil mean?" asked Clara.

Dominic's father let out a sigh.

"It was strange. Phil's right. Something happened and Eddie was never the same after that. Or maybe he was never the same in my eyes, anyway."

"What happened?" Clara swatted away a fly that had landed on the faded green tattoo of an anchor on her favorite brother's forearm.

"It happened when we were living in the apartments on Winfield Avenue, across from the small park there, right before we moved out and bought the house in Rosedale. There was a hodge-podge of tenants there—Irish, Italians, Poles, Portuguese, Puerto Ricans, even some Jews. Mostly vets from the war. The landlord didn't care much about who was renting as long as they paid the rent. And I guess most of us as first-generation Americans come back from fighting overseas together, well, we were indifferent to culture differences at that point. We all just wanted to get on with our lives. Just glad we had made it back in one piece."

Dominic scanned the facial expressions of the grown-ups sitting there, each lost in their thoughts remembering another time; maybe thinking of where they precisely were and with whom in recalling the period his father was speaking to; his father continued.

"A number of the guys there placed bets with Eddie. He would come around once a week, usually Monday, sometimes Tuesday to collect from the losers and pay any winners. I'd run into him once in a blue moon, depending on when he showed up and if I was around. There was one tenant that I always had a funny feeling about. Couldn't actually explain it but he kind of gave me the creeps. He had been a tenant before any of the rest of us had arrived. He was an older man; I think he might have been retired. Kept to himself, never really stopped to chat with anybody though he would say hello if your paths crossed. He was very pale looking and thin, bony hands, gray haired with psoriasis, with that far away stare in his eyes. Like I said, creepy looking."

He reached for his can of beer, took a swig and then picked up his cigar.

"There were a number of young kids who lived in the apartments.

They'd play in the park across the way or sometimes in the street in front of the brownstones. Sometimes when I came home from work, they'd be out there playing and I would spot this guy watching them."

"Watching them?" asked Aunt Giovanna.

"Not looking after them, no. I mean like staring at them. He'd be in the alley way, out of view, or he'd be sitting up in his apartment window on the third floor that faced out that way. The moment he saw me taking notice of him, he scampered away out of my sight. One time I pretended to keep walking up the steps to enter the building, waited a minute or two, and then jumped back down and looked up at his window and he'd be back staring. And when he spotted me, he again leaned back out of view."

Dominic noticed as some of the grown-ups shifted in their chairs, some leaning forward, listening more intently as his father spoke. Others reached for their cocktails or another cigarette. Uncle Phil sat back in his chair, slowly smoking his Pall Mall. It was obvious he knew the story.

"There was one boy in the apartments, he was sort of slow, didn't talk much, awkward. The other kids neglected him. They weren't necessarily mean to him but he couldn't keep up with the games they played so just left him out. Usually, he would just sit on the stoop and watch. Sometimes they sent him around the back of the building to grab the garden hose and had him pull the hose around so they could get some water after running around and working up a thirst. A few times I noticed that the old man from the third floor would be standing down by the stoop, watching the others along with the boy, talking with him. I didn't think much of it. The boy seemed to appreciate the company."

"This story going anywhere," interrupted Marty.

"God damnit, zip it, Marty, or so help me God, I'll…" Tino glanced around as though he was looking for something to throw at him.

Aunt Clara frowned at Marty while Lena hushed him and smacked him in his arm with the back of her hand.

"Go on, Sal," Aunt Clara motioned to her brother.

Dominic watched his father take another sip of his beer and then re-light his cigar before continuing.

"It was a Monday, around dinner time. I had just cleaned up and sup-per was almost ready. I could hear the kids in the hallway coming in from playing outside. I decided to do a quick trash run. I passed some of the kids in the stairwell on my way down to the dumpsters out back of the building. Coming out the side entrance, I bumped into Eddie. He liked to hit the fellas up at dinner time as he figured they'd be home and be quick to make the transaction so as to not draw attention from the wives. He gave me a smile and a salute as I nodded hello to him. He was making his way to wait in the entrance to the basement area in the back of the building, opposite from where the dumpsters were. Each tenant was given a small space for storage in the basement. The coal bin for the supply that fueled the furnace was also down there. As I walked over to the dumpster to drop off the trash, I noticed a couple of guys milling around, shooting the breeze and having a smoke, obviously waiting for Eddie. Eddie had reached them and wads of cash were being handed to him and new bets placed. By the time I closed the dumpster and turned to walk back to the apartment, Eddie was standing alone.

> *"How ya doing there, Sallie?"*
> *"Good, Eddie. Can't complain. How about you—calling it a day?"*
> *"Just one more and I'll be on my way."*
> *"Ok, tell Daisy I was asking for her, have a good night."*
> *"Thanks, you too, Sallie."*

"I was walking along the side of the building back to the side en-trance when something in the alley way caught my eye. I paused to see if I could make it out. I drew closer to the object and realized it was a baseball cap. I picked it up and figured one of the kids must have dropped it when they had come in for dinner. As I held it, I thought it looked particularly familiar. Then I remembered where I had seen it before. The slow kid who sat out front—it was his. I'd seen him wearing it before. I figured I could hold on to it and give it to him next time I saw him or just place it in the vestibule near the mailboxes out front. As I turned to go back in, Eddie was walking toward me, rapidly walking, almost a half-hearted jog. He had a look on his face I had never seen before. It had gotten darker and the two-sided flood light above the side entrance illuminated the alley way and Eddie's face. Eddie didn't say a word when he passed me and his eyes made momentary contact with mine and I saw it. I saw that look—that look of haunted fear in his eyes; the kind of fear that Eddie was used to seeing when someone was looking back at him—looking back at him as he hovered over them, threatening to inflict a beating on them that they would never forget; maybe even the look he's received right before he's felt a man's last breath on his hands. He didn't say a word. And just like that he was gone."

Sal stopped talking. Dominic watched the other grown-ups but no one made a move. After a moment, Uncle Marty cleared his throat and was likely going to say something but Uncle Tino's icy stare caught his eyes and he just shifted in his seat and dropped his head. Dominic looked at his father and waited.

"I was trying to figure out what had happened to put that kind of fear into Eddie. Had he lost the mob's money? Did he take a bad bet? Did the cops finally turn the tables on him? But I was thinking it had to occur within what, five or ten minutes of when he was in his not-a-care-in-the-world mood. I looked toward the back of the building and then started to walk in that direction—when who turns the corner quickly and comes out of the shadows but the guy from the third floor. He stops abruptly when he sees me before him, guess he wasn't expecting to run into anyone. I have to admit, I jumped back when he suddenly appeared out of the dark as the sun had disappeared by now. His eyes were frantic as they glared into mine and then dropped to my hands. They seemed to widen when he took note of the hat I was holding. Suddenly he bolted past me—he almost knocked me over as I stood there a bit dumbfounded. I guess my mind was racing so fast, trying to piece together the unfolding events. The kids in the hallway—Eddie—the dumpster—the hat—Eddie—this guy—the hat...I started to slowly walk toward the back of the building. I swear as I looked down that alley way it suddenly appeared like it was as long as a football field and every step forward that I took the length became another ten yards longer. I was holding the hat out in front of me like it was contaminated and I didn't want it to touch anything on me. As I was nearing the end of the building, another figure turned the corner, emerging from the shadows. It was the slow boy. He nearly walked right into me. We both halted as soon as we spotted each other. I was standing over him as he looked up at me. His face was pale and his eyes withdrawn and frightened. His arms hung listless at this side. His appearance was disheveled, his shirt and pants in disarray. He didn't say a word as his eyes dropped from mine and settled on his hat. He stuck his hand toward the hat, and I handed it to him. And then he gave me a slight smile as a streak of a tear fell from each eye, and he walked past me and I heard him enter through the side door."

Dominic surveyed the grown-ups as his father stopped speaking. Uncle Tino blew out a steady stream of cigarette smoke from his mouth as if he had been holding it the whole time Dominic's father had been talking. The others had scrunched up faces, their eyes ranged from intensified scrutiny to wide-eyed surprise. No one, not even Uncle Marty, stirred. No one seemed to even be breathing. They were waiting.

"I turned around and went up to the apartment. I put on a clean shirt and went down to the precinct. I told the desk sergeant what I had seen, leaving out any mention of Eddie. They sent a couple of men down to investigate. Never sure what happened with that. But the following week, I saw an "apartment to let" notice on the wall in the vestibule and it was for a third floor flat. Never saw that guy again. And the slow boy—never saw him anymore either."

Dominic watched as the grown-ups reacted. Some sat back, others sat up straight with a puzzled expression, while Uncle Tino and Uncle Phil remained motionless, just smoking. He guessed they were all trying to figure out if that was the end of it, as he was. They didn't have to wait to find out.

"Not too long after that night, cousin Daisy sent me a message that she wanted to meet for a cup of coffee at the diner. She didn't say why but I figured I already knew what it was about. It was early on a Saturday morning, before the breakfast crowd hit. When we met there, she asked for a booth in the corner. There weren't many others in the place, just a few patrons sitting on the stools at the counter. We sat down and the waitress brought us coffee and menus. She made some small talk and then cut to the chase as was always her style. She wanted to talk about that night and what had happened. I told her that I didn't see or know much. She wasn't impressed.

"You're not talking to the cops here, Sallie."

"I know that, Daisy. But I don't know what you want from me."

"Eddie appreciates you keeping him out of it."

Sal nodded, took a sip from his coffee, and looked out the window, watching the various delivery trucks begin their trek around town or up to the turnpike.

"You want to know what Eddie saw?" she finally asked.

"If you want to tell me, sure. But don't feel you have to." Sal was curious but didn't need any more trouble in his already troubled existence.

"Eddie was waiting in that doorway, for his last pay-off. The guy was already late and Eddie figured he was a no-show and he'd catch him the next day. As he went to go, he thought he heard something from the basement. It was a strange sound—at first, he thought it was some rats scampering around. But then he thought he heard like a hushed voice, angry, and then a whimpering sound. He shook it off and turned to go but then he heard more of a commotion and a silent shrieking sound and a hushed accented voice telling someone to shut up. Eddie quietly made his way down a few steps and then bent over to have a look around. It was dark down

there and at first, he didn't see much. But then he heard those sounds again and it drew his attention over by the coal bins. He took another step down and now could see a faint light coming from over by the bins. He squatted down to get a better look at what or who was over there. And that's when he saw it."

She paused to drink some coffee. Her voice had been cold and steady, very matter of fact.

"Saw it? Saw what?"

"He saw a young boy bent over the lower side of one of the empty coal bins. Behind him stood a grown man, with his hands on the boy's backside."

"How did he see this in the dark?"

"There was a lantern turned down low resting on a post to the right of the bin. He could see the boy's skin reflecting in the light, and the man's hands clutching the boy's hips. The boy was obviously experiencing excruciating pain as the man standing behind him thrust himself forward against the boy."

"What the...." Sal was speechless.

"Yes, I know. Sick bastard."

"What did Eddie do?"

"That's the strange thing, Sal. Eddie didn't do anything. He froze. He just froze up like he was paralyzed. I would have expected him to go down there, tell the boy to get out, and then break that bastard's neck. But he didn't. He didn't. Instead, he went to step backwards up the narrow stairs and tripped over his feet and fell back. The man heard him and realized that there was some one there. He pushed the boy aside and turned out the lantern and waited. Eddie turned himself on the stair and scrambled on all fours to get out as fast as he could. That's when he passed you in the side alley."

Sal sat back in the booth, his arms falling limp at this side. His stomach was churning as his thoughts imagined and then chased the images from his mind.

"And then?" he asked.

"And then I think you know the rest as well as anyone. It appears the bastard's left town. You going to the cops assured that."

"Or maybe he recognized Eddie and didn't want to stick around for an introduction."

"Could be."

"And the boy?"

"Your guess is as good as mine. After the cops spoke to the family, they disappeared as well. Not sure what the arrangement was."

"Arrangement?" asked Sal puzzled. His cousin looked back at him with a steely gaze. "Forget it. I don't even want to know." Sal finished his coffee and snatched the check. "You ready?"

Daisy went into her purse and pulled out a cigarette case and an envelope that she placed on the table. She lit up a cigarette, inhaled, and blew the smoke out of the corner of her mouth, down and away from her cousin. She put her hand on top of the envelope and pushed it over to her cousin.

"We're almost done here. Take this. Eddie wants you to have it. He appreciates that you kept his name out of it. And he appreciates that you won't ever discuss it with anyone. Anyone. Understood?"

Sal pushed the envelope back to his cousin. "Eddie didn't have to send you here to tell me this. And I don't need that." He tapped the envelope and pulled his hand back.

"I think you should take it. Heaven knows you could use the money."

"Thanks, but that's alright. Eddie doesn't have to worry about me. But I'm sure he knows people see and hear things and people talk."

"Yes, but they don't know for sure and no one believes or trusts them anyway. But not Salvatore Manterra. The man of integrity and honor. Loyal and trusted patriot. Honest to goodness Sallie. It's different if you're the source."

"You can tell Eddie that I'm deaf and dumb. I'll be moving anyhow. I need to go now." He stood up, looked at the check, stuck his hand into his pocket, pulled out some coins and placed them on the table next to his empty cup. "See you around, Daisy."

He paid the check and left.

Dominic eyes were opened wide. It was a scary tale and the fact that it was a true one made it scarier still. The grown-ups snapped out of their collective trance and there were murmurs and heads shaking as what they heard sunk in and they considered the chain of events.

"See, he was a real chicken shit," muttered Uncle Phil.

"Yeah, I guess you never how someone's going to react in a given situation," added Uncle Marty. Once in a blue moon, even he could flash a little insight.

"Dominic? How long have you been here? Why Dominic have you been sitting there all this time?" It was Aunt Clara who discovered his presence.

"Why aren't you with the others?" asked Uncle Tino.

"I didn't feel like going for a swim," he answered.

"The silent listener. We'll have to take roll call next time," remarked Aunt Giovanna.

"Get along, Dominic. These conversations aren't meant for impressionable ears," his father sounded annoyed.

Dominic stood up and looked across the field. The other kids were making their way back from their swim. He walked over to meet them.

PART ONE

DOMINIC, HER LITTLE PRINCE

I.

RITES

I t always occurred in late August—like intoxicating ether clandestinely seeping in from an unseen time-release capsule circling from above. It would furtively make its way in circuitous routes in and around the heart and soul and senses of the unsuspecting. Introspection and digression were its symptoms, leading to sustained periods of anxiety and longing. Unlike early April's cruelest intentions that inevitably would pave a path to rebirth and hope as barren landscapes burst into collages of colors and scents, August ushered in the forlorn. Perhaps it is the predestined fate that every viable birth lends itself to certain death. Then we struggle to fill the span in between those two markers with what we refer to as a life, all the while our time is running out. Such is the burden that late August brings with nature's final thrust of its palette of wondrous hues before she dulls and fades and cracks like a fair maiden's lips as they are kissed by passing time. September arrives abruptly with indicators both natural and manmade that signal a shift, and with it she brings yearnings and yawns. Dominic referred to it in his private conversations with himself as an internal vacancy—an empty feeling of inevitable alienation. A feeling of solitariness that over a prolonged and sustained period produced a state of being that was best identified as numbness. At first it was foreign to him—as he could do

nothing but feel every experience through an emotional prism that reflected an innate ability to empathize. This was real passion—true passion, and the curse of poets, saints, and lunatics. Then the engineers
were called up in time to dig the moats and construct the high walls that
provided protection and defenses, and the ultimate emotional sanctuary
that was needed. Yes, an emotional hermitage of sorts was established–a
place safely remote, invulnerable, impenetrable-and terribly alone.
Dominic could feel everything while feeling nothing. Self-preservation
and detachment manned the towers and were his relentless guardians. It
was apparent to Dominic that the bridge had been raised too late and
the few vermin that had crossed over carried with them a strain of a
plague so unmercifully cruel that it would not kill but only torment. It
was irony most treacherous—trapped inside the hiding place with the
very thing you were hiding from to begin with—all wrapped up in hurt.

DOMINIC SAT STRAIGHT UP in the leather chair. He was looking out
the window but not really looking at anything in particular. He was
only looking to avoid seeing anything. His eyes searched for something
to focus on, to come to a stop and rest upon some item, some place, some
spot, some something—anything. But there was nothing, and his eyes
would return to his hands. He would either have them clasped in front
of him, palms up, or resting one on each knee, quietly tapping out some
work of Beethoven or Mozart that provided some semblance of relief.
Eventually the silence would be broken with an inquiry:
   "Is there anything you would like to talk about, Dominic?"
   Dominic lifted his head to acknowledge he had heard the question.
His expression, however, remained blank, which had been the extent of
it, thus far. But this time—this time he had buckled. And she saw it. It
was ever so slight a gesture that anyone would have been permitted to
miss it, but to her credit, she did not. And in turn, her recognition of it
was met with a matched subtlety. Her left eyebrow raised itself ever so
delicately in response to Dominic having ever so slightly tilted his head

to the right as he gazed at her as if actually seeing her for the first time. She momentarily held her breath, waiting, hoping...

Dominic saw that she was very pretty. Her dark brunette hair extended just below her shoulder, full and thick. He could imagine her taking the length of one side in her long, thin fingers and pulling it across her face, to smell its fragrance or feel its softness against her skin. Her dark-blue satiny blouse was snug over what he suspected were ample breasts accented by her thin waist. She wore a grey skirt that rested right above the knee, her legs smartly crossed. From across the short distance that separated them, Dominic caught a hint of eau de parfum. Her hands were folded casually in her lap as she sat straight and tall in the corner of the cushioned settee. Between them was a low glass coffee table upon which rested a closed shorthand notebook with a wire binder at the top, a fountain pen set on top of it.

The initial sessions were with an older gentleman with glasses and a graying beard and mustache that were neatly trimmed, who wore dark suits that reeked of cigarettes and conventional cologne. He was followed by a younger gentleman who sported turtleneck sweaters and had really white teeth and skin bearing the ravaged consequences of battling adolescent acne. He may have won the war but it was a pyrrhic victory for sure. Both men had sat across from him in their respective offices with pen and pad in hand poised to write—what exactly, Dominic couldn't figure out. Thoughts? Observations? Images? His words? In the end, he wore them down with the unbearable sound of his silence.

And now this nearing middle-aged damsel with a scant touch of makeup and no jewelry had been called in to break the impasse. *A femme fatale, perhaps—it only makes sense*, thought Dominic. He decided to peek through the balistraria.

"What do you want to talk about?" he asked quietly.

She exhaled as she sought to catch herself and not convey any hint of being caught off guard. They had briefed her on Dominic's background and history, and, of course, she had reviewed his file. But cutting through the clinical assessments, the evaluations, the observations, the interviews and other information her conclusion was, textbook analyses aside, that he basically remained an enigma. But now there was a breakthrough, and she didn't want to screw it up.

"We could talk about anything you like...would you like to talk about how you're feeling? *How are you feeling?*" as soon as the last question left her lips, she immediately kicked herself in her thoughts. The words rang so hollow in her own ears.

Dominic smiled. He recognized it was the first time he had done so in about fourteen months. But he wasn't going to let her off easy. He sighed and thought, *Aw com'on, you can do better than that?* He shifted in his chair and placed his left elbow on its arm and then rested his head on his hand.

She let out a breath, his tone and body shift relaxing her, and she smiled back at him and responded with an acknowledgement of understanding the message of his body language. "You're right, that sounded so lame. Let's try this again, shall we?"

Maintaining his current sitting position, Dominic nodded his head. She stood straight up for a moment and paused, as if she were an actress in a commercial collecting herself for "take two"—all that was missing was the clapboard and camera loader.

"My name is Cheryl Lynn. I see that your name is Dominic, but do you have a preference?"

"What's in a name? A rose by any other name would smell as sweet," quoted Dominic.

"From *Romeo and Juliet*. Is that a favorite play?" asked Cheryl with a naturally inquisitive manner.

Dominic straightened up in his chair, sitting back and stretching his arms out on the arm rests. "It is...one of my favorites, yes. My mom used to say that one to me, when I was growing up."

Cheryl simply nodded her head. This was a start and she wanted to proceed at his pace.

"Are we out of time?" asked Dominic, looking at the small round desk clock set on the table in between them. The back of the clock was facing him.

"No," she softly replied, not bothering to look at the clock, "we still have time." She wondered if her eyes had wandered to take a look at the clock while he was responding, but she was certain they hadn't.

"OK, good. Nick is fine, Cheryl Lynn. Is that your first name?"

"Actually, that's my first and last name. You can call me Cheryl."

"Oh, alright. Well, Cheryl, what's new in your young and exciting life?" asked Dominic.

Cheryl smiled broadly. "I don't believe we're here to discuss me, Nick."

"Well, I just thought maybe, you know, you needed someone to unload on, and hey, I'm all ears," Dominic smiled back.

"I appreciate that, Nick, that's very thoughtful of you but we really need to focus on you, and talk about...*you*."

Dominic nodded his understanding. He scanned the room until his eyes found what he was searching for. "Do you think I could have a cup of water, please?"

Cheryl sat up. "Oh, certainly." She turned to look around the room. "I think there may be——"

Dominic stood up and walked over to the water cooler in the corner of the room, pulled down a paper cup from the dispenser, filled it, and then returned to his chair.

"Have you ever read *The Little Prince*, Cheryl?" he asked as he sat down.

"Yes, a long time ago. I'm fluent in French—I minored in it in college. I actually read it in French. Why do you ask?" Cheryl was curious.

"Do you remember what rites are?" asked Dominic.

"Rights? As in civil rights?"

"Rites as in r-i-t-e-s," explained Dominic as he finished the cup of water. "From the conversation the little prince has with the fox."

Cheryl shook her head, "I'm drawing a blank."

"Maybe if I said it in French that would help you remember." He smirked and crumpled the paper cup. "Anyway, rites are actions too often neglected, at least that's how the fox explains it."

Cheryl winced at his abruptness although she was kind of amused at the same time. She tried to remember the book. "Oh wait, yes, now it's coming back to me. It's when the little prince is looking for friends," Cheryl said, recalling the story.

"Friends? Ah, yes...friends..." Dominic sat back and his disposition immediately changed. He crossed his arms and crossed his legs. Cheryl watched as he closed himself up right before her eyes—if he could have folded himself up and just disappeared, he would have done it. She drew herself to the end of the settee where she sat and leaned forward.

"Dominic, what's wrong? What's changed?" she spoke softly, endearingly with genuine concern. Dominic looked at her. "Do you want...to talk...about...the fox?"

"Is it true that one becomes responsible forever for what you have tamed?" he asked her.

Cheryl brought her hand to her chin, settling back in the settee, and considered his question. She recognized those words—the phrase stirred her memory. She believed she was beginning to understand. She looked into his eyes—they seemed to be pleading for her to understand! Oddly enough, it really was starting to make sense to her. Dominic wasn't just going to talk to anyone—not on their terms anyway. The dilemma wasn't that he wasn't ready to talk to them—they weren't ready to talk to him. Or more importantly, listen to him. And Dominic knew it.

"Yes," she firmly answered.

"Yes?" he questioned.

She realized he needed her to confirm it. "Yes, it is true—one is responsible for what one tames. But then there are those tamers who neglect their responsibilities."

Dominic unfolded his arms and legs, placing his arms on the arm rests and his feet on the ground. He looked at her and smiled. "Where should we begin?"

"Wherever you want to begin, Nick."

Cheryl reached over to the clock and placed it face down on the table.

II

ONE WAS TAKEN,
ONE WAS LEFT ALONE

H is eyes were shut tight with every atom of energy in his being dedicated to the effort so that not a sliver could permeate his eyelids. He lay still like a corpse stretched out on a coroner's table, holding his breath for long periods of time, and then only exhaling and inhaling intermittently with the stealth of a cobra scoping its prey. He believed if he could sustain this state of inertia, then he would escape detection and harm from the strangers that surrounded his bed. He didn't know who these strangers were but he knew they meant him harm. His blanket was wound snugly around his body like he was a mummy wrapped in wool cellophane. He sometimes pulled the blanket over his head as an added layer of defense. He would listen intently for any stray or unfamiliar sound and quickly consider its possible source. He would identify a dripping faucet, the hissing heat from the radiator next to his bed, the wind whispering through a window screen, a tree branch close to the house scratching the siding, the murmuring voices of folks out for an evening stroll, car doors opening and closing. Sometimes he would wake up in the middle of the night and swear he could feel their presence. They would be circling his bed, searching for an opening or exposed area. They would place their faces close to his, waiting for him to open his eyes and make himself vulnerable to their power. Occasionally he would be startled by the whistles of the passing trains on the tracks a block from the house, trains racing through the night, with no pause at the small town's abandoned railway station. The trains whistled like the eerie screaming of lost or abandoned children being swooped upon and snatched by giant condors. Eventually, he would succumb to the exhaustion brought on by such intense vigilance and he would fall into a deep slumber. The forces of evil would be held off another night as the creeping streams of dawn dissipated their presence.

DOMINIC MANTERRA DONNED HIS daily standard fashion statement of navy-blue slacks, white collared shirt, and clip-on school tie. He put on his black shoes with their cracked and faded leather, tying the frayed and worn shoelaces with a delicate and deliberate touch so as to not break them. Picking up his bookbag with his school books and notepads, he quietly made his way downstairs to the kitchen. He quickly downed a bowl of shredded wheat. He took from the fridge the brown paper bag that contained the peanut butter and jelly sandwich he had made the night before. From the hall closet, he fished out his coat, headed back through the kitchen, snatched his bookbag, and exited the back door of the house.

He walked along the broad avenue toward the grammar school he likened to a torture chamber of sorts. Not that there was any actual physical abuse rendered in subterranean pockets of the brick and steel edifice. It was the *threat* of such abuse that tortured him. The weapons of choice for the executioners in black and white weren't an axe or a guillotine. No, their preferred method of inflicting anguish and pain was humiliation. The verbal dressing down in front of his classmates was far worse than any other imaginable form of punishment. The effectiveness of this tool in maintaining control was not lost on him. Each child was categorized into one of two groups based on gender. With the exception of the gender label, all other forms of uniqueness were denied. The boys all wore the same shirt and tie. The girls all wore the same plaid blue and green skirt and vest with white blouse. In the classrooms, seat assignments were arranged alphabetically. All desks were the same. Their textbooks were the same. There was a stationery store within the school where all students were required to buy identical pencils and notebooks. No exceptions. The students sat at their desks with their hands folded when not engaged in writing numbers or letters. The only distinctive characteristics were the sizes and shapes of the students. Other than that, the uniformity of the student body was enforced through dress code, materials, and discipline. It was by this means that a nun (who stood four feet eleven inches in her black patent leather shoes, with a face contorted into a square rigid cloth-covered plastic habit that he believed left a permanent red square outline on the nun's face when she removed it in her solitude) maintained control over a classroom of fifty snot-nosed kids. That was the early years, when the last of the ancient sisters of the Order of St. Mary of the Divine Way were still hanging on with everything they could.

Around each rotund waistline was a thick braided rope belt with a heavy crucifix tied to the end, which they sometimes twirled like a baton. These lady knights of Christ would make their way up and down the aisles, inspecting for any deviation from the norm whether in dress, schoolwork, or personal quirks. Their thick-rimmed glasses gave many a student a false sense of security, as the students had no appreciation for these lady knights' acute sense of hearing and smell, poised to detect a quick whisper or a wisp of chewing gum. They had eyes in the back of their habits. Though they had no reservation about employing the ruler or open palm if they felt the infringement warranted it, they preferred appealing to the mob mentality to dole out the severest humiliation. Subtle sarcasm was highly effective and the air of scorn was intensified with the appeal to the classroom chums of the unfortunate victim. The phrasing was key: "Well, class, what have *we* here?" And the mob mentality made the other students almost gleeful with the proposition that if someone else was the victim, then you were safe. For the moment.

For this reason, he adapted a mode of survival that he believed was the best defense: invisibility. His strategy was simple—sit as still as possible when not engaged in taking notes or problem solving or paging through the text, and always have your gaze fixed on the back of the head of the classmate sitting in front of you. Avoid all eye contact even when spoken to—especially then! Keep your eyes on your shoe-tips and your arms straight and lifeless at your side. Always sit up straight. Accept no notes being passed whether for you or someone else. Be certain to do all home-work assignments. Do not share test answers. Don't cough or sneeze. Don't run in the schoolyard. Don't throw snowballs. Sing loud in church services. Walk in a single straight line, especially during fire drills. Do not write on books. Obey the rules. Respect the elders. Read the signs. Never question authority.

He was usually one of the first in the schoolyard. Any other early birds who were there ahead of him, were kids whose parent dropped them off while on the way to work, or older students who wanted to meet up before school. He found his way to his usual waiting spot near the back of the church, by the altar boys' entrance. He sat on the ledge at the top of the steps, placing his bookbag down next to him. The morning air was crisp and fresh as a new linen shirt. Inhaling deeply and exhaling slowly, his breath condensed before him like a smoke-breathing dragon. The air felt and tasted clean and untainted. He considered his attire. His shoes were worn, his coat even more so, and the knees of his pants were shiny, a sign of thinning material. The knitted gloves on his hands were too small and had several holes, but they managed to keep out most of the cold.

"Hey, Dominic."

His only friend, Danny Petersen, gave him the usual bump on the shoulder greeting as he down next to him.

"How you doing?" Danny asked while placing his own bookbag down between his feet. He reached into it and took out a small chocolate Nes-tle crunch bar. He broke the bar in two and handed half to Dominic.

"Thanks. I'm fine." The two friends unwrapped their pieces of candy and munched away.

"Did you do the homework assignment for Mrs. Boyle?" asked Danny as he chewed.

"Yes, of course, what do you think?" replied Dominic.

The two friends, both fully aware that they might as well not even show up for school, laughed. While they sat chatting, the schoolyard filled up around them and they paid little attention to the sea of young faces now present. At the appropriate time the bell would ring for assembly. Just prior to that, starting with the older classes, the students would have already begun to fall into formation. Each class formed two straight lines while the teachers emerged from the school's two rear entrances. Starting with the highest grades, the two vertical lines would march toward the school's entrance and be met by their respective teacher, who would escort her class into the school. Dominic and Danny stood and waited next to each other in line. Dominic spotted Danny's older sister, Angela. He waved and she smiled back sweetly. Angela was an excellent singer. Sometimes at Sunday mass, she would go to the pulpit and sing a hymn during the reflection period after communion. Dominic thought she was very pretty when she played Dorothy in *The Wizard of Oz* at the summer recreational center. She was a favorite of the nuns and Dominic thought she would eventually become one.

"Hey Dominic, when's the rain supposed to start?" snickered Danny.

Dominic gave a puzzled glance to his friend.

"Isn't this how Noah got the animals in the ark—two by two?"

Dominic chuckled and gave Danny a gentle push. "Corny one, Danny."

Their line began to move, and the two became serious as they filed past the inevitable gaze of Sister Weatherby Constance. Dominic, stealing a quick glance at her, thought her scrutiny of the lines of students not unlike General Patton assessing the battle readiness of his Third Army troops.

"I don't remember ever enlisting," Dominic thought to himself as he listlessly walked by her, his eyes facing straight ahead.

. . .

THE PAIN WAS INTENSE, like being stabbed from inside his body. He clutched his right side, fighting to stay still to prevent triggering another round of throbbing pain. He felt small and vulnerable. He knew this was more serious than eating too much too fast or playing too soon after eating. He'd even be willing to puke if that would make the pain stop—and he hated throwing up more than anything. But he knew this pain wasn't resolving in that manner. No matter how still he stayed, the pain increased and the intervals between the throbbing reverberations lessened. Dr. Grusich, the family doctor from around the corner, was called. Dominic lay motionless on the couch while his shirt was lifted up to his chin. The stethoscope's coldness felt good against his feverish skin as the doctor listened a moment in a few different spots before dropping it and then pulling the buds from his ears and uttering "Uh-huh," affirming what he had heard. He then pressed several spots around Dominic's abdomen and asked, "Does this hurt?" while Dominic said nothing. When the doctor applied pressure to his right lower side, Dominic answered with a screech of anguish.

His shirt was pulled down and the blanket placed back over him. Dominic had his eyes closed but could hear the grown-up voices speaking as if he wasn't there.

"Yes, I believe that's what it is."

"Is it serious?"

"We caught it in time. He'll need to go to the hospital."

"When?"

"Now."

"Ambulance?"

"That won't be necessary if you leave right away."

"We will. We don't want another tragedy."

"Please do. Yes, that was a most unfortunate event."

Dominic's eyes were half closed but he could see Doctor Grusich looking down on him, as he patted Dominic's head.

"Hang in there, little man. We'll get you to the hospital and fix you up in no time. "

The car ride over to Elizabethtown General was a blur. When the car pulled up to the hospital emergency room entrance, an orderly was waiting with a wheelchair. Dominic, crouched over in pain, was transferred to the wheelchair. Peeking through the slits of his eyes, he could see that he was surrounded by people dressed in blinding white clothes. Everything seemed to be brightly lit and white. He didn't understand what was happening and, despite the pain, he attempted to become invisible. But the sharp stabbing in his side was relentless in exposing his presence. Everything was becoming a blur of lights, the images beginning to streak like clouds at sunrise, thinning and stretched out against a blue-orange canvas.

He was stretched like one of those clouds on a hard bed with bright lights shining down on him. He felt a sequence of pointed jabs in his left arm. He heard the hushed and steady chatter of voices around him. Another stabbing pain in his right arm, with someone pressing down on the spot, brought his eyes wide open. Above him, he saw a sea of eyes. The heads and mouths were covered. He heard muffled voices and beeps and various radar sounds. Suddenly a face appeared parallel over his, the head blocking out the bright lights like an eclipse of the sun.

"What's your name, son?" The voice was kind and friendly.

He managed to mutter, "Dominic."

"Hello, Dominic, I'm Dr. Schneider. I know you're not feeling too well but we're going to take care of you and you'll soon feel all better, OK?"

Dominic nodded his head.

He heard another voice, a female voice. He imagined it belonged to the same person who was gently stroking his arm because it came from the same direction.

"Dominic, a sweet name for a sweet boy. Do you know what that name means, Doctor?"

"Isn't it some religious name?" the same voice who quizzed Dominic replied.

"It is from the Latin. Dominicus. It means 'of the Lord.'"

"I see that nursing education at Holy Name Academy was well worth the money," he quipped.

Dominic began to squirm as the pain had intensified and was not letting up.

"OK, little Dominic, just a minute or two more and you won't feel a thing." It was the doctor's voice again. "What is your favorite hobby, Dominic?" he asked.

Dominic shook his head from side to side. The hand that had been stroking his arm stopped and then he felt a hand on the side of his face and on this forehead. The female voice spoke again. "The fever appears to be breaking." He felt the hand rest on his head.

"Oh, I'm sure you have some hobby, something you like to do. Collect stamps, perhaps? Any sport teams you like?"

"Reading," Dominic managed to whisper.

"Reading? Really. Quite impressive for a little boy. Nurse, I think we're about ready."

Dominic felt the hand on his head lift slightly but then he felt something soft and flat make something like an x on his forehead, and then the hand moved.

"OK, Dominic, what do you like to read about?"

"Bible stories."

"The Bible? Fairly heavy reading for a little boy. My, aren't you a smart lad? OK, let's see, Dominic. Do you know about Jacob?"

Dominic nodded his head yes.

"You do? Huh. He had twelve sons, you know that, right?"

Again, Dominic nodded yes.

"Well, can you name his twelve sons? Let's see how many you can name. Start now."

Dominic thought and he began to recite the names, "Joseph...Judah... Benja...."

Then—the closest experience to being in the womb.

. . .

WHEN HE AWOKE, his body felt drained and weighed down. His eyelids were heavy and the pinching in his arm was superseded by the pain on his side. However, it was an uncomfortable soreness and not the throbbing, sharp pain that tormented him before he fell asleep. Asleep? He began to recall the events that had occurred. Wait. What time was it? It was dark now. Where was he? A weakness permeated his body as if all his strength had been sapped out of him. He tried to raise his head but his neck and shoulders were too stiff to accommodate him. It was quiet except for beeping sounds that were similar to the ones he had heard while watching movies with submarines in them. He realized he was in a hospital. With the pain in his side now more or less gone, he could think more clearly about the chain of events. He was now recalling the snippets of dialogue that he had managed to hear. An appendix. Yes, that was the word. He didn't know what exactly it meant, but it was what the grown-ups had discussed. He concentrated for a moment on his right arm and managed to budge it from the invisible weight that seemed to have it locked in place at his side. He brought his right hand up to his right side and could feel a large bandage over the spot from which the pain had emanated and caused him to curl up in agony. Slipping his arm back down to his side, he closed his eyes and listened intently. In the distance he could faintly hear intermittent footsteps and fragments of conversation. Screwing up all the strength he could muster, he pushed hard against the bed with his arms and legs and torso in order to lift his head and look between the bed rails to get a view of the landscape around him. He could see the light from the main corridor barely illuminating the entrance to the room he was in; it seemed like a large room, like the school cafeteria, only much narrower. There was a large walkway down the middle separating two rows of beds. He dropped his head back down onto the pillow. He didn't know if all the other beds had anyone in them. It was very dark and the faint light from the main corridor reflected various shadows from the IV stations and other monitoring devices at each bed. In unfamiliar surroundings, his body in a weakened state, Dominic felt very vulnerable. His standard rituals to avoid detection and maintain security were not available to him here, his visibility very apparent. He was exposed and defenseless. He closed his eyes tight, inhaled deeply, held his breath, and lay very still. With calculated deliberation he exhaled as quietly and motionlessly as possible. It didn't work. He felt very alone. His lower lip began to quiver and tears streamed from the corners of his eyes, streaking down his temples, and parting ways around his ears. A muffled whimpering sound escaped from him as he fought to control the emotion. He could hear his own sobbing echoing in the room. Footsteps quickly approached, their echo overwhelming his own pathetic whimper.

"What's the matter?"

The nurse was checking the monitor and looking at his IV. She lifted his blanket and examined the bandage. She noted the sheets were dry. Satisfied, she lowered the blanket down. Another nurse had joined her, picking up the chart hanging at the foot of the bed.

"Everything OK?" the second one asked, not looking up from the chart.

"Appears so. Just having a bad dream, I guess," answered the first.

"Dominic Manterra. He had the appendectomy. Seems like it was routine. Although that was yesterday. He's been sleeping most of the time. Hasn't eaten."

"Well, they'll bring him some breakfast in a few hours."

Dominic opened his eyes.

"You OK, honey? Bad dream?" the first nurse asked, patting his head. Dominic could smell the scent of Jergens hand cream. He nodded yes.

"His doctor will be making rounds tomorrow afternoon," remarked the second nurse. "I don't think anyone has been up to see this one. And no one was in the waiting room post-surgery either."

The first nurse had pulled a tissue out of a box on the table next to his bed and patted the sides of his face and around his ears.

"Don't be afraid. Be a good boy and go back to sleep. I'll check on you later."

The second nurse returned the chart and the two walked away whispering to each other. Dominic closed his eyes and fell asleep.

DOMINIC EMERGED FROM HIS appendicitis experience with a scarred side and a reduced stature. He felt he had shrunk in size because everything that seemed big before was even bigger now. The avenues were wider, the buildings taller, the cars larger, the grown-ups around him appeared like giants. What really had grown was his sense of fear. Obstacles of all shapes and sizes surrounded him and he was in a constant struggle to protect and preserve himself from these harsh elements. Other children, especially those in the upper grades, were mean-spirited and vicious in their words and how they contorted their faces. Everyone else seemed to be projected on a jumbo-sized movie screen and he was overwhelmed with their magnitude and scope. The only advantage he could garner from his reduced stature was that he should be able to achieve invisibility with greater ease. He also found another means of escape. His other secret weapon was reading. Opening a book was like opening a secret trap door that no one else knew existed. He could climb down between the two covers, slip into the center crease, slide down into the binding, hide out among the words that filled the pages, and be lost in another world where others could not find him. They wouldn't even know how to begin to look for him there. It was a world of characters and places that he totally immersed himself in—a world where he felt safe and not so alone. When he was reading, the only real world he inhabited was the one before his eyes, brought to life by his imagination. He became the paint instructor of white picket fences; the forever youthful raft rider of the Mississippi trying to figure out justice from the law; the funeral orator to sway the mob; the hero who blows up the bridge and sacrifices his life for others; the drifter who spared his friend from the lynch mob though it broke his heart to do so; the catcher of children in the rye field; and the World War II pilot who could never catch a flight home. Every book became his escape hatch from a world that he saw as threatening and scary. And whenever anyone did seek him out, usually for a purpose or reason that served him no use, when they finally discovered him in a corner or behind a chair, crouched over a book, they halted their advancement:

"Oh, there you are, Dominic. What are you doing, reading? What are you reading?"

He would flash the cover at them, and depending on their own erudition, the interrupting party would either comment, "Oh, haven't read that, is it any good?" or, "Oh, that's a good book. A little advanced for your level, no?" In either case, the questions were rhetorical and they would beat a hasty retreat while Dominic smiled slightly and quickly made his way back down the secret door.

He had spent his time recuperating from the surgery reading a pile of books. It was a very enjoyable time. It was not lost on him, however, that he seemed to be especially left to his own devices. Interruptions were few and far in between, though there were quiet whisperings and the avoidances seemed deliberate. Something didn't seem right but he couldn't tell what was wrong. He hadn't even heard from his best friend Danny and that bothered him as well.

THE SCHOOL AUDITORIUM WAS full of people. It was Dominic's first appearance with a large crowd since he had been in the hospital. It was very quiet and everyone had sad faces. People were crying and saying, "I'm so sorry" and, "it's such a shame, so sad." People he didn't know were coming up to where he sat and patting him on the head. He was feeling very uncomfortable and his extreme shyness kicked in. He didn't understand what was going on or why he or anyone was here. He had overheard the voices talking low at home but couldn't figure out what was being discussed. He figured it had something to do with where he was right now. He just sat motionless and stared at the floor. Everyone around him was so much larger than him. He couldn't see much from where he sat. Suddenly it got quiet and some people appeared on the stage. A man began to speak. Dominic couldn't hear him too well though he looked familiar. He sat down while a woman stood up and read from a piece of paper. She paused every now and then, struggling to read from the paper. A few more people followed and it became harder for Dominic to hear because those around him were crying and consoling each other. Dominic felt very uneasy and lost because he didn't understand what this was all about. Finally, a person was introduced and Dominic recognized the voice when she spoke. He strained to look over the adults sitting in front of him to confirm who it was. He could barely see her, but it was indeed Angela Petersen. She had her long hair pulled back into a ponytail and looked upset. Dominic immediately thought of Danny, and that he might be here too. He had wondered why Danny hadn't called him or stopped by to visit him at all but when he asked, he was told that the doctor said no visitors and that he should focus on getting better. Dominic started to look around to see if he could spot Danny. His scan proved futile as he couldn't locate his friend. But it was eerily quiet and he could hear Angela better now.

"...whom I will always love. And he will always live in my heart, even though I will miss him every day. And so, I would like to dedicate this song to my brother Danny."

At his point, Dominic was sitting as high as he could, straining his neck to get a better glimpse of Angela, practically standing on his tippy toes, stretching to see her on the stage. He had heard Angela mention Danny's name and so he thought maybe he was up there on the stage with her. His eyes met Angela's and when she saw that it was Dominic, he smiled and gave her a little wave, blushing because he thought she was really pretty. Angela seemed to gasp and then Dominic saw that her eyes welled up. She spoke up again.

"And to his best friend Dominic."

People seemed to turn their heads and look at him. He immediately became self-conscious and sat back down on his chair. At the same time, Angela began to sing.

"Somewhere…over the rainbow…"

Dominic liked that song. He remembered it was Danny and his favorite part of *The Wizard of Oz*. He was wondering where Danny was sitting. It all felt very strange to him because Angela was singing but her voice kept cracking and it sounded different to him. Besides, a lot of people were crying around him and he was getting very scared.

"…oh why…oh why…can't I…"

Angela finished singing. The auditorium was totally silent except for the muffled sounds of tears and coughs and hushed, consoling voices. Dominic sat motionless in his chair, staring down at the ground. Something wasn't right, he could sense it—he could feel it though he didn't understand it. Folks began to stand up and head towards the exits. Dominic stared at the shiny hardwood floor beneath his feet, fixated on the grainy design in the oak. He looked up to a clear view of the stage and he could see an easel near where Angela had stood and sung. On it was a poster-size photograph of Danny's smiling face.

"Come on, Dominic. It's time to leave."

He lay in bed that night, the blanket wrapped especially tight around his body. He had opened the bedroom window a little so that the cool late-autumn air could seep through and he caught the scent of decaying leaves and wood burning from a nearby chimney. They had spoken to him and explained to him what had happened. Danny had a pain in his side as well but it had been too late. His appendix had burst. And the angels came and took him to heaven.

Dominic stared out the open gap of the window at the stars and the moon and the background of blackness.

"Goodbye, my friend."

III.

THE PUPPET SHOW

Dominic's cheeks burned. He didn't understand why he would feel a surge of heat in them whenever he saw her. And whenever he could catch a glimpse of her, he would stare until she would notice and she would smile and then give him a little wave. Embarrassed by being caught like a cow in a pasture mesmerized by passing traffic, he would quickly turn his head away or divert his eyes to the ground. Her hair was long, golden like a season's first winter wheat, with blonde highlights, courtesy of the sun's rays. Her eyes were hazel but in certain light the green shone brighter and made her look like a princess in a story book. Occasionally Dominic would be near her in the schoolyard and could see her close up. She was perfect beauty—symmetry of cheeks and flawless skin not unlike a porcelain doll that Dominic had seen in a picture book. Her lips were shiny red and her smile or the sound of her laugh made Dominic's heart leap up in his chest, especially if she was smiling at him. Her name was Anna and he wanted to be her friend more than anything else in the world. She was the reason he woke up in the morning, and the reason he raced to school, and the reason he didn't want the school day to end. When the bell rang to let out the students, Dominic would watch as she walked to the back of the classroom to fetch her coat, chatting with the other girls, and his eyes followed her as she left the classroom. He would pause a minute or two and then quickly leave the classroom, leaving a safe distance so as not to be discovered stealing his last moments of seeing her until the next morning. Once outside he would saunter over by a nearby tree and watch as she ran to her mom, and the two would walk off hand-in-hand. And then he would turn to start his own journey home in quiet solitude. This was his daily ritual and Fridays were the worst, for he knew he wouldn't see her for two whole days. Weekends with a Monday holiday were even more torturous.

His refuge from this forlornness was found in his armies of fighting warriors. Dominic owned a collection of toy soldiers that numbered more than ten thousand, which he knew from counting them. On every occasion when someone asked him what toy or gift he would like, the answer was the same: toy soldiers to add to his warrior empire. The military throughout history was well represented: The Roman legions, the barbarian horde, the knights and Vikings, the Prussian regiments, the Napoleonic armies, the Redcoats and the American Revolutionists, the Union and the Confederates, the American Calvary and the native Indians, the Russians, the Germans, the Japanese, the British, and the American GIs of the great World Wars. He had them by land, sea, and air; on horseback, on galley ships, and in tank formation. There were forts, there were mountains and valleys and open plains. He re-enacted the great battles of history, based on the various history books that he liked reading. Those were his two favorite pastimes: reading books and creating battles with his toy soldiers. He spent many hours alternating between his two worlds of reading and soldiering, and was most content in his sanctuary of isolation. Both hobbies basically let him slip into another universe where he would commune with the heroes and villains in their eras and lands. His imagination soared across boundaries of time and space, and he was able to supersede any obstacles because nothing was real, yet everything mattered. And it was up to him to play his part well. The biographies were his favorites, especially of generals and presidents and saints. He learned that sometimes all three could be the same;

and at other times, not. He was given a children's Bible when he was six years old, and that was the book he read and re-read most of all. He liked the stories of Noah and the flood, Joseph and his brothers, Moses and the Egyptians, David and Goliath, the prophet Elijah, Jonah and the whale, the miracles of Jesus, and the adventures of the apostles, especially Paul. There was also a collection of old encyclopedias in the house, and he would pick out a volume, and skim through the entries. At first it was mostly the entries with pictures that caught his eye that he would take time to read. But eventually he would read those that had topics or descriptions that attracted his interest. He liked the maps as well. He enjoyed fictional stories and immersed himself in Mark Twain and John Steinbeck. *Tom Sawyer* became his favorite book, and he dreamed of life on the Mississippi, although he had never left his own state on the East Coast. With the Joad family he traveled across the dust bowl states to the promised land of California, the journey ripe with injustice and the harshness of human nature. But hope was often seeded and he always believed in its harvest. Sometimes he attached book characters to people in his everyday life, and so Anna became his Becky Thatcher.

By chance his seed of hope one day sprouted, and for a moment, albeit brief, he was Tom Sawyer and he would finally be with his Becky Thatcher. The class was abuzz regarding a contraption that was present on the side wall of the classroom that hadn't been there that past Friday. It looked like a stand that one would see at a carnival or country fair, or like a proscenium arch one would see in a stage theater. Dominic had seen a picture of his very thing in an encyclopedia. He recognized it and knew it was used to put on puppet shows. He wondered what it was doing in the classroom.

The teacher entered the classroom and the class hushed its chatter. The teacher took the attendance and then was writing something. The class waited in anticipation to see what she would say about the stand. Eventually she looked up from her desk and began to address the students. She drew their attention to the stand, asking if anyone knew what it was. Dominic was sure he knew, but his shyness to raise his hand would not be easily overcome. The teacher waited and her eyes scanned the room and Dominic thought she was searching for an answer on someone's forehead. Her eyes met his and to his shock, she seemed to be reading his forehead. She spoke:

"Dominic, do you know what this is?" she said as she made her way over to the stand.

It seemed like every head in the class turned to look at him. As though it was someone else using his voice, Dominic heard himself respond: "It's a stage setting used for puppet shows. The people hide underneath and behind the curtain stand, while they wear the puppets over their hands, and then they say their lines and match the hand movements with what they are saying."

"Very good, Dominic, that's exactly what it, is." She had begun to push the stand, which was on wheels, toward the front of the class. "I thought we'd have a little fun this morning, as the school year is drawing to a close, and see if we could put on a puppet show."

The kids in the class began to chatter among themselves with anticipation. Dominic figured they were all excited because the school year was nearly over and the summer break was on their minds. In the fall, when they all would be back for the new school year, he would listen as they spoke about their summer vacations and all the places they visited. Most would drive down to Florida or rent beach houses for the summer; others would travel to national parks or attend summer camps. Dominic would make more trips than all of them combined, and visit more places in more countries around the world, meeting so many people from many different walks of life: all this without ever leaving his block. His thoughts were interrupted by the sound of his name.

"Dominic, since you seem to know so much about this lost art of entertainment, why don't you come up and be one of our puppeteers?" The butterflies exploded in Dominic's stomach and the perspiration flowed. He froze.

"Come on, Dominic, come on up here, please." The teacher addressed him with an encouraging tone, clearly impressed with his knowledge and explanation. Dominic felt a gentle nudge on his back from the boy sitting behind him, which broke him out of his trance. He stood up and started to make his way up to the front of the classroom.

"Who wants to put on the puppet show with Dominic? Do I have a volunteer?" asked the teacher.

Dominic reached the front of the class and turned around to see a raised hand and to hear the words he could not believe he was hearing.

"OK, Anna, you want to be Dominic's partner? Good, come on up, dear."

The teacher gave Dominic a knowing smile as his face turned to crimson. He watched as Anna made her way up to the front of the classroom where he and the teacher stood waiting. She was graceful and confident as she strode up the aisle and took her place standing next to Dominic, giving him an assuring smile.

The teacher provided direction. "Anna and Dominic will each have a puppet that they will pick from a box of puppets and they will take their places behind the stand, where you won't be able to see them. And then the puppets will appear on the stage above them, and they will put on a sort of little play. They will do what is called "improvisation," making up the conversation as they go along. We will give them a few minutes to get themselves ready and then the show will begin. I will need everyone to be very quiet so we all can hear. OK, are the two of you ready?"

Anna answered "yes" while Dominic just nodded his head. Anna took hold of Dominic's arm and gently led him to the back of the stand. She found the box of puppets and quickly sorted through them. She picked one out and held on to it while she continued to rummage through the collection until she found another one that met with her approval. She turned to Dominic.

"Here, Dominic, I found two puppets we can use." She handed him one of a man dressed in a cardigan sweater and a turtleneck shirt. He noticed her puppet was dressed like a stewardess.

"OK, we'll pretend we're married and it's Friday evening, and you have just come home from the college where you are a professor, and I have just arrived home from the airport. Let's see, I have just flown in from Boston. And we're both tired and are trying to make dinner plans, OK?"

Dominic nodded and was beginning to feel more relaxed. Anna held the curtain skirt open and waved for him to go under the stand, which he did. She joined him and put her puppet on her hand. Dominic struggled to get his puppet on, and she took hers off and then helped him securely fit his puppet on his hand. He watched as she concentrated on putting the puppet on his hand, blowing her breath up to push her hair bangs out of her face, reaching up to push the golden strands behind her ear. He could smell her peppermint breath, and her big eyes gleamed like Egyptian emeralds he had seen in pictures. She looked up to see him staring at her and smiled and whispered, "Stop!" and then asked him, "Are you ready, Dominic?" He believed it was the first time he had ever heard her say his name. He nodded. "OK," she breathed, "let's put on a show!"

They raised their hands through the opening above them. She looked at Dominic and nodded her head once for reassurance and then she began:

"Hello, darling! It's so good to be home at last. It was so crowded at the airport! I am just wiped out!"

"Hello, my dear! Yes, I can only imagine how relieved you must be to have both feet firmly on the ground at last."

They could hear their classmates giggling.

"Oh, I've so missed that witty humor of yours. Your students at the college must so enjoy your lectures. At least the ones that manage to stay awake."

They could hear the teacher let out a laugh and Anna glanced at Dominic, motioning for him to speak next.

"Are you hungry? What would you like to do for dinner?" Dominic asked.

"Yes, I am famished. Did you go grocery shopping this week?"

"Um, was I supposed to go grocery shopping?"

The class continued to laugh as the two puppeteers managed to match the movements of their hands with their words.

"That's OK, Dominic, we can make my usual favorite!"

Dominic's puppet placed its hand to its head, scratching and thinking. "Hmmm...lasagna?"

"No, silly, dinner reservations at the club!"

Dominic brought both hands up to his puppet's head and began to shake his head back and forth.

Anna continued. "Speaking of reservations, did I mention my mother was coming for a short stay?"

Dominic brought his puppet's arms down to its side and turned it to face the class and it shook its head no in an exaggerated motion. He then abruptly stopped his shaking.

"Any chance we can convince her to change that to a longer stay? As in stay away?"

The class and the teacher roared with laughter.

"Come now, Dominic, you know how fond she is of you."

"Well, Anna, absence does make the heart grow fonder. I only want her fondness to increase, so..."

The two went on for another three minutes or so before bringing their little act to a close. When they emerged from under the stand, the class and the teacher broke out into wild applause. Dominic was grinning ear to ear and Anna curtseyed. She took hold of Dominic's hand and whispered into his ear, "On the count of three, let's bow." She counted out and then the two bowed. The teacher approached them, clapping.

"Excellent! Excellent! That was very, very good!"

The rest of the day was a blur for Dominic. He seemed to take on celebrity status. It was like everyone wanted to talk to him. He was surprised at his own easiness in chatting with his classmates. He even found himself sitting at the lunch table with Anna and her friends, although Anna sat on the other side of the table, down one person to his left.

Every now and then he would catch her eye, and she would look back at him, tilt her head to one side as though she was sizing him up, and slightly shake her head, raise her eyebrows, and then look away.

At the end of the day, when school was dismissed, Dominic resorted to his same routine, waiting for the classroom to empty out before he gathered up his books and made his exit. However, when he looked up from his book, Anna was still in the classroom, speaking with the teacher leaning against her desk. Dominic gathered up his books and headed out.

"Oh, Dominic, hold on. Anna and I will walk out with you." Dominic could feel his shyness had been restored as Anna turned to face him with her confident eyes piercing his sensitive nature.

"You were great this morning, Dominic!" she gushed with genuine enthusiasm.

"Thanks, Anna, but you were the real star," Dominic managed to stammer, his shyness making a full recovery.

"*We* made a great team!" Anna gave him a playful slap on the arm. "It was so much fun! I'll always remember it."

Her last remark caught Dominic's attention, as it sounded strange to him, so...final.

"Let's go, you two." And they followed the teacher out.

They made their way out of the school and stepped into the late spring sunshine. The teacher and Anna bantered back and forth while Dominic followed quietly behind. At the end of the walkway waited Anna's mom. Dominic had never been this close to her before. He noticed she was wearing some kind of uniform. Then he recognized the scarf around her neck and the wings on the front of her dress. Of course, she was a stewardess.

"You should be very proud of Anna, Mrs. Stravinsky, she was terrific this morning. She and Dominic here put on a show for the class that was very entertaining."

"Oh really, how lovely!" responded Mrs. Stravinsky.

"Yes, it was like they had rehearsed it beforehand. Very natural and quite funny."

"Dominic was really good, Mother. He was just like Dad would be with you," Anna chimed in.

"Well, that is quite a compliment. Your dad is a tough act to follow!" Mrs. Stravinsky winked at the teacher.

"We will really miss Anna next year. She's has been such a joy to have in class."

"Oh, thank you for saying so. We will miss it here, too. But my husband 's job is relocating us, and because of my line of work, it's easy enough for me to transfer as long as there's an airport nearby."

Anna's mom and the teacher stepped away from the two classmates to continue their own conversation.

Dominic now knew what a sledgehammer to the jaw felt like. *Anna was leaving? Moving? What the...?* Anna was suddenly silent and stared down at her feet.

"It was really swell this morning, Dominic. You were really, really good. You should be more like that. Not so quiet all the time." She raised her head up and smiled at him. "I will miss you, Dominic." She took his hand and then leaned over and kissed him on his cheek. "Please take care of yourself."

"Are you ready to go, young lady? We really should get moving. Have you said goodbye to your friend?" asked her mom.

The teacher bade them farewell and good luck, then turned to head back to the school. Anna and her mom also turned and headed toward their car. Dominic stood watching in silence. Once they reached their car, Anna opened the passenger side door, paused to look back at Dominic, and gave him a wave. She then pushed back her hair behind her ear, smiled at him, and disappeared into the car, closing the door behind her. The car pulled away and his eyes followed it as it drove down the block, made a turn, and was out of sight.

Dominic sighed, touching his cheek where her warm lips had bid him farewell. Then the little professor turned on his heels and headed home.

IV.

A GODLY MOTHER

What are you reading, Dominic?"

"I am finishing a biography," he answered.

His mother smiled and continued to knead the dough. "Who is it a biography of?" she asked.

"A saint—Peter the Hermit. He led a crusade. I want to be a hermit when I grow up."

"A hermit? Why would you say that?! A hermit lives by himself and never sees anyone," explained his mother.

"I know. I think that would be good. I can read all day and not be bothered." His mother smiled at his earnestness but was uneasy about his response.

"But that means you wouldn't want to see me? Or your father or your brothers?" she had taken a break from kneading.

Dominic thought about it. "I guess not. I would let you come and visit me."

"And where would I be visiting you?" She scooped up a handful of flour and spread it over the ball of dough and the surrounding counter-top.

"In my cave, of course."

"And how will you eat?"

"I will have a farm. Hmmm, or maybe just a garden. I won't need much."

"Just books, right?" She began to knead the dough again.

"Yes. I guess it will have to be a cave near a library. But I will bring some of my own books."

"Your Bible?" she asked.

"Yes, I will bring my Bible, the one you gave me."

"It is good to read, Dominic. Always remember, you wouldn't fill your stomach with garbage, so don't fill your head with garbage. Promise me that, OK?"

"I promise, Mom."

"And promise me you won't be a hermit. It would make Mommy sad to think you were all alone."

Dominic did not answer this request as he watched his mother knead the dough. She did not look at him but waited to see what her young son would say.

"Do you want me to organize your pots and pans?" he finally asked.

She sighed, knowing this was his usual ploy to avoid things he didn't want to talk about, his diversionary tactic.

"Sure, dear, Mommy would appreciate that, but first do you want to hear a poem I learned as a child?"

Dominic nodded yes and closed his book. He jumped up, went over to the lower cabinet next to where his mother stood, and started to pull out its contents.

"I'm nobody," she said, "who are you? Are you nobody too? Then there's a pair of us! Shh! Don't tell—they'd banish us, you know!" She looked down at her son at her feet as he looked up at her with his intense blue eyes. She smiled and continued, "How dreary to be somebody! How public like a frog, to spend the livelong day, with an admiring bog." She knelt down and kissed her son on the forehead.

"Did you write that?" asked Dominic.

"Oh no, no, Mommy is not that talented. That was written by Emily Dickinson."

"Who was she?"

"Interestingly enough, she was what you would call a hermit." She smiled at the irony. "Do you like it?"

"What's a bog?" he wondered aloud as he went back to organizing the pots and pans.

"Dominic, you didn't promise me that you wouldn't be a hermit?" She paused her kneading.

He was stacking the stainless-steel bowls according to size, and then he began to recite, "I'm nobody! Who are you? Are you nobody too? Shh, don't tell—they'd banish us, you know!"

She smiled a sad smile and went back to kneading her dough.

DOMINIC LOOKED UP FROM his reading. "Mom, why did Peter deny he knew Jesus?"

She looked up from her sewing and smiled. "Because he was afraid."

"What was he afraid of? If he knew Jesus was God, then what was there to be afraid of—Jesus could do anything He wanted."

She put down her needle and thread. "That's a good question, Dominic. Peter said that Jesus was God, but he didn't really understand what that meant or what Jesus's mission was as the savior of the world."

Dominic pondered the explanation. "Does that mean Peter didn't really believe in Jesus?"

"You can say that to a certain degree. But Peter and the others had a different belief on not only who the Messiah was going to be, but what the Messiah was going to be. Peter was human, and he was very proud. Jesus tried to warn him that he was going to be tested."

"And he failed that test, right?" Dominic sounded judgmental to his mother.

"Yes, he did. But—"

"He failed his best friend, just when his friend needed him most," Dominic persisted.

"Yes, he did, but Peter was very sorry, so sorry that it is said that he had furrows under both of his eyes from how bitterly he wept over his denial. And Jesus forgave him."

Dominic went back to his reading for a minute and then glanced at his mother. "Mom, is Peter as bad as Judas?"

She pushed her sewing aside and patted the cushion next to her on the couch, beckoning Dominic to come sit beside her. Dominic went and sat next to his mother.

"Peter denied Jesus because he was afraid, and although he felt he let Jesus down, Jesus already knew Peter was going to do what he did. And Peter regretted what he did. Judas, on the other hand, betrayed Jesus, and basically helped those who wanted to harm Jesus."

"Was Judas sorry?" asked Dominic.

She ran her hand through her son's hair. "That's hard to say. True, Judas ended up regretting his decision, and then he hung himself. But we can't know for sure if he did that because he was sorry or he was just scared."

"Scared like Peter?" asked Dominic.

She considered the question carefully. "No, Peter was scared that the people who had arrested Jesus would also arrest him. Peter was afraid of being put in jail and being punished by those people. Judas was afraid that since he had betrayed Jesus, he would be punished in a different way. Peter was sorry and repented and asked forgiveness. Judas was scared but didn't repent and didn't ask for forgiveness."

Dominic listened intently. "Would Jesus have forgiven Judas?"

"Hmmm, good question. I would say yes, Jesus would have forgiven him. But I think the difference between Peter and Judas is that Judas never really believed in or loved Jesus."

"Did Jesus love Judas?" asked Dominic.

"Yes…yes, I believe He did. Jesus as God loves all His children. But God doesn't force any of His children to love Him, that is what is called free will. The Bible says that we must be like a child if we are to be a part of God's kingdom in heaven. And because God loves all His children, He doesn't want anyone to lead His children astray. Jesus said it would be better for a man to tie a millstone around his neck and to cast himself into the ocean than to lead a child astray."

"What does it mean to lead a child astray?" asked Dominic.

"That means to lead them away from the open arms of Jesus," she said lovingly.

"I will remember that," stated Dominic in a matter-of-fact tone.

"Good. And remember that your body is the temple of the Holy Spirit. God lives inside you, in your heart. His power within you is greater than the power outside in the world. Your body is a very special place—because inside it holds the Holy Spirit and that connects you to Jesus and to God our Father. There is a part of a psalm that will help you remember that—'Who shall ascend the hill of the Lord? Or who may stand in His holy place? He who has clean hands and a pure heart; who has not lifted up his soul to vanity, or sworn deceitfully. He shall receive blessing from the Lord, and righteousness from the God of his salvation.' Dominic, promise me you will always keep yourself pure and avoid anything that would hurt God. Remember this saying—the true test of character is not the resistance of temptation but the avoidance of temptation."

"I will remember," promised Dominic.

"And never lose hope, Dominic. Always hold on to hope, no matter how bad things may seem. Hope is very important. Peter loved Jesus. He faltered in his faith but he still had hope in Jesus. And it turned out alright for him. Judas didn't love Jesus, he didn't believe in Jesus, and so in the end, he had no hope. And that is why he took his own life."

Dominic nodded his head. "I will remember, Mommy."

She embraced her young child and Dominic hugged his mother with all his might.

. . .

DOMINIC CAME THROUGH THE side door, crossed the kitchen and placed his bookbag on the floor in the hallway. By the counter, his mom was preparing dinner. "Hi, Mom."

"How was school today, Dominic?" queried his mom.

"It was OK. Gerard and Thomas were being mean to Colleen Jones at lunchtime."

"How so?"

"They were making fun of the way she looked. It wasn't very nice. No one was helping her."

"And?"

"Colleen was getting upset. It looked like she was going to cry." Dominic paused. "Can I have a bowl of cereal?"

"Sure, but don't have too much, or you will spoil your dinner."

Dominic got a bowl and spoon out of the cabinet. He poured some Corn Flakes into the bowl, then some milk, and spread a teaspoon of sugar over the top. He sat down and began to eat.

"What happened next, Dominic?"

"Huh? Oh, I felt bad for Colleen. I told Gerard and Thomas to knock it off."

She smiled. "And did they?"

Dominic nodded. She reached over and kissed him on the top of his head. She went to continue with her dinner preparation, but then paused and listened. She laughed. Dominic looked up from his reading of the back of the Corn Flakes box.

"What's so funny, Mom?" he asked.

"The sound you're making."

"What sound?"

"The hmmm, hmmm sound as you're eating your cereal. It reminded me of when you were a baby, and I would give you your bottle of milk. You would look up at me with those baby blue eyes and make that same sound."

"Mom!" Dominic shook his head.

"Was that the end of it? I mean with Colleen Jones. Did she say anything to you afterwards?"

"She was telling the other girls about it. They were saying that we were boyfriend and girlfriend now. Dopes."

"Do you like her?" She was curious.

"No, Mom! I don't like her at all. Even Gerard and Thomas were saying that because I told them to leave her alone."

"Then why did you stop them?" she said half teasingly.

"Because it wasn't right. They were going to make her cry and she wasn't bothering them. But that doesn't mean I want to be her boyfriend or that I like her. What Gerard and Thomas were saying about her was true—she is sloppy and does sometimes smell."

"So, what made you defend her?"

Dominic shrugged his shoulders. "I just felt sorry for her. Maybe those things are true but maybe there's a reason for it and it's not her fault. I don't know. I didn't think they should be mean to her."

She rinsed her hands in the sink, dried them with a dish towel while sitting down in the chair across from Dominic.

"Now, Dominic, that was very noble of you to stand up for Colleen, and you are correct, that was the right thing to do. But I want to tell you that you must be careful when it comes to a girl's feelings. You must be sensitive to how a girl thinks about things a boy says or does."

Dominic finished the last of the cereal in the bowl, and then picked up the bowl and slurped the remaining milk. He placed the empty bowl down on the table, letting out an "ahh," and wiped his mouth with his sleeve.

"Dominic, are you listening to me?" asked his mom.

"Yes, Mom, I am listening. I didn't tell Colleen I liked her or wanted to be her boyfriend. I just didn't want her to be treated meanly."

"I understand that, Dominic. But Colleen and the other girls for that matter interpreted your actions differently and it is important you are aware of how your actions and words can make a girl feel. You don't want to ever send the wrong message. Do you understand?"

"Yes, Mom, I understand."

"Good. Now go do your homework for a little bit and I will let you and your brothers know when dinner is ready." Dominic pushed himself away from the table and with an "OK" grabbed his bookbag and went upstairs. Iolanda Manterra scooped up the bowl and spoon while contemplating the difficult road ahead for her little knight errant.

V

CAPITAL OFFENSE

The bronze man with outstretched arms, his legs neatly placed one over the other, and a crown with points that looked like shark teeth on top of his head, appeared to look down over the classroom, although his eyes were closed. Dominic Manterra wondered if the bronze man was as bored as he was. The classroom was neatly arranged in rows of desks, filled with boys and girls dressed in their school uniforms. All sitting up with their hands folded in front of them, all looking straight ahead, while their teacher, Mrs. Carson, sat at her desk, reviewing something, wearing a stern expression. Dominic could feel the sweat on the back of his neck begin to trickle down to his collar and seep slowly onto his back. He glanced to the left to look out the open windows to see if the branches on the trees were moving at all, in the hope of some breeze of relief forthcoming. The trees were as motionless as the students at their desks. Dominic paused to admire the beautiful auburn hair of Moira Toomey, with whom he had been madly in love ever since he first set eyes on her. She had the face of a Barbie doll, and in September she returned from summer break with a bronze tan that made her perfect teeth seem whiter than the chalk by the board behind Mrs. Carson. Dominic turned back to re-focus his gaze onto the back of the head of the classmate sitting in front of him but froze when his returning eyes met Mrs. Carson's icy stare squarely focused on him. He had taken too much time admiring the secret love of his life.

Fortunately, the door to the classroom opened, and a cool breeze swept the room as the air from the hallway followed the entrance of the principal of St. Mary's grammar school, Sister Catherine Michael. On cue, the students stood up straight and tall next to their desks and in unison sang out the expected salutation, "Good morning, Sister Catherine!" Sister Catherine paused her forward progress and responded, "Good morning, children." And then, waiting a beat, she followed her greeting with, "You may be seated." The classroom complied with her order by sitting back down at their desks, once again folding their hands and staring into the back of the head of the student sitting in front of them. Sister Catherine made her way over to Mrs. Carson and the two turned away from the class. They whispered to each other while both tried to keep an eye out for any trespasses from one of the captive students.

Dominic wanted to put his head down on the desk and take a nap. He was tired. He was restless. He was hungry. He was bored. He felt sticky. He could smell the pancake syrup the boy sitting behind him had for breakfast. He could see the traces of white specks in the hair of the student in front of him. Every now and then he caught the smell of flowers from just outside the classroom window mixing with the odor of the floor cleanser disinfectant. And he could smell the fruity aromatic shampoo of Moira Toomey's hair, which made him dizzy and mischievous. He felt disconnected and out of place. He was always described as quiet and shy, which he was. This was not the result of bashfulness or a special reserve or even a social awkwardness as much as he was just afraid. He was afraid of everyone and everything. He didn't feel safe. This fear was driven by the proposition that someone would take notice of him and then humiliate him: whether it was to mock his name, his looks, his clothes, his haircut, his speech pattern—anything. It was for this reason that Dominic practiced being invisible. Whether at school, on the playground, in church, at home, or anywhere else in public—Dominic imagined that he wasn't really physically present and that no one could actually see him. He had convinced himself this unique power actually worked.

"Well, Mrs. Carson, what are the children learning today?" Sister Catherine intruded on Dominic's thoughts. The two had finished their furtive chat and were now both facing the students.

"I was just about to hand back the test that the students took yesterday."

"And how did everyone do?" inquired Sister Catherine.

"Overall, the class did well. Some students really studied hard, and others will have to do more studying. Only one student got every question right."

"Really? And who was our gold star student?" asked Sister Catherine.

"Oh, he correctly answered every question; however, he won't be getting a gold star."

Dominic was looking straight ahead, listening to the dialogue between the two grown-up figures, when he took note of a pause in the conversation and realized that Mrs. Carson was glaring directly at him, with a sadistic grin on her face.

"Dominic Manterra was the only student who correctly answered every question on the test."

Dominic wanted to slump down in his desk and hide behind the classmate in front of him. But it wouldn't have mattered. All the other students had turned to look at him. Dominic was tempted to make eye contact with Moira Toomey to see if she was impressed with his accomplishment and would talk with him at recess. However, Mrs. Carson was about to obliterate any such chance.

"Why no gold star for Master Manterra?" Sister Catherine sounded genuinely surprised.

"Because Master Manterra decided he was going to write his name at the top of the test in all capital letters, although I specifically told the students not to use all capital letters. Obviously, Master Manterra is a big baby and can't follow simple instructions."

Dominic felt the blood rush to his face and sweat soaked his forehead and back. His mouth was dry and his hands were shaking. He wanted to disappear into thin air, to instantly be invisible.

"A big baby!" Mrs. Carson repeated. The other kids began to giggle and sneer. Mrs. Carson extended her arm and held out the test paper in Dominic's direction.

"Come on up and get your test, Dominic the big baby! You would have gotten an 'A' but because you decided to be a big baby and write in all capital letters, you get a 'C.' You must learn to follow directions, if you want to succeed in life! Come get your paper."

Dominic rose from his desk and walked up to the outstretched hand holding the folded paper. He could feel the disdain emanating from both adults, and the mocking eyes of his classmates upon his being. When he reached the front of the class, Sister Catherine addressed him:

"Well, you have anything you want to say for yourself, Master Manterra?"

Dominic paused for a moment. He considered the person dressed in black from head to foot except for two pieces of white cardboard—one to cover what Dominic surmised was a rather large set of breasts and the other that appeared to be pasted to her forehead. Her face was squared off in the headdress habit, which pushed in her prune face and accentuated the wrinkles more than necessary. He looked at Mrs. Carson's varicose hands, wrinkled and boney, holding forth his capital offense. He defiantly met each woman's gaze rather than looking down in shame.

"Yes, I just like capital letters. Is that such a sin?"

He reached up and snatched the test paper out of Mrs. Carson's hand. He turned around and walked back to his desk. The class seemed to have ceased breathing and by the expressions on their faces, Dominic could only imagine the punishment the two women would cook up for him.

VI.

LITURGICAL DEBUT

At lunch, especially in the autumn and the spring when the weather permitted going outside in the schoolyard, the favorite pastime for the boys of St. Mary's grammar school was playing keep away. It basically was an alternate form of rugby where one side would have the ball and the other side would try to steal it back. The side having the ball had the goal of keeping it away from the other side. The boy who actually held the ball would run with it but could pass it off to a teammate. The teammate would then become the runner. The other side would try to catch the runner and steal the ball from him. When the runner was caught and couldn't escape the clutches of the other team's players, it usually resulted in a "pile on". The runner would find himself on the bottom of a pile of boys while his hands and arms were peeled and pulled and twisted until he coughed up the ball. This activity was totally forbidden by the nuns of St. Mary's. In fact, running in the schoolyard at lunchtime was forbidden, period. To be caught playing keep away was almost a mortal sin in the eyes of the nuns.

Dominic loved to play keep away. And of course, he got caught playing it. And of course, he was caught playing it by Sister Catherine, who never forgot any student's prior transgression. As with any transgression at St. Mary's, there was consequences. Dominic had feared that the punishment would be his suspension from his recent entry into the corps of the altar boys. However, the consensus was that he needed to spend more time in church examining his conscience and repenting of his defiant ways. That and a week of detention praying the rosary out loud with other "ruffians" and "rambunctious boys" was ample restitution. As the week went on, volume of the praying of the rosary became increasingly louder and louder. So much so that by Thursday, the shouting of "...full of grace, the Lord is with thee. Blessed are thou amongst women and blessed is the fruit of thy womb..." could be heard throughout the corridors of the school, reaching the ears of Sister Catherine sitting in her principal's office. Sister Catherine quickly made her way down to the detention room and stood in the doorway. She fixed her glare on Dominic and without saying a word, transmitted daggers of death at his head. Dominic got the point, and brought the fervor of the praying down to a quieter pitch and a slower cadence. Sister Catherine nodded her head and then stalked back to her office. Dominic glanced over at Miss Svarickova, the teacher on detention room duty for that week. She caught Dominic's gaze and gave him a brief subtle smile as she returned to marking the stack of papers in front of her. Dominic liked Miss Svarickova. She was younger than most of the teachers and didn't seem to fit in with the rigidity of the system. She wasn't exactly pretty—perhaps her exotic looks were too sophisticated for the simple taste of the small town of Rosedale—yet she had a mysterious air about her like a French movie starlet. And Dominic felt a strange secret connection to her.

The Friday night service was to be Dominic's altar boy debut. Altar boys were assigned in teams of two. Dominic scanned the assignment sheet until he found his name. His eyes widened when he read the name next to his: John Nebbenshultz. John was one of the nerdy kids—horn-rimmed, Coke bottle glasses that were held together with an assortment of tapes and glue. His white shirts had the look and feel of pantyhose material. He had sported a hint of a mustache since first grade and was paler than a whitewashed fence, with a thick head of greasy, dirty-blonde hair that he parted neatly on the side. And he had a unique

talent for spontaneously mimicking any sound that the body could make
from deep-throated belches to the wettest farts, in addition to an astounding catalogue of animal sounds, cows being his forte. Dominic
figured he was basically harmless, amusing for sure but a beacon for
trouble since he had no restraint.

Why does he even want to be an altar boy? Dominic asked himself.

The mass on Friday evening started at 7:30. It was a short mass, about
twenty-five minutes long. For their debut as altar boys, Dominic and
John would be serving a priest that was fairly new to the parish—Father
Chou. Father Chou was from Taiwan. He was a very humble man whose
spoken English was very difficult to understand, but this did not deter
him from praying out loud during the Sunday masses during the time of
reflection right after communion. He would bring the microphone close
and share his prayer aloud with the startled parishioners who were aghast
at the fact they could barely understand a word Father Chou was saying
(it could have been Latin to them) and because he was expressing himself
so intimately. Dominic suspected most felt uncomfortable, some were
amused, and the rest were indifferent. Dominic would watch from his
pew and then look up at the little statue of a crowned, bearded, and
mustached white man with piercing blue eyes, his hands stretched out
and his legs hovering above the raised altar. If this manifestation of the
savior was holding a microphone in his one outstretched hand and a mic
stand in the other, Dominic imagined he could have stood in as the front
man for Led Zeppelin or Aerosmith. But in any case, the expression on
the statue never changed when Father Chou prayed aloud, so if it didn't
bother the person the whole event was honoring, then it was OK with
Dominic.

From the side of the altar, straight from the sacristy, Father Chou led
as Dominic and John followed piously behind. Father Chou took his
post up in front of the altar and John and Dominic moved to the side,
where two chairs and kneelers were set up. Father Chou greeted the
people in attendance.

Immediately, John began fidgeting.

"These damn cassocks are so itchy." John was running his fingers between the collar and his neck. "God knows it took a while to find one of them that didn't reek of b.o. It's like no one heard of freakin' deodorant. Don't they ever wash these rags? How about you, Nicky boy, did you find a clean one?"

Dominic couldn't disagree with John's observation. The red cassocks were hung in wooden lockers in the altar boy room and for the most part they all smelled foul. As soon as Dominic opened a locker the pungent odor of pubescent teenage boys' underarms smacked him like an iron door. He went through a number of lockers before finding one that didn't totally repulse him.

"Christ, can you understand a word this guy is saying?" John chuckled. "Confucius say one egg foo young and one shimp roll with dumping prease, water and wine on the side."

Dominic started to sweat.

"John, be quiet. We're in church. Now's not the time." Dominic looked at Father Chou, who appeared to not have heard John.

"Nicky, how long does this thing go on? I'm hungry. The old lady sent me here without dinner. I don't know why she even signed me up for this torture anyhow."

Dominic noticed that Father Chou had managed a few quick puzzled glances at where he and John were sitting.

"Do you hear that, Nicky? It's my stomach growling like a junkyard dog: one that hasn't eaten. Man, I could eat a cow right now!" At these last words, John turned his face toward Dominic and mischievously grinned. "You know what that means, right?"

Dominic knew what it *might* mean. "John, you have to quit it," he whispered as seriously as he could.

John just smiled as if looking right through Dominic. "Relax, Nicky boy. Just having some fun with ya."

Soon, John seemed to settle down, remaining mostly silent, although he would let out an occasional belch or a farting sound when there was a quiet moment. Unfortunately, the slow but steady theatrics along with the build-up of nervous tension started to break Dominic. He became delirious with containing his laughter, fighting to stifle an outburst, which only served to egg John on in trying to break his resolve.

"Show time, Nicky boy!" John interrupted Dominic's thoughts. Dominic realized it was time for them to bring up the water and wine to Father Chou. They walked over to a side table and John flipped Dominic a large chalice and the linen towel. John grabbed the water and wine as he grinned at Dominic.

"Let's go!"

They marched up to the side of the altar where Father Chou stood waiting. He wore a very serious expression that reflected hurt more than anger, and Dominic felt bad. Father Chou could not even look at them as he conducted the cleansing ritual with the chalice and towel held by Dominic. He then held his priest's chalice in front of John, who poured some of the water into it, and then some of the wine, but as Father Chou went to pull back the chalice, John decided to be generous.

"Hold on, Fadda, here's a little extra vino for ya." And John promptly emptied the cruet of wine into the chalice.

Dominic noticed that the chalice was shaking. He figured that Father Chou was really angry now. But when Dominic looked up, he noticed that Father Chou was straining...not to laugh. He was looking down and avoiding eye contact with them. He waved them off and they turned around, returned the items to the table, and knelt down on the kneelers. The two boys had agreed that John would take care of the Sanctus bells and that Dominic would hold the communion plate when Father Chou served communion. The Sanctus bells were next to John, out of view so that when they were shaken it would appear mysterious as if something miraculous was occurring on the altar. Dominic figured the real miracle to occur would be that the two altar boys weren't burned at the stake.

A choking, chortling echoed in the nearly empty church.

"Whoa, I knew I should have eaten something before I left the house," murmured John. "The stomach is growling like a bear. Nicky boy, I could eat a—cow..."

Dominic shot a look at John who just stared straight ahead and smiled. Father Chou held the host up. At this point in the Mass, John was to ring the Sanctus bells. Instead, John went with a different sound effect:

"Mmmmmmooooooooooo...."

It was a perfect inflection of a cow's bellow.

Without missing a beat, Father Chou placed the host down and held up the chalice. And again, right on cue, John bellowed:

"Mmmmmmooooooooooo...."

It all became too much for Dominic to bear. He tried swallowing his lips, biting down on his tongue, pinching his crossed arms—it didn't matter. John had broken him. He began to laugh uncontrollably.

John was chuckling as well. "I knew I'd break ya, Nicky boy. The cows out of the barn always get 'em."

Dominic sat back in the altar chair and buried his face in his hands, trying to calm himself down. He managed to regain his composure as he looked up at Father Chou, who was waiting at the altar with the chalice full of communion wafers. Dominic stood up, picked up the communion plate, and met the priest at the altar rail where communion was served. The attendees slowly lined up to receive communion. Each person paused to glare at Dominic before acknowledging Father Chou's invocation of "Body of Christ" and responding with an "Amen" and an outstretched tongue.

Dominic figured this would be his first and last Mass. Sister Catherine would no doubt have him expelled. He would be ex-communicated by the Pope as a modern-day heretic. He'd have to go to public school and most likely never graduate high school. And end up digging ditches for the rest of his miserable life. The image of a shovel in a ditch from the pamphlet *High School or Else* came to his mind.

The communion phase ended. Father Chou moved quickly to bring the Mass to an end. The two altar boys followed the priest off the altar.

"I'm outta here," grunted John and he quickly turned and headed for the altar boy room as he began to pull off his surplice and unbutton his cassock. Dominic looked up at Father Chou but the priest avoided his gaze and hurried into the priest's changing room and closed the door. The sound of the door to the back entrance opened and closed as John made his getaway. Dominic took a deep breath and slowly made his way to the altar to complete his altar boy tasks, his head weighed down in guilt and shame. He immediately froze. In front of the altar rail there stood a small mob of angry parishioners.

"You should go to confession right now! What shameful behavior!" charged a stocky young woman. "Blasphemy! Nothing short of blasphemy! Sacrilege!" cried out an older woman, her head covered by what looked to Dominic like a white doily, its corners snugly tied under her chin.

Others in the crowd murmured their approval of these remarks while adding their own comments. Dominic stepped quickly away and, extinguished the candles on the altar and returned to the sacristy.

He noticed that the priest's changing room was dark. Dominic felt remorse for his behavior, especially in light of the pious priest's devotion and humility. He removed his altar boy garments, turned out the lights and exited through the back entrance. The crisp air of the autumn night felt refreshing as he took in a deep breath and climbed the shallow steps. He stuck his hands in his coat pockets and started down the walkway. The night's events were weighing on his mind and the weight trickled down to his feet as each footstep felt like it had been dipped in cement. A voice slightly higher than a whisper startled him from his thoughts of shame.

"Dominic!"

Dominic recognized the voice, but the tone was different. Once the speaker emerged from the shadows he understood why. Miss Svarickova never called him Dominic. She had always addressed him as Nick. She was the only teacher who did.

"Oh, hello, Miss Svarickova." Dominic blushed at being alone in the presence of a teacher, especially at night.

"Hi, Nick. How are you feeling?" she asked, not taking her eyes off of him.

"OK, I guess." Dominic suddenly felt awkward.

"Quite a performance in there tonight," Miss Svarickova nodded her head toward the church building.

"Wait, were you...were you...at Mass tonight?" asked Dominic, as he could feel his cheeks flush with blood and the sweat form on his forehead and neck.

"Indeed, I was," she replied. "I would have thought a week of hail Mary's, our Father's, and blessed this and that would have had a different effect on you." She looked askance at Dominic and he dropped his head. Suddenly she let out a soft laugh and touched Dominic's elbow. "Head up, Nick, it's not the end of the world."

"It isn't?" he asked dejectedly.

"Well, I don't believe Sister Catherine will be amused, I suppose."

"That's for sure," Dominic mumbled.

"Come walk with me, Nick." And Miss Svarickova slipped her arm around Dominic's and escorted him down the path toward the main sidewalk. Dominic could feel the blood flushing his cheeks turn hotter.

Dominic had never been this close to a grown-up that wasn't a relative. His eyes scanned over Miss Svarickova's hands and then her neck and the side of her face, as they slowly walked, her eyes fixed clearly ahead of them. His arm felt comfortable in hers, natural—safe and reassured. Dominic could smell the sweetness of her perfume in the crisp autumn air, like she had just stepped out of a bath. Her soft voice broke up his thoughts.

"Nick, *what* do you think God is?"

Dominic paused for a moment. "The creator of the universe?" he replied.

Miss Svarickova smiled. "Yes, but that is more a role than a substance."

Dominic thought harder but couldn't come up with any other answer.

"Give up?" she inquired gently. Dominic nodded.

"God is love. Never forget that, Nick. He's not a ritual nor a set of rules. He is unconditional love."

She pulled away her arm and turned Dominic to face her, placing her hands on his shoulders and looking straight into his eyes.

"I don't know what was going on in there tonight, nor would I condone your behavior as appropriate for the setting, but I don't want you to beat yourself up over it. Although I believe religion has a place and purpose in our world, it is not what defines God. Do you know what defines God?"

Dominic was too mesmerized to respond with any intelligence. Standing this close to Miss Svarickova, with her hands on his shoulders, and the sweet aroma of her person filling his senses, he could see for the first time she was very beautiful. She dropped her right hand from his shoulder and, placing it on his chest over his heart, she whispered softly.

"He's defined by the love you hold inside you, the love in your heart for Him and for others, especially the least of His children. We're all His children, Nick. And He loves us all. He is not defined by laws and regulations. The laws and regulations are defined by Him. And the heart of His law is grace, and His rules and regulations are written in mercy."

She brought her right hand up to Dominic's chin, her fingertips nudging his chin up. Her fingertips and palm felt warm and tender against his skin.

"Nick, there are two paths in life before us. One path is understanding that leads to enlightenment. The other path is judgment that leads to condemnation. Depending on which we choose, we either find freedom or bondage. Choose carefully, my young friend."

Dominic felt a stirring in his belly, a nervous, exhilarating sort of feeling as he observed her eyes and cheeks and mouth beaming with a sort of angelic glow. Then she turned and disappeared down the path into the night. After that school year, Miss Svarickova left St. Mary's and Dominic never saw or heard from her again. But later in life he would think of her every so often and reflect on that night's encounter and the path he had chosen.

VII

REVELATION OF
AN OLD SOUL

Mrs. Bruning waited patiently at the corner. Dominic spotted her first and tapped his best friend, Jack Bruning, on the arm to draw his attention to where his mom stood. Mrs. Bruning was a slight woman with a very white complexion and blue eyes that glowed even on the brightest days. Her son Jack was her spitting image with bright red hair that matched his mom's. Dominic always thought of her as a serene person, quiet and reserved, and always in a pleasant mood. Dominic liked her because she never raised her voice or said a negative word about anything or anyone. At the same time, Dominic felt sorry for her. He imagined she was really sad inside. Her husband, Mr. Bruning, was a very strict disciplinarian. Dominic felt nervous around him. He seemed to have a problem with holding on to a job—Dominic thought this was probably the reason why Jack was always moving to a new apartment. Dominic would watch as Mr. Bruning would interact with other parents at various school functions and notice how he comported himself as a friendly and care-free person, with everyone believing he was such a swell guy. But to Dominic it was a stage act. Dominic believed that Mr. Bruning abused his wife and son—maybe not in an actual physical way, but with the fear and intimidation that he would resort to an open hand or closed fist if he felt circumstances warranted such action.

"Hey, Mom, why are you waiting over here?" Jack questioned her in a curious tone. He was as gentle and harmless as she was.

"So that you could easily see me, Jack." She smiled at him and then turn to Dominic. "Hello, Nick."

"Hello, Mrs. Bruning." Dominic blushed and looked down. It felt funny when grown-ups addressed him as Nick and not as Dominic. Mrs. Bruning was one of the few grown-ups who did.

"Besides," Mrs. Bruning turned her attention back to Jack, "this is the corner closest to our new place."

"A new home?" Jack asked.

"Yes, a new apartment. It's the second-floor unit of a two-family house. Your father and I moved our furniture and clothing and other belongings into it while you were in school today. Remember we had been talking about it for the past few weeks. It's a bigger place, we'll have more room and space."

"Is Dominic going to be able to stay for dinner?"

"Yes, he is. That's the plan, anyway. Come, let's walk."

Mrs. Bruning turned and headed up Third Avenue, and Jack walked beside her. Dominic followed close behind, breathing in the late-autumn air and noting the bright colors of the leaves that dotted the sidewalk and front lawns of the houses they passed.

"How was school today?"

"Boring, as usual," answered Jack. "The day takes so long."

"Thanksgiving and Christmas will be here before you know it," responded Mrs. Bruning. "Hopefully you boys have been good so that Santa can bring you some nice presents."

"You know what Miss Svarickova said about Dominic in class today?" piped up Jack. Dominic wondered where Jack was going with this.

"No, what did Miss Svarickova say?" Mrs. Bruning asked with an earnest interest.

"She said that Dominic was like a forty-year-old man," laughed Jack.

Dominic looked down, embarrassed. He remembered that Miss Svarickova said that to him in front of the class and all the other students laughed at him. He wanted to crawl inside a desk and hide. Miss Svarickova had hushed them and had walked over to Dominic to pat him on the back, a gesture Dominic thought meant she regretted saying it, and Dominic heard her whisper to him, "Don't worry, Nick, they don't understand." Dominic didn't understand either. And although he was hurt and angry at the moment, he wouldn't hold it against her. He loved Miss Svarickova because she made him feel special. Maybe it was because he was different like she was.

"That was quite a compliment Miss Svarickova paid to Nick," Mrs. Bruning said quietly.

"What? How can that be?" laughed Jack. "She called him an old man!"

"No," Mrs. Bruning continued in her quiet but confident manner of speaking, "she didn't say Dominic was an old man. She said he was like a forty-year-old man."

"Well, forty is way old!" Jack said with emphasis. Mrs. Bruning shot her son a look and smiled before continuing her explanation.

"What Miss Svarickova meant was that for a fourth grader, Nick is very mature. He's old beyond his years in his understanding of life and how he handles himself with others." Dominic looked up to catch Mrs. Bruning gazing back at him and she winked at him reassuringly as though to say that Miss Svarickova was correct in her assessment.

"How much further?" asked Jack.

"We're here," replied Mrs. Bruning.

They stopped at a large colonial house painted grey with dark-green shudders, a wrap-around front porch, and a neatly trimmed lawn with a bed of garden flowers in front. It was the nicest-looking place that Dominic could recall that Jack had ever lived in up to that point. Dominic glanced at the second floor with its big picture window centered over the front porch and noticed Mr. Bruning standing motionless, watching them without any expression on his severe face. Dominic looked at Mrs. Bruning and she was staring up as well.

"This is a cool place, Mom!" Jack's glee was apparent.

"Yes, it's very nice," added Dominic. "I'm sure you will all be happy here."

Mrs. Bruning placed a hand on each boy's shoulder. "Come on, boys, dinner will be ready soon."

"THAT WAS NOT BAD but I know you can do much better than that—especially since we are singing to our Lord!" Sister Marianne's voice echoed in St. Mary's Church as the assembly of fourth, fifth, and sixth-grade students struggled to quietly sit and pay attention to her musical direction. "Let's take it from the top with *Shout from the Highest Mountain*. And let us sing with our hearts so God knows how much we love Him!"

"Dominic! You better put down the missalette and start singing," Jack cautioned his friend in a hushed tone. "You don't want Stoneface to catch you! You're sitting on the end so you're easy to see."

Dominic looked up to take note of the nun's position, knowing it was prudent to heed his friend's warning. Sister Michael Parsons had earned that moniker due to her austere, square-faced countenance that instilled fear and loathing in the students. The nickname also aptly captured her overall disposition. He placed the missalette in the holder on the back of the pew in front of him and picked up the paper handout with the words of the five hymns. A shadow fell over his paper. He slowly looked up to see Sister Stoneface herself standing next to him. Fortunately, she was just on a reconnaissance mission scanning the pews for gum-chewers, nappers, non-singers, and talkers. Jack's advice could not have been better timed. Immediately she shot away like a hawk ready to pounce on an unsuspecting hare. A violator was spotted and needed to be stoned.

"OK, everyone, now we're all to give it our best effort here. I need you all to stand-up straight and tall. I am really counting on the boys to step it up here! The girls so far have been doing the majority of the singing,

I want to hear you boys raise your voices louder. Remember, singing is praying twice! Let's sing so it makes the heavenly angels flap their wings with joy!" Sister Marianne lifted her arms to conduct the chorus of students. "Everyone on the fourth beat! One, and two, and…" Her hands began to gesture as the chorus of voices sang out.

Dominic held the paper in his hands but didn't need to read the words. They have been singing most of these songs since first grade. Every now and then the song list would be updated with a new hymn from some priest or religious brother whose job it was to come up with a new batch of worship tunes. The missalette was full of numbered songs that Dominic had never even heard sang in school masses or on Sundays for that matter. Dominic didn't mind the singing for the school masses as he thought it sounded much better than the singing at the Sunday masses. Maybe the parishioners needed to practice with Sister Marianne. They finished the song with a flourish and Sister Marianne appeared pleased.

"Excellent! Excellent! I think Sister Michael will agree that sounded inspired!" Sister Marianne glanced over at Sister Michael who was now on the other side of the church at a different guard position. Sister Michael managed a smile (that Dominic feared would create cracks in her face) and nodded her head in approval. Actually, Dominic felt sorry for Sister Michael as he figured she was so mean in her disposition because deep down inside, she was really unhappy. And that made Dominic feel sad for her. He wouldn't want anyone to be unhappy, especially if serving the Lord. He then caught a glimpse of auburn hair in the pew that Sister Michael was standing next to…yes, it was her: Moira. He leaned and stretched to get a better glimpse of her. And found himself staring right into the eyes of Sister Michael, who motioned with her fingers for him to look forward and pay attention. Dominic snapped to it.

"Alright, let's remain standing and sing the next song, *Come Back to Me*. It's a more solemn song but that doesn't mean we sing it with any less spirit, just a gentler spirit. This will be our Communion song so remember to keep singing while you are walking up to receive the Eucharist." Once again Sister Marianne raised her hands to conduct. "On my count!"

This was Dominic's favorite hymn of all and he loved the words. He imagined them to be the words the Savoir sings to every soul that has strayed and lost its way, hoping any little lost lamb would hear the Shepherd's voice and return to His waiting arms. To him, it was a song of forgiveness, reconciliation and peace. As Dominic sang along with his schoolmates, he leaned forward to gaze at his love...

VIII.

AT THE FAIR

Timmy Stefano and Ernie Damon, two of Dominic's closest friends at St. Mary's, waited for him at the corner of Fourth Avenue and Poplar Street.

"Is it me or are we always waiting for this guy?" asked Ernie with exasperation.

Timmy chuckled. "Calm down, here he comes now."

Dominic reached his two friends and the trio started walking down Fourth Avenue toward St. Mary's.

"What in God's name is it with you and being on time?" snapped Ernie.

"Com'on, Ernie, it was just a few minutes," Timmy said, seeking to calm any tension.

"Sorry, fellas, was watching the 4:30 Movie on channel 7 and lost track of the time. Brando as Marc Antony was about to deliver the funeral oration for Caesar. And no wisecracks about me being late for my own funeral needed."

"You should worry that I don't arrange for your funeral," answered Ernie with mock anger as he punched Dominic in the arm.

The boys reached the St. Mary's schoolyard, which was brightly lit up like a combination amusement park and Christmas bazaar. It was the St. Mary's summer fair and there were rides and attractions and food stations scattered across the breadth of the grounds. It was an annual event that brought all the folks that belonged to St. Mary's parish and other people from around Rosedale as well as neighboring towns. The place was already bustling with an ocean of adults and children scrambling to take in all the activities of the fair.

"My number one goal for this evening, Nicky boy, is to get you on the bullet." Ernie flashed a devilish grin at Timmy.

Dominic frowned. He gazed over at the aforementioned ride, situated next to the St. Mary's convent. The ride was basically a large capsule connected to a windmill that went round and round. Every year, Ernie made the same threat. And every year Dominic was able to avoid it. He had no reason to believe this year would be different.

"I don't think so, Ernie. I just ate a big dinner, my mom's pasta e fagioli, and a meatball sandwich. Probably not the best idea to go on the bullet. Not tonight anyway." Yes, Dominic would be avoiding the bullet once again.

"Well, look who it is? Heading our way to boot. Hey, Nicky, aren't you going to say hello?" Ernie's mind was already working on a plan. Timmy and Dominic turned to see what Ernie was referring to and instantly Dominic's stomach started twisting into knots. Coming towards the boys was none other than Moira Toomey and two of her friends, Anne Conley and Betsy Sullivan.

"Hello, ladies!" Ernie greeted the three girls while giving Dominic a shove towards Moira.

"Hi, guys," responded Moira. "What rides have you been on so far?"

"Oh, we just got here," Timmy answered.

"That's right, but Dominic here, he wants to start off with the bullet, ain't that right, Dominic?" Ernie winked at Timmy.

"I'm thinking we don't have to start off with that ride. We can play some of the arcade games first." Dominic was suddenly nervous.

"The wait for the bullet is the longest. You may just want to get on line now and get it over with. That's what we did. It was wild," Betsy replied, her two friends shaking their heads in agreement.

"It's the best ride here," added Moira. "It's my favorite. It's fun and fast and scary all at the same time. I'm sure you like things like that, Dominic!" Moira smiled at her not-so-secret-admirer.

Dominic managed to stammer out a response, "Yeah, that sounds like it's right up my alley."

"Great!" exclaimed Ernie while slapping Dominic on the back. "We'll head over there right now! And maybe meet up with you girls for some cotton candy or popcorn afterwards and compare notes!"

The three boys made their way over to the ride. Timmy was shaking his head, broadly grinning at Ernie's perfectly executed plan. They quickly got on the end of the line.

"Hey, Nicky boy, snap out of it!" Ernie waved his hands in front of Dominic's face. "You're never going to get anywhere with Moira if you freeze up whenever you're around her, being all tongue tied. Girls like her are looking for a real man, not a shy antelope. You have to work on being cool."

Timmy cracked up. "Dominic turns into an ice cube every time he's around her. Can't get any cooler than that."

"Alright, I get it. I was just caught off guard. Besides, it doesn't matter. It's not like she knows how I feel." Dominic was getting annoyed and also apprehensive as they drew closer to their turn to enter the bullet.

"God no, Nicky boy, Moira hasn't a clue that you're madly in love with her and spend all your time pining away for her. You hide it so well!" Ernie's faux tone of sincerity made even Dominic laugh.

Before Dominic knew it, the boys were passing through the turnstile and climbing into the bullet...

DOMINIC WAS HUNCHED OVER by the side of the barn-house, gasping for air while Timmy held on to his arm so he didn't fall over into the pool of vomit in front of him.

"Geez, how much did you eat?' Ernie could barely contain his laughter.

Dominic managed to get out a "fuck you" in between retches. Timmy started to laugh, and as Dominic realized he had emptied all he had, even he began to laugh.

"Maybe we can get you cleaned up somehow and get over to the cotton candy booth to share our experiences with Moira and the girls?" Ernie was enjoying the moment. Dominic shot him a look and shook his head. "On second thought, maybe not such a good idea."

The boys went to see if they could get into St. Mary's to use the bathroom and get Dominic some water.

IX

PLAY BALL!

Dominic and Timmy walked along Fourth Avenue carrying their baseball mitts, heading to the try-outs for St. Mary's Little League Baseball. It wasn't technically a try-out as much as an evaluation as all boys that signed up were more or less guaranteed a spot on a team. This exercise was just for the initial entry into the league as once a boy was assigned to a team, future team assignments would be based on the actual playing experience of the athletes. The volunteer army of fathers who served as coaches, assistant coaches and umpires set-up various stations for the boys to pass through to assess their skills at catching, fielding, hitting, throwing and running. At each station, one or two of the fathers would coordinate the activity while other fathers stood around with clipboards, making notes and negotiating among themselves. This was the process for assigning the boys to various teams and ensuring that the skill and talent were fairly spread.

To Dominic, it always seemed to be the same core crew of fathers who organized and ran different events or activities at St. Mary's. Whether it was the little league baseball, Cub and Boy Scout troops, church and school fundraisers, helping out in the school cafeteria, sponsoring dances and social events for all the parents, and assisting at church services as readers and ushers, these men were on the job. From the school grounds to the baseball diamond to the campground to the Sunday services, these fathers were the backbone of a community held together by faith and family. To be clear, they weren't just there because of their own sons and daughters. In their minds, each child of St. Mary's and of Rosedale itself was *their* son and daughter. And these men succeeded because of the wives and mothers who partnered with them to make living in Rosedale and belonging to St. Mary's a wonderful life.

Dominic and Timmy walked into the St. Mary's Academy for Girls High School gymnasium which had been temporarily converted into a baseball clinic. Some boys had already lined up along the one side of the gym. Dominic recognized some of his classmates and friends waiting a turn to show their stuff. He spotted Ernie Damon and his brother Rick, already reputable ball players from the sandlot games and summer rec-reation baseball. Ernie's pitching was legendary. His arm strength was such that the Rosedale Bowling Alley had banned him from bowling any games there as the owners feared he would damage the bowling lanes with the way his bowling ball raced down the lane and sent the pins flying like it was shot from a Howitzer cannon. Standing next to them was another outstanding athlete, already taller than most of the other guys, Billy Feeney, both an excellent hitter and infielder. George O'Grady was better known as a venom on the gridiron but his hitting skills were well respected. Sporting his Mets hat, Mark Stephens, the smartest kid in Dominic's class, was standing next to Joey Cerratano, wearing his signature Yankees cap (and a pair of baseball pants, of course) probably discussing sporting stats. Between Mark and Joey, Dominic figured there wasn't a sporting event, milestone, player, team, league, distance, time, inning, round, quarter, period, match, overtime, ice rink, court, stadium, referee or umpire's call that they didn't know any and everything about; and would argue with you as though life and death depended on it. They were much better statisticians than athletes. Dom-inic was also in Cub Scouts with Joey. Mrs. Cerratano, Joey' s mom, was their Den Mother. She was a gentle and kind woman, with a dignified and graceful presence. She was no pushover though, and was a firm and strong leader, sophisticated and savvy, who had taught the boys in her den that brain-power triumphs over brawn when skillfully applied. The assistant Den Mother was Mrs. Feeney, Billy's mom, another formidable woman of quiet strength and resolve. They always had the best snacks at the den meetings.

The lines moved fast and the boys all had their turns at each station set up by the fathers. Dominic observed how the fathers were able to balance the serious purpose of the try-outs with humor and jokes among themselves. While he thought this was another time-consuming endeavor for men who were already busy working and raising their own families, it seemed they were having a lot of fun and laughs. But it wasn't totally without controversy. Dominic could sense some tension at times. He figured it was that everyone wanted the Damon brothers on their team. Dominic couldn't say he blamed them...

IN THE ST. MARY'S Little League all the teams were sponsored by various businesses in Rosedale as well as other organizations. This applied to all three levels in the league: junior, intermediate and senior. From pharmacies to funeral homes to liquor stores to auto repair shops to florists to the Police Athletic League and the Rosedale Fire Department, the commercial, economic and public sector enterprises of Rosedale were well represented.

The teams had been set and the game schedules distributed. Uniforms with baseball hats, baseball pants, and brightly colored t-shirts that would be worn well beyond faded recognition were picked up. It was time to play ball!

Dominic ended up on Pat's Liquors, which had the special perk that the owner, Mr. Rincanello, always sent a cooler of soda to each game for the players and coaches. Timmy ended up on Ritzman Travel Agency, which his older brothers had played on before, and still had the same coach, Mr. Strand. George was on Lorraine Drugs while Joey was playing for Mullins 5 n 10, and Mark ended up on Lazelli Brothers. Woody's

Crematorium, coached by Mr. Mullaney, was where the Damon brothers landed.

The first few games on the schedule went by quick. There was always anticipation in the Junior league as the teams were assembled based on the impressions made at the try-outs. The coaches were able to assess how they did in distributing the talent evenly across the teams. For the most part, the teams seemed fairly matched. There were a few surprises. Cruziano Plumbing & Heating became an early standout with Marco Leonardo (who was better known for his basketball ability) combining with Tony Silvitano and Kenny Williams for a formidable three-four-five hitter line-up. The other team to beat (or more likely, to get beat by) was Woody's. Besides Ernie and Rick Damon, the team had picked up the stalwart Billy Feeney at third base. Woody's, with these three players as their core was taking no prisoners and they were the next team for Pat's Liquors to play.

Dominic was fully aware of Ernie Damon's fastball. He had watched most batters be embarrassed by it playing in the summer recreation league. But he was on the same team as Ernie then, so it didn't matter. True, Ernie would have some fun during batting practice but for the most part, he would go easy on his teammates. But being on a different team made it a whole new ballgame. As luck would have it, Ernie was on the mound for the scheduled game against Pat's Liquors.

"Batter up!" The umpire adjusted his clicker as Dominic stepped into the batter's box. Ernie just stood on the mound, grinning from ear to ear. He lifted his baseball hat off his head and then brought it down to set the bill lower in front. "OK!" shouted the plate umpire who set himself in a standing crouched position behind the catcher. Ernie kicked up his front left leg then in a quick motion whirled around his right leg and pitching arm in one smooth motion and launched the baseball toward the plate. Dominic jumped back from the plate as the pitch came in high and inside.

"Ball one!" barked the umpire. Dominic shot a look at Ernie as he caught the baseball the catcher had thrown back to him.

"That was a little too inside, Nicky boy. I promise to give you some more room next pitch." Ernie winked at Dominic. The next pitch came in just as fast but was toward the outside of the plate.

The umpire shouted "Ball!"

The next pitch was a change-up that floated high over the plate and the umpire called it that way.

Ernie stood off to the side of the mound and smiled at Dominic. "I know I'm down in the count, Nicky, but I'm thinking those last two pitches were your best chance. Anyway, the next three will be right over the plate, if that helps ya!" He moved to the rubber.

With that, Ernie threw three fast balls straight down the middle and Dominic swung but as the saying goes, you can't hit 'em if you can't see 'em. Yeah, Ernie was that fast. For his next two at bats, Ernie showed him some mercy. He just threw the six pitches straight up and struck out Dominic right away.

After the game, the teams lined up for the traditional "good game" exchange. Ernie's face beamed with a big smile as he smacked his glove against Dominic's. "Nicky boy, I always told you were better on the hardcourt with a basketball in your hands! Nice game!"

Dominic shook his head. "Just remember us little people when you're playing for the Bronx Bombers, Ernie. I expect World Series tickets— free!"

Mitchell Manterra was leaning against the fence, waiting for his younger brother, Dominic. "I guess Woody's Crematorium lived up to its name," Mitchell laughed.

"Yup, pretty much creamed us. Or at least I got buried."

"Ernie looks like he's ready for the pro's now. Or at least the Senior League."

"Let's get home. I need some of mom's cooking. At least that will be a homerun!"

X.

LEADING THE WAY

S omebody please, shoot the bugler!" shouted a scout from within one of the tents that squared out the campsite for Boy Scout Troop 60. It was 6:30 a.m. and the troop was being called to assembly courtesy of the Scoutmaster's son, Bobby "Babs" Wilson, and his bugle. Dominic opened his eyes to the faint rays of sun shooting through the screen window of the tent. Unzipping the side of his sleeping bag, he pushed himself on his elbows, yawned, and glanced over at his two tent mates, Billy Mickler and Eddy Garvis.

"Up and at 'em, boys. We have a long day ahead of us. Got to get going here."

Eddy was still in a sleep coma but Billy stirred in his bag, turned, lifted his head without opening his eyes, muttered, "More of a reason to catch a few more z's," and dropped his head back down.

Dominic chuckled. He got out of his sleeping bag and donned his wool cap. His two buddies hadn't budged.

"Come on, guys, we only have fifteen minutes to get in formation after reveille sounds. Let's go!"

The two mummies ignored his cajoling. Dominic shrugged. He then proceeded to climb over both of his companions, crawling on all fours, and making his way to the tent door amid the sounds of their gasps and protests.

"Son-of-a-bitch, how much do you weigh, fat man!" yelled Eddy.

"Funny comment coming from you, lard ass," Dominic responded. He stepped out of the tent. Dominic inhaled the clean mountain air through his nose and then exhaled the air through his puckered lips in a slow, steady stream of frosted breath.

"Morning, Nicky boy! Did I wake ya?" greeted Babs as he sauntered by with his shiny brass instrument of torment.

"Nice playing, Babs. Could have used a little more boogie-woogie, though."

"I'll remember that for tomorrow morning. Ready for the mother of all hikes?" Babs didn't wait for an answer but continued on to his own campsite.

Dominic scanned the campground as his fellow scouts emptied from the warmth of their tents to gather into formation for the flag raising. He trekked over to a pine tree to relieve himself and returned to the tent site. Eddy and Billy were up and dressed, with Eddy already incessantly talking while Billy was busy prepping a fire. Billy shot Dominic a knowing smile as he noticed the annoyed expression on the senior patrol leader's face.

"Weren't you just in a coma five minutes ago?" asked Dominic of Eddy.

"Well, good morning to you, too, captain." Eddy grinned. Eddy had skin thicker than an alligator and took no offense to anything. Despite his loquaciousness and proneness to severe odiferous flatulence, he was a solid scout and Dominic liked having him on his patrol team that they self-named the Hawk patrol. Billy was likely the best scout in the troop and both he and Eddy were the best fishermen.

"Good job on the fire-building there, Billy. After assembly, we can light it and have a quick breakfast. You boys piss yet?"

"I've been telling Eddy to piss off since we woke up but he hasn't stopped talking long enough to hear me." The three scouts laughed and headed over to the center of the campsite to join their fellow scouts already lined up by their respective patrols.

"Ten-hut!" Mr. Lyons shouted. The troop stood at attention as the Scoutmaster, Mr. Wilson, stood alongside his assistant. Babs was already standing near the flagpole, his bugle tucked underneath his arm.

"Color guard!" shouted the assistant scoutmaster, and three scouts from the Mountaineers patrol marched toward the flagpole. They halted at the pole and proceeded to hoist the stars and stripes. Babs played "To the Colors." The morning breeze caught hold of the flag as it reached the top and the bright red, white, and blue cloth stretched out in its full glory. It was a picture-perfect morning with the sun shining in a clear blue sky above the surrounding treetops in the pristine Adirondacks. Babs finished playing and then the whole troop recited the Pledge of Allegiance. Once the pledge was finished, Mr. Wilson nodded to Mr. Lyons, who called out to the scouts, "Bow your head, boys!"

The scouts bowed their heads, and Mr. Lyons continued, "Lord, we thank thee for the gifts of thy natural world and this beautiful morning. Watch over our troop this weekend and keep us safe on our hike today."

A voice came out from among the assembled scouts "...and from Babs stinking up the latrine!"

Mr. Lyons raised his head with a perturbed expression. Dominic glanced at Mr. Wilson, who still had his head bowed and managed to keep his slight smile from breaking out into a full-blown grin.

"Amen!" shouted out Dominic and the boys released their stifled laughter, as Mr. Wilson stepped forward, smiling and called them all to parade rest. Babs and the color guard joined the rest of the troop. "I know that was you, Eddy Garvis," called out Babs with a smirk.

"Good morning, boys." Mr. Wilson was a short man with a slight build, thinning hair, and a pleasant disposition. He was a Korean War vet who had two sons in the troop, Babs and his brother Johnny.

The scouts responded with a unified good morning, and Mr. Wilson continued.

"Thanks to the color guard this morning and to Bobby for getting us all up on time. He paused for the comments from the peanut gallery, and then raised his hand to signal for quiet.

"We're going to have our breakfast, and then we'll need to prepare our backpacks for the day's hike up the mountain. Be sure to fill your canteens with water. We'll have lunch on top of the mountain. Troop dismissed!"

THEY MADE THEIR WAY up to the side of the mountain on a rocky trail that made the hike a real challenge with a backpack. Mr. Wilson kept the pace steady but also paused so they could take note of the spectacular views. The boys engaged in their usual banter although it came in spurts as the physical demand of the climb required their energy and focus. A number of times they were fooled by a false summit, and Mr. Wilson clearly enjoyed their temporary dismay at "almost there" turning out to be not all that near, although the three chaperoning fathers did not appear as amused.

Nevertheless, the troop's enthusiasm was undaunted and they were rewarded with awe-inspiring views when they reached the mountaintop. The troop had their lunch while admiring the surroundings and chattering away. After about an hour, the assistant scoutmaster gathered everyone for a troop photo and they started their descent.

Mr. Wilson had timed the climb right and they were able to get back to the campsite just as the sun slipped down behind the treetops. The evening campfires were lit and a tired and hungry troop vigorously chowed down their dinners. Dominic and the other patrol leaders had prepared the bonfire for the Saturday evening activities where each patrol put on a skit and led a campfire song. Mr. Wilson provided some challenges on scouting techniques and shared some folklore. Then the boys turned in for the night. It was a long day of adventure and camaraderie, and it was what Dominic loved to do.

Dominic finished putting out the last of the bonfire flames, making sure the ambers were snuffed out. Mr. Wilson was smoking a cigarette as he stood watching Dominic. Dominic finished and gave Mr. Wilson a wave good night. The Scoutmaster nodded his head as he threw down his cigarette and stamped it underfoot before entering his tent.

As Dominic approached his tent, he could see the glow of the flashlights and hear the laughter of the occupants. Obviously, the hike hadn't zapped all their energy. Inside the crowded tent were Billy and Eddy, joined by Eric Montes and Drew Beekman from the Comanche patrol. They appeared to be in an extra silly mood. Dominic was met with a chorus of greetings. It took a moment, but the aroma reached Dominic's nose and he smelled trouble.

"What are you guys thinking?" he whispered harshly. "Don't even tell me you are drinking in here!"

"Shh, not so loud!" Billy hushed him. "Eric here brought something to warm us in this cold weather."

"Ugh, I don't want to hear it or know about it," replied Dominic.

Eric spoke up. "It's just some rum from my dad's cabinet, Nicky. No big deal. We're just having some fun." He held the bottle out to Dominic.

"No, that's OK, Eric. I'll pass. Look, you guys need to keep it down. Maybe you should go off into the woods a bit but not too far, so you don't wake the other tents. And not for long. It's already late." Dominic glanced at Drew Beekman. He appeared to be a bit dazed and unsteady.

"Drew, you feeling OK?" asked Dominic.

"He's fine, ain't ya, Drew?" responded Billy, slapping Drew on his back. The four boys laughed. Dominic reached out his hand for the bottle. He passed it by Eddy's flashlight and noted it was over half empty.

"You think you guys had enough?"

"We'll be OK, Dominic. We'll just finish it off so we can ditch the bottle. Don't worry," assured Billy. "We'll sneak out over to the firewood shed."

"OK, but just be very quiet and don't do anything stupid."

Dominic climbed out of the tent and studied the leadership tents for a moment. No activity, the area was completely dark. He figured the hike had caught up with the adults. He pulled back the tent flap and whispered into the tent: "OK, just be really quiet."

The four lads crawled out of the tent and headed toward the firewood shed.

"Don't be long!" whispered Dominic, and they all flipped him the bird in response.

Dominic crawled back into the tent and got into his sleeping bag. He listened for a moment, closed his eyes, and fell fast asleep.

"Manterra! Get the hell out here!"

Dominic immediately pulled himself together and crawled out the tent entrance into the shining lanterns held by Mr. Wilson and Mr. Lyons. He quickly pulled on his boots and jumped to his feet. He raised his hand to block out the intense illumination and managed to squeak, "What's going on?"

Mr. Wilson lowered his lantern, although the assistant did not follow suit. Dominic's eyes adjusted, and he could see the four boys lined up, with one of them, Drew, bent over a bit. They were swaying as they stood, shivering in the night cold.

"You awake?" barked Mr. Wilson.

"Yeah...yeah...yes, sir. I am awake," answered Dominic.

"Good. These scouts, appear not to be turned in for the night. And in fact, appear to have been drinking alcohol behind the firewood shed."

Dominic glanced over at the four boys, nodded his head and replied, "Yes, sir."

"In fact, they have nearly finished off a bottle of rum." Mr. Wilson held the bottle up to the light and Dominic could see that it had not much rum left in it. "Drew here has been throwing up for a bit and was close to passing out. Fortunately, Mr. Lyons heard the retching sounds while he was relieving himself and went to investigate. Did you know anything about this, Manterra?"

"Yes, sir, I was aware that they were drinking. It was my suggestion that they go over by the firewood shed, although I did tell them not to overdo it." Dominic shot a look of disdain at Billy and Eric, who were handling the liquor better than Eddy, who was straining to stay awake, and Drew who may well have been sleeping while standing up.

Mr. Wilson turned to the assistant. "Get these four squared away. Have Drew clean himself up a bit and get him something from the first aid kit to settle his stomach. Manterra, come with me."

Dominic followed Mr. Wilson to the center of the parade ground where they halted.

"Stand at attention!" snapped Mr. Wilson. Dominic could tell that Mr. Wilson was specifically angry with him. But he couldn't understand why.

"You're wondering why I am angry with you?" It was like Mr. Wilson was reading his mind.

"Yes, sir. I'm not sure I understand. I didn't drink any of the rum and I didn't bring it, so I don't see why any of this is my problem."

"You think you're off the hook here because you didn't bring the rum and you didn't drink the rum, and that makes you an innocent bystander, as if you have no responsibility for this incident?"

Dominic considered the question for a moment, and then replied, "Yes, sir. This was their doing and I warned them not to overdo it."

Mr. Wilson stepped back for a moment and folded his arms. After a few minutes he broke the silence.

"What are you, Manterra?"

"What do you mean, sir?"

"What is your role in this troop?"

"I'm a Boy Scout. A senior patrol leader, if that's what you're asking, sir."

"Those are titles. But in the big-picture scheme, what are you really?"

Dominic was trying to figure out what Mr. Wilson was after but he was drawing a blank.

"Give up? I will tell you then. Nick, you're a leader, a natural born leader with the potential for great leadership because of your good heart, sound mind, and noble spirit. But that gift of leadership comes with great responsibility and accountability. A leader is only a leader because people follow him. People follow him because they trust him, respect him, and rely on him to do the right thing. When? Always. And because that leader accepts and embraces his responsibility with commitment and fortitude. As a leader, your first priority is to always protect your people, not only from others but most importantly from themselves. Protect them from poor choices and decisions that they might make. And the most effective tool for that challenge is to underscore the consequences of poor choices and decisions."

Mr. Wilson paused to let his words sink in. His tone was now softening so that Dominic understood his intent was to educate, edify, and encourage. Dominic took a deep breath and remained standing at attention. Mr. Wilson continued.

"You failed tonight, Nick. You failed your scouts, the boys that you lead. You allowed them to create a situation that could have had disastrous consequences. They could have gotten lost in the woods. One could have fallen into the lake and drowned. Or tripped and cracked his skull open. Or passed out, gotten sick, and choked on his own vomit. Thank God those things didn't happen. You failed their parents, who know you and respect you, Nick. They feel secure knowing that your presence and example can influence their sons. How would they feel knowing you did nothing to prevent these actions tonight? And you failed me, Nick. You let me down."

These words stung Dominic and his heart sank. He respected Mr. Wilson more than any other role model in his life. He appreciated the manner in which Mr. Wilson interacted with him, taking time to teach him and give him insight to human nature and how to carry himself.

Mr. Wilson had quiet strength and no ego. He put others first and demonstrated no arrogance. He was patient and kind-hearted, yet strong and resolute. Letting him down was the last thing Dominic wanted to do.

Mr. Wilson put his hand on Dominic's shoulder. "Nick, I don't tell you this to make you feel bad. I tell you so you understand that as a leader—an effective leader who makes a difference—you must always guard your integrity. Great leaders don't pursue popularity—great leaders pursue accountability. They are accountable to those very things we pledge in the Scout Oath and the Scout Law. Son, I want to tell you here and now that those principles aren't just for scouting, they are for your whole life. There will be those who mock those virtues when you go out into the world, and they will think you're naïve and a fool for believing in them and for living by them. But they are the real fools. What happened tonight was a learning experience. Whether or not it is an invaluable learning experience depends on how you respond to it. Resiliency often is an underestimated virtue. But resiliency when combined with the virtue of courage, guarantees all the others."

The hand on Dominic's shoulder gave him a gentle squeeze. "Let's go get some sleep, Nick, it's been a long day." Mr. Wilson passed in front of Dominic to head back to his tent.

"Mr. Wilson?"

Mr. Wilson turned around.

"Sir, I heard everything you just said and will take it to heart. I apologize for my failure of leadership, for letting down the guys and their parents, and for disappointing you—but most of all for letting myself down. I will always remember what you told me tonight, in the hope that as much as I can, I will always step up to be the kind of leader you would be proud of. Thank you, sir."

"I know you will, Nick. One other thought to sleep on. A lot of people want to be *in charge*, Nick. It's the real leader who *takes charge*."

Dominic walked over to Mr. Wilson, who put his right arm around the shoulders of his young protégé. As they approached the split for their respective sites, Mr. Wilson handed his lantern to Dominic so he could make his way back to his tent, and he headed off to his own tent.

Dominic reached his tent where his tent mates were fast asleep. Even Babs playing inside the tent couldn't wake them. He slipped into his sleeping bag and caught up with them in no time at all.

XI

MOIRA IN THE MORNING

W hat do you think, Mom? Can I do it?" Dominic waited for his mom's response.

Iolanda Manterra considered her young son's request. She had no desire to deny him a chance to do something he enjoyed. Her Dominic loved scouting and hiking and camping. But a whole week away at Boy Scout Camp was different than a weekend away with people she knew and saw on Sundays at St. Mary's or at school functions. It was the idea of her impressionable and innocent child being away from home for a whole week with strangers that gave her concern.

"If it's the cost for the camp, I am going to get that paper route and will pay for it myself." Dominic had planned out all his points of persuasion ahead of time.

Iolanda fixed her gaze upon her son's blue eyes, so fearful of disappointment. Of all her seven children, Dominic held a special place in her heart. True, the first born, her daughter Maria, was her closest ally. And she loved all her other sons with the kind of unconditional love that only a mother could give. But her other five sons were their father's pride. Dominic was his mother's joy. His sensitivity and compassion were a direct connection to her heart and soul. They shared an innate empathy that enabled them to see the hurt of others. She knew this insight was both a gift and a curse.

"Don't you trust me?" he asked.

Iolanda sighed. "Of course, I do, Dominic. It's the rest of the world that I don't trust. I know you will always do the right thing. But not everyone believes in doing the right thing. Not all the time, anyway."

"I will be alright. Like you always say to me—'the Lord give His angels charge over you and protect you in all ways you go, and their hands will uphold and guide you'—so I will be safe!"

Iolanda smiled at her son. How could she say no to that guarantee? "We will have to make sure your father is in agreement." She reached down and warmly hugged her joy.

THE BITTER COLD OF January on an early Saturday morning was giving Dominic second thoughts about Boy Scout Camp. He could already feel the wind-burn on his face and his feet didn't feel like they were there anymore. With his birthday arriving this month, he was sure to receive money that he could put toward the camp. But he would still have to make up for the rest. He had made good on his promise to obtain a paper route. Unfortunately, the only available route was on the other side of town, off of Rivertown Road near the Apostles of St. Mary High School. His mom offered him encouragement, telling him that the paper route and its location would teach him endurance. Right now, all he wanted was to be home in front of the fireplace. It was brutally cold!

In the neighborhoods surrounding the high school, Dominic carried the satchel of papers, walking up to each house, and dropping off a paper on the front steps. It was a weekly local paper, *The Suburban Scoop*, more a circular of ads than news articles, that every house received. Although the newspapers were thin, there were a lot of them. The paper bundles were dropped off at his house early enough that he could start his route by 6:30 a.m.

The early morning in winter was especially desolate and eerily quiet. Dominic barely saw another person while delivering on his route. Occasionally he would catch a glimpse of someone arriving home from the graveyard shift or running out for an early Saturday morning errand.

On this particular morning, after rounding the corner onto Wheatley Road, which was the last section of his route, as he zigzagged his way through the row of houses, he heard the sound of a screen door, its hinges creaking against the cold and wind of January. It was nearby and he paused to see who was brave enough to venture out into the arctic freeze.

A young girl in a green peacoat appeared.

Her long, thick auburn hair glistened in the morning sunlight, framing an angel's face. He recognized her in an instant. Dominic's heart raced as he watched her step down from the small porch of her yellow house and disappear around the corner, down the driveway toward the back. Yes, it was definitely Moira Toomey. Dominic had only seen her in school and church, at the fair, and once in the local bakery over on the main road in town, Sycamore Street, after twelve o'clock mass one Sunday. She was there with her father, who was one of the church ushers and with whom she bore a close resemblance. Now he knew where she lived. He had fallen in love with her the moment he first saw her in the schoolyard at St. Mary's. She was very smart and a talented artist. The teachers favored her as she always carried herself with a certain poise and maturity and exuded a confidence and independence the other students didn't possess. She was a year ahead of Dominic, as she had been moved up a grade, so he didn't see her as much in school classes. As Dominic stood watching the spot where Moira appeared, he thought to himself *She probably doesn't even know I exist.*

He waited as she returned from around back and made her way up the front steps. She lingered for a moment and seemed to turn toward where Dominic was standing. Sudden embarrassment shot through Dominic and he could feel the blood rushing to his already wind-burned cheeks as he felt he was caught staring at her. In a state of paralysis, he attempted to wave. After hesitating, she turned and went into her house. Dominic exhaled. He wasn't sure she even noticed him.

"Moira Toomey. The love of my life," Dominic whispered to himself as he finished off his route.

FOR SOME REASON, Dominic wasn't feeling at all nervous. As shy as he knew himself to be, he was actually relishing this moment. The sixth-grade class English teacher, Mrs. Dotson, had assigned the class to read Marc Antony's funeral oration from Shakespeare's *Julius Caesar*. *Julius Caesar* was one of Dominic's favorite plays and the funeral oration was one he had memorized as soon as he first read it. He had recited it countless times at home when no one was around. Mrs. Dotson was one of Dominic's favorite teachers—she was always upbeat and enthusiastic. She was the mother of one of Dominic's classmates, Mike Dotson. She was the rare teacher at St. Mary's who was always talking *with* the students instead of *down* to them. The sound of laughter was heard in her classroom more than all the other classrooms in St. Mary's combined. Dominic thought of the irony in that because Mrs. Dotson was a widow, raising three children on her own, but she always had a smile on her face and an encouraging word. The assignments that she gave were the best, too. The class would have to do weekly book reports called tic-tac-toe. The tic-tac-toe squares were filled with the choices of a novel, play, poem, or short story. The student would have to choose any three-way combination and complete a report on each type of reading in the sequence. Mrs. Dotson had cool assignments and she was really cool.

Mrs. Dotson had decided she was going to have some of the students come to the front of the classroom and read the funeral oration. She asked for volunteers. Mary Mullin's hand shot up first. Dominic wasn't surprised. He had overheard Mary talking about how she planned to be a Broadway actress and a writer. Mary's reading was fairly good and the class politely clapped. Mrs. Dotson asked for another volunteer and Mary

Hinckney went up next. Dominic had to believe that half the girls in the school were named Mary.

"That was very good, Mary. OK, we have heard from two of the ladies, do we have any of the boys ready to take the stage?" Mrs. Dotson asked, looking at the boys for any takers. Immediately, the boys dropped their heads down to avoid any eye contact. Except for one. Mrs. Dotson was almost shocked to see Dominic Manterra's hand raised. Although she was quite impressed with his book report selections—*Macbeth* being one of his first—Dominic rarely said a word in class. She was pleased he was volunteering.

"Dominic! That's great! Yes, come on up." Mrs. Dotson retreated to the back of the classroom while at the same time Dominic made his way up to the front of the class. Mrs. Dotson was at first puzzled since Dominic wasn't carrying a book. Dominic stood in front of the class and gazed at his classmates for a moment, as if sizing up the mob gathered in the Roman Forum. Then he extended his right arm while his left hand took hold of the collar of his imaginary toga.

"Friends, Romans, Countrymen! Lend me your ears!" he bellowed out and for the next four minutes or so, Dominic walked back and forth, reciting the whole funeral oration from memory, lowering his voice, bending down, adding pathos, and persuading the crowd. When he was done, he stood at attention, and slightly bowed his body forward. For a moment, Mrs. Dotson and his classmates sat in astonished silence. Then Mrs. Dotson began to clap as she made her way up to where Dominic stood, the class joining in on the applause.

"That was amazing, Dominic! Just amazing!" She offered her hand to Dominic, who shook it with a big smile on his face. "Class, Dominic is obviously a little familiar with this piece from Shakespeare and has provided us with a tour de force performance of the whole funeral oration. Excellent, Dominic, excellent!"

Dominic sat back down at his desk and returned to his anonymity.

XII.

I F

Dominic turned the corner onto the block where he lived. He kicked some chestnuts that had fallen, scaring off some foraging squirrels. As he approached his house, he noticed an unfamiliar car parked in the driveway. A station wagon with contact paper wood paneling on the doors. *Company*, he thought as he made his way down the driveway and to the back door of the house.

Once inside the door, pausing on the small landing, Dominic could hear a man talking to his mom. The smell of cigarette smoke was thick coming from under the kitchen door. The smoking surprised Dominic since his father had banned all smoking in the house (except for when he wanted to enjoy a cigar or any of his sisters were over for a visit). The ban was a result of his brother Jack's friends always smoking in the kitchen and being very loud with their anti-American sentiments. The main culprits were Tim McCurley, John Cord, and Freddie Bowen, who had all served in Vietnam and were less than thrilled with the experience.

Dominic climbed the steps and opened the inner door. His mom was leaning against the counter by the sink, holding a cup of coffee, with an expression that struck Dominic as both apprehensive and yet full of anticipation.

At the kitchen table was sitting a man with an ashtray already filled with a large number of butts. A thin man with slicked-back silvery gray hair, wearing a short-sleeved collared shirt with a bolo tie and a turquoise buffalo clasp. He wore lowcut cowboy boots and blew out a steady stream of blue grayish smoke when he saw Dominic.

"Dominic, my boy!"

Dominic scrutinized the stranger. He hadn't seen this man before who addressed him by name with a certain familiarity. He was wary and did not return his greeting. He looked toward his mother for an explanation when the man addressed him again.

"You're Dominic, aren't you, my boy?" he said it more as a statement than a query. He paused, took a long, slow drag from his cigarette, and then exhaled the smoke quickly, adding, "Or don't you know?" He smiled disarmingly, revealing teeth that were yellow stained from years of chain smoking and drinking.

"I know who I am, who are you?" countered Dominic in friendly defiance. For some reason he could not explain, he was amused by the stranger's overt histrionics with a cigarette and the affected way he enunciated his words.

"Me? I'm nobody? Are you nobody too?" the stranger stamped his cigarette into the ashtray without looking down, and had another cigarette lit and between his lips so fast that Dominic thought it was a sleight of hand trick. Now Dominic's attention was fixed as the secret code just transmitted was well-received. Now his mom broke into a smile as she shook her head.

"Or perhaps the whining schoolboy with his satchel, and shining morning face, creeping like snail, unwillingly to school?" The stranger recited the words with a faux snarl as the performance continued. It struck Dominic that this stranger was more like Picasso's *The Actor* than the Will Rogers he dressed like.

"And the curtain comes down. Performance is over. My dear nephew Dominic, I am your uncle. Your Uncle Tony to be exact. We have never had the displeasure of meeting, so I am here to rectify that. And although you have probably never heard about me, I dare say, I know about you. Or more precisely, at least a piece of you."

Dominic stepped back. He knew all his uncles, on both his father and mother's sides. This man was not among either group.

"By the look on your face, my young nephew Dominic, I can decipher that I am at best a well-kept secret, and at worst, a black sheep who has been kept far apart in order not to contaminate the rest of the flock. I can assure you—I'm neither. I am your mother's brother, her only brother, and though she may have been more mum on me, she was not on you."

Now Dominic was dumb-struck. In studying the stranger's features more closely, however, the resemblances to his mother appeared more striking. Actually, the stranger—or as he presented himself, Uncle Tony—shared the same good looks as Dominic's older brother Salvatore. His uncle turned sideways and straightened himself up.

"How about a profile view? Does that give you more of a reference point? Take note of the prominent Roman nose. You'll likely be sporting the same trademark one day. Hopefully you'll also retain the slim and sleek contours of your uncle's paratrooper physique—82nd Airborne, 101st Screaming Eagles—oh how those Dutch ladies expressed their appreciation! But on further observation, I think you'll be cursed with your father's barrel-chested brawn. That's OK—maybe you'll be another Burt Lancaster."

He turned to face Dominic. "Have I passed inspection, my young nephew?" His hand reached up for his cigarette and with a wide swoop of his arm, he removed the cigarette and blew the smoke out of the corner of his mouth, up and away from his face and the direction of Dominic.

Finally, Dominic's mother interceded. She explained that this was indeed her long-lost brother who fell out of contact with his four sisters but had now re-emerged from the past. As Dominic listened to his mom, he noticed that she maintained a combination of wariness and relief at

seeing her brother after so many years. A good number of years considering that Dominic and his three siblings closest in age had never even
heard about him and the three oldest siblings never mentioned him.

"I need to run and pick up your brother Jason. I shouldn't be long.
Dominic, sit with your uncle and keep him company in the meantime."
With that, Iolanda grabbed her purse and car keys and was out the door.

"Why are you here? What do you want?" asked Dominic in a matter-
of-fact tone.

Uncle Tony laughed. "You are my sister's son! How you begin! The
hardest questions in life for anyone to answer, at least with any certainty.
Mind you, my young nephew, people will always be able to tell you why
not, and more specifically what they don't want. But what they really,
truly want—now that is an elusive and haunting question that most
take with them to the grave, unanswered. Don't be one of those fools!
Being that you raised the question—I will share with you this gem: tell
me what you want, and you tell me who you are. Remember that one,
my young nephew. But let's move on, shall we? You presume I want
something—more precisely, I want something *from you*. Perhaps, I am
here to give you something. Although I was tempted to say I'm here to
share things with you—no, no, we can do better than that—to share
truths with you, *because I have your best interests in mind*." Dominic had
moved closer to get a better look at this man who came from out of nowhere as he continued to listen.

"Lesson two: be wary of the phrase 'your best interests in mind'—a
phrase usually uttered by someone who has only *his* best interest in
mind, and likely at *your* expense. Only two entities get to use the phrase
'your best interests in mind'—one conditional, one unlimited. Your parents, being one of those entities. They can have your best interests in
mind, mostly because they are accountable for you. But then there comes
the day when they can no longer be accountable for your actions, that
being the age of majority. There are those few insightful souls who realize that the sooner they wrest the chalk from their parents' hands the
better chance they have of filling up the res tabula with their own

choices—not necessarily better but at least their own. It's quite a vanity for parents to overcome—that belief that they can do a better job at managing another's life purpose, meaning, and happiness than the individual whose life it is. Parents need to move—sometimes must be forced—to the sidelines, where they can *hope* the best for you, the wiser ones knowing that each of us has a different notion of what's best for oneself."

He paused to puff and check in with Dominic. "You keeping up? Or am I going too fast?"

Dominic shook his head. "No, I am with you. Go on."

"The other entity being God Almighty Himself. He can lay claim, always, to having your best interests in mind. Do you know why?"

"He controls it all anyway?" offered Dominic.

Uncle Tony laughed. "That's one way of putting it, though that sounds so unbenevolent. Let's rather say, because He already knows how it all ends."

"And He loves us, unconditionally?"

"Like a mother, thank you, Dr. Fromm," replied Uncle Tony.

"So, you are sharing this because you have my best interests in mind?" Dominic slyly questioned, thinking, *Check*.

"Ah, the power of language! I said *I was tempted to say*—I did not actually express that I had your best interests in mind. Although I do have your education in mind—and hence, the lessons have begun. Question for you my young nephew, what are you most afraid of in life?"

Dominic pondered the question. His uncle deftly eluded his check, and now was back on the attack, advancing with his queen. But with what other pieces, he could not be sure. Dominic quickly responded with his best gambit.

"The unknown, of course." Dominic smiled smugly as his uncle's face betrayed a hint of satisfaction with the response.

"Can you be more precise? Precision being the key to effective communication," countered his uncle.

"Ignorance?" offered Dominic without waiting a beat. "Or not under-

standing. It leads to fear of the worst kind—judgment and condemnation." *Thank you, Miss Svarickova,* thought Dominic.

"Very impressive, my young nephew. Someone has mentored you
well. But there is something much more to fear in life. Although it is
mistaken for ignorance, its real root is in vanity." He added a butt to the
ashtray and lit another cigarette. "That which is to be feared more than
anything else in life is the person who says there is no God. Do you
know why?"

Dominic's mind raced but the best he could come up with was. "That
person is lost?"

"That is true indeed, but only if it were so that it began and ended
there. But while that person is living, they have no restraint—and they
are capable of doing anything to anyone at any time in any way and anywhere subject to their own relative notion of right and wrong. That is
fear both real and with respect to knowing the interest and motivation
of that individual—an unknown of horrific proportion and potential."
Dominic considered the case made and found himself in agreement. It
was a compelling position, one that he had contemplated but had not
yet clearly defined as his uncle just did.

"Final lesson for today," continued his uncle. "No, actually, this is an
assignment—one that comes with reward." Uncle Tony reached into the
inside pocket of his sportscoat hung on the back of the kitchen chair and
pulled out a card that had been folded in half. He handed it to Dominic.
"Here, take this—it is your assignment."

Dominic took the folded card, unfolded it, and read its cover.

"*If?*" he read aloud. Dominic was puzzled.

"Written by Rudyard Kipling. It is on a greeting card, yellowed and
crinkled with age, yet the print is quite readable. The card was never
actually used. Your assignment is to take that card, memorize that poem,
ponder its meaning, and be prepared to recite it and discuss it with me
a week from today. In return, I will give you a crisp twenty-dollar bill."

Dominic's eyes lit up. "Twenty dollars? For real?"

"Ah, my young nephew, twenty dollars in cash and a guide for your life that will prove priceless. The poem will provide the insight you will need to survive and maintain sanity while dealing with all the *if's* and *if only's* that you will face in life." He paused to light another cigarette. "Do we have a deal?"

Dominic glanced at the card in his hands and then back at this uncle who just invaded his universe. He was unsure of what to make of this strange encounter but was intrigued. "Memorize a poem for twenty bucks—no problem."

His uncle stuck out his hand, "To next week here, then." Dominic shook the thin, calloused hand extended before him.

"That is all for now, my young nephew."

Dominic's mom arrived back and she instructed Dominic and Jason to do their schoolwork while she prepared dinner. The boys went up to their bedroom, with Dominic pondering Uncle Tony.

XIII.

NEW KID IN TOWN

A re those hands even moving?" Dominic wondered to himself, staring at the clock on the wall. He could swear it had been forty minutes after nine for the past half hour. His stomach was rumbling as he tried to quell the sound lest anyone around him hear it.

The classroom chairs were arranged in a pattern like a c-clamp with the teacher stationed in the center, aligned with the first column of desks on each side of her. This gave Dominic a full view of the girls sitting in the opposite section. There were those girls who were mindful of the view and had their plaid school skirts pulled down over their knees. Some of them managed to cross their legs although the nuns did not approve of this position as it was deemed unladylike (obviously they weren't seeing things from Dominic's point of view). Occasionally Dominic would be staring too long and a hand would slowly slip between the girl's legs, blocking the view, and a middle finger would be flashed. Dominic would look up and the girl would be crossing her eyes and wildly whirling her tongue outside of her mouth, while her friends giggled at him. His face burned crimson and he averted his eyes, usually down at his notebook or at the teacher, who it always seemed, would have her eyes locked on him.

"What are you up to, Dominic?"

Dominic, still flustered by the various images, was slow to respond.

"Manterra! I'm talking to you. Look at me when I'm speaking to you." Dominic was suddenly pulled into reality.

"Sorry, Ms. Prudhomme. What was the question?" Dominic murmured.

"Never mind, it was rhetorical. I don't know where you go, Manterra, but go there on your own time. Pay attention, please!"

Dominic looked over at the other side of the classroom and the same girls were now covering their open mouths with their one hand while pointing at him with the other and mockingly laughing and alternately flipping him the bird. He looked back at Ms. Prudhomme, who was still glaring at him but then shifted her gaze to the other side of the classroom, where the same girls were now sitting up straight with their hands folded, angel-like.

Angels of Lucifer, Dominic thought to himself.

"Little teases," whispered Denny Massilli, leaning forward from the desk behind Dominic, so only Dominic could hear him.

There was a knock on the classroom door and everyone turned their attention to it. Standing in the doorway was the principal, Sister Catherine.

"Don't these nuns ever die," hissed Denny to Dominic. Dominic contained his impulse to laugh.

"Ms. Prudhomme, do you have a moment?" inquired Sister Catherine.

"We certainly do, Sister."

Sister Catherine smiled. "Oh good, this will only take a minute." She entered the classroom and the students all stood up.

"Good morning, Sister Catherine," they said in unison. Dominic was amused at the sound of these words six years after they first started this ritualistic greeting.

"Good morning, students. Please take your seats."

Everyone followed the directive and the hands were folded on the desk in front of them.

"I want to take a moment to introduce you to the newest member of our parish family. He's actually a former member of our parish, who attended St. Mary's when he lived in Rosedale as a youth. He went on to college, and while pursuing his studies, heard the calling from our Heavenly Father. He now has returned home, so to speak, as a priest here to serve the Holy Trinity and all of us. May I introduce to all of you our newest parish priest, Father Bumbry. Father, please do come in."

All of the students turned their heads to the door to see who this mystery man was. There was a momentary delay and then his head appeared as if he was looking around a corner. He looked at Sister Catherine and then at Ms. Prudhomme standing next to her. He smiled, and then his shoulders, arms, torso, and the rest of his body caught up with his head and he finally walked into the classroom. He was a hefty fellow with glasses, a beard, and a mustache. He reminded Dominic of King Tut, the villain from the *Batman* series on TV.

"To serve all of us?" whispered Denny to Dominic, "What—to serve us for dinner?"

Dominic chuckled. "Yeah, that might just cover the appetizer." Then King Tut spoke.

"Good morning, class, and Ms. Prudhomme. Thank you, Sister Catherine, for that introduction. I just want to say what an honor it is for me to return to St. Mary's. I have so many fond memories of my growing up here, and really look forward to meeting each and every one of you, and getting to know all of you. I hope we can all become good friends. I plan on establishing the St. Mary's youth ministry and promoting relationships with the youth of the parish through connection and mutual understanding." He paused, looking at the blank faces sizing him up. "That's all just a mumbo jumbo way of saying we're going to have a boatload of fun while finding fulfillment."

"Then why the hell didn't he just say that instead," murmured Denny.

"You're on a roll today, Denny," whispered Dominic.

"Yeah, well, roly-poly man here is whacked."

"How do you know that, Denny? You don't even know him."

"I can just tell."

The three adults were making small talk near the doorway and this gave way to the students chatting among themselves. Finally, the small talk was over.

"OK, class, quiet please," Ms. Prudhomme said, seeking to regain control. Sister Catherine stepped forward to again address the class.

"Thank you for your attention, students. I am sure you will join me in making Father Bumbry feel welcomed to St. Mary's and getting re-acquainted with the parish while assisting him in his mission. Father Bumbry, anything you'd like to add?"

"Thank you, Sister. Only to reiterate how excited I am to be back at St. Mary's. I look forward to getting to know all of you on a personal basis."

With that, the man and the woman dressed in black left the class-room, Ms. Prudhomme resumed teaching her lessons for the morning, and Dominic returned to daydreaming.

DENNY, HENRY, AND DOMINIC walked out of the schoolyard of St. Mary's and made a left down Fourth Avenue. This was the street Denny lived on, about two blocks from the school. Denny was in a foul mood and Dominic was attempting to draw him out of it.

"It's no use, Dominic. I am so tired of all this bullshit. I don't give a crap about school, about people, about anything. Screw it all."

"It's not all bad, Denny. It's just the way life is sometimes. We need to go through these phases in life and hope we can get through it without being overwhelmed. It really doesn't matter in the long run. Think about it—in five years, we won't even remember most of these people or any of the things that they've said or done. You just can't let it bring you down or take it all so seriously."

"You should talk, Dominic, you're the most serious person there is," said Henry.

"That's not what I'm talking about, Henry. Looking at things respon-
sibly or in a mature way is not the same as being too serious about life."

Henry wasn't buying it. "Yeah, yeah, I know. It's different for you,
Dominic! Always different for you! Talk about bullshit."

"Wait a minute? Did you just fart?" Dominic asked.

"Jesus, what did you have for lunch?" clamored Denny. "That's toxic!
Holy shit!"

Henry started to laugh. "Hey, wait, it wasn't me!"

"Yes, it was! Damnit, let's walk faster!"

"No, it wasn't me! It was you, Dominic. He who smelt it dealt it!"

"You're a moron! And you were just questioning my maturity? You're
an ass, you know that!" Dominic was cracking up, as was Henry. Even
Denny started to laugh at Henry's goofiness.

They reached Denny's house.

"You guys coming in?" Denny asked.

"I got to go straight home," answered Henry. Henry turned to Dominic, "You staying or going?"

"Why don't you hang out for a while, Dominic?"

"OK, I can hang for a bit. We'll see you tomorrow, Henry."

"See ya tomorrow, Henry," added Denny. "Stay away from those freaking pork n beans, too."

"Not pork n beans, I'm Cuban! *Arroz y frijoles, mis amigos*!"

"Stay away from that shit too, then," snapped Denny.

Dominic followed Denny up the driveway and through the front door
of the empty house. It had the makings of a nice home and there were
hints that it once was but had now been given over to neglect. It had
been invaded by dust and indifference. Faded curtains hung in the windows. The wood floors were bare and dull while the painted walls were
peeling off colors that were out of style. The uninviting rooms were
barely furnished. The kitchen did not have a table. The only item that
struck Dominic as odd was the grand piano in the family room. It was a
beautiful piano with an oak finish but sorely in need of a tuning. The

pianist of the house was Denny's mom, though Dominic had never heard her play it. He wasn't even sure if Denny ever heard his mom play it.

Despite the dismal setting of the house, one step through the closed door into Denny's bedroom, was like stepping into a different dimension, or a different house for that matter. The room was pristinely clean and organized. There were books of various topics neatly arranged on shelves. Charts and maps adorned the wall. A telescope was positioned under a skylight. Balsa wood models of World War I airplanes hung from the ceiling, among other items of curiosity that filled the room. Denny was basically a genius but the only person who seemed aware of it was Dominic. How they became friends was purely by chance. Whereas Dominic was terribly shy, Denny was a genuine loner. Before Henry introduced them, Dominic's only interaction with Denny was as second graders, when Tim O'Malley had a birthday party. Tim invited over a dozen boys but only two showed up: Dominic and Denny. Tim's mother was so pleased with the two of them that she gave each a half-gallon of ice cream at the party to try to finish if they could, and they gave it their best shot. It was the best party as the three of them still played every game and sang happy birthday and had as much birthday cake as they desired. The only other time Dominic noticed Denny was when he overheard other classmates mocking Denny as he crossed the schoolyard one morning.

"Get a load of Massilli, will ya?" pointed Billy McHugh.

"What the hell does he have on? Is that his sister's coat?" laughed Pete Finer.

"I think that's his knapsack from first grade! He can barely move his arms. Jeez, he's a mess."

Dominic turned his head to see the object of their ridicule. True enough, Denny was wearing a girl's coat, and his arms hung out at his side, locked in by the knapsack he wore on his back that was clearly too small for him. He appeared disheveled, with a terribly painful looking cold sore in the center of his bottom lip that was split open and raw. He moved slothfully as if every step was agony. He didn't acknowledge it but seemed aware that his appearance was a form of entertainment for others, and Dominic wondered if the performance wasn't deliberate. Still, Dominic felt sorry for him.

IT WAS THROUGH HENRY that Dominic's friendship with Denny was first established. Henry was somewhat of a class clown but was so good-natured and funny that Dominic got along well with him. One day while walking home after school, Henry spoke to Dominic about his new friendship with Denny. He couldn't stop talking about the interesting things that this Denny had in his house. Dominic was surprised to hear so much about this kid that did not seem to match the non-descript person that existed in class.

"Let's stop by his house on the way home," suggested Henry. "I want you to see this building he made."

"He made a building? What are you talking about?" Dominic was skeptical.

"It's made out of steel and beams and stuff. It's pretty cool. It's on the way. We won't stay long. He's by himself anyway. Maybe we can get a Coke or 7UP while we're there."

"Alright, but I can't stay long. I have to get home to do my schoolwork and practice piano." Dominic was curious.

The two friends made their way to Denny's house. They mounted the stone steps up to the front door and just as Henry went to knock the door slowly opened.

"Enter, if you dare!" a voice rang out with mock trepidation.

Henry went to move forward but Dominic grabbed hold of his arm and pulled him back, with a doubtful look.

"It's OK, Dominic. That's Denny behind the door." Henry pulled his arm free.

Suddenly Denny's head popped from behind the door. "Hey, fellas, how ya doing?" he said with an exaggerated friendliness that made the three of them crack up.

"Denny, this is my friend Dominic. Dominic Manterra—Denny Massilli."

Dominic extended his hand. Denny hesitated as if considering what to do, and then shrugging his shoulders, placed his hand in Dominic's and shook it.

"Nice to make your acquaintance, Mr. Nick," Denny was impersonating Peter Lorre from Casablanca. "Tell me, Nick, do you still like to write your name in all capital letters, hmmm?"

Dominic jerked his head back. "Wow, you remember that? That was a long time ago. Were you in that class?"

"That I was. And I remember even better the look on those two bitches' faces. It was classic. And daring."

Dominic decided he already liked Denny Massilli. Denny gave a quick tour of the downstairs and then directed them toward the second floor.

Henry interrupted. "I'm parched, Denny. Mind if I have something to drink?"

Denny didn't even look at him. "Cokes are in the fridge, Henry. Grab a can for yourself. Nick, you want one?" Dominic shook his head no. Henry wandered off to the kitchen while Denny took Dominic upstairs. There was a sign over Denny's bedroom door that read "let no one enter here who has not geometry."

"Fan of Plato, eh?" Dominic remarked.

"A student of the classics, I see." Denny was impressed.

"Sign over Plato's Academy in Athens."

"A guy walks into a tailor shop, hands the tailor his pants and the tailor says 'Euripides?' The customer responds 'Eumenides?'"

"That's pretty corny," said Dominic, "but I'll still use it."

Denny unlocked the bedroom door and then pushed it opened and extended his hand, inviting Dominic to proceed first, and Dominic entered into Denny Massilli's world. And thus began the friendship of two kindred spirits.

. . .

"Hey, what are you looking at so intently?" Denny's somewhat hostile tone broke up Dominic's concentration. He had been studying a pencil drawing that was taped to Denny's closet door. The intricacy of the detail and the flawless shading were remarkable.

"You know, Denny, they are having an art contest at St. Mary's. Any student from the fifth through eighth grade can enter. It can be a portrait or landscape or flowers or any subject the student wants. And it can be oil, watercolor, charcoal, pencil—any medium."

"How about horse shit on asphalt?" Denny sneered.

"Com'on, Denny, I'm being serious. You could definitely win. I have no doubt about it. No one has your talent." Dominic considered his words, thinking to himself, *not even Moira*, although she was considered the best artist in school. "You should submit one of your drawings."

"And why would I want to do that?"

"Because you would win. They probably have a nice prize for the winner, and a trophy or plaque. You will get recognition. They will likely hang the winning artwork in the school lobby. I think it would be cool." Dominic was suddenly determined to have his friend enter the contest.

"What the hell do I care about recognition, their crappy prizes, or even their opinions of anything, especially my artwork? Screw that!" Denny was laughing, incredulous that Dominic even suggested it.

"You know, Denny, I know you don't care about what people think about you or anything like that. You sort of relish the fact they think you're an oddball and some kind of problem child. But the reality is that you don't really believe any of it. Take a look around this room—it's organized like a library or museum. It's spotless and organized with everything in its proper place. I mean, Denny, your model airplanes are suspended from your ceiling in such a way that you can't see the wire they're hanging from, and they're angled to maximize their details."

"It's my room, I spend a lot of time in here so I want it to be comfy and cool looking."

"That's my point, Denny. You do care about things like that and most of the things in here you created. But art isn't meant to be hidden. It's meant to be exhibited and shared and admired. Art is a gift in talent to the one who creates it, and it's a gift in beauty to others who can enjoy it and identify with it, whether in touching their heart, inspiring their mind, or just giving them a sense of pleasure. It's almost a sin to hide that kind of talent and to keep that gift from others."

Denny was listening to his friend and although he was always amused at Dominic's idealistic view of things, he was genuinely moved by his sincerity.

"So, you really believe I could win this contest, eh?"

"There's not a doubt in my mind," responded Dominic with complete confidence.

"Does that include beating out your precious Moira for top honors?" Denny couldn't resist.

Dominic grinned. "Yes, I think even Moira takes second honors to you." Dominic paused. "You going to enter?"

"I will think about it," Denny answered. "The thought of the nuns having to hand me the first-place prize in front of the school does have a certain appeal—that alone may be worth the effort and actually be the bigger prize."

THE FACT THAT DENNY actually entered the contest did surprise Dominic a bit. What really surprised Dominic was that Denny didn't just submit one of his existing masterpieces—he actually created a new piece. The subject matter was even more of a surprise: Denny drew a family scene, of a father, mother, older sister and younger brother, and even a dog, with a grand piano, too. It was a happy scene with plenty of bright colors. It was hands down the best entry as far as Dominic was concerned.

The judges all agreed—Denny won first place. Dominic was so happy for his friend because the smile that Denny flashed was genuinely thrilled—not a trace of cynicism. Denny was standing up on the stage next to his winning picture, holding the first-place plaque, grinning ear to ear. He glanced over at Dominic and gave him a thumbs up. Denny also nodded his head and raised his eyebrows in the direction of the second-place winner standing next to him—Moira Toomey, sporting a burgundy French beret. Dominic imagined her sitting along the Champs-Elysees painting portraits of little children.

Sister Catherine Michael appeared at the podium and waited for the conversations among the students in the school auditorium to cease. It always impressed Dominic how the nuns had such command and control over the school body just by their sheer presence and stern demeanor. The auditorium was now completely silent and Sister Catherine adjusted the microphone connected to the podium.

"I want to thank everyone who submitted an entry into the art contest. You should all know that just by participating in events like this, you are already a winner. May we have a round of applause for all of our participants." The students applauded but it was understood how loud and long the applause would be. Sister Catherine waited a moment and then spoke again. "But there is no point in having a contest if there isn't recognition of those students whose work is truly outstanding and considered the best. And with that, I want to give kudos to our first and second place finalists, Denny Massilli for his watercolor *Happy Family Gathering* and Moira Toomey for her watercolor landscape *The Ridgeway River in Autumn*. Congratulations to you both!" And without Sister Catherine saying a word, the whole auditorium broke out in applause.

"WHAT ARE YOU READING?"

Dominic's second-oldest brother turned his head sideways to glance at the book Dominic was holding.

Dominic looked up from the book. "A book Sister McKenna told me I should read called the *Silent Spring*. Kind of boring."

His brother David grinned. "I do not miss those wonderful Catholic school days."

"Must have been a different school."

"Not if you still have the same teachers we had," remarked the oldest Manterra brother, Jack, who walked in to overhear. The two brothers had stopped by for a quick visit. "How are things going at old St. Mary's?"

"Pretty much the same. Oh, a new priest has arrived. He went to the school. Probably around the time you went. I'd say he's about your ages."

"Maybe we did. What's his name?" asked Jack.

Dominic thought for a moment, trying to recall. "Uh, Bumbry. Father Bumbry."

"Arnold Bumbry?" asked David.

"His first name was never mentioned. He had a beard and mustache, wore glasses, and fat."

"Well, Arnold Bumbry was a fat kid growing up." Jack glanced at David. "Guess I'm not surprised he became a priest."

"You guys know him?" asked Dominic.

"His grandmother lived two houses over from here. He was the youngest of four brothers. The three older brothers were athletes—pretty good on the gridiron and in the outfield," explained Jack.

"Not so much Arnold," added David.

"He didn't look like he'd be winning any hundred-yard dashes," commented Dominic. Dominic closed his book, sat up, and stretched. "Are you two leaving?"

"Soon. What are you up to?" Jack feigned a cross and hook at Dominic.

"Heading over to Timmy's house to shoot some basketball."

Mitchell walked in. "Only for a couple of hours. Dad wants us here when he wakes up to help on some project around the house, so you better get going."

"Alright. See you guys soon." Dominic left his brothers.

"Mitch, what's this about the new priest? Have you heard anything?" asked Jack.

"Yeah, they made an announcement over the loudspeaker at ASM last week. Some former student of St. Mary's. I don't remember the name, wasn't paying that much attention to it, who cares."

"Was it Bumbry?" asked David.

Mitchell thought for a moment. "Yeah, that sounds right, something like that. Why? Does it matter?"

"He was a strange bird. Different, you can say," David answered.

"How so?" Mitchell was curious.

"Not sure it was his fault. He was the youngest kid. After three boys, his mom really wanted a daughter. Not sure if they were hoping for a girl with one of the prior kids. But Arnold arrived, and then when he was probably two or three, Mr. Bumbry died of a heart attack. Jack looked at this watch. "Dave, we better get going."

"So why does that make him a strange bird?" wondered Mitchell aloud.

David answered. "Rumor has it that Mrs. Bumbry got her daughter after all. She used to dress Arnold up like a little girl, had him wearing dresses and girly outfits. Even put makeup on him when he was a little boy. He would walk around the house that way. A couple of times, he was seen like this in the backyard at his grandmother's. I mean, we even saw him once."

"That's sick!" Mitchell shook his head in disbelief.

Jack sighed, "Yeah, it was unhealthy to say the least. One of the older brothers found out and made his mom put a stop to it. But, uh, I think the damage was done."

"It's a wonder he grew up normal." Mitchell was shaking his head.

Jack glanced at David. "Let's hope for the best. OK, Mitch, we're outta here. Tell Mom and Dad we'll see them soon." Jack stuck out his hand and Mitchell slapped him five and David gave a salute. The older brothers left and Mitchell went to check for something to eat in the fridge.

TIMMY STEFANO WAS ONE of Dominic's best friends. They had spent many a summer afternoon shooting hoops in Timmy's backyard and sitting on Timmy's front steps watching the days of their youth slowly pass them by while discussing anything and everything. They would walk down to the corner to Uncle Milton's for carton pints of iced tea. They would walk up town for sub sandwiches or a slice of pizza and a fountain Coke at Naples Pizzeria. At night, they would go see a movie and then walk to the diner for a cheeseburger and French fries with brown gravy or get dropped off at the Friendly's for ice cream—a Jim Dandy for Nick and a sampler for Timmy. Theirs was basically a carefree life. Sometimes they were joined by another of their classmates, Ernie Damon. The three friends lived within two blocks of each other like the points on an equilateral triangle. Denny Massilli lived outside that triangle but right around the corner from Ernie. Sometimes other classmates would show up or there would be brothers or cousins visiting. Board games would be played—mostly Monopoly or Risk. Dominic wasn't all that enthusiastic about Monopoly—that was Timmy's preference—but he loved to play Risk. They would also spend a good deal of time listening to records. The Eagles' *Greatest Hits* and *Hotel California* were shared favorites and were dominating the airwaves. They had started to listen to a New Jersey artist that had made a huge mark on the music scene with his *Born to Run* album and they were hoping to see him in concert. Simon and Garfunkel's records were usually played as well. They agreed their ideal job would be to stuff envelopes and listen to their favorite music all day, of course while being paid big bucks, like ten dollars an hour.

Timmy was standing at the foot of his driveway bouncing a basketball as Dominic turned the corner. The two friends exchanged head nods and then walked to the backyard, where a backboard and hoop hung over the garage. Timmy halted at the border of the concrete pavement that marked the beginning of the makeshift court, about the length from the top of the key on a real basketball court, and launched a shot. The ball swished the net and ricocheted back to Dominic, who caught it and then bounced it behind his back to pass the return shot to Timmy.

"So, what did you think of the new priest?" asked Timmy as he set for another shot.

"Bumbry? Not much. My brothers remembered him. He seems harmless enough."

"Yeah, I guess so. Ms. Boutaine and Sister Marie spoke to me a couple of days after Sister Catherine brought him around."

"Really? About what?"

"They said that he met with them and asked for some students who could serve on his youth committee. They wondered if I was interested. They also mentioned you as a possibility."

"What did you tell them?"

"Said I would think about it. What do you think?"

Dominic shrugged his shoulders. "I don't know. What does it involve?"

"They said that Father Bumbry is a man of action. He wants to make good on his youth ministry pledge. I'm thinking about it." Timmy paused. "You think you'd be interested?"

Dominic motioned for the ball and Timmy bounce passed the ball over to him. Dominic threw up a shot. Without much arch on the shot, the ball hit the front of the rim and ricocheted straight down and bounced high up back to Timmy.

"If you want me to do it, Timmy, I'll do it."

THE SCHOOL LIBRARY FOR St. Mary's was separate from the newer brick school building. The library was an old Victorian house with large sash windows and three full floors. While part of the first floor had a few administrative offices, and the third floor included a large, separate room that served as a meeting room, the rest of the space housed the library's book collection. Dominic had spent a lot of time in this library and it was one of his favorite places.

Dominic waited in the meeting room next to Timmy while across from him sat Moira Toomey. In addition to being the object of Dominic's love and one of the most beautiful girls in school, she was also one of the smartest students and had even moved up one grade, although this had saddened Dominic at the time because he saw less of her. Despite his feelings for Moira, he knew it was hopeless. He was fairly confident Moira never gave him a second thought. Or even a first one, for that matter. Sitting next to Moira was Kelly McGlinchey, a girl whom Dominic was not fond of as she was one of the "hard" girls from the west side of town that liked to torment him. There were also two older boys from the boys' high school—The Apostles of St. Mary's High School, or ASM as it was called—and two older girls from the girls' high school— St. Mary's Academy for Girls, which was connected and adjacent to St. Mary's grammar school. The eight students had been selected to participate on the Youth Ministry Council that Father Bumbry was creating. The students sat in silence waiting for the new priest to arrive. Keeping watch over them was Mrs. Bailey, the school librarian, who did not sit at the table but stood in the doorway reading over a report of some kind while keeping an eye out for the tardy priest.

"You have any brothers that go to ASM?" one of the older boys asked Dominic and Timmy. Timmy shook his head no.

"One of my brothers goes there," answered Dominic.

"What's his name?"

"Mitchell."

"Manterra?"

"Yup."

"I know him. He's a douche bag. Are you a douche bag?"

Dominic's face turned red.

Kelly McGlinchey answered for him, "I don't know if his brother is but yes, Dominic's a real douche."

Dominic wanted to snap back at her but thought better of it.

Mrs. Bailey reacted as a sentinel spotting a returning scout and the group straightened up.

"Good morning, Father Bumbry, the students are here and ready to begin."

Father Bumbry appeared in the doorway and reached out his hand and touched Mrs. Bailey's folded arms. "Good morning, Mrs. Bailey, sorry I'm late, tending to some paperwork that took longer than I anticipated. I hope I didn't hold you up from anything." He glanced at the table full of waiting students. "Good morning, folks. Be right with you." He turned back to Mrs. Bailey and they stepped out of the room.

"What's your name?" asked one of the high school girls. Dominic looked to see who she was asking. She was staring straight at Kelly.

"Kelly," came the answer in a defiant tone.

"Kelly what?" pressed the older student in a calm and steady voice.

"McGlinchey. Why, what's it to you?" Kelly replied in a more defiant tone.

"Well, Kelly, my name is Debbie Whitmore. I am one of the student advisors to the Admissions Committee at SMA, and if you have any plans or hope of attending SMA, I would advise you clean up your act and your filthy mouth. You can begin by apologizing to Dominic here."

All the other faces except for the other high school girl showed surprise. Dominic noticed Kelly's face was flushed. He even noticed Moira giving him a quick knowing glance and a slight trace of a smile. It was obvious Debbie Whitmore was not joking and Kelly lost her air of defiance as she looked at Dominic and said, "I'm sorry, Dominic." Dominic didn't know what to say but managed an "OK."

Debbie Whitmore wasn't finished. She turned to the high school boy next.

"As for you—Jonathan, is it?—I am sure my uncle, Mr. Whitmore— yes, I think the last time I checked, Athletic Director at ASM—will really find your behavior here interesting if his only niece decides to fill him in. Or you can just apologize to Dominic as well."

He made a good show of planning to blow her off, but Dominic could tell he was scared. He turned and gave Dominic a half-hearted "Sorry, kid." Dominic just nodded, although he noted an ever so slight reaction in Debbie Whitmore's eyes that he clearly read as disapproving. Finally, she turned to Dominic.

"Sorry that you had to be subjected to that, Dominic. I happen to know your brother Mitchell from Social Action Club and the Tuesday Bowling for the Special Needs kids, and he's a really good guy. Tell him Debbie said hi." Again, Dominic just nodded. She was his new hero. He glanced at Moira, who winked and gave him a smile, seemingly pleased with Debbie's command of the situation.

Father Bumbry entered the room, closing the door behind him. He removed his coat and scarf and placed them on a chair set against the wall. He took a deep breath and gave everyone a big smile as he made his way over to the table. He sat down at the table opposite Dominic.

"Look at all these serious faces! I think someone sent you the wrong memo! This is going to be a fun experience! You have my word." He glanced around the table at each of the faces. "As you may have heard, my name is Father Arnold Bumbry—Father Arnold is fine—and I'm the new priest here at St. Mary's. I apologize for being late. Before we start, let's go around the table and you can introduce yourself and share a little of your background. Who wants to start?" he fixed his gaze on Debbie, who took the bait.

"Good morning, Father Bumbry, I can start us off. My name is Debbie Whitmore and I am a senior at St. Mary's Academy...."

They went around the table, ending with Dominic.

"Good morning, Father. My name is Dominic Manterra and I—"

Father Bumbry interrupted him, "Excuse me, what's your last name?"

Dominic spoke louder, "Manterra."

The priest laughed. "I could hear you, Dominic. It's just that name sounds familiar. Do you have older brothers?"

"Yes, Father." Dominic wondered if Father Bumbry was going to refer to any of them as douches.

"What are their names—John and David?"

"Yes, Father."

"OK, I know them. Well, I knew them growing up. The family still lives over on Second Avenue?"

Dominic nodded his head yes, a little uncomfortable with the focus on him.

"My grandmother lived two houses over from you. After we're done here, stay for minute, I'd like to talk to you, ok? Alright, I'd like to begin by—"

"Excuse me, Father Arnold?" It was Debbie.

"Yes, Debbie?"

"While we were waiting for you, we were talking about the committee amongst ourselves and, uh, well Jonathan here is a little shy about bringing it up with you but…he really doesn't think he has the time to commit to this endeavor."

Dominic's eyes opened wide. Jonathan's eyes were even wider as he questioned her. "I don't?"

Debbie didn't miss a beat. "Yes, because you are already stretched too thin between your studies and your year-round interscholastic sports participation. You just can't afford to jeopardize either of those, while pursuing possible college scholarship money."

For the first time, Dominic noticed the varsity jacket hanging on the corner of Jonathan's chair. *So that's how she knew his name,* Dominic thought. He tilted his head a little and read on the varsity jacket sleeves the three different sports Jonathan lettered in—one each for fall, winter, and spring—*and why she brought up her uncle.*

"Oh, that's too bad, but yes I fully understand, Jonathan, you can't put your future at risk," responded Father Bumbry understandingly.

"Uh, um, yeah, sorry about that, Father, it certainly would be, uh, best for me," Jonathan stammered, still not sure of what had just happened.

As Jonathan stood up and reached for his jacket, Debbie's voice once again filled the room. "Father Arnold, if you're looking for someone to replace Jonathan, I have a recommendation."

"Really? Gee, Debbie, that would be very helpful."

"Mitchell Manterra, he's a junior at ASM and I think he would be an excellent addition to our committee."

Game, set, match, Dominic thought to himself as he watched Jonathan, already halfway to the door, stop and whirl around, then shake his head and bolt out of the room. She *really* was his hero. Dominic saw that Moira was busy doodling something in her notebook. He stretched his neck to catch a glimpse. She had sketched two little portraits—one looked like him and the other like Debbie Whitmore. Moira noticed his focus, put down her pencil, and closed her notebook, raising an eyebrow at him. He quickly sat back and looked down at his own notebook.

"Done deal. I take it that's another older brother, Dominic? How many of you are there now?"

"There's seven, Father," Dominic answered, his cheeks burning.

"Seven! My, your parents were very busy!" exclaimed the priest. Dominic's face dropped and he lowered his eyes. Timmy shot a look at him and then at the priest. Father Bumbry bit his lower lip, realizing his faux pas, then decided to just move on.

"Thank you for that recommendation, Debbie. I will reach out to Mitchell. Perhaps, Dominic, you can fill Mitchell in on today's meeting if you have the opportunity when you see him?" Dominic nodded his head.

"OK, let's get this meeting started!" Father Bumbry handed out a meeting agenda and walked the group through his plans. Everyone participated in giving their ideas and point of view on the various topics discussed. They met for ninety minutes, then Father Bumbry ended the meeting after planning for the next one.

Father Bumbry chatted with Timmy, Moira, and Kelly. Dominic sat back in his chair, trying hard not to stare at Moira and waiting to see what Father Bumbry wanted to talk about. Debbie stopped next to him.

"How are you feeling, Dominic?"

"Oh, I'm good, thanks. Thanks for...everything." Dominic was very appreciative.

"I remember being bullied when I was younger, Dominic. It's a terrible feeling, especially this one time in the schoolyard, when these boys were making fun of me in front of everyone, and they were pretty vicious about it."

"I'm sorry to hear that," said Dominic.

"Thanks, but it turned out alright."

"It did?"

"Yes, someone came to my defense, stood up to them, and those guys backed down. Even made them apologize to me. My hero that day was your brother Mitchell." She gave Dominic a big smile. "Take care of yourself, Dominic. See you next meeting." Then Father Bumbry called her over for a moment.

WHILE DOMINIC SAT WAITING for Father Bumbry to finish his good-byes to the other students, he thought about the conversation with his brothers. Their expressions and their reactions betrayed a suspicion of the rotund priest. However, based on the meeting, Father Bumbry seemed friendly and kind, more easy-going and approachable than the other priests. True, he was younger than most priests that Dominic had interacted with, and maybe a little less religious, but this just made him appear more, well, Christ-like. The priest finished speaking with Debbie and took a seat next to Dominic.

"Thanks for waiting. Dominic? Nick? What do you go by?"

"Dominic is fine."

"Great. Thanks for waiting—Dominic—I just wanted to take a few minutes of your time to get to know a little bit more about you, and how things are going in my grandmother's old neighborhood."

"I guess things are alright in the neighborhood. My two brothers—

Jack and David—remembered you when I mentioned that you were the new priest in the parish."

"And how are Jack and David doing?" Father Bumbry asked perfunctorily.

"They're alright."

"Good, good. Give them my regards when you see them." Father Bumbry was intently looking at Dominic. "And what about you?"

Dominic was puzzled by the question. Father Bumbry wore a keen expression of expectation. After a long pause, Dominic responded, "What about me what?"

"How are you doing? How's Dominic Manterra doing?" Father Bumbry asked earnestly.

Dominic thought this was an odd question. After a short pause, he responded, "I'm as fine as wine, Father Bumbry."

Father Bumbry smiled, sat back in the chair, and stroked his beard. He liked Dominic Manterra. *What is there not to like? He is young, good looking, shy, smart, eloquent, and, above all else, innocent. The shy, smart, and eloquent assessment comes courtesy of the nuns. The innocence is apparent: this idealistic youth has no guile or malice, a regular Boy Scout type.*

"A good vintage wine, no less. Well, Dominic, I have heard very good things about you from your teachers and knowing your family background, I certainly will be looking to you to help me lead the charge on the youth ministry initiative. And I hope we can become very good friends in the process."

Dominic felt good to receive such compliments. "I will do what I can to help make the youth ministry a success, Father Bumbry."

"Please—Father Arnold. You can even call me Arnold if you like."

Dominic didn't feel comfortable addressing grown-ups, especially ones in positions of authority, by their first name. He was willing to meet him halfway, though. "OK, Father Arnold. Was there anything else? Can I go back to class now?"

"Sure, Dominic. Thanks for giving me a few minutes. I am sure we will be seeing a lot more of each other as things start to fall into place. And I am looking forward to it."

Dominic responded "OK," and got up to leave. Father Bumbry stood up as well.

"I will walk out with you, Dominic, as I am heading out anyway."

"WHAT DID FATHER BUMBRY want to talk to you about?" Timmy asked. They had just sat down at a corner table in Naples Pizzeria. Dominic blew on his slice of pizza and then took a bite, looked across the table at his friend, sat back, and shrugged his shoulders. Timmy was waiting for his slice to cool and for Dominic to finish chewing so he could answer.

Dominic gulped his soft drink. "Nothing really. Asked me some questions and then went on about helping with the youth ministry."

"He's definitely serious about that. He's asked Pastor Downey if he could have the old barn-house to convert into a youth center."

"How do you know that?"

Timmy's expression responded "How do you think I know?" Dominic thought about it, and then realized the obvious. Timmy's father was an accountant and as part of his services to the parish, he oversaw the budgets and reporting that Pastor Downey had to provide to the archdiocese.

"What did the Monsignor say?"

"He didn't say yes and he didn't say no. It would need a lot of work even if they found someplace to put all the stuff that's in the building." Dominic nodded his head in agreement. The barn-house was basically treated as a storage facility. There were desks, chairs, tools, shovels, lawn mowers, holiday decorations, bags of rock salt, and an assortment of other items.

"I guess he wasn't kidding about his commitment. What did you think of him otherwise?"

Timmy finished his last bite of pizza. He sat back as he chewed it down, followed by draining his paper cup of Coke. "He seems OK to me. A little too much on the relating and getting to know everyone talk. But according to my dad, he thinks highly of you and me. Told the Monsignor we were *outstanding* and *fully engaged* at the meeting he had in the library." Timmy rolled his eyes.

Dominic chuckled. "You have to give him credit for recognizing our brilliance!"

"Yes, he must have been a mind reader because I think neither of us said much." Timmy crumpled up his paper plate and cup. "You ready?"

"Sure, let's head over to the Rosedale Library. They're having a used book sale."

"...THE AMERICAN CIVIL WAR represented a classic struggle encompassing not only the conflict between culture and geography, but also industrial versus agrarian economics, federal versus state power and..."

A light knock on the door of Ms. Boutaine's classroom, followed by the appearance of Father Bumbry's face in the window, interrupted her teaching lesson. She paused her writing on the blackboard, putting her chalk down on the ledge and wiping her hands as she headed toward the door. Father Bumbry opened the door as she reached it.

"Sorry to interrupt, Ms. Boutaine. I was wondering...." She stepped out of the classroom into the hall and the echoing of the voices in the corridor distorted the clarity of the conversation. She stepped back into the classroom.

"Yes, Father, not a problem, hold on I will summon them for you. Timmy Stefano and Dominic Manterra!" She waved the two boys over. "Pack up your books."

"Thank you so much, Ms. Boutaine, I really appreciate it."

"You're welcome, Father."

"Thanks a million! Please come with me, boys."

Timmy and Dominic followed the priest down the corridor toward the exit that led out to the schoolyard. Once they were outside, he guided them toward the barn-house building.

"How are you two doing?" he finally asked.

The boys responded with a "good" and an "OK," looking at each other wondering what this was all about and waiting for an explanation.

"Why did I pull you out of class? Well, one of the perks of serving on the youth committee is helping me get the project off the ground. That has to happen during the week. So occasionally we will be getting together during the school day to take care of some of the housekeeping chores that need to be done. How's that sound?" He gave the two friends a big smile.

Timmy and Dominic nodded their approval.

"I thought so. Fortunately, you two are excellent students so the teachers are not opposed to you missing some class time. I won't try to make too much of a habit to pull you out of class...." He paused.

"I wouldn't worry about that, Father...Arnold, we can manage the school work.," Dominic interjected.

Bumbry grinned. "I am sure. Alright, let's have a look at the inside of this barn-house..."

He opened the padlock, then the deadbolt, and finally the doorknob before pushing open the door with an "open sesame!" Inside the building the contents were an organized chaotic mish-mash, part storage facility and part dumping ground.

"Well, we certainly have our work cut out for us," mused the priest.

And so it began. The boys would be pulled out of class to assist with the barn-house clean-up, with altar boy services (funerals and school masses), and other odd job assignments that Father Bumbry cooked up. The activities began to include outings for lunch at a local sub shop or grabbing a cheeseburger after school at Friendly's. Most of the time it was just the three of them, but there were times when it would only be Father Bumbry and Dominic. Dominic found that Father Bumbry was easy to talk to, and at times not very reverent. He shared a lot of grown-up stuff with him.

"That Downey is giving me such a hard time. Any idea I have, it's like I have to fight with him every step of the way. His response is always the same," Father Bumbry said as he was driving his car. It was brand new and sporty, but Dominic didn't care for the color—fluorescent lime green.

"What does he say?" asked Dominic.

"Basically, to kiss his ass!" Father Bumbry sounded exasperated.

"And what do you tell him?"

"Mark a spot!" laughed Father Bumbry.

Father Bumbry slowed the car down as they approached Dominic's house. "There it is—Grandma's old colonial." He had rolled down the window to get a clearer view. Dominic thought it was a nice-looking house with a lot of character. It had a big back yard. "Lot of memories there," Father Bumbry went back in time in his own mind. "Yes, indeed," he sighed.

He pulled the car up in front of Dominic's house and put it in park.

Father Bumbry wanted to chat some more with his young friend. "Dominic, I...uh..."

"Thanks for the lift, Father." Dominic released his seat belt. "I guess I will see you next week."

"Well, OK," Father Bumbry murmured quietly.

Dominic hesitated as he unlocked the passenger door and placed his right foot on the curb. "Everything OK?"

Father sighed. "Yes, yes...it is. Have a good night, son."

Dominic climbed out of the car, closed the door and waved before heading up to his house. Father Bumbry watched him go around the house to the back door. He looked into his rearview mirror, straight into his own eyes. *What was that feeling? It was a mixed-up feeling—a mixed-up feeling indeed.* Alone and frustrated, he shifted the gear into drive and pulled away.

XIV

IN DEFENSE OF HIS WOODY

The rite of passage for eighth graders of superior knowledge and talent from St. Mary's grammar school to the two high schools was the Scholastic Olympics. The event was an academic competition that the Apostles of St. Mary's held each year for all the Catholic grammar schools in the surrounding towns. For St. Mary's, the representatives in each category, one girl and one boy, were chosen by the nuns and the lay teachers. Dominic Manterra was chosen to represent St. Mary's in the speech competition. He had won speech contests for reciting Lincoln's Gettysburg Address and JFK's Inaugural Address in the seventh grade and had established a solid reputation as a future orator. For the Scholastic Olympics, the speech to be delivered was Victor Hugo's "In Defense of His Son," an impassioned plea to spare a condemned man from the guillotine. Dominic liked the speech and had managed to quickly memorize it. But he was challenged by some of the phrases and unfamiliar words. For this reason, Sister Tamblerin, St. Mary's coordinator for the Scholastic Olympics, was concerned Dominic wasn't getting enough practice. She believed he required more exposure in giving the speech before an audience of strangers and worried about Dominic's nerves once he found himself in front of the judges at ASM. Sister Tamblerin found a solution.

"Good afternoon, Ms. Boutaine!" Sister Tamblerin suddenly appeared at the doorway to the classroom.

"For Christ's sakes, can't we get someone to put a bell on these nuns!" hissed Denny into Dominic's ear. "The way they just materialize out of thin air. Scares the be-Jesus of out of you!" Dominic just shook his head.

"Good afternoon, Sister Tamblerin. To what do we owe the pleasure?" The classroom of students found themselves in a state of confusion, as Sister Tamblerin had not actually entered the room and had not addressed the class. The students were unsure of whether to stand and provide the formal greeting. Sister Tamblerin sensed the apprehension and provided a hand gesture that was interpreted by the students to just sit tight.

"I was wondering if I may borrow Dominic Manterra for a little while. We are going to do some prep work for his upcoming speech at the Olympics." Sister Tamblerin winked at Ms. Boutaine.

"But of course, Sister. Dominic! Please go with Sister Tamblerin."

"Thank you, Ms. Boutaine. Come along, Dominic." Dominic followed the sister out of the classroom, his cheeks red with the attention being placed on him.

As they walked down the pristine corridors of St. Mary's, Sister Tamblerin spoke quickly and excitedly.

"We were discussing at dinner last night over at the convent what we could do to better prepare you for the upcoming competition. Sister Margaret McShea came up with a brilliant suggestion!"

Dominic didn't recognize the name. He didn't believe it was a sister who taught in the grammar school.

"Oh, Sister Margaret teaches at St. Mary's Academy next door. You may not know her, Dominic. Anyway, she has taught public speaking and she suggested that she meet with you to give you some pointers. And then she came up with the idea that you give your speech to one of her classes. How is that for building confidence!"

Dominic's stomach began to churn as he now realized they were heading toward the big gray metal door that separated St. Mary's grammar school from the attached building that was the St. Mary's Academy for Girls High School. There was a stairwell behind that door and a small landing that led to another metal door of the same design that opened into the girls' high school auditorium. Among the boys in St. Mary's grammar school there was this belief that as soon as the girls walked through those doors to the Academy side, a total physical transformation of extraordinary proportions took place. This transformation involved hair, breasts, hips and buttocks: in all colors, shapes, and sizes. Once they crossed that threshold, the girls of St. Mary's became Academy Amazon Warrior Princesses and were not to be messed with—and any grammar school boy's glance that seemed impolitely sustained was met with a venomous stare down. Sister Tamblerin opened the door and ushered Dominic through it onto the landing. Sister Margaret stood there waiting.

"Oh, there you are, Sister Tamblerin! I wondered if you had forgotten our little plan!" Sister Margaret was a tall woman with broad shoulders and a beaming face. "And is this our little Demosthenes?"

"Sorry that I'm late, Sister. Yes, this is Dominic Manterra. Dominic, this is Sister Margaret."

"Good afternoon, Sister Margaret." Dominic was a bit nervous.

"Good afternoon, Dominic. We're good, Sister Tamblerin, you can leave Dominic with me for now. We will return him hopefully in one piece."

"Thank you so much for doing this, Sister. I'm sure this will make the difference in the competition. Good luck, Dominic! You're in good hands with Sister Margaret." Dominic watched Sister Tamblerin depart through the metal door. He turned to meet Sister Margaret's studious but gleaming gaze.

"I want you to relax, Dominic, and to get yourself calm. The best way to achieve that sense of calm resolve is by the simple act of breathing." To add emphasis to her words, Sister Margaret drew a big breath through her nose and then slowly exhaled out her mouth. Dominic got a good whiff of the tuna fish the nun apparently had eaten for lunch. She repeated her breathing demonstration but this time Dominic managed to hold his breath to avoid the catch of the day effect.

"Now you try it with me." Sister Margaret added hand motion with her breathing technique. Dominic followed her lead. They repeated this exercise several times, Sister Margaret's gaze fixed upon Dominic to ensure he was keeping stride with her lead.

"Very good, Dominic. Tell me, do you feel more relaxed now?"

Dominic nodded his head yes, while continuing to breath with a deliberate and steady effect.

"Good, good. Now, the next pointer I have to tell you is one I have often used myself, and I find it to be most settling in getting me ready to present in front of an audience. It may sound a bit off color but let me assure you, it's a sure-fire technique."

Dominic's last breath was more a sigh, as he now wanted to be done with this exercise. Sister Margaret's chirpy, upbeat disposition was not something he was used to from the nuns, although he realized she was only trying to help him.

"When I get up in front of an audience, I take a few deep breaths, I stand up tall, look around at all the people sitting before me and then— I imagine that they are all stark naked!"

Dominic couldn't believe his ears. Did Sister Margaret actually just say that to him—out loud? The good sister couldn't contain her glee.

"Yes, it works every time! Once you imagine they are all sitting there naked, it immediately puts you at ease and you are able to focus on delivering your speech or presentation. The silliness of the whole notion just totally relaxes you!"

It struck Dominic how Sister Margaret was quite pleased with herself and her suggestion. Dominic also realized she was clueless to the hormonal horrors at war within the body of an eighth-grade school boy.

"Are you ready?" With a flourish, Sister Margaret opened the metal door that led into the auditorium of the girls' high school. Dominic had not expected this. He wasn't sure if it was the whole high school assembled, but it was more than enough. Sister Margaret escorted him to the front of the auditorium. As the good sister spoke, all Dominic could see before him were the bright yellow, pink, and blue colors of the uniforms the girls wore. These were button-down dresses with collars and matching knee-high socks. Dominic was trying his best to not make any eye contact but at the same time didn't know where to fix his eyes. He figured staring down at his shoes would make him appear pathetic. He managed to look up and scan the audience when his eyes were met by Sue Ellen Buckley. She was one of the lead Academy Amazon Warrior Princesses. Even in grammar school she seemed ten years older than she was. She was a physical specimen—a well put together package that one could imagine would qualify her for the *Sports Illustrated* swimsuit edition. Sitting next to her was Maria D'Argento, another Warrior Princess, with her black Neapolitan locks that flowed down past her shoulders onto her ample breasts. The two girls smiled knowingly at each other and then focused their attention on Dominic.

"And so we have as our guest this afternoon Dominic Manterra from St. Mary's, next door, and he will…" Sister Margaret was busy giving her own speech as Dominic tried to stay focused but Sue Ellen and Maria had caught his attention. Sue Ellen started with running her hand through her long brunette hair and slowly folding it back behind her ear. Meantime with her other hand, she had unbuttoned her dress a bit, and exposed her cleavage. She sat back and let her hands slide down to her sides. She slowly pulled up the hem of her pink dress over her knees and spread her legs a little. In full view of Dominic's direct line of vision were Sue Ellen's pure cotton white panties. Dominic quickly averted his eyes but they found themselves staring at Maria's heaving breasts, which were in full view as she was now sitting slightly bent over, leaning forward as Dominic witnessed the emergence of the twin peaks of Maria's marbled chest of perfection.

"Without further ado, I present to you Dominic Manterra, reciting Victor Hugo's *In Defense of His Son*." Sister Margaret walked past Dominic to take a seat and whispered to him, "Remember what I said about the audience!" Sister took her seat.

The actual speech was a blur to Dominic. He was unsure how it sounded but managed to get through the whole speech without a hitch. When he finished, he was kind of taken aback by the girls' reaction. They broke out into wild applause and whistling and some stood up to cheer. He felt his cheeks burning.

Later that week, Sister Tamblerin passed along kudos from Sister Margaret. "Sister Margaret said you really rose to the occasion, Dominic! She was quite impressed how you expanded beyond the boundaries of your comfort zone and showed the audience your reach!"

The irony of Sister Margaret's observation wasn't lost on Dominic the following day when he crossed paths with Sue Ellen and Maria and their classmates in the schoolyard. Sue Ellen called out to him.

"Well, look who it is, girls! It's the speechmaker! Hey, how's it hanging, *Woody?*"

A red-faced Dominic quickened his pace as the girls' laughter echoed in his brain.

XV.

DREAMS

There seemed to be an ocean of them. In every shape and size and color and taste and texture and smell—beautiful and pleasant in every aspect of eyes and hair, curves and points, delicate hands and graceful legs. All ravishing, totally naked women who seemed to all share one desire—to have their way with Dominic Manterra –who was drowning in the middle of this ocean of nymphs. He lay in the midst of this overwhelming barrage of feminine desire and erotica while arms and legs enveloped him and lips covered him with countless kisses. They could not get enough of him. He could not get enough of them. To Dominic they were endless. Where did they come from? Who were they? Why were they all naked? Why was he here with them? He kept kissing them and touching their bodies—their faces, their lips, their breasts, their everything! It was unreal. He wanted to love them all. He wanted to kiss them all. He wanted to touch them all. He wanted… never…to…wake…up….

But he did. And as he lay there in his bed, Dominic wondered to himself. Why was he having these dreams? He had never even seen a real woman naked except in a magazine. He really didn't have any knowledge or experience beyond that. After all, he was only eleven years old when they started. But he knew that since the dreams began to occur, his penis took on a life of its own. Every night as he started to doze off, and in the morning when he awoke, it was stiff and throbbing. And throughout the night his dreams were a constant barrage of naked affection.

Then one night, a different dream occurred.

It was her—his love, his very heart's desire.

Moira.

She was ethereal, comely, and demure. And she was alone and was actually clothed. With a diadem of flowers upon her head, her long, shining auburn mane flowed down her back and over her breasts. Her lips were luscious red. Her eyes were bright with a constant glow of anticipation about them. She sat on a flower-covered swing effortlessly swaying as petals fell like rain. She glided back and forth, gazing at Dominic with a smile that combined mischievousness with innocence and vulnerability. She wore a sheer, silk robe loosely tied at the waist. Dominic strained to get a better view and he could feel a sudden and overwhelming desire to touch her. With a laugh, she stretched out her legs on the swing as she went back and forth. This motion blew open the robe and Dominic now had a better view of her torso and patch of red hair that adorned her perfection. Dominic had to have her! She halted the swing, leaned forward and tucked her legs under the swing. She bit her lower lip and seemed to stop breathing as she waited with eyes full of anticipation. Dominic moved toward her, and then as if by magic she vanished and reappeared behind the swing separating her from Dominic. She leaned forward with one hand resting on the swing and the other holding one of its ropes, fully revealing her sublime breasts. Shimmering as if in a body-size halo, her cheeks were flush and Dominic imagined it was because she was feeling the same desire that he was. But she wasn't going to make it easy. Dominic went to take hold of her hand, she pulled it back and laughing, ran from him. Dominic was left in darkness. But then she suddenly appeared, her illumination lighting up the darkness. Dominic could see her from a short distance and also hear her breathing with gentle giggles as if she was right next to him, whispering into his ear. He could smell honeysuckle and flowers of all sorts. As the world around them brightened, Dominic found himself transported to a meadow, filled with lush greenery, and surrounded by trees. She always seemed to be just out of his grasp. Her beauty and delightfulness kept increasing as the chase continued to mount. Dominic sensed she was deliberately slowing her pace as the distance between them lessened, and she came closer and closer to being within reach. She paused near a short garden wall covered with ivy waiting for Dominic to catch up to her. Dominic's heart was racing like a thoroughbred down the stretch. She extended her arm toward him and motioned with her hand for him to come to her. As he reached out his hand to touch her waiting fingertips, she pulled back slowly and skipped through an opening a few feet away. With a sigh, Dominic followed her. On the other side of the wall, she stood waiting for him, surrounded by light seeming to shine from everywhere. Dominic sensed she was not going to move this time. He drew close to her, standing right in front of her, within arm's reach. She let her robe fall from her shoulders and down along her arms, landing at her feet, completely revealing her beauty to Dominic. With her arms spread wide, the tip of her tongue slowly licking her lips, her eyes beckoned for him to come to her...

Dominic erupted. Like the shooting waters of a garden park fountain piercing the bluest summer sky, he spewed forth and she let herself be covered in the creaminess of his desire; it streamed out of him and all over her—her stomach, her breasts, her arms, and her thighs. She smiled with delight and encouraged the flow to continue, and the more he gushed out, the more pleased she appeared. Nick felt weakness in his legs and slowly dropped to his knees. He leaned forward as she stepped toward him, and he wrapped his arms around her and pressed the side of his face against her body. She placed her arms around his neck, and hugged him close while gently running her fingers through his hair.

Dominic woke up. For a moment, he opened his eyes and looked at the ceiling above him. He was alone. He immediately wanted to go back to her, to be with his love! He felt the wetness about him. Smiling, he closed his eyes and fell fast asleep.

PART TWO

MOIRA, HIS
PRECIOUS ROSE

XVI.

SOUTHERN DISCOMFORT

Henry and Dominic reached Denny's front door and found it opened. They noticed there were no cars in the driveway and figured Denny was home alone. They entered and could hear voices coming from the basement along with the stereo blasting loud with Kiss' *Rock and Roll All Nite*. They found Denny sitting with another classmate—Marco Leonardo. Marco was the tallest kid in class and the center on the basketball team. He was lean with dark, Italian good looks that, according to Denny, "made all the girls want to squeeze his limoncello." He and Dominic spent a lot of time together during the basketball season as Dominic played forward on the team. They all exchanged greetings.

"You guys ready to go to the dance?" Dominic asked the group. It was their first high school dance, and it was at St. Mary's Academy.

"Sure," answered Denny, "but Marco and I thought we'd celebrate with some libations before we went."

"That's alright, I already ate dinner at home," Henry said and sat down on a chair, "but you guys better eat fast if we want to get there before they close the doors."

"No, you dumbass, we're not talking about eating anything," laughed Marco. "Show them what we got, Denny."

Denny pulled out a bottle of liquor from behind the sofa cushion. "Gentlemen, what we have here is a little *al-key-haul* to get the party started."

"I don't know about this," demurred Dominic. "I think we should skip it for tonight."

"You said that last time," responded Marco, "after we won our first basketball game and Coach Conrad got us the bottle of Jack Daniels."

"You say that *every* time," chimed in Denny, "but we're not listening *this* time." He peeled off the wrapper on top of the bottle's cap. "Look, we have to drop our IQs to an enjoyable level."

"I vote we have a few rounds," Henry added his two cents.

"See," pointed Marco, "even Henry's up for the party!"

"Yes, especially compelling from someone who thought you were talking about hors d'oeuvres two minutes ago," responded Dominic.

"Aw, com'on, Nicky boy, let's have a little fun. Loosen up a bit. Maybe you'll get some real cojones and actually talk to Moira Toomey instead of just lusting at her from a distance," cajoled Denny. "Either way, I'm drinking." He raised the bottle to his lips, took a big gulp, and passed it to Marco, who did likewise. Marco then handed it toward Dominic. Henry reached for it and Marco handed the bottle to him. Henry pulled up his sleeve with his hand, wiped the top of the bottle, and then took a swig. He handed it back to Denny, who took another drink but this time a longer one. He bristled as he swallowed it down and then let out a laugh and handed the bottle to Marco, who was laughing as well, and he took a big gulp. Marco turned to Dominic and extended the bottle to him. "Com'on, have some. It doesn't taste bad. It's kind of sweet."

"It's Southern Comfort," added Denny. "It tastes like cherry cough syrup. Very good. Go ahead and try it for Christ's sake."

Dominic accepted the bottle, glanced at the label, considered the red amber liquid inside, took a sniff, raised it to his lips, and paused, conscious of the three pair of eyes on him. He lowered the bottle. "Do you have a cup?" he asked.

"Aw, com'on already, will ya!" cried out Denny.

Dominic continued, "Even a paper cup, it doesn't—"

"Just drink it already!" barked Marco, who was annoyed now.

Dominic raised the bottle to his lips, paused, and then swallowed a mouthful. Denny was right. It tasted like cough syrup—with a lot more heat. His three companions gave shouts of approval and the bottle went around a number of times. For the next fifteen minutes they drank from the bottle without pausing.

Henry checked his watch. "We better get going, it's getting late." He stood up quickly, let out a "Whoa!" and then fell forward right at Denny and Marco, who caught him and prevented him from falling flat on his face. The three of them busted up laughing.

"Sit down, Henry, before you crack your skull open," Denny said, feeling no pain. "We just have a little more left. We can finish it off really quick."

"No more for me," said Henry, "the room is moving too fast." They all bellowed with laughter.

"That's right, no more for you!" Denny's eyes were tearing he was laughing so hard.

"That's enough for me, period." Dominic was feeling very loopy himself, outright giddy.

"Let's just finish it—the three of us as fast as we can!" challenged Denny. "I'll start. We'll just keep passing it around until it's done. Whoever finishes it off—the others will pay his way into the dance tonight. Ready, set, go!" Denny drank and passed the bottle to Marco, who took a quick gulp and passed it to Dominic, who was a little slower on the uptake but managed to swallow some and pass it back to Denny. Three more rounds and Denny finished off the bottle.

They managed to make the trip from Denny's to the schoolyard without falling down too much. The fresh air was a big relief to Dominic as the pendulum in his head and body swung back and forth from euphoria to uneasiness. Henry was giggling like a lunatic. Denny was plain silly while Marco was acting like he was in total control—although Denny would mockingly imitate Marco's attempt at showing a cool composure and they would both go into a laughing fit.

They stopped in the schoolyard, over in the shadows of the barn-house to re-group and prepare themselves before they went into the dance.

"Hey, Nicky boy, isn't this the place you and Father Bumble-ass fixed up for the youth minstrels," asked Denny.

"It's the youth ministry. And his name is Father Bumbry."

"Whatever. Anyone got gum?" Denny's euphoria seemed to be wearing off as well.

"Here, everybody should have a piece." Marco came prepared.

Everybody chewed vigorously and took deep breaths. Dominic studied the outline of the brick building where he had attended school for eight years. Strangely, it already seemed like so long ago.

"OK, let's all be really normal-like here. We don't want any of the good sisters of St. Mary's Academy to suspect anyone here has unnatural intentions towards their young charges," counseled Denny.

"We don't?" asked Henry earnestly.

"OK, show time, you idiots. Let's get the game faces on." Marco wanted to get into the dance.

The four would-be Lotharios sauntered over to the entrance to the dance and without a hitch made their way into the darkened gymnasium that had been converted into a disco ballroom with flashing lights and streamers strung overhead. Chairs and tables were scattered around the edge of the makeshift dance-floor while a deejay blasted loud music. The deejay exhorted students to get on the floor and shake their booty to the sounds of the Bee Gees. No doubt the *Saturday Night Fever* soundtrack and Meatloaf would be the featured music of the evening along with a spattering of the Stones, Aerosmith, Elvis Costello, Blondie, Styx, The Cars, Van Halen, Billy Joel, the Eagles, and of course, the Boss. The last song was always the same: "Free Bird" by Skynyrd.

They saw some of their other friends gathered around one of the tables and Marco motioned to head over that way. As they did, a group of girls crossed their path and Marco stopped to make some small talk. That was one big difference at ASM high school—no girls. After eight years of attending school with girls, Dominic was now in a classroom of all males. Truth be told, it was a much less stressful environment. He realized he hadn't seen some of these former female classmates in a while but it now seemed like years. He was struck by how grown-up they acted now. He guessed it was true about crossing that threshold from the grammar school to the high school.

"Am I wrong or have we just landed on the island of the Academy Amazon Warrior Princesses?" murmured Denny under his breath to him. Dominic could tell that the gum's effect had worn off and the scent of alcohol was noticeable on Denny. He immediately wondered if that was the same for him. But before he could pursue that thought, one of the aforementioned former classmates approached him. It was none other than Kelly McGlinchey who took it upon herself to drop off the youth committee after that first meeting.

"Oh, hi, Dominic! It's so good to see you again!" She spoke with genuine sincerity that caught Dominic off guard. What further caught him off guard was her leaning in to greet him with a kiss. Unfortunately, he wasn't expecting it and her mouth landed on his, and Dominic ended up swallowing a wad of whatever lip gloss she had caked on her lips. It grossed him out but he managed to recover.

"Hello, Kelly. How's tricks?"

"Couldn't be better! Oh, did I get my lip gloss on you? Here, let me take care of that." And she went to give his mouth a little swipe of her thumb, which basically smudged it over his cheeks and chin.

On the stage, another former classmate from St. Mary's had commandeered the deejay's spot and mic. Mary Jane Swanson had cued up Dion's *Runaround Sue* and was now belting out the lyrics with her own unique brand of panache and bravado.

"Look, Mary Jane's getting the party going! You want to dance, Dominic? Com'on!" Kelly grabbed Dominic's hand and tugged him toward the dance floor. He didn't budge.

"Uh, no, um, really no, don't want to dance right now," he said quietly.

"Aw, why not? Com'on, it will be fun! Don't be a stick in the mud all your life!" she insisted.

"Sorry...I...can't...dance...right...now...." He wasn't sure if she was even talking to him or where she was standing, because the room was spinning. Or was he spinning? It felt like the dance floor was a deck of a ship, a ship that was on a stormy sea with violent waves thrashing each side so that it kept keeling from side to side. He wanted to grab on to something so that he didn't tip over. He heard someone calling his name. He turned his head and Denny seemed to be shouting out his name at him. Then Marco's head appeared next to Denny's head and it appeared as if both of them were shouting at him in unison in slow motion but he could barely hear them over Mary Jane's singing. Suddenly he felt like his body was now leaning forward as if his feet were blasting straight up, forcing his whole body through his skull, and he was going to end up in a headstand. In an instant, his mouth was very dry and he didn't feel well at all. He needed fresh air. He turned his head and saw a red-and-white lighted sign. It looked like it said "EEXXITTT," so he headed that way.

He made it to the doorway out of the gymnasium. The bright light in the corridor was abrupt and he put his hand up to temper the intensity. Some of the teachers and nuns were out there chatting and turned to face him with various smiles and greetings directed at him. It was just a blurred montage of faces and sounds and he just nodded his head in any direction that he thought a voice was addressing him. He finally found the exit door to the schoolyard.

The fresh air felt exhilarating, but he knew what was coming and that there would be no way to avoid it. He walked around the St. Mary's Academy building to the side that shared a walkway with St. Mary's Church. He figured if he could find a spot to sit down and maybe get some rest, then he would feel better. He made his way down the walkway to a spot where there was a little alcove. As he drew near, he could see what appeared to be the outline of two stretched out legs. He approached with caution.

"Hello, Nicky! How ya doing?" Henry laughed. "Pull up a seat!"

"Henry, what are you doing out here?" Dominic was feeling very queasy as he sat down with his back against the cool brick. "I didn't even see you leave."

"I felt sick and I knew I was going to puke so I came out here while you guys were talking to the chickadees." He coughed. "I got sick behind that bush there." He raised his arm and pointed in no particular direction. "You might want to do the same. You'll feel a whole lot better."

Dominic could smell the stench coming off Henry's shirt. No points for neatness. Dominic thought he would feel much better if he could stop everything from spinning. He sat down a few feet from Henry and placed his hands on the ground to balance himself. But it didn't really help. Henry managed to get up on his feet. He let out a deep breath that Dominic got the brunt of—"Henry! You're gonna make me puke!" snapped Dominic.

Henry laughed and then started to walk away.

"Where you going?"

"Home."

"Now?"

"I can't go back in there smelling like alcohol and old cheese, can I? I'll be alright. Talk to you later."

Dominic watched the blurry image stumble to the stairs at the end of the walkway and then disappear from view. He leaned back and closed his eyes. If only the spinning would stop. His stomach did not feel right and his body began to shiver. He was trying to remember what he had eaten that day when his mouth began to water. His body started to shake and his chest began heaving forward like a hand had plowed through the brick wall and was jabbing and pulling him from behind. He leaned to his left and the vomit exploded from his mouth like a volcano top blowing out hot molten lava. He hated throwing up. It was the worst feeling in the world as it felt like he couldn't breathe and was going to choke. He stopped for a moment and took a deep breath. He was glad that was over. Wait. Not so fast. A spasm shot through his body and again his body lunged forward and more vomit sprouted out. He dropped back against the wall. That had to be it—he couldn't possibly have anything left in his stomach. He had to admit that Henry was right—he felt much better. He tried to stand up but lost his balance and slid back down to the ground. He was weak—obviously he and alcohol were not a good pairing. He took another deep breath and pushed himself up onto his feet. He looked to his left and to his right down the walkway. He opted to go the opposite direction from Henry. He didn't want anyone to see him, so when he got to the end of the alleyway he cut over to the pathway between the church's back entrance and the end of the rectory property. He made his way to the sidewalk and turned right to head toward Fourth Avenue. When he reached the corner, he looked up to the second-floor windows of the rectory. He noticed the lights on in the corner room. He could make out the figure of the occupant and he could see it resembled Father Bumbry. He had no idea what time it was but figured it wouldn't be a good idea to show up home in the shape he was in—he too probably smelled like alcohol and old cheese. He could see Father Bumbry's shadow occasionally moving around—and thought it must be him. He went to the auxiliary door on the porch underneath the lighted room. He hesitated. He opened the screen storm door and gave the heavy painted oak door a few sharp taps, and then stepped back to wait.

The porch light came on and then he could see Father Bumbry pull the window curtain aside to see who it was and then the porch light was quickly turned off. The door opened and Father Bumbry waved for Dominic to enter. Once inside, Father Bumbry closed the door, brought his right index finger up to his lips, and signaled Dominic to go up the stairs. Dominic walked quietly up to the top of the stairs and paused on the landing while Father Bumbry made his way up. Once Father Bumbry made it to the landing he took hold of Dominic's elbow and guided him to a door that was ajar, fully opened the door, and led Dominic into the room, closing the door behind him.

"Have a seat, Dominic." Dominic looked around and sat down on an easy chair next to a small book case. Father Bumbry disappeared around the corner of the rather large room. Dominic glanced around—there was a sitting area with a coffee table, a sofa, a large console television, and a single wall unit with books, record albums, and a stereo system with a phonograph and cassette tape deck as well as a receiver. Next to him was a chair and desk with a typewriter and a telephone on it, as well as an appointment book. On the wall was a cartoon of a large foot surrounded by a multi-colored group of people looking up. At the bottom of the poster were the words "Now a message from our Creator"; and in the poster above the heads of the group were the words "love one another." Around the corner Dominic could see the opened bedroom door that Father Bumbry disappeared through and the bedpost of a footboard.

Father Bumbry came back through the door carrying washcloths, a towel, and some other items. He walked over to Dominic and handed him a washcloth.

"Here, wash your face and hands." Dominic accepted the soapy washcloth and passed it over his face, giving extra attention to his nose and mouth; he rubbed his hands.

Father Bumbry reached out his hand. "Alright, give that one to me and take this one." Dominic handed him the soapy washcloth and took the other washcloth, which was wet, and repeated the same motions. When he was done, he exchanged it with Father Bumbry for the towel. The towel felt very plush and soft as Dominic dried off his face and hands.

"OK, now here's a toothbrush and some mouthwash. There's toothpaste in the bathroom. Follow me." Father Bumbry turned and Dominic stood up and trailed him through the bedroom door, into the bedroom past the bed to a bathroom on the other side of the bedroom.

"You can brush your teeth and gargle in there; and if you have to go to the bathroom. Do you feel like you're going to be sick again?"

Dominic shook his head no.

"OK, I will be in the other room at my desk. Take your time." Dominic nodded and watched him walk back into the other room. He went into the bathroom and brushed his teeth and gargled. He looked in the mirror and saw his pale complexion and his drawn cheeks. "Man, I look like crap," he said to himself.

On his way back through the bedroom he noticed a painting of a crucified Christ he had never seen before. It was a very austere setting, Christ held in place between a square-shaped cross and square pegs. There was no blood and the body looked unblemished. There was one other figure in the painting—probably Mary, His mother. It was an interesting painting but he thought it was probably blasphemous.

"Are you familiar with Salvador Dali?" Dominic turned around. He hadn't heard Father Bumbry walk back into the room. "That painting is called *Corpus Hypercubus*—probably my favorite painting."

"It looks kind of sacrilegious," commented Dominic. "Is the woman in it the Holy Mother?"

"No, that is Mary Magdalene. It's modeled after Dali's wife, Gala. I think it's a beautiful painting. Do you like it?"

Dominic looked back at it. He shook his head. "Not really sure. It's kind of strange."

"Come on back to the sitting room and tell me what happened."

Dominic sat down in the chair. Father Bumbry reached into a mini-fridge that was next to the desk and handed Dominic a can of Coca-Cola, which he was very happy to see. He opened the tab and drank half the can before coming up for air.

"Thanks, I really needed that."

"So, what was the poison of choice tonight?" asked Father Bumbry as he opened a can of soda for himself.

"Southern Comfort. I will never drink again." Dominic spoke with a solemnness that made Father Bumbry smile.

"Oh, I'm sure you will find the courage to drink again. Might I suggest you stay away from the liquors and stick to beer? And refrain from drinking if you are going anywhere in public like a school dance full of nuns?" Father Bumbry chuckled. "But I must say you kept yourself fairly unmarked for someone who got sick," continued Father Bumbry, "or we would have had to get you undressed and I don't believe my clothes would fit you. Cheers!" And he held up his can for Dominic to bump his against.

Dominic sat and chatted with Father Bumbry. His eyes found themselves focused on the bookshelf and an unusual-looking book. It stood out from the rest because of its height and cover design.

"What's caught your attention?" Father Bumbry was curious.

"That one book sticking out—may I?" asked Dominic.

"Certainly, help yourself."

Dominic grabbed the book off the shelf and opened to the title page. It was a book of Shakespeare's sonnets. The pages were crisp and stiff, like the book had barely been opened.

"Have you read the Bard's sonnets?" asked Father Bumbry.

"No, I have only really read his plays. Not so much his poetry."

"His sonnets are classics. Very beautiful and moving. It is said that certain sonnets were written to a woman who scholars suspect was of African descent because of the words Shakespeare chose to describe her physical characteristics."

Dominic listened intently. Father Bumbry paused, amused by the youth's concentrated curiosity.

"There are also sonnets that they believe are written to another man." Bumbry took a sip from his soda.

Dominic frowned. "Another man? He wrote poems to another guy?"

"Yes, is that so unusual? Shakespeare believed a bond between two men was closer than a bond between a man and woman."

Dominic shook his head. "I don't know. Never really thought about it." Dominic thought of his own feelings for Moira.

"Well, maybe Shakespeare was referring to the special friendship that two men can have." Father Bumbry thought it best to leave it at that for now. "Why don't you take that book, Dominic. It's yours."

"Oh no, Father Arnold, I don't want to take your book from you." Dominic went to place it back on the shelf.

"Take it, Dominic. I want you to have it. A special friend gave it to me. And now I give it to you as my special friend. Anyway, you can see from its condition, I really don't read it. You will get more use out of it. Maybe you can pick out your favorites and read them to me sometime."

Dominic considered the book in his hands. It would be a nice addition to his book collection.

"OK, Father Arnold, if you really don't mind, I will take it. Thank you very much. What time is it?"

"It's probably time for you to head home if you're feeling sufficiently recovered." Dominic nodded his head in agreement and finished off his third can of soda.

"Thanks for everything, Father Arnold. I'm sorry if I interrupted you or kept you from anything important."

"Not to worry, Dominic. Just another exciting Friday night in the St. Mary's rectory with the wild crew of priests that live here. Father Chou is likely praying and flagellating himself. Father Vincenti is probably thinking about Father Chou flagellating himself. I suspect Father Downey is reading the *Sporting News*. And Father Bob is working on his sermon over his third scotch and soda."

"And you?" asked Dominic innocently.

"Me? Why, I'm ministering to the youth of the parish," laughed Father Bumbry.

He walked Dominic down to the door and opened it but hesitated for a moment: "Dominic, you did the right thing coming here tonight. You should always feel free to come here if you ever are in trouble or need my help, OK?"

"Sure, Father Arnold, I appreciate that. Thanks for everything. Have a good night."

Dominic walked down the steps and headed down Fourth Avenue toward Denny's house. He figured he'd wait for Denny and Marco there.

Father Bumbry closed the door and hurried to a window to watch the youth. His pulse raced with excitement.

In the shadows of the next room Father Downey stood watching his newest charge with an uneasy feeling.

XVII.

DESPERADOES AT THE
POOL PARTY

L et's just be clear—nobody do anything stupid!" Ernie held up his
finger and went from Timmy to Dominic to Denny to Marco with
a threatening intent. "*Capito?*"

"Screw you, *Ernest*!" Denny shouted at him with fake disdain.

The boys cracked up. It was the first house party they had been invited to and they were all fairly excited. It was at Belinda Donaldson's
house. Belinda was one of the "three damsels" of Landon, the town next
to Rosedale. The other two were Annette and Trish—all three were
sweet, beautiful girls who were inseparable. One of Belinda's older
brothers was Harry Donaldson, who was a year ahead of the boys and
played soccer for ASM. The boys received the invite from Andy Terrolla,
a classmate at ASM, who was good friends with Annette and Trish. It
was billed as a pool party but no one was expected to really go swimming. Nonetheless, Denny had asked Dominic to bring his swim trunks
with him.

Meatloaf's *Bat Out of Hell* album was booming from a record player
that had been set up outside. There was already a fairly large crowd of
kids in the backyard of the Donaldson residence, with an even mix of

girls and boys. Belinda's parents were out for the evening at a local Knights of Columbus affair and had given permission to Belinda for the party, with the understanding her two older brothers, Harry and Willie, would be around.

"Well, get a load of all the babes here, Nicky boy." Denny's impersonation of Ernie was spot on. Dominic smiled and nodded.

Belinda walked over to say hello to them.

"Hi, fellas, glad you could make it. There's soda in the cooler and there's chips and pretzels for snacking. We ordered some pizzas for later."

"Thanks, Belinda. Very nice of you to invite us." Dominic couldn't help hearing the sincerity in Belinda's greeting.

"Hey Belinda, are we still allowed to take a swim?" Denny asked.

"Sure, Denny. Did you guys bring your swimsuits?"

"I sure did!" replied Denny. "And Nick brought his, too."

Dominic shook his head. "I forgot them at Ernie's house when I used his bathroom. Sorry, Denny."

"That's OK, Dominic. I'm sure my brother Harry has a pair you can borrow. Go ahead inside the house and up the stairs. I think Harry's up there now listening to records in his room."

"I'm going to jump in the pool, Nicky boy, and get this pool party going!" Denny headed over to the above ground pool while Dominic headed toward the back door.

"Hey, Harry, what are you listening to?" inquired Dominic as he entered Harry's bedroom.

"New Kinks album, *Misfits*."

"How is it?"

"It's alright. Not one of their best. How's the party?" Harry was turning the record over.

"It's good. A lot of people. You going to come down?"

"Eh, I don't think so. I can basically catch the action from up here. Lot of my sister's pretty friends are here though." Harry winked at Dominic.

"They sure are. Hey, Harry, you have an extra pair of swimming trunks I can borrow? I left mine at Ernie's house and Denny's insisting that we go for a swim."

"That freaking Denny is a crazy dude. In a fun way, though. Yeah, second drawer there should be a pair that will fit you."

Dominic went over to the half-open drawer and grabbed the blue trunks that were at the top. "Mind if I just change here?"

"No, go ahead." Harry walked to the window overlooking his backyard. "Yup, a lot of pretty girls here."

Dominic finished changing into the blue trunks. "Fit like a glove. Are you sure you don't want to join in on all the fun and games?"

"Maybe when the pizza arrives, I will come down. For now, I'll just enjoy the view from up here."

"OK. Thanks for the trunks!"

The water was freezing at first immersion but Denny assured Dominic he would get used to it. It was just the two of them in the pool and Denny was busy making wisecracks. Dominic was enjoying the comments although he thought Denny had an extra sharp edge tonight. The sunset was quickly fading and the crowd of young teenagers had grown to a good size. Their conversation was interrupted by a female voice.

"How's the water, boys? Mind if I join you?"

The voice belonged to Kim Gordon—and was attached to a body that was all curves, roundabouts, and jug handle turns. Without waiting for a response, Kim climbed the ladder, paused as she reached down with her left foot, and dipped her toes in the water.

"A tad on the cold side but I'm sure if I need to be warmed up, you two would be up for the challenge." Kim gave the two a leering smile. She was wearing a pair of tight cut-off jean shorts and a white T-shirt that strained to hold back the biggest breasts that Denny and Dominic had ever seen this close. Kim slowly and deliberately climbed down into the water. Almost on immediate contact with the frigid surface, the nipples on her two breasts popped out like erasers on brand new number two pencils.

"Oh my, I guess the water's a bit chillier than I thought." Kim glanced down at her chest and then back at the two boys. She chuckled and then submerged herself in the water for a moment. She came back to the surface and pushed back her wet, shoulder-length hair, being sure to showcase her wares to her entranced audience. She swam past the boys and pulled up opposite them, her back against the side of the pool. Her breasts were like two huge white buoys floating on top.

"Didn't anybody ever tell you it's rude to stare?" Kim's feigned offense annoyed Denny while Dominic quickly averted his eyes.

"I see you came dressed for the occasion, Kim." Denny wasn't going to be intimidated. Besides, he liked a big bosom, especially with binky-sized nips.

"Oh, you think? I don't know, I feel I'm a bit over-dressed." And with that comment, Kim reached her hands back, unsnapped her bra, pulled it out from under her T-shirt, and hung it over the ledge of the pool.

"That feels so much better." Her knockers looked even bigger now, like two mammoth beasts unleashed from their cages. "There aren't any water snakes I need to watch out for in this pool, are there?" Kim inquired with mock fear.

Denny accepted the challenge. "There might be a couple of pythons lurking about, but they're usually picky about their prey."

"Pythons? Oh, that sounds dangerous! But promising! Then again, I've heard guys brag about pythons and then only an earthworm shows up, if you know what I mean. What's a girl to believe?" With that, Kim stretched herself out on her back while holding on to the pool's edge, her voluptuous body floating on top of the water.

Harry was watching the pool scene from his bedroom window. Kim was a senior at Mother Theresa High School in Clarksville, one town over from Landon. She lived in the neighborhood and she had attended the same grammar school as he and his older brother Willie. Harry was an eyewitness to Kim's growing in all the right spots.

"Damn, Kim, that's a magnificent rack," Harry muttered to himself.

"Hey, little brother, what are you up to?" Harry hadn't heard Willie enter the room. Willie had just graduated from the Police Academy and shared a bedroom with him. He walked over to the window to see what had caught his brother's interest.

"Kim showing off her assets. Or breast set, I should say." Willie chuckled. "Wouldn't mind doing the breaststroke with her, if you know what I mean? Why not go down and mingle with the ladies instead of watching it from up here? It will do you some good. You may even get lucky." Willie slapped his brother on the back.

THE CONVERSATION IN THE POOL began to wane. Kim was getting bored while Denny was getting annoyed. Dominic concentrated on not staring at Kim's chest, which he imagined was beckoning to him with every deep breath she took. A tall, muscular guy appeared at the side of the pool. To Dominic, he appeared to be a senior in high school or maybe even already in college.

"There you are, baby. I was wondering what happened to you."

Kim glanced over her shoulder. "Thank God, you showed up. I believe I was in real danger here."

The guy glared menacingly at Denny and Dominic. "These punks giving you a hard time?"

"If only! God no, I meant in danger of being bored to death. Can you grab me a towel?"

As the boyfriend fetched a towel, Kim stood up, grabbed her bra, and put it back on under her T-shirt while staring back at her captivated two boy audience. "Show's over, fellas. Be gentle with me tonight in your beds. Wait, on second thought, be extra rough. I'll like that. Ta-ta!"

Her boyfriend showed up with the towel. Kim got out of the pool and disappeared into the crowd.

"That little tease!" Denny sneered.

"Little is not an adjective that I would use to describe Kim." Dominic shook his head as if to snap out of a trance.

"You know what, Nicky, I think it's time we shake things up around here."

Dominic didn't like the sound of this suggestion as he knew his friend was prone to impulsive and rebellious notions. Denny referred to these impulses as unconventional. Dominic saw them as unwise.

"I have an idea. Oh yes, I do! We're going to have some real fun now. We'll show this wench and the rest of them. Yes, we will!"

Dominic didn't like the sinister voice coming from Denny or his use of the word "we."

"What are you thinking, Denny? Remember, we're guests here."

"What are you worrying about, Dominic? Always worrying about what others think."

"I like the fact that we were invited to a party with a lot of pretty girls. I do worry about not getting invited to any in the future, if that's what you mean."

"Trust me, Dominic. Follow my lead here, and we'll be invited to *every* party!" With that comment, Denny pulled down his swim trunks and swung them over his shoulder. "Come on, Nicky boy, time to step up to the diving board."

"What the hell...are you out of your mind?" Dominic was in complete disbelief.

"Come on, come on, take 'em off. You and me are climbing out of this pool, walking across this yard, grabbing some towels, and giving these ladies a show of our own."

"Denny, that's not a good idea, no, no, not at all. Let's just get out of the pool, dry off, and have some pizza. And, uh—"

"No! Damnit, Dominic, I never ask you for any favors. Never. Whenever you want or need something, I don't ever hesitate to be there for you. I'm calling in my favor now. How long have we been friends? A long time. All I'm asking is that you do this for me. I just want to show these chicks once and for all that we're not their little panting puppies. They shake their titties and asses in our faces all the time, and get their jollies making us salivate after them. To hell with that! Drop them, now! Or don't ever call me your kindred spirit again."

Denny 's face expressed no room for compromise. Dominic couldn't argue with Denny always being there for him and never asking anything in return. And Dominic could relate to his friend's perspective on the ladies, especially after the pool encounter with Kim—and his experience with the now infamous "In Defense of His Woody" speech, as it became known. Dominic quickly pulled off his trunks and slung them over his shoulders.

"Crazier person, first."

Denny grinned and nodded his head at his friend. Dominic watched as Denny climbed the stairs, his bare buttocks emerging from the water. It was now officially night as the sun had totally disappeared and the only light shining over the yard was from the spotlight above the back-steps of the house. It was positioned perfectly, almost like a stage setup, in direct alignment with the pool. Dominic took a deep breath and climbed out of the pool. He was about six feet behind Denny. At first, no one appeared to notice but then some of the party goers caught sight of them. Kids began to shout and point and some started to run back and forth. For his part Dominic tried to avoid eye contact and kept focused on Denny. It struck Dominic how comfortable Denny seemed, like he was out for a leisurely stroll yet proud as a peacock displaying his array of feathers. Suddenly, reality of the situation burst upon everyone present and complete chaos broke out.

"What the fuck!" Ernie came running toward Dominic, grabbing a lawn chair, on the way. "Nicky! Jesus Christ, what are you doing?" Ernie stumbled a bit as he held the chair at an angle, trying to cover Dominic's lower torso. Ernie dropped the chair, bent over laughing hysterically. Meanwhile, Marco and Timmy stood frozen watching their two friends' exhibition.

Marco turned to Timmy. "Denny's crazy—for sure. But what's with the Monsignor? Has he gone nuts?"

Timmy reacted fast. "Obviously, since he's showing them to everybody." Timmy ran and grabbed a towel off a nearby table and hurried over to Dominic and handed it to him. "Dominic, you got to get dressed! Like now!" Dominic accepted the towel and wrapped it around himself. Dominic looked to see where Denny was. Denny had made it to the backsteps where Trish, one of the three damsels of Landon, was sitting, reading Yes's *Tormato* album cover, seemingly oblivious to the commotion around her. Dominic watched as Denny walked up to Trish and tapped her on the shoulder.

"Hi, do you know where I can get a towel?" Denny asked politely as Trish turned her head and came eye to eye with Denny's one-eyed python. The album cover went flying as Trish jumped up with a shriek.

"Guess not. What's a guy have to do to get a towel around here?" Denny asked no one in particular. Marco ran up to Denny and threw a towel at him. "You crazy loon! What the hell are you doing? *How* did you get Dominic to do it?" Marco sounded impressed with Denny's power of persuasion.

From the second-floor window, Harry and Willie observed the whole scene. Harry was in a state of shock while Willie was grinning ear to ear, shaking his head.

"Let me get down there and address this. You coming, Harry?" His brother just shook his head no.

Willie had managed to get Denny and Dominic out of the backyard and onto the front sidewalk a few houses down from his home. At first, he maintained a stern disposition, expressing deep disapproval and disappointment with the boys' behavior. But he couldn't contain his true feelings about the event.

"You two are out of control! That was too funny, though. You guys got some real cojones—no one can deny that!" He chuckled. "Unfortunately, you can't stay because my sister and her friends are quite upset. Don't worry, they'll get over it. It's not as if my friends and I didn't pull off-the-wall stunts like this. But we were usually stoned out of our minds. It's very apparent to me you two couldn't be any more sober. And that's what really makes it hysterical. If I didn't have to chaperone, I'd take you guys out for some White Castles! It was that good a show! Just be careful getting home."

Denny and Dominic walked in silence as they made their way back to Rosedale. Finally, Denny spoke.

"You mad, Dominic?" Denny sounded a bit remorseful.

Dominic glanced at his friend. "No, not really."

"No?"

"Not the least bit. I hate to admit it, Denny, but you were right. I mean, we'll probably never get invited to another party. Not by Belinda or Annette or Trish anyway."

"There I think you're wrong, Nicky. I think we get VIP invitations to every one of them. Trust me on that, my friend. VIP all the way."

"I don't know, Denny, did you see the look of horror on Trish's face? You scared the crap out of her!"

Denny responded in a Boris Karloff voice: "Of course she was scared, Nicky, she came face to face with my monster python!"

The two friends erupted in laughter and quickened their pace. Maybe there was a White Castle they could hit on the way home.

XVIII.

BREAKFAST IN THE
MANTERRA'S HOUSE

Dominic stood outside the barn-house, waiting for Father Bumbry. He kept an eye on the back entrance of the rectory anticipating the priest's appearance. Father Bumbry had called him with the request to meet him at the barn-house to give him a hand with some stuff. It was a Saturday morning, and Dominic did not have anything else going on so he agreed to meet him at ten o'clock. Dominic was aimlessly kicking stones across the empty parking lot when the priest's "Good morning, Dominic!" greeted him and he looked up.

"Good morning, Father Arnold." The priest approached Dominic and gave him a hug with another "Good morning, my son." Dominic kept his arms at his side and grimaced while the priest held the hug for a moment.

"So glad you could help me this morning. They just laid the new carpeting in the barn-house this past week and some of the furniture was delivered yesterday. The Knights of Columbus agreed to donate a pool table and a ping pong table so things are starting to come together and we'll be able to meet here soon instead of the school library. Remember our first meeting there? It seems so long ago now."

Dominic nodded his head. He wished Timmy had come with him.

Father Bumbry unlocked the barn-house door and flipped the light switch, then they went inside. Sure enough, a brand-new wall-to-wall carpet had been installed and the scent of the new rug filled the whole place. On one side of the room were couches, chairs, and various tables that had been delivered.

"Let's remove our shoes so we don't muddy up the new carpeting," Father Bumbry suggested. Father Bumbry kicked off his shoes, then took off his raincoat and threw it on one of the chairs. Dominic removed his shoes, took off his coat, and hung it on the knob of the utility closet door adjacent to the entrance door.

"What do you think?" Father Bumbry asked.

"It came out nice. This place has really been transformed. You did a lot of work here, Father."

"*We* did a lot of work, Dominic. You've been a great big help in making this happen. Thank you so much!"

"The whole team made it happen, Father. Without everyone's help it would have never come together."

"You just can't take compliment or credit for anything, can you?" Father Bumbry teased. "Anyway, how do you think we should set up the furniture?" Father Bumbry started to stroke his beard, envisioning the layout of the furniture. He turned to Dominic. "How about some music?"

"OK, sure."

"There's a cassette player over on the countertop by the kitchen galley with a case of cassettes next to it. Choose one you want to listen to while we're setting up the room."

Dominic went through the row of tapes picked out the Police's *Outlandos D'Amour* and stuck it in the cassette player and pressed play.

"Good choice," Father Bumbry remarked. "Let's each grab an end of this couch and we'll move it over there." Father Bumbry motioned toward a corner of the room. Dominic moved to the opposite end of the couch and lifted it. They spent a couple of hours moving the furniture around until all the pieces had been assigned a spot. Father Bumbry stood by the entry door of the barn-house and surveyed the final result.

"Looks good, Dominic, looks really good. What do you think?"

"Yeah, it looks sharp. And there's still room for the recreational tables you mentioned."

"I love this carpeting, especially the color. It's so plush." Father Bumbry went over to the open area where the recreational tables would be going and plopped himself down on his butt. He ran his clawed hands in circles through the thick pile of the carpet. "Come on over, Dominic, and have a seat."

Dominic walked over and sat down on the carpet, keeping some distance between Father Bumbry and himself.

"Do you feel that—it's so soft and cushiony." Father Bumbry smiled at Dominic. "Go ahead and touch it, Dominic."

Dominic placed his hand on the carpet. "Yeah, it's pretty soft. But, I mean, it's brand new and it's carpeting, so it should be."

Father Bumbry let out a sigh and shrugged his shoulders. He then rolled to his side and stretched out on the carpet, rolling onto his back, staring up at the crossbeams above them. "Oh, this feels so good, this is so comfortable!" He closed his eyes. "Dominic, why don't you lie down on the carpet and see how good it feels?"

Dominic hesitated. He didn't really want to lie down on the carpet but instead wanted to know if they were finished so he could go home.

Father Bumbry opened his eyes. "Come on, Dominic, just for a minute. I want to share some things with you. Here, lay your head here next to mine." Father Bumbry patted a spot above his big round head. His eyes stared into Dominic's and to Dominic they seemed to reflect a mixture of pleading and sadness. Dominic stretched out on the carpet, opposite Father Bumbry, the top of their heads not quite side by side. Dominic heard Father Bumbry let out a deep sigh.

"What did you want to talk about?" asked Dominic, hoping to get the conversation over with as quickly as possible.

"You know, Dominic, sometimes it gets, well, very lonely. Do you ever feel that way?" Father Bumbry's tone was very serious and soft.

"Who gets lonely?" asked Dominic.

"I do," answered Father Bumbry in a hushed tone.

"Why?" Dominic sounded incredulous. "How can that be?"

Father Bumbry was casually drawing little circles in the carpet next to him with his index finger. "Well, because I am alone and by myself and sometimes, I have these feelings and a need—"

"That doesn't make any sense," Dominic interrupted, "that doesn't make any sense at all."

"Why do you say that?" Father Bumbry tried not to sound put off or annoyed at the interruption and Dominic's tone.

"Why would you ever feel lonely? *How* could you ever feel lonely?" Dominic sounded more demanding than inquisitive.

"I'm human, Dominic, just like you. I have feelings…uh, certain feelings and there are times when I feel I need—"

Again, Dominic interrupted, "But Father Bumbry, you're a priest!"

"Yes, I am, but that doesn't mean—"

"You're not alone at all. Jesus is with you all the time. How could you ever feel lonely when Jesus is always with you? You're one of His priests, one of His chosen servants—He's closest to His servants. You should never feel alone or lonely because of that." Dominic's earnestness was emphatic. Father Bumbry was quiet. Dominic continued, "I envy you, Father Arnold. You get to spend all your time and energy devoted to God. That is very special and you have a very unique relationship with God because you are His priest."

Father Bumbry's eyes stared down at his feet. He let out a deep breath through his mouth and rolled his large girth to his side, and pushed himself up to a sitting position. Dominic stood up and brushed some of the carpet strands off his pants. Father Bumbry waited and then extended his hand to Dominic.

"Would you mind?" he asked. Dominic took hold of his hand and pulled while Father Bumbry pushed himself up, first onto his knees and then up on his feet. "Thanks," he said, "we better get going." Dominic put on his shoes and then his coat while Father Bumbry grabbed his raincoat and made his way to the door to put on his shoes as well.

"How about some lunch to thank you for your help today?" offered Father Bumbry.

"Sorry, Father, no can do. I have to get home to help my dad. I told him that I would only be a couple of hours and I am already late."

Father Bumbry bit his lower lip and tried to hide his disappointment at Dominic's response. "Oh OK, I thought we could go grab something to eat but if you have to go, I understand."

"Alright, Father Arnold, the place came out great. See ya next week." Dominic turned to go.

Father Bumbry suddenly changed his expression. "Dominic?"

Dominic paused. "You know we're friends—I consider you a very close friend. I want you to know that."

"OK, Father Arnold. I appreciate that." Dominic looked at the clock on the wall. He didn't want to keep his dad waiting.

"Dominic, I want to share a sign of that friendship that was common in the days of Jesus and his disciples. It's called a liturgical kiss." Father Bumbry smiled. Dominic made a face—he could only remember one kiss described in the Scriptures with respect to Jesus—and it didn't turn out too well for the Lord.

Father Bumbry edged closer to Dominic and continued, "I would like to share that sentiment with you." Before Dominic could respond, Father Bumbry hugged Dominic and gave him a peck on the cheek.

Dominic bristled, pushing himself from the priest's embrace. "OK, Father Bumbry, I gotta go." Dominic opened the door and quickly stepped out of the barn-house into the midday sun. He scampered away from the barn-house and headed home.

Father Bumbry slammed the door shut and stood inside the empty barn-house; a tinge of elation consoled the feeling of rejection. He sighed, then looked down at himself while locking the door, shifted his gaze to the light switch, and flipped it to off.

. . .

IOLANDA MANTERRA MIXED THE pancake batter while bacon sizzled in the frying pan. Jon Jasper sat at the Manterra's kitchen table reading the sports section of the *Star Ledger*.

"More coffee, Jon?" asked Mrs. Manterra, holding forth the coffee pot.

"Yes, please, Mrs. Manterra, thanks."

"You want your eggs the usual, over easy? Short stack of pancakes on the side?"

"Perfect, thanks." Jon neatly folded the newspaper and placed it on top of the *Daily News* he had picked up for Mr. Manterra. "I have to tell you, Mrs. Manterra, this is the best breakfast deal in Rosedale."

Mrs. Manterra smiled at her adopted sixth son as her boys Mitchell and Jason walked into the kitchen and joined Jon at the table. Jon looked at his watch. "You guys are running late. I'm already on my second cup of coffee and buttered roll." Mrs. Manterra placed a plate of bacon and eggs in front of Jon, who dug right in.

"What time did you get here, Jon?" asked Jason.

"I've been keeping your mom company since about 6:30. Here, I brought some rolls and apple turnovers. Help yourselves."

Mrs. Manterra set a platter of pancakes in the center of the table. "Help yourselves, boys!"

"See, early bird gets the hot 'cakes! Thanks, Mrs. Manterra!" Jon ate his breakfast while Mrs. Manterra filled a glass of orange juice for him.

"Did the Yankees win last night?" Mitchell stretched his neck to check out the folded-up sports section.

"Nah, they lost. Billy and Reggie having their issues. But I'd be surprised if they still don't win the American League this year. Is Sal coming down?"

"He's still getting ready. You know how he is." Jason replied.

"How many miles did he run this morning?" Jon asked between bites.

"I think he said seven miles." Mitchell accepted a plate of scrambled eggs from his mom.

"Is that all? That's just seven more than I was planning to run." The earnestness in Jon's tone got a laugh out of Mitchell and Jason.

The sound of someone entering the backdoor and climbing up the steps caught everyone's attention. The kitchen door slowly opened and Father Bumbry's head popped out from behind the door. "Good morning, folks! Mrs. Manterra, is there any extra grub?" Father Bumbry was stopping in for his weekly breakfast visit.

"Of course, Father Arnold, always enough! Come on in. Have you had your coffee yet?"

Father Bumbry greeted everyone and pulled up a chair next to Jon Jasper. "How are you, Jon? I saw on the Rectory schedule that your dad is meeting with Monsignor Downey later. Hope all is well?"

Jon pushed the plate of apple turnovers toward the priest while Mrs. Manterra placed a cup of coffee down in front of him. "I believe they're just meeting to discuss the assignments for the Sunday Mass readings. Doesn't want my dad to be overwhelmed. I believe the Collingswood sisters will be attendance as well."

"Where's Dominic?" Father Bumbry noticed his favorite Manterra was not present.

"The Barry Gibb wannabe is upstairs blow-drying his hair. Shouldn't be much longer." Sal Manterra answered from the adjacent dining room. "Jon—you ready to roll?"

"Just finishing up this delicious breakfast your mom whipped up. Did you eat already?" Jon popped the last of his pancakes in his mouth and washed it down with orange juice.

"I had a protein shake after my run. So ready when you are."

"Thanks for another great breakfast, Mrs. Manterra! Tell your husband I will see him on Saturday morning."

"You're welcome, Jon, Saturday then? French toast for a change?" Mrs. Manterra winked at him as she picked up his empty plates.

"Mrs. Manterra, you could serve dry toast and it would be special! Ok, not as special as your pizza…"

Jon and Salvatore said their goodbyes and went out the front door.

"Maybe I will take a walk upstairs and nudge Dominic along." Father Bumbry stood up.

"Ok, I will have your eggs and pancakes ready by the time you two come down," responded Mrs. Manterra.

Father Bumbry made his way up the stairs and could hear a radio playing *More Than a Feeling* with Dominic Manterra singing along. The priest paused on the top stair and watched the would-be rock star preening before the mirror, hairdryer in one hand and a hairbrush-microphone in the other. He listened carefully as the song ended to hear the words that Dominic was singing: "until Moira and I walk awaaaaaaaaaaay..." *Who is he singing about?* the priest wondered.

"And the audience goes wild and shouts for an encore!" Father Bumbry clapped his hands.

A startled and embarrassed Dominic turned off the radio. "Hey, Father Arnold, I didn't see you there. You scared me a for a second!" Dominic put away the hairdryer and brush.

"Nothing to fear, my son, I come in peace. When's the next set and do you take requests?"

"Hopefully it's a request to end it!" Mitchell brushed by Father Bumbry on the way to his room.

"Hey Dominic, who sings that song—Boston, right? Let's keep it that way!" Jason pushed by Father Bumbry's other side. He slipped into his room, re-appeared within moments and swept right by Father Bumbry down the stairs. "Mom says she has your guys' breakfast ready! Mitchell, I'll be in the car!"

Mitchell followed behind his youngest brother. "You better get moving there, Joey Ramone! See ya later, Father Arnold."

Father Bumbry shrugged his shoulders at Dominic. "Everybody's a critic! Don't listen to them. They're just jealous."

Dominic laughed it off. "Denny tells me I have a singing voice made for silent movies so I'm used to it. Let me grab my tie and then we can have a quick breakfast." Dominic walked into his bedroom, took his tie from his bed post, turned around and almost ran smack into Father Bumbry. "Whoa! Didn't see you!"

Father Bumbry didn't flinch. "Oh sorry, figured since I was up here, I'd check out your bedroom."

Dominic hesitated for a moment. "Sure, but mom's got breakfast done and I have to get moving if I'm going to be on time to meet Timmy and Ernie."

Father Bumbry sat down on Dominic's bed. "Ahh, this is where you sleep?"

"Yup, and that's Jason's bed," Dominic pointed to another bed on the opposite side of the room.

"Dominic, come sit down for a moment."

"Father, I really have to hurry."

"Just for a moment, Dominic. That's not too much to ask from a friend?" Father Bumbry persisted.

Dominic sat on the opposite end of the bed from the priest.

"Thank you. You know now that you're at ASM, we don't see each other as much as we did when I first arrived at St. Mary's. That's why I like to stopping by for breakfast when I can, so the two of us can stay connected." He reached over and put his hand on Dominic's shoulder.

"I understand Father Arnold. My schedule is fairly busy right now. There's only so many hours in a day. I'm realizing I can't do everything and need to decide what I want to keep participating in and what I'm going to have to give up."

"I hope I am in the keeper column of that list!" Father Bumbry voiced with seriousness.

"Sure you are! No worries there. But, seriously, Father, we need to get going!" Dominic stood up and headed for the stairs without waiting for a response. Father Bumbry sighed deeply although he felt good about Dominic's answer. As they made their way down the stairs, a thought came to Father Bumbry.

"Why don't I just give you and Timmy and Ernie a lift to ASM? This

way you don't have to rush through your breakfast?" Dominic considered it and nodded his head. "And maybe next time I stop by for breakfast, I will come a little earlier and we can hang out in your room for
a bit."

Dominic had already scooted off to the kitchen leaving Father Bumbry to wonder if he had heard his last suggestion.

XIX.

THE SEED

The sun couldn't decide if it wanted to come out. Every now and then it peeked from behind cumulus clouds and streaked through the curtains of Monsignor Downey's office in the rectory. James Downey stood at the window glimpsing the sky and pondering what the sun's final decision might be. He scanned the vacant schoolyard of the grammar school, and the adjacent all-girls' high school. He could see the barn-house where the Youth Ministry group met on Wednesdays and Sundays for social activities and events. It was Saturday morning and there were no cars in the parking spaces by the rectory except for his, those belonging to his small contingency of priests, and Mrs. Taylor's old Chrysler. She cooked, cleaned, and did the clergy's laundry.

He turned away from his observation post and sat down at his desk. He opened the slim drawer in the center of the desk and took out his pack of L&M cigarettes. After lighting one up and exhaling, the nicotine fix in place, he looked about his office. A quick assessment of his years of ministry was that he didn't have much to show for it. Shelves stacked with books, covering topics from pastoral leadership to liturgical rites to discourse on the Roman canon. Most he hadn't read and those he had, he had very little recall of, or use of for that matter. None of them had the answers to the questions and challenges he faced on a daily basis anyway. None of them really could tell him why we were here, why we treated each other the way we do, and why suffering seemed to be the only constant. True, they offered explanations and theories and so-called insights. But nothing of any real value when administering last rites to a dead teenager who had plowed his car into a bridge buttress after finishing off a bottle of Schenley's in the back of the girls' high school. The same teenage boy who after consuming the bottle, had sauntered into the dance empowered with confidence and bravado but alas, no increased social skill. It didn't take too long before he realized he was no more noticed or wanted anyway and then left the dance to escape his torture and ended up at his meeting with destiny at the bridge. Monsignor Downey would stand up from the dead body as the parents arrived and broke out in the hysterical shrieks and cries that would later echo in his head as he lay in his bed at night staring at nothing. A sibling or close friend would no doubt show up to add to the pathetic scene and he always slightly bristled with their not atypical comments such as "Where the fuck is Jesus when you need Him?" Where, indeed. Monsignor Downey wanted to tell them that Jesus was right there but of course that would only elicit disdain in the form of, "Oh, really? Then why didn't He do something?" and other such comments that are the momentary relief of what will be permanent pain. He simply said nothing, posted like a sentry, motionless with a lugubrious face. He had fears that this had become his actual everyday face, forged by the countless rituals he had presided over throughout his thirty plus years in the priesthood. He wondered when the numbness had taken over—at what number of baptisms, weddings, sicknesses, funerals, the countless encounters of broken hearts and souls and minds that he had engaged—at what specific moment did the indifference seep in and the routine of motion take over? He wondered when his just going through the motions had denigrated into just pretending to go through the motions. He knew it wasn't an indifference borne of real apathy. Not at all. It was indifference as a means of survival. But Monsignor Downey wondered whether despite surviving, if irreparable damage had been done.

Monsignor Downey did not drink, as his witness of the harm it could cause to families and friends alike turned him off to the bottle at a young age. He was withdrawn and shy as a child and never really developed the charm and personality for attraction with the opposite sex. His mom had seemed to worry about this and abetted the choice of a vocation. He went willingly to the gallows of celibacy and never looked back. Perhaps the roots of survival had taken hold earlier than he imagined.

Continuing with his inventory assessment, there were knick-knacks from his trips abroad—Ireland, for sure, to visit County-who-really-cares to meet up with distant relatives whose pastime was drinking in dark pubs with somber music, and who enjoyed showing off their photos of JFK and the current Pope. The Vatican, of course, where members of the Roman Catholic clergy might pilgrimage at least once in their life, like their ecumenical brethren, the devout Moslem who journeys to Mecca. He presumed the trek to Rome held many more comforts and delights: better accommodations and food, no doubt, and less agony and ecstasy. Finally, there were his tribute items to Notre Dame—the Fightin' Irish, not the French cathedral. College football was his passion, the one thing that brought him pleasure in life. He permitted himself two vices in life: smoking and wagering. He liked the horses and he liked the Irish. He was not reckless or extravagant and did not skim the church funds. He only used his own money. As an only child, his parents' estate, though modest, all came to him. He invested most of it but kept some for entertainment. He knew to be prudent because when his stint in the parish life was over, he would be on his own. The Church may keep you sheltered and fed while in service but not much was waiting for the parish priest when he was discharged from duty, especially those who were not the princes in the hierarchy.

He glanced down at his watch and stamped out his cigarette, placing the ashtray on the windowsill behind him. "Is the man ever on time?" he said out loud to himself, annoyed.

"The man" in question was Father Arnold Bumbry. The Monsignor was torn about his feelings for Father Bumbry. True, the young priest was not his cup of tea, and they didn't have much in common. He was part of the up-and-coming new breed of priests who were of a more liberal bent than the old school of tradition that had forged and shaped Monsignor Downey's generation. Bumbry was touchy-feely with a tinge of flower child mysticism and mumbo jumbo lingo that Downey found undignified and entitlement-minded and irresponsibly immature if not downright out of touch with the realities of life. Father Bumbry was in charge of the youth ministry outreach, as he referred to it, serving as its director, and had no common sense as far as Downey was concerned. In meetings with the parish council, discussing budgets and finances, Bumbry would push for items for the youth group's barn facility, such as new furniture, recreational games, a television, a music system, and it would be even better if they could get a kitchen installed and sleeping quarters built. The parish council members would sit and stare at Bumbry in silence. Bumbry was not put off by this but persisted in what he called his championing of the parish youths' needs and rights. Downey would interrupt and acknowledge that although these pursuits were noble perhaps the feeding and clothing and sheltering of the poor, the abused, and the abandoned in the parish as well as ministering to the sick and dying, might take precedence. Bumbry would eventually back off red-cheeked and pouting at the Monsignor's rebuff. Maybe Downey didn't like Bumbry because Bumbry was a drinker. And perhaps more so because he had heard rumors that Father Bumbry would imbibe with some of the youth of the parish in his rectory apartment at night. The Monsignor had made subtle overtures to Bumbry to let him know he was aware of this possibility and that he disapproved and would have no tolerance of it, as he could only see it leading to trouble and scandal. When the Monsignor found out later that Bumbry had installed a private buzzer on the side entrance under his room that connected directly to his rectory apartment, he was furious as he saw no purpose for this and no good coming from it. Father Bumbry argued that sometimes youth in the parish were in hostile and abusive situations at home, and his motivation for installing the private and direct connection was to avail an avenue of escape at all hours, in order to alleviate the possibility of significant or permanent physical harm not to speak of the emotional and mental trauma. Considering the logic, Monsignor relented on that score, but warned Bumbry never again to take any such actions without his express permission.

Downey had one other reason for his dislike of Father Bumbry. Spirituality. Bumbry appeared to have a calm and serene comfort with his own spirituality. There were no struggles of guilt or doubt or even an air of gravitas with Bumbry. He was at ease with his relationship with God, a relationship that appeared to focus on free will and promoted Bumbry's free-spirit approach to his priestly duties. Bumbry had a knack for connecting with the folks of the parish, and they liked him. He was affable, sensitive, and approachable. Downey realized these were not attributes readily identified with his person. His appeal was to the old guard members of the Knights of Columbus and the elderly parishioners who had known him many years, in fact were part of his brand of spiritual family. These select few seemed to harbor a dislike of Father Bumbry, if not an outright distrust of his manner and style. They preferred that old-time religion and Bumbry represented to them an erosion of the security they felt in the rigidity and structure of their vision of church. Decorum, protocol, and ritual were the foundation of their church and they had no use for any fresh approach represented by young upstarts like Father Bumbry, whose eagerness and enthusiasm for folk music masses and multi-colored banners to decorate their sacred altar they found to be anathema. Besides all that, Father Bumbry was out of shape, had a flamboyant air, and had zero interest in sports. While he was popular with the youth, and some of the more "hip" parents, there had been more than one occasion when the eyebrows rose or the heads shook.

He heard approaching footsteps and looked up as Bumbry sauntered into his office, collar off and a brightly colored sweater announcing his arrival in advance of his actual appearance.

"Good morning, Jimbo, hope I haven't kept you waiting."

Downey bristled at the greeting. He resented Bumbry's familiarity and casualness with him.

"Good morning, Father Bumbry. I take it you've had your coffee this morning?"

"Oh yes. Mrs. Taylor fixed me up with her usual hearty breakfast. I'm all set, thanks." Bumbry plopped himself into one of the leather chairs in front of Downey's desk.

Realizing that the subtleness of his annoyance was lost on Bumbry, Downey proceeded to the matter at hand.

"Have you given some thought to how you will be handling the Carbonni matter?"

Bumbry took his eyes off the Monsignor and looked down at the back of his outstretched hands resting on his lap. He studied them for a moment and let out a slow and steady sigh.

"I have. It won't be pretty, no matter how one approaches the subject. Carbonni is an old-school Italian and this is his only daughter. He has two older sons, one who is known to be a hothead. But this kind of news could make the other brother angry as well. There's no telling what the father's reaction will be when he finds out his seventeen-year-old baby girl is with child but it could get ugly real fast."

Downey sat motionless in his chair on the side of the desk opposite Bumbry. Already the parish priest's cavalier tone had begun to get under his skin, although his analysis, while simple, was fairly spot on: Mr. Carbonni was a long-time parishioner, a pillar of the Knights, and the owner of a construction company. His only daughter was with child and the only people who knew were the two men currently discussing the topic, the girl, and presumably the father of the baby within the young Miss Carbonni. Interestingly enough, Bumbry had volunteered to be the one to accompany the girl and meet with the parents to break the news to them.

"How have you arranged telling the parents?"

"Well, I have been counseling the young lady, to discuss her options, and whether or not she wanted to keep it." Bumbry paused. He knew that his choice of phrasing irritated the Monsignor and this gave him both amusement and pleasure. He waited a beat and continued on. "Of course, she is not open to the option."

"The *option?*" the Monsignor inquired.

Bumbry paused before responding. "The option of giving up the baby for adoption. We'll have to see how her parents react. The shaming factor of a pregnant teenage daughter is certainly going to greatly unsettle the old man, but the prospect of his blood line floating out there whereabouts unbeknownst may override his trepidation of the public spectacle."

The Monsignor glared at Bumbry and waited. Bumbry's own defiant stare met Downey's eyes.

"Don't worry yourself, Monsignor Downey. The possibility of termination was not raised."

Downey looked away and slowly counted to forty before returning his gaze to Bumbry.

"Father Bumbry, it may not occur to you, given my long years as a priest and the generational gap that may exist between us, but I am not without understanding in these matters. For instance, it is clear to me that it is not a case of the young lady not wanting the child as much as it is her not wanting to be pregnant."

Bumbry fidgeted a bit as he realized he might have pushed the Monsignor too far. But he was not going to cower either.

"Well, that certainly puts a nice spin on the matter but it doesn't really account for the concept of free will, now does it? I believe that would be a concept that involves choices."

Downey's smile was taut across his face. "Free will is a contemplation *before* the act that would constitute a sin. It is not a solution to be employed *to escape* the consequence of sin. Consequences, or rather our dealing with them, shape our character, Father Bumbry. I would, uh, *pray* that you keep that in mind as well as the tenets of our Church which we have vowed to uphold as sacred and constant."

Bumbry stood up. "I will be driving Miss Carbonni and the father-to-be this evening to sit down with the parents. I will let you know how it goes."

Downey arose from his chair and made his way around the desk to accompany Bumbry to the door. He desired to cut the distance and tension between them. He spoke quietly. "Arnold, I do realize this is not an easy task and I appreciate your efforts here to handle it with sensitivity and dignity. I will be praying it goes well as can be. Good luck."

Father Bumbry glanced at Downey, nodded his head, and walked out. Downey went back to his chair, pulled open the drawer, and took out his cigarettes. It was going to be a long day and a longer night.

BUMBRY KNEW AGNES CARBONNI fairly well. She was a nice girl, not too pretty but pleasant looking enough to have the boys take notice of her. That and the fact that she was a conduit for getting them summer jobs working at her dad's construction company. She was a regular at the barn-house youth meetings and although not a stand-out, she was certainly a steady-eddy for community projects and the like. Bumbry did not know the boy involved here and that gave him cause for concern: the boy had never been to any youth meetings and Agnes had only spoken sparingly of him, usually in response to Bumbry's inquiries as to why she had not been attending recent meetings and social events. The boy was obviously not a member of the parish, or at least not an active member. Bumbry pulled his bright lime green Oldsmobile coupe in front of the diner and then, giving it a second thought, pulled into the parking lot and took the first open space. He cut the engine and looked around. It was 6 p.m. on a Saturday night, in between the early bird patrons and the pre-movie crowds. He had agreed to meet Agnes and her boyfriend for a quick discussion before heading over to her parents' house. He presumed the two had spent the day together gathering up their courage. At least that was what he hoped, and that they were not carrying on in other ways. "Not that it matters now," he said aloud to himself.

After a little time had passed, the headlights of a Ford pickup flashed across the parking lot as it pulled in rather quickly and parked in the row over from where Bumbry sat in his vehicle. He recognized Agnes right away but if the boy had ever stepped inside the confines of St. Mary's, he must have been stealth about it. Bumbry had no recollection of him; perhaps a closer look would reveal a knowable face. Bumbry got out of his car, closed the door rather softly, and took a few steps and waited. There was what he perceived to be an intense dialogue still lingering between the two expecting parents. The boy was quite animated in the expression of his thoughts as his arms gestured emphatically. Agnes appeared to have surrendered to the occasional head nod, though she was not nodding in agreement, a head that seemed to hang in defeat. Finally, the two emerged from the Ford and slowly approached Bumbry.

"Hello, Agnes. How are you feeling?"

"Good evening, Father Arnold. I am doing well, thanks for asking."

The boy said nothing.

"And this must be...." Bumbry paused for someone to take their cue.

"Oh, this is Peter, Father."

"Peter...?"

"McInerny," the boy broke his silence. Something about the boy's tone struck Bumbry as odd. "Peter McInerny. And I am sorry to make your acquaintance under such circumstances. You must think me a real loser," he said more as a statement than an inquiry.

"It is a pleasure to meet you, Peter," Bumbry replied. Bumbry extended his right hand and Peter took hold of it firmly, while at the same time Bumbry thought to himself, *And no I don't think of you as a loser as much as an idiot and clueless wonder who has no idea what he's gotten himself into.* It appeared Peter may have been reading Bumbry's thoughts because he immediately looked away as he took back his hand.

"Can't say I recognize your face," Bumbry continued, "from Sunday mass or any of the youth activities?"

"Oh, I'm not a member of St. Mary's, Father. I'm not even Catholic."

Bumbry shot a glance at Agnes, whose eyes immediately looked down. He caught himself. She didn't need another going over after the exchange in the car, and this he understood.

"I'm a Presbyterian. Or at least that's what my parents said we were," Peter continued with a smile.

"Well, we're all God's children, despite our religious upbringing. Or lack thereof. Shall we go inside for a cup of coffee and to discuss our game plan?"

Once inside and seated at a booth, Bumbry had a better look at Peter in the dining room lights. The boy's face seemed to fit the voice better under closer inspection. It clearly reflected the situation, considering the great deal of stress he imagined the boy had likely been dealing with this past week. Yet, he appeared older to the priest than seventeen. Bumbry ordered a coffee, black, as did Peter. Agnes requested a glass of water with lemon. Bumbry did not know too many teenage boys who drank black coffee. It suddenly dawned on him that the conversations he had had with Agnes centered on her pregnancy, her family's reaction, and what she wanted to do. Bumbry really knew very little about the boy sitting across from him. Up to this point, Peter was more a bit player in the unfolding drama, whose role had only been referenced while he was off stage. Although he was a main catalyst in the drama, he had not been its focal point. Until now.

"So, Peter," began the priest after the waitress delivered their order and departed, "what school do you attend?" Peter shook two sugar packets in his hand and after tearing off the tips of them, poured their white crystal contents into the black pool of his cup while stirring with a teaspoon.

"I'm outta school, Father Arnold."

Bumbry watched as Peter raised his cup of coffee to his lips and drank from it without blowing on it to cool it off, all the while staring right back at him. Agnes interrupted their staring contest.

"Peter works at an auto repair shop, Father. He's an auto mechanic. He fixes cars. He's very good at it."

Peter seemed to sneer at Agnes's adulation. A knot started to form in Bumbry's gut as an uneasiness took hold of him and the table in the booth seemed to crowd him. He could feel the perspiration form on his temples.

"How long," Bumbry seemed to be forcing the words through his lips and teeth one by one, "have you been an auto mechanic?"

"A few years...yeah, a few years," Peter answered and took another sip of his coffee, without taking his eyes off the man in the collar. Bumbry watched as Peter looked away from him and to the coffee cup Peter was holding. Peter's eyes followed the cup as he placed it down on the table and kept his gaze fixed on it for a moment. He then looked up directly at Bumbry.

"Any more questions, *Padre?*"

"Peter, you said you wouldn't be like this. Father Arnold is here to help us." Agnes spoke with a shrill voice that instantly annoyed Bumbry.

"I didn't ask for his help," retorted Peter.

Bumbry interjected. "But Agnes did. And from what I am gathering now, she certainly needs it and I suspect you will need some help as well. Probably help I am not qualified to give you."

"But Father Arnold you said you could be there for us. You promised to help us get through this. Why has that changed?"

Bumbry sat back and collected himself. The facts of the matter were beginning to come clear to him but obviously Agnes was not seeing them with any clarity at all. Her innocence that may have been quite endearing at one point in time was now startlingly irksome.

"Agnes, I did say I was going to help and I intend to keep my promise. But....it...uh." Bumbry struggled as his mind raced ahead of his thoughts and words.

"Father Arnold, what is it?"

Bumbry finally blurted out, "Agnes, how well do you know Peter here?"

"Father, we've been through this. I love Peter. He makes me feel special. He treats me very well. He pays attention to me and listens to me and makes me feel wanted. He doesn't treat me like a child like everyone else does."

The knot in Bumbry's gut had grown to the size of an entangled cobra. *Options*, he thought. *There are options here.* He shot a glance at Peter.

"How old?"

Agnes looked at Bumbry, then at Peter, and then back at Bumbry. Peter did not look at her but met Bumbry's eyes with a glare.

"What?" she asked.

Bumbry ignored her. "How old are you? Really."

"Father Arnold, what is going on? Why are you taking that tone with Peter?" Agnes asked imploringly.

Peter lowered his eyes, which Bumbry immediately claimed as victory. The tough shell was only a veneer and not mahogany. Bumbry pressed his advantage now by staring down at Peter and waiting for a response. He began to tap his index finger against the coffee cup without taking his eyes off Peter. Waiting. Waiting. Waiting. Peter looked up.

"Twenty-eight."

Immediately Agnes's two hands joined at her mouth as she gasped and her eyes widened. Tears began to well. The cobra in Bumbry's gut had lurched into his throat. He pressed back against the booth cushion.

"Twenty-eight," he managed to utter softly when the cobra finally recoiled. The utterance was more in disbelief than affirmation. Peter was closer in age to him than he was to Agnes. Peter reached for a napkin from the stack the waitress had left and handed it to Agnes. Bumbry shook himself from his momentary shock and turned his head to Agnes, to make sure she had taken a breath. Her hands now covered her face and Bumbry could see the tears seeping through her fingers as she wept silently, sitting straight up, her body shaking as she fought to hold in the sobs. Bumbry took off his eyeglasses with his right hand and raised his left hand to his own face and rubbed his eyes, bringing his thumb and index finger into the corners of them, then opened his hand and rubbed down his face, over his beard, and let his thumb and index finger meet at the tip of his chin.

"We have a lot to discuss and not much time," he said quietly.

THE THREE OF THEM climbed into Bumbry's Oldsmobile, Agnes in front and Peter sitting in the back seat. They were already thirty minutes late. Actually, only Bumbry was late. He had managed to get himself invited to dinner at the Carbonnis' for this Saturday evening. He thought the best approach was to not give any hint as to the conversation that was about to occur as he did not want to alarm the family or give the old man any time to react in a rash and irrational manner. He had wanted it to be just Agnes and himself but the girl had insisted on her boyfriend being there. Bumbry was against this but relented against his better judgment. Now that it had been determined that the boyfriend was a twenty-eight-year-old man, there was a horrific new spin on the whole ordeal—yes, the fact that Peter was older than both her brothers put a twisted perspective on the matter indeed. Not to mention the legal implications due to Agnes's age. This was a far more complicated matter than Bumbry had anticipated and he knew he was ill-prepared for what the evening had in store for them all.

LIFTING HIMSELF UP FROM the heavy wooden chair with the bright red velvet cushioned seat and back, Monsignor Downey stepped down to the altar. He bent and kissed the center of the cloth-covered marble table and then turned to face the two altar boys who approached him from the right of the altar. His body was going through the motions and his lips and tongue mouthed the words, but his thoughts were elsewhere. They were in an anxious and fearful state of affairs. The altar boys had reached him and stood in silence awaiting his next motion—one boy holding the porcelain bowl with a towel draped upon his arm and another holding a small glass pitcher of water. He looked right through them for a moment and then shook off his distraction and placed his hands over the bowl. The altar boy with the pitcher poured some water over the lingering hands as the Monsignor quietly spoke. "Lord, wash away my iniquity and cleanse me of my sins." He took the towel, dried his hands, and returned it to the boy's arm. The two boys slightly bowed their heads and returned to their chairs on the side of the altar. Downey turned to face the gathering of Saturday night church goers. He thought to himself, *Why are they here, on a Saturday evening? To revel in the company of their Creator? To seek comfort and peace in the presence of the Almighty? To get closer to their Lord and Savior? Not really. They are here so they won't have to be here on Sunday. They are here to fulfill their obligation. Fulfill their obligation? Yes, that's what a loving and pure and holy and righteous and perfect and all-powerful God wanted: people who were putting in their time allotment with him because it was an obligation.* He stared at his flock with a blank expression and they stared back at him with the same look. *Yes, considering the statue behind me of a figure on a cross, it's the least they could do.* He stole a glance at his watch, feeling the heavy perspiration on his forehead. *How is it going with Father Bumbry?* He looked up at his captive audience, some looking curious about the delay in the action. *It certainly is the least they could do, fulfill their obligation*, he sighed to himself. He took hold of the gold chalice in front of him and continued his part in the obligatory dance.

FATHER BUMBRY DROVE THROUGH the neighborhoods, down the narrow streets, and past the familiar landmarks of the small town of Rosedale. No one spoke as he made his way to Agnes's parents' house. He knew the way as he been invited to dinner with the family a few times which he gladly accepted. Every so often, Bumbry would steal a glance at Peter sitting there in the back seat. At first Bumbry couldn't make out the meaning of the expressions that swept across Peter's face. Was he nervous? Afraid? Angry? Trapped? Did Peter have the stamina to sustain the evening's fireworks? Peter noticed the set of eyes upon him and Bumbry looked away, focusing once again on the road ahead.

"Father Bumbry?" Peter's voice was quivering with anxiety. Bumbry glanced back at Peter in the rearview mirror and he could see that the color of Peter's complexion matched the severe tone of his voice.

"Yes, Peter, what is it?" Bumbry seemingly snapped at him.

"There's something else I need to tell you. Tell you and Agnes." Peter's voice had dropped to a whimpering whisper.

"What is it? What do you have to tell us?" Bumbry's voice projected alarm. Agnes quickly turned to look at Bumbry, obviously shaken by the priest's tone, then turned around in her seat to face Peter. For a moment, all three had stopped breathing in heightened anticipation of what Peter had to share.

"I'm married, Father Bumbry."

Bumbry managed to avoid hitting a parked car as all the energy drained from him and he veered sharply to the left before screeching to a halt.

BUMBRY PULLED UP IN front of the rectory. He turned off the car, shut his eyes, let out a heavy sigh, and dropped his head onto his hands, which gripped the top of the steering wheel. It was after midnight. His Roman collar was off and on the seat beside him. His shirt was soaked with perspiration and his heart was still racing. He was physically exhausted and the weariness of his mind was on par with his body. His head was pounding, as the echoes of the shouts and screams and sobs and shrieks of the past several hours ricocheted within the walls of his skull like the little silver balls in a pinball machine. The old man was beyond angry, beyond livid, beyond the realm of rational thought or reasonable indignation. It was a rage that Bumbry had read and heard about but never actually witnessed. The veins in the old man's neck swelled with a purplish pigment that created crazy patterns of blotches and color across his skin. He had to be restrained by his two sons, who were doing everything they could to contain their own rage. Agnes could not stop weeping and her mother at first had struck her a few times before grabbing hold of her and hugging her in a locked embrace, her body shaking with her own sobs. Bumbry had stood in silence next to Peter, torn between hatred and pity for this foolish stranger.

Bumbry opened his eyes and pushed himself back from the steering wheel. He opened the door and slowly slipped out of the car. He stood for a moment in the street and looked about the neighborhood. All was still and no lights shone except for the crescent moon that hung motionless in the sky. Bumbry slowly made his way to the entrance beneath his apartment. From a window in the darkness of the rectory, Monsignor Downey watched in resigned silence.

The door to Bumbry's room flung open and Bumbry quickly stepped in, closing the door behind him. He rested his head on the door for a moment before turning around, walking into his bedroom, and falling face down onto his bed. Lying outstretched, he clasped his hands above his head, and began to speak in a hushed tone.

"Oh God, please... please...please God...take this baby! Make her miscarry! Let her not have to deal with this...her family either. Please God...let the baby die now! Let there be a miscarriage! Make this go away! They don't deserve this. You can fix this. Please, God, show some compassion and mercy and let her have a miscarriage. It's the right thing to do. Oh God, please do this...for Agnes, for her family, for me."

Bumbry stopped speaking. He listened as his heart began to slow down and his breathing began to stabilize. He lifted his head and studied the crucifix on the wall; he marveled at how after all the years the man hanging from it never changed his expression, his posture, or his position. He just hung there suspended in time.

The Master. The Master of Plaster, thought Bumbry. *Why was it necessary to make things so difficult? There were many women, married women, who wanted a baby but couldn't have one. Why didn't He permit one of them to get pregnant instead of this little seventeen-year-old girl? If He was in control, why didn't He make more sense of the events that occurred? What's the point of being an all-powerful God if you don't do anything right with the power?*

He made his way over to his desk and opened the bottom drawer and pulled out a bottle of Seagram's whiskey. He reached for some ice cubes from his mini-refrigerator and a glass from his desk. He poured himself a drink and paused to consider its amber color. He raised the glass to his lips, the sweet odor filling his nostrils, and then drank from the glass. "Why didn't He just come down off that cross for once and do something about all the problems in this fucked-up world He created?" he asked no one in particular. He poured some more whiskey into the glass and then stood still to listen. *Was that...?* Yes, the private buzzer sounded. Bumbry downed his drink and headed toward the door. Another young person in trouble.

XX.

THE ROSE

The field of grass and flowers spread out before him like a plush tapestry of blue and green and yellow and red hues blended and strewn into a calm sea of color with no beginning or end. Dominic's feet barely touched the top of the blades of grass. He seemed to sail effortlessly above the tranquil sea beneath him, drawn to an object in the distance, shrouded in billowy fog and a shadowy mist (though the sun shone brilliantly in a cloudless sky that was bluer than lapis). His heart was racing, yet he did not know why. Did it have to do with what hid behind the fog and mist? He thrust himself forward and churned his legs as strenuously and ferociously as possible to propel himself faster but his body only drifted, indifferent to his desire or will. As he drew closer, the fog and mist lifted and, in the clearing, he could see it: a tree—a most majestic one— taller and wider than any other with countless sculpted limbs and branches, sinewy and full, carved with detail worthy of Michelangelo; with leaves of varied tints and tones that could inspire the gardener of Giverny. Dominic's body floated toward the tree, and as it descended, he began to discard his clothes. He arrived in front of the tree, standing totally naked, in awe of its beauty and mystery. He felt surges of warmth shoot through his being and in an instant a cooling breeze swept over him and his skin tingled with a soothing sensation. The breeze trickled through the leaves of the tree and he heard the sounds like the gentle plucking of strings and the sensuous whisperings of woodwinds. The smell *of orchids and wisteria and alyssum and gardenias and jasmine carried on the breeze and filled his nostrils with an intoxicating fragrance. He was suspended in light and air, time and space. He had not a care or concern in the world, not even a hint of a worrisome thought. Laughter pierced the serenity surrounding him like an arrow through a shadow. It was a girl's laughter and he turned his head in its direction. There she stood, his love! She with the flowing auburn hair and sparkling eyes imbued with the color of sapphire. Her countenance was glowing and she reached out her hand, beckoning Dominic to her. Dominic extended his hand to her and his body followed suit. But he hesitated and glanced back toward the tree as its limbs and branches began to stir and shake—Dominic became unsure. He felt a tug on his arm—he turned to face his love and she fixed her sapphire eyes upon him. While reaching both arms to him, her eyes drew him to her with an irresistible allure. He drifted into her arms and she embraced him to her to breasts. Her skin was the scent of the fragrances carried on the breeze; her breasts were warm, tender, and lush. Her hands cupped his face and she brought her lips to his, and slipped her tongue playfully into his mouth and she tasted of wild honey and sweet berries. Her tongue plunged deeper in his mouth and a heavy warm breath exuded from her nose, her arousal surging as she unlocked the excitement of his desire for her. She swirled her tongue in his mouth and she took hold of him, as his hands found their way to her breasts. The sky around them grew dark, then darker, until it was suddenly night and the clear sky was littered with thousands of flickering lights. She pulled away from him and he turned his head to glance at the tree. The leaves of the tree glistened in the starlight for a brief moment and then transformed into a black silhouette against the shimmering lights in the sky. When he turned back to her, she was gone. He sat in the field of grass alone and naked. In the spot where she lay, he could see a quivering light—a reflection of the night sky. Dominic reached down, sliding his hand through the grassy spot. His fingers found it and grasped it. It was a rose—a perfectly precious rose—its delicate petals without any blemish or bruise. He turned to face the tree and his body suddenly flung back and started to fly away from the tree. He fought hard to run back toward the tree but it grew further and further from view. He pushed and struggled with all his might, all his strength, but he kept moving further and further away from the tree until it was totally out of sight. The rose became increasingly heavy in his one hand and he grasped it tight with both hands. But the petals were coming loose and he strained to hold on to the withering flower. He sailed through the air faster and faster and the weight of the rose grew heavier still. He could not hold on to it any longer and as he passed over a body of water, what remained of the rose slipped from his hands into the depths below. Dominic was spinning and tumbling, losing all his sense of bearing. He slowly, steadily drifted to the ground until he landed in a field of chrysanthemum and fell into a deep sleep.*

When Dominic awoke, he was stretched out on the great lawn on the Mansion Hill of the Featherstone Estate. He had come out alone to watch the sunrise over the Hudson River. The quiet stillness of Esopus surrounded him as the sun began its ascent. He got up on his feet and made his way back to the main path. He licked his lips—he could still taste her mouth. A sense of sadness overcame him as he remembered the rose.

XXI.

ON BROADWAY

Tim and Ernie stood on the corner, waiting.

"At least it's not raining," Tim offered.

"I'm not waiting for him once it starts getting cold," countered Ernie.

"Hold on, here he comes now."

Dominic was jogging around the corner and up the street to the corner where his two classmates waited. He slowed to a quick walk when he got within a hundred feet of them to catch his breath.

"Sorry, fellas, won't happen again."

Ernie punched Dominic in the arm. "That's what you said yesterday!"

"Ow! Dude, someone's been overdosing on Wheaties."

"Dominic, you got to get here on time. We won't be waiting in the rain." Tim shook his head as to reinforce his seriousness.

"And screw you come the winter," added Ernie. "Which means you will miss out if my mom decides to drive us if the weather is too bad."

"Alright, alright, just keep in mind that I'm the first one eligible to get his driver's license," Dominic laughed.

"Talk to me when you have wheels and a license," Ernie shot back.

The three friends commenced their one-and-a-half-mile walk to ASM.

The teaching order of brothers, the so-called Apostles, was founded by a French cleric, who, inspired by the sister of Lazarus and Martha, felt compelled to educate young boys to prefer the "good part" as Mary had, in following Jesus's examples and teachings. All of Dominic's older brothers had attended ASM, and he was the fifth Manterra to be a student at the school. His younger brother Jason would be the next and last.

The three talked about school and sports. The transition to the high school from the grammar school was rather seamless and uneventful. The biggest adjustment in addition to the walking distance to school was the absence of girls in the classroom, including the teachers. They went from having no male teachers to having almost all male teachers, albeit some of them still wore dresses.

"They're not dresses, Ernie," snapped Dominic, "they're cassocks."

"Oh, I didn't realize they were part of the Russian Orthodox Church," he barked back.

"I thought they were habits," interjected Tim.

"Let's hope they don't drop 'em like a bad one, if you know what I mean," laughed Ernie.

"Yeah, well did you ever get Terry Cartwright to drop anything for you?" sneered Dominic, "I still remember that night when we were coming back from one of the school dances and we were all debating the ranking of the girls in class. Do you remember that one, Timmy?

"Indeed, I do, but your memory does it so much more justice," he replied.

"Let's see if I can recall the passion of the moment with the right precision…oh yes…it's coming back to me…I believe Ernie shouted loud enough to wake up the neighborhood—'how about Terry Cartwright—she's got the biggest tits of them all!' I believe is how Ernie expressed the sentiment."

"You guys suck, you know that?" a red-faced Ernie muttered.

Timmy and Dominic high-fived. "What do you make of this Brother Corwin clown?" inquired Ernie. Timmy shrugged his shoulders.

Dominic offered his opinion. "Kind of over the top. It's like he's on stage giving a performance."

"Yeah, kind of like that," agreed Timmy.

"He should be performing alright. He's a little flamboyant, if you ask me," replied Ernie.

"You can say that about any of these clergy," countered Dominic, "but they're an easy target with their commitment to celibacy."

"But that's the whole point—why would anyone make that kind of commitment unless there was something, uh, not right with them?" argued Ernie.

"Maybe they're answering to a higher calling," replied Dominic, who wasn't necessarily convinced himself. From what he observed, they also liked not having any bills or responsibilities in the real world. Everything was handed to them.

"That's a bunch of horseshit." Ernie wasn't buying any of it. "These so-called *Brothers* and not just Corwin have a few screws loose. They are definitely not cut from the same cloth as my dad, that's for sure!"

"Nor my dad," laughed Dominic.

Timmy spoke up, "Everyone's dad, for that matter. Let's just hope they don't kill us with the homework and term papers, like Ms. Boutaine used to warn us about. It was bad enough that we had that summer book reading list come in the mail in June."

"That wasn't so bad." Dominic smiled.

"Yeah, coming from the guy who had read those books already, jackass." Timmy shook his head.

"We better take it up a notch or we'll be late." Ernie looked at his watch. "Make that a really big jackass for keeping us waiting. Not happening again." And with that the three friends picked up their pace.

"You want to split a caramel chew bar quick before the next class?" Marco asked hurriedly.

Dominic thought about it. "Sure, we have another hour before lunch.

I'm starving. And Coach Grogan will have us running wind sprints on the field until we drop at soccer practice."

Dominic looked up and saw Mr. Copper heading down the corridor, his head tilted to the right, his arms swinging in syncopation with some unheard melody as he dragged his feet along the linoleum floor.

"Don't be late for class, boys," he advised as he sauntered by them.

"Hey, Mr. Copper, did you mark those exams yet?" asked Marco as he waited for the candy bar to drop.

"Not yet, Mr. Leonardo. How do you think you boys did?"

"Piece of cake," answered Dominic with a confident tone.

"Some people choke on cake, Mr. Manterra, so I wouldn't be licking the icing off the spoon just yet," Mr. Copper responded in the same monotone voice as he continued swinging his way down the hall.

"I'm sure a spoon isn't what he has in mind," muttered Denny as he joined his two friends. Marco laughed and Dominic just shook his head and they headed to their next class.

The classroom of students quietly chatted as Brother Corwin wrapped up a conversation with Mr. Gavin, one of the lay teachers and the moderator and director of the Drama Club. The two men finished talking, and Mr. Gavin exited stage left. Brother Corwin wrapped his knuckles loudly on the desk and all the students stopped their chatter and turned their heads.

"The Ironman knuckle strikes again! Now that I have your attention, I hope it's not an inconvenience to commence with today's lesson." He let go a deep-bellied laugh that was part mad man, part goofy clown—and totally obnoxious. Annoying. A number of the students just rolled their eyes. Some looked at him with disbelief. Most just ignored him.

"What the hell is up with this whack-a-doo?" whispered Denny to Dominic.

"The circus wasn't hiring?" whispered Marco. Dominic struggled to hold back his laughter.

"As I am sure you gentlemen will remember, you had an assignment for me last week. And that assignment was to compose an essay based on the title *What Is Man?*" He paused to take in the various expressions of his audience. Undaunted by their indifference, Brother Corwin proceeded with his the–show-must-go-on theatrics.

"And I was prepared to dazzle you with references and rhetoric and erudite citations but then going through the various essays, it appears one of your stalwart colleagues has stolen my thunder!" Brother Corwin then fixed his gaze on Dominic. Dominic met his gaze and then looked down at his desk.

"Oh, no!" hissed Denny.

"Mr. Manterra, were you a mouse secreted away in my chambers who absconded with my daily lesson planner?"

"Probably wished he had stored them in his pants if that were the case," muttered Denny. Dominic slightly turned his head to Denny and muttered out of the side of his mouth, "Will you quit it!"

"I'm sure he likes little furry things in secret places," sneered Marco.

"Well, Mr. Manterra? We're waiting." Brother Corwin stood with one hand on his lecture podium and the other hand on his hip, like a stage performer waiting for his antagonist to remember his cue and line.

"*We?* I could give a crap, just so you know, *Mr. Manterra*," snarled Ernie from another row.

Finally, Dominic raised his head and responded to Brother Corwin. "I'm pretty sure I was never in anyone's chambers, Brother Corwin. Not to say I haven't looked for a chambermaid now and then, but the search goes on."

"That's because you're always late," called out Ernie and the class-mates cracked up. Brother Corwin moved quickly to regain control. He tapped his "Ironman knuckle" loudly on the podium and the class qui-eted down again.

"Thank you, gentlemen. I will remind you that our time is short as it is and I would appreciate keeping interruptions and distractions to a minimum."

"My God, someone doesn't want the spotlight diverted," Denny said with annoyance. Brother Corwin shot Denny a perturbed look and Denny sat straight up in his desk while at the same time furtively giving Brother Corwin the middle finger under it.

"Mr. Manterra opened his essay with the very quote from Shakespeare's *Hamlet* that I was planning on opening this lecture series with, although I was planning on using the version from the musical *Hair*. Have you seen that musical?" he directed the question to Dominic. Dominic shook his head no.

"Have any of you seen that musical?"

The crickets were especially loud. Evidently ten years after its debut, the musical had lost most of its follicles as well as a generation to Led Zeppelin, Black Sabbath and Kiss not to mention the Ramones and the Clash. Unfortunately, the class was not going to be spared. Brother Corwin placed a record on a turntable and cranked out some tunes from this musical that no one could relate to—those that were actually paying any attention.

Mercifully, Brother Corwin's session ended when the bell rang for next class. As the boys gathered up their books, Brother Corwin addressed Dominic.

"Mr. Manterra, if I could see you a moment before you leave.

"Oh, fun for you," Denny commented.

"Maybe he wants to discuss a mouse trap with you," snickered Ernie as he passed.

Dominic packed his notepad into his bookbag and walked up to Brother Corwin's desk. Brother Corwin was busy writing something.

"You wanted to see me, Brother Corwin?" Dominic interrupted, mindful of getting to his next class.

"Ah, yes, Dominic. I was very impressed with your essay. It was the best essay I have ever read from a student in my teaching experience. I would like to discuss it in more detail with you as well as get to know more about you and your background. When do you think we can get together, preferably after the school day?"

Dominic felt good about the comment on his essay as he had put a lot of thought into writing it. "To be honest with you, Brother Corwin, I have a fairly full schedule with soccer practice and homework after school."

"Maybe we can grab a burger after practice one night?" Brother Corwin persisted.

Dominic paused. He didn't want to be late for his next class, as Mr. Bonner was not only the teacher for American Lit, he was also the Vice Principle for Student Discipline.

"I will check my schedule and let you know," Dominic replied. "If that's all, Brother, I need to get to Mr. Bonner's class before the bell rings."

"Of course, you don't want to be late for Boner's class." Brother Corwin let go one of his mad man guffaws as Dominic hurried on by him, shaking his head, asking himself, *Did he really just say that?*

DOMINIC REMOVED HIS SWEATY gym clothes from his locker and placed them in his gym bag along with his lock. Timmy, a few lockers over from him, put on his jacket and asked him if he was ready to go.

"Sorry, I forgot to mention that I am meeting up with Brother Corwin."

"Corwin? What for?" Timmy was surprised.

"He wants to discuss my essay." Dominic shrugged his shoulders.

"OK. Will see you in the morning at the corner. Don't be late. I don't want to listen to Ernie complaining," Timmy laughed.

Dominic nodded. "See you then."

Dominic watched Timmy leave through the locker room side exit. Dominic grabbed his gym bag and headed to Brother Corwin's classroom. Walking across the empty gymnasium, he made it to the doors before the janitorial crew had locked up. He turned down the corridor past the administrative offices, past the nurse's station, both on the right, and past the cafeteria on the left. At the end of corridor, he turned right and went past the darkened classrooms. Brother Corwin's was the last one on the right and it still had its light on. He proceeded to the open door and gave it a light knock to announce his presence to Brother Corwin, who was sitting in one of the student's desks with his shoes off and his feet up on another desk, reading through some papers.

"Brother Corwin?"

Brother Corwin looked up and his face broke out into a big smile. "Dominic! How are you, little brother?"

"I'm good." Dominic felt somewhat awkward.

"Good, good. You must be hungry, no? I will just pack up really quickly here and we'll go to a diner, if that's OK with you?" He put his feet down into his shoes and wiggled them on while he gathered up the papers on the desk in front of him. Dominic simply nodded his head and waited. Brother Corwin made small talk while getting his things together and as they walked across the parking lot over to the Brothers' residence Dominic listened quietly, not saying much. They arrived at the back entrance of the residence and they went inside so Brother Corwin could grab the car keys and sign out one of the community vehicles. It was the first time Dominic had been in the brick residence and it reminded him of the convent that the nuns lived in at St. Mary's grammar school. Dominic stood in the main hall waiting for Brother Corwin when two teachers came down the stairs talking—Mr. Bonner and Brother Colenza.

"Ah, Mr. Manterra, what brings you to the residence? Brother Colenza, do you know Dominic?" An Irishman with a rather large girth, Mr. Bonner had red hair both on his head and his face. Brother Colenza was a short Italian man known for his short temper that matched his height. His reputation was that of a borderline dictator in his interactions with the boys in the classroom, and he did not suffer fools. The sign over his classroom door was a line from Dante's *Inferno*: "Abandon all hope ye who enter here." Dominic did not like him much, as he conjured up "Napoleon Complex," standing outside his classroom in between classes, eyeballing students while twirling his roped crucifix that hung off his waist like a lasso. Dominic imagined a demon trying to capture souls who got too close to the inferno's abyss in order to drag them down into hell.

"Manterra? You're not one of the Manterra brothers, are you?" Brother Colenza gave Dominic a side-ways glance and then a once over. He smiled a crooked grin. "By the looks of you, yes you are. Sal and Mitchell's brother?"

Dominic just nodded his head yes.

"Yes, he is," Mr. Bonner interjected, "except he's a lot smarter than those two. What brings you here, Dominic?" Mr. Bonner appeared curious.

"He's going to grab a burger with me," Brother Corwin answered as he returned from obtaining the car keys. Dominic detected a defensive tone, almost hostile, in Brother Corwin's response.

"A burger, how nice!" Brother Colenza countered, "maybe even some melted cheese on top between the buns. Fries and a Coke!"

"I don't know about you, Brother Colenza, but I'm getting images of a Norman Rockwell picture," added Mr. Bonner. Brother Corwin released one of his goofy guffaws and then motioned to Dominic. "Let's go, Dominic, don't want to keep you out late on a school night."

"Yes, mustn't do that, Brother Corwin, you don't want to set a bad example. And I'm sure Mr. Manterra has some schoolwork to get done before turning in for the evening." Mr. Bonner winked but Dominic wasn't sure at who.

"Nice to make your acquaintance, Dominic. Say hi to your brother Sal for me, won't you." Brother Colenza's eyes widened as he stared at Dominic. Dominic just nodded and followed Brother Corwin out.

They walked to the brown Ford Fairmount and Dominic waited as Brother Corwin got in on the driver's side and then leaned over to unlock the passenger side for him. He opened the door and got in the car. Brother Corwin drove them over to the Rosedale Diner, which wasn't too far from ASM. As he drove, Brother Corwin talked.

"Apparently Mr. Bonner and Brother Colenza know your siblings who attended ASM before you. Quite a few of you."

Dominic just nodded his head.

"I only know one of them—probably your oldest brother. I believe I was a few years ahead of him."

Dominic's eyes widened. "You attended ASM?"

Brother Corwin smiled and let out a modified version of his guffaw, "Yes, I did. Class of '66. You seem surprised."

Dominic was but he didn't know why. "Did you have any of my other brothers in your classes?" he asked.

"No, this is my first year back at ASM, as a teacher. It's is sort of a homecoming for me."

"You lived in Rosedale?"

"Nope. I was from Elizabethtown. Lived in the Maggie Boulevard section. Familiar with that neighborhood?"

Dominic shook his head no.

"Maggie Boulevard is where all the broken families lived. Alcoholics, druggies, single-parent homes. It was the low-life section of town."

Dominic was a little unnerved. He didn't know why Brother Corwin was telling him this. He just continued to look straight ahead.

"Your older brother—Jack, right?—he was a basketball player, if I remember correctly?"

Dominic smiled and a tinge of pride surged through his body. His brother Jack was his hero—he was everybody's hero. Out of the corner of his eye, Brother Corwin noted this reaction as he pulled the car into the dining room parking lot.

"He was supposed to be a pretty good point guard. Did he ever keep up with that?"

Dominic responded, "He's a teacher." For some reason, Dominic didn't think that Brother Corwin really cared about sports. They went into the diner and were seated at a booth.

"See anything you like?" inquired Brother Corwin. Dominic closed the menu and put it down on the table. "Yes, I'm ready." Brother Corwin made a mischievous grin while looking down at the menu and then abruptly closed it and stated, "Me, too."

The waitress came over with two glasses of water and placed them down on the table. She whipped out her pad and pen. "Hi, what can I get you guys?"

Brother Corwin motioned to Dominic to order.

Dominic looked up at the waitress, checking to see if she had on a name tag. She didn't.

"What's your name?" he asked innocently. The waitress looked up from her pad and assessed the inquirer. She smiled. "My name is Missy. What's yours?"

"Hi Missy, I'm Dominic. I would like a cheeseburger and an iced tea, unsweetened, please."

"You want the deluxe? Comes with fries and tomato and lettuce. Otherwise, you just get a pickle and coleslaw."

"That's fine, I don't need the deluxe. Thanks."

Brother Corwin's observation of the exchange was interrupted by the waitress. "And you?"

"Oh, I will have the cheeseburger deluxe. And a cup of coffee."

The waitress picked up the menus. "Cream and sugar?"

"Black."

"Be right back with the iced tea and coffee."

"So, Dominic, we finally have a chance to talk." The waitress dropped off the drinks as Brother Corwin leaned back to give her room.

"What did you want to talk about, Brother Corwin?" asked Dominic as he stuck a straw into his iced tea and took a sip from it.

"Well, for one, that essay you wrote. I don't believe I have had such a young student with that kind of insight or literary references who could present them so soundly in an essay. You must be very well read to be quoting the Bard. And Albert Camus for that matter."

Dominic sat back and looked at Brother Corwin, unsure of what this clergyman wanted from him. Brother Corwin stared back, waiting for a response. Dominic shrugged his shoulders. "I like to read."

"That's commendable, but Shakespeare and Camus are not exactly light and fluffy."

Dominic considered the comment. Timmy always said that Dominic was interested in Shakespeare because he liked the sound of the language when it was read aloud, and that was true. Dominic recalled the time, in Mrs. Dotson's class in fifth grade, when he recited the funeral oration from *Julius Caesar*. It was the first Shakespeare play that Dominic had read, and he fell in love with Shakespeare from that moment. The love affair was solidified when Dominic watched Zeffirelli's *Romeo and Juliet*. The scenes where Romeo discovers Juliet, and the balcony kiss they shared, filled Dominic with a sweet longing that haunted him whenever he saw Moira Toomey. It was his first fix of romantic heroin.

"I wouldn't fill my stomach with garbage. Don't want to fill my head with it."

Brother Corwin lifted his cup of coffee to his mouth while keeping his eyes fixed on Dominic, who stared blankly back at him. He placed the coffee down and let go an *"ahh."* The waft of coffee smell reached Dominic and he recognized the odor from Brother Corwin's classroom. It wasn't pleasant and Dominic's face screwed up in reacting to it. Brother Corwin grinned.

"I love my black coffee the way you like your Shakespeare!"

Dominic nodded his head. "Never use cream or sugar?"

"Never! Always black and hot!"

Dominic stole a glance at the clock on the wall behind the counter. He was hoping this would be over soon. The waitress came through the kitchen door carrying two plates and made her way toward their table. He was a little disappointed when she continued past their booth.

"Would you say Shakespeare is your favorite?"

Dominic reflected for a moment before responding, "Yeah, I would say that. As far as plays go. Of those I have read, *Hamlet* is probably my favorite, although I don't believe it's his best play."

The waitress returned with their orders and placed them down. "Cheeseburger deluxe for you...and cheeseburger non-deluxe for Dominic." She smiled at Dominic. "Will there be anything else for now?"

Dominic shook his head and smiled back. "No, thank you," he said while Brother Corwin responded, "Not right now." She smiled again at Dominic and moved on to another table.

"Help yourself to my fries," instructed Brother Corwin. Dominic just nodded as he reached for the ketchup.

"Which play do you think is his best?"

"*King Lear*," answered Dominic matter-of-factly in between chews of his cheeseburger.

"Hmm, interesting choice. Why do you say that?"

Dominic put his cheeseburger down and wiped his mouth with a napkin. He finished chewing and replied, "Because he takes a universal theme—parent and child relationship—and explores it on three levels: the royal class, the middle class, and the working class. And it covers the power of loyalty and friendships and how these concepts work in relationships, including those people who act as models to others—like a father figure when someone really isn't your father." Dominic picked up his fork and started on his coleslaw. Brother Corwin sat up straight and shook his head, thinking, *Who is this Fauntleroy sitting across from me? Young, knowledgeable, mature—yet seemingly innocent and impressionable and naive.*

"Have you ever seen a Broadway play?" asked Brother Corwin.

"No, I haven't," answered Dominic. He had downed the coleslaw and was finishing off the cheeseburger. He kind of regretted not getting the cheeseburger deluxe. He was still hungry. He eyed Brother Corwin's fries.

"Go ahead, help yourself to the fries. I won't eat them all anyway," Brother Corwin pushed the plate toward Dominic.

Dominic grabbed a few and put them on his plate. "Thanks."

For the remainder of the time, Brother Corwin asked questions, mostly about Dominic's literary preferences, with an occasional inquiry on his family background, and Dominic answered them. Eventually, the waitress brought the check. Brother Corwin had another cup of coffee while Dominic ate the rest of the fries. After paying at the cash register near the entrance, they were back in the car.

"I can give you a ride home as it's late," offered Brother Corwin.

"That would be great, if you wouldn't mind." Dominic still had some homework to get done and didn't want to be up too late. Or be late in the morning and keep the fellas waiting.

"No problem, little brother."

Dominic provided directions to his house and Brother Corwin pulled up to the front door and put it in park

"Thanks for taking the time to have a bite with me." Brother Corwin was suddenly low-key in his tone.

"Yup. Well, thanks for the grub, Brother Corwin. You know how to get back to the residence?" Dominic paused as he got out of the car.

"I'm sure I can figure it out. See you tomorrow at school, little brother."

"Alright, good night." Dominic got out and shut the car door. He headed around to the back door of the house, watching as Brother Corwin pulled away and turned right at the corner and drove down Second Avenue. He had a lot to do before he could call it a night. And he was still hungry.

DOMINIC SAT ON THE stone steps of his house and waited. It was an overcast, chilly Saturday morning, and he pulled the zipper on his coat up to his chin. He noted it was close to 9:30, which was the agreed-upon time for being picked up.

A car turned the corner and Dominic recognized the Ford Fairmount and the outline of Brother Corwin's wavy, unkempt haircut. He stood up and walked down the steps as the car made a U-turn and coasted around to pause in front of him standing on the curb. He opened the door and climbed in to the passenger seat.

"Good morning, little brother," greeted Brother Corwin.

"Good morning, Brother Corwin." The smell of coffee breath hit Dominic like a tsunami.

"Ready for our adventure in the big city? There's a donut in the bag for you. The powdered one is jelly and the other is crème. Take the one you prefer. It doesn't matter to me. There's a bottle of O.J. as well."

"Thanks." Dominic reached for the crème donut and the O.J.

Brother Corwin jumped on the New Jersey Turnpike over by the Elizabethtown Refinery and headed north toward New York City. Despite living a thirty-minute train ride from the heart of Midtown, Dominic had not been to Manhattan all that much. Most of his travel had been confined to either his aunt's house in Freehold or to an uncle's brownstone in Jersey City. He had two standard landmarks that he kept an eye out for: the Gold Bell Diner on Highway 9—that's where they turned off and he knew they were close to his aunt's house—and the World Trade Center's Twin Towers. When he saw them, he knew it was only fifteen minutes or so before they'd be back home. Dominic had finished his donut and drink. Brother Corwin was playing a cassette tape of a Broadway musical—the songs were unfamiliar to Dominic. Brother Corwin took note of the puzzled look on Dominic's face as he stared at the cassette player and listened.

"Have you heard that before?" he asked. Dominic shook his head no. Brother Corwin reached into the side panel of the car door and threw the cassette box in Dominic's lap.

"*Sweeney Todd, the Demon Barber of Fleet Street.* Sondheim." Brother Corwin announced it like a prayer.

Dominic started to read the cassette cover.

"Have you heard of Sondheim?" asked Brother Corwin.

Dominic lifted his head and gave it some thought. "Yes, he wrote a song that I have heard. I only remember because Frank Sinatra mentions it in his little intro before he sings the song. I believe it's about bringing in clowns."

Brother Corwin grinned. "'Send in the Clowns'—from *A Little Night*

Music. I would pay to hear Stephen Sondheim sing the ABCs. Just as I would pay to hear Olivier just recite the alphabet. Have you seen any movies with Olivier?"

Dominic thought about it. "No, I haven't but I know he's a famous Shakespearean actor."

"Yes, he's considered the sublime Shakespearean actor but he's so much more than that, as both an actor and a director."

They went through the Lincoln Tunnel and then Brother Corwin drove around until he found a place to park the car.

"I'd thought we'd walk around the city a bit before we headed to the theater. Have you ever been on the Subway before?" he asked.

"No, I haven't. I really haven't been to Manhattan all that much." Dominic was a little embarrassed.

"No problem, little brother. We will correct that for sure. Let's grab a train downtown." With that, Brother Corwin scampered to a nearby Subway entrance and bounced down the steps with Dominic close behind. He obtained some tokens and handed one to Dominic. He explained to Dominic how to determine which direction to go—whether uptown or downtown—depending on what part of the city one was looking to get to, and also the differences between the various subways and how the tracks ran. He walked up to the turnstile and showed Dominic where to insert the token and then passed through first, followed by Dominic. They waited on the subway platform until a train's lights reflected in the distance in the tunnel, and then pulled into the station. The doors opened and they boarded the train, finding some empty seats and sitting down. The Subway experience—from coming down from the street level to actually boarding a Subway train—was totally new to him. Besides the people, the other element that struck Dominic was how dirty everything appeared to be. Brother Corwin turned into a tour guide, providing historical facts about the city as well as commentary on landmarks and interjecting anecdotes about his own life growing up in Elizabethtown. Evidently, Brother Corwin was fairly independent early in life and was going to the city on his own at an early age. He loved plays and the theater and so explored that world as soon as he was able to afford tickets. They took the E Train downtown and got off at the West 4th Street Station near Washington Square Park. They walked up the stairs to the street level.

"I had always imagined that I would end up as a participating member of the theater but alas it didn't happen," sighed Brother Corwin.

"Because you answered to the life of a higher calling?" asked Dominic.

"Huh? What do you mean?" inquired Brother Corwin.

"The higher calling of the vocational life instead." Dominic returned an equally puzzled look.

"The vocational—oh yes! Yes, I, uh, answered that calling," grinned Brother Corwin, letting go one of his signature obnoxious laughs. "Have you thought of the, uh, vocations, for yourself? Have you heard the call of, uh, God, in your life?" Brother Corwin asked.

"I had thought about it in the past but I don't believe it's the right path for me." The earnestness in Dominic's tone amused Brother Corwin. He was struck by Dominic's total lack of malice.

"I have a book recommendation for you," Brother Corwin said, shifting the conversation. "Have you ever heard of Herman Hesse? No? I have one of his books I think you would appreciate. I will give it to you next week."

"What's the name of the book?" Dominic was curious.

"Narcissus and Goldmund."

They crossed the street and entered the park. Brother Corwin provided a brief history of the area including its famous inhabitants, past and present. Dominic listened attentively. Dominic wondered if Brother Corwin was always so overly dramatic. They sat down on the steps near the fountain, facing the arch. Dominic leaned forward, resting his arms on his knees, continuing to take in the surroundings. Brother Corwin leaned back, resting his elbows on the stone steps. City folk filed into the park for their daily walks, to meet friends, to practice their yoga or tai chi, or to sit on a park bench and read a newspaper while drinking their coffee.

"How do you like the city so far?" asked Brother Corwin.

"It's different from Rosedale that's for sure! It's very interesting though." Dominic continued to people watch. This world was a totally foreign universe to him.

"I feel right at home here." Brother Corwin sighed as he studied the expression on Dominic's face, a mixture of curiosity and confusion. "We better start heading back up to Midtown soon so we don't miss the show." They were going to see *Deathtrap*—it was the first time that Dominic was going to a Broadway show, and he was quite excited about it. Although he didn't know much about the play, Brother Corwin assured him it was both fun and entertaining. Brother Corwin was also hoping to stage a production of it himself for a small theater group he belonged to back in Texas, which was where he'd taught before returning to ASM. As they made their way to the theater, Brother Corwin revealed more and more details about his own life. They arrived at the theater, where a crowd of theater goers were trudging through the doors to get to their seats. Brother Corwin handed a ticket to Dominic as they passed through the doors and Dominic presented it to the usher, who directed him to the upper mezzanine section, to the left. Dominic found his seat and Brother Corwin sat down next to him.

"Well, little brother, welcome to Broadway!" Brother Corwin patted Dominic on his shoulder. Dominic looked at him and smiled and said, "Thanks!" The lights dimmed and flickered, and then a minute later, they went out and the stage curtain went up. And so, the play began....

ON THE DRIVE HOME, they discussed the play. Brother Corwin was impressed with Dominic's understanding of the mechanics of the stage craft and the development and structure of the play itself. However, he realized how little he knew or understood of the ways of the world.

"What did you think of the end of the first act, after the two men had caused the death of the professor's wife?" Brother Corwin inquired.

"It was necessary for the play that the student was writing. It really worked to develop the play within a play," answered Dominic.

"And the relationship between the professor and his student, during the second act?"

"I think the professor was jealous of the student. It was obvious they didn't really trust each other. I was wondering if there was insurance money on the wife that the two men would split so they could then have the means to write."

Brother Corwin smiled and thought to himself, *Ah, such innocence! It's terribly endearing, in its own way.*

"Were you born in Elizabethtown?" asked Dominic.

"Yes, I was. Spent most of my childhood and youth there. After I graduated from ASM, I went off to college where I, um, answered the call to my vocation." Again, Brother Corwin smiled broadly.

"Did you live at the ASM Novitiate at Esopus?" asked Dominic.

The question caught Brother Corwin off guard. "What do you know about Esopus?"

"I have been to it. It's a beautiful place. We visited my brother Jack when he was living there," answered Dominic. "We stayed at the mansion. I was with my father and my brother Jason."

"Your brother was in the Novitiate?"

"Yes, but only for a short time. I don't believe the vocations were for him."

"I see," mused Brother Corwin. "It's not the kind of life for everyone, little brother."

"Why do you say that?" Dominic had a quizzical look upon his face.

"Well, because you have to give up certain things in life that other people are free to pursue," Brother Corwin replied with an air of mystery.

"No, I mean why do you say little brother to me?" asked Dominic.

"I think it's because of the little brother that I had. Or should I say, was taken from me." Brother Corwin replied in a serious and introspective tone.

"Taken from you?" Dominic asked.

"In a manner of speaking." Brother Corwin paused for a moment before continuing, as he observed Dominic out of the corner of his eye while exiting the Lincoln Tunnel and proceeding on 1/9 South. "My upbringing was somewhat tragic, you might say."

Dominic looked out the passenger window for a moment while Brother Corwin waited for him to consider the appropriateness of asking more questions.

Dominic turned his head and gazed up at Brother Corwin. "Why, what happened?"

"Well, my mother and father never really got along. My mother always seemed to be angry with my father for some reason or another."

Dominic nodded his head as he listened intently.

"One evening while we were having dinner, the conversation turned acrimonious as it typically did, and my mother was berating my father while he sat quietly eating his dinner, every so often glancing at me with that combination of appeal for sympathy and here-we-go-again-can't-we-ever-just-have-a-nice-quiet-meal look, when suddenly she blurted out, 'I wish you would just drop dead!' and that was a bit much even for my mother. My father gently put down his fork, looked over at me to ascertain whether I had heard those words my mother spoke, and then gazed back at my mother and simply shook his head no, and whispered, 'Please, for the sake of the boy, refrain from saying such vile things that you really don't mean.'" Brother Corwin stopped there, letting out a deep sigh.

"And then?" Dominic asked.

"A couple of days later, my mother got a phone call. My father had a massive heart attack at his job and died."

"Oh my God!" exclaimed Dominic. "That's terrible!"

"Yes, it was most unfortunate," Brother Corwin continued. "Of course, my mother blamed herself because of her declaration at dinner, believing she had caused my father's death, and was eventually overwhelmed by guilt."

"That is very sad," murmured Dominic.

"It was just the three of us then. My mother, myself, and my little brother, who was still but a toddler. Each morning, I would go into his room to greet him and to help him get out of his crib bed. This particular morning, when I entered the room, my little brother wasn't standing, holding on to the side rail as he normally did. He was still lying down, asleep. When I stood over him and tried to wake him, he didn't stir. I kept calling his name and gently nudged him but he didn't respond. I called out his name louder and louder, and nudged him a bit harder, but still, he wouldn't wake up. Finally, I heard my mother's voice behind me. I turned to look at her. I still remember what she said."

Dominic was watching Brother Corwin, who seemed to be in a trance as he stared straight ahead, not at the road in front of him, but straight into the past as if he was standing in his brother's bedroom standing at that crib looking back at his mother. Dominic waited.

"'He can't hear you, now, William. Not here and now, anyway,' is what she said to me. And I shouted, 'What have you done?! What have you done, Mother?' But she didn't say another word."

Dominic was perplexed. "I don't understand. Did something happen to your little brother?"

Brother Corwin broke off from his trance-like state. He glanced over at Dominic and slowly nodded his head. "Yes, something horrible had happened to him. I realized my mother had gone into his room at some point during the night and, in her despondent state of mind, suffocated my little brother while he slept. Now I was truly left alone. No father, no brother, and for all practical purposes, no mother."

Dominic didn't know what to say. This was truly a horrible story, the worst he had ever heard. He felt sad for Brother Corwin.

"I am sorry you had to go through that, Brother Corwin. I truly am. That is so sad," he said after a while.

"Thanks, little brother, I appreciate that." Brother Corwin gave Dominic a smile and ran his hand through the top of Dominic's hair.

"What happened to your mom?"

"She had lost her mind. She was institutionalized, which is where she has spent all her life after that ...incident."

Dominic pondered the story he had just heard as he gazed out his window.

"Do you see her?" he finally asked.

"Every so often, I will pay a visit." Brother Corwin cleared his throat, reached for the empty Styrofoam cup in the holder to see if he could coax another drop of coffee from it, and sought to change the subject so as not overwhelm his target audience.

"Have you ever thought of joining the drama club?" he asked, changing the subject.

"Who, me? No, not really." Dominic continued to focus on the traffic.

"Why not? You like reading plays so much, and Shakespeare is your favorite, it would only make sense that you would try your hand as an actor on the stage."

Dominic shrugged his shoulders. "I just never really thought about it. Although I have recited speeches in front of an audience, it would still make me nervous having all those people stare at me."

"It's a wonderful art form—acting, that is. Think about it—you can pretend to be someone else and the better you are at it, the more the people love you."

"But it's not really *you* they love if you're pretending to be someone else," countered Dominic.

Brother Corwin grinned and let out his obnoxious laugh. He nodded his head, reminded as it were that as innocent as Dominic may be in worldly ways, he was quite a number of steps ahead in the spiritual realm than most.

They eventually pulled up in front of Dominic's house.

"Thank you very much, Brother Corwin, for taking me to see the play. It was really cool." Dominic was sincerely appreciative.

"Oh, you're very welcome. My pleasure, little brother. Will see you next week at school."

"For sure, thanks again." Dominic opened the passenger door and stepped out of the car. As he turned to close the door, Brother Corwin leaned over.

"Hey, give it some thought about joining the drama club. Auditions are in a couple of weeks for the spring show. I think you'd really be good on the stage and would have a lot of fun as well."

Dominic nodded his head. "I'll give it some thought, good night," he said and he closed the door.

Brother Corwin watched as Dominic made his way up the walk and then cut over to the side of the house and disappeared. He put the car in drive and pulled away from the car. His thoughts flooded with the memories of his own youth, of that last dinner with his father, of that fateful morning in his little brother's room, of his own first Broadway play with Brother Gerald. Where was Brother Gerald now? Eventually Brother Gerald took the wrong student to a Broadway play, and then he was shipped abroad. *Can't make that mistake*, Brother Corwin thought to himself, *must be patient. All things come to those who wait.* For now, he wanted to get himself a cup of black joe.

XXII.

RUSSIAN ROULETTE

What's are you reading?"

Dominic looked up from the book he was reading to see his brother Jack in the doorway of his bedroom. "Hey, Jack, I didn't know you were stopping by today."

"I was just dropping something off for Dad. What book is that?"

"*Why Am I Afraid to Tell You Who I Am?* Have you've read it?"

"No, never even heard of it. Why are you reading this book?"

"Brother Corwin lent it to me, thought I might enjoy it."

Jack picked his head up. "Billy Corwin?"

Dominic thought for a second. "Yeah, I guess, since his first name is William. Do you know him?"

Jack nodded yes. "So, he's a brother of the ASM Order?"

"Yes, he is. He mentioned you were at ASM when he was there."

"I was a few years behind him. I believe he graduated when I was a sophomore. I barely knew him."

"He knew that you played basketball."

"Yeah, well, he didn't. Hey, I'm meeting David for a late lunch, you want to come?"

"That's OK. I have some schoolwork to get done and then I'm supposed to meet Timmy later to go to the movies."

"What movie are you going to see?"

"*The Deer Hunter.*"

"Isn't that rated R?" asked Jack.

"Yeah, I believe it is." Dominic noted the page he was stopping at in the book.

"How were you planning on getting in, then?" inquired Jack.

"We're going with Brother Corwin."

Jack thought for a moment. "I see. It's supposed to have some pretty intense violence..." Jack's voice trailed off.

"I'm sure I can handle it. It can't be much worse than *The Godfather.*" Dominic raised his head and smiled at Jack. Jack chuckled, remembering that Dominic had read *The Godfather* even though he couldn't actually see the movie in the theater.

"Good point. Let me know what you think of it."

"I will. Tell David I will see him next time."

Jack left and Dominic checked the desk clock for the time. Timmy would be meeting him here at the house in two hours. He figured he had some time before he needed to get ready for the movies.

THE DEER HUNTER HAD been intense. Although the three of them went to a diner afterwards, he and Timmy had done most of the talking, while Brother Corwin seemed distracted. They had dropped Timmy off and now Brother Corwin was driving Dominic back to his house. Brother Corwin was in a very serious mood, uncharacteristically silent as he drove. Dominic broke the silence.

"Did you like the movie, Brother Corwin?"

"Like the movie?" he snapped. "Like the movie? What kind of asinine question is that? Those fools in the theater cheering when DeNiro killed the Viet Cong in the Russian roulette scene! I was shaking in there! I wanted to stand up and scream at them all and their phony, ill-conceived notion of heroics! Bunch of assholes!"

Taken aback, Dominic fell silent and didn't say a word.

"What do they know, anyway? What did they suffer? Where were they when I got the news? Did they try to stop him? I know I did. But it's because of the false bravado that they label manhood and if you act like some Neanderthal warrior that it really means you're a real man—what a load of bullshit!"

Dominic was feeling a little scared now as he had no idea what Brother Corwin was talking about and at the same time, he was feeling somewhat guilty because he also cheered during that scene. Dominic didn't think it was so wrong to want to see the Americans win. Especially since the way they were being tortured was cruel to him. Brother Corwin seemed to break off his trance as he turned to gaze at Dominic.

"Oh, sorry, so sorry, little brother, I didn't mean to go off like that. No worries—it's not, uh, you. It was a very emotional movie for me. Especially that last scene in the warehouse. It brought back memories, bitter memories for me."

"You were in Vietnam?" Dominic asked, surprised.

"Huh, who, me? Ha, ha, no, no, Dominic, I wasn't in Vietnam," Brother Corwin's mirthful disposition returned for a moment.

"But you said it brought back memories?"

"Yes, yes it did," once again Brother Corwin's manner was subdued, "but from the vantage point that I once pleaded with someone not to go to Vietnam. Someone that I lo—someone very close to me. I begged him not to go. But he wouldn't listen. And he died when his helicopter was shot down."

"He was your best friend?"

Brother Corwin glanced at Dominic. "He was more than that."

"Like a brother then?"

"Did you ever go hunting?" Brother Corwin changed the subject.

"No, but I would like to," answered Dominic.

"Really? You don't have a problem killing animals?"

"Well, I wouldn't just kill an animal for sport, if that's what you mean. I wouldn't want to put an animal's head on a wall so I could show off to everyone about it. But I don't have a problem if you go hunting and eat the animal," explained Dominic.

"Oh, so killing them is OK as long as you eat them?" countered Brother Corwin with more than a hint of sarcasm.

"You don't eat pork chops or steak or fried chicken or veal cutlets?" responded Dominic. "I am pretty sure they were all living animals at one point. Does it really make a difference who pulls the trigger or swings the blade? They still end up on the dinner table."

Brother Corwin smiled and thought to himself, *So smart in so many ways, and yet so much like a little lamb being led to the slaughter.*

The car pulled up in front of the house and Brother Corwin put the gear in park.

"Thanks for taking us to the movies," said Dominic, "and sorry about your friend."

"Thanks for saying that, I appreciate it, little brother. Hey, what did you think of the one scene with Christopher Walken?"

"Which scene was that?" asked Dominic.

"The one with the Vietnamese prostitute?"

Dominic sort of shook his head, a little puzzled. He didn't think it was that key of a scene to the rest of the story. It wasn't even that long of a scene. All he remembered was a baby crying and a song he liked playing in the background, *Midnight Train to Georgia.*

"You don't remember the scene, where the whore tells him, 'I make you crazy! I make you crazy!' She told him 'Not like the girls home in USA!' That scene?"

Dominic felt a knot forming in his stomach. "Oh yeah, that one."

"Back when I was teaching in Texas, when the boys turned fourteen, the fathers would take them to the local whorehouse and let their sons get laid, get all the horniness out of their system. It released all that pent-up frustration, not to mention sperm. It basically released the tension and stress. I imagine those whorehouses were similar to the ones in Vietnam. You will probably have a dream about that tonight, maybe?"

Brother Corwin spoke softly. The knot in Dominic's stomach grew tighter. He didn't say anything.

"You know it's OK if you have to masturbate, little brother, you know, jerk off. Sometimes you have to do it just to unload all that sperm build-up and get to sleep. There's nothing wrong with that."

Dominic just nodded his head, opened the car door, and lifted himself out of the car.

"Good night, little brother," Brother Corwin maintained the same tone. "Sweet dreams!"

"Good night, Brother Corwin," responded Dominic, closing the door behind him without turning around. Dominic made his way to the back door. He listened to the car pull away and feared the knot in his stomach might cause him to throw up.

XXIII.

ONE WAY OR ANOTHER

Dominic, wait up for a moment, will you, please?" Father Bumbry motioned toward one of the chairs. Dominic acknowledged the request with a head nod and went over and collapsed in the easy chair. He waited while Father Bumbry finished speaking with one of the other youth ministry members. Dominic glanced at the wall clock. It was already getting late and he hoped Father Bumbry wasn't going to be much longer. His thoughts were interrupted by the priest.

"Don't worry, I can give you a ride home if you want," Father Bumbry said, "but this will only take a minute." He plopped himself down in a chair across from Dominic.

"That's OK," blushed Dominic, embarrassed that his mood was so obvious. "What's up?"

"I just wanted to let you know that I was able to obtain tickets for the hottest concert tour in the country." Father Bumbry could hardly contain himself.

"Really, which one?" asked Dominic, only slightly curious.

"Which one? There is only one!"

Dominic was drawing a blank. He had never been to a concert, so it wasn't like he was up on all the concert tours. He heard enough ads on the radio but didn't pay much attention to them.

Father Bumbry's enthusiasm was a little dampened by Dominic's lack thereof. "You really have no idea?"

Dominic shrugged. "Not really. The Eagles?"

Now Father Bumbry was even more deflated. "No, my son, not the Eagles. Bigger than the Eagles. Are the Eagles even together anymore?"

Dominic stole another quick glance at the clock. "I don't really know that either."

Father Bumbry finally coughed up the information. "The Bee Gees! Aren't you a huge fan?"

Dominic did listen to them, but his brother Mitchell was more of a fan than he was. "Oh yeah, I guess they are the hottest band right now."

"I think they have most of the songs in the Top Ten list if I'm not mistaken," replied Father Bumbry. "Anyway, I have tickets and you and I are going."

"OK, cool," replied Dominic. He wondered if he could leave now to go home. But Father Bumbry wasn't done.

"Now, I have three tickets as I was planning on you and your brother Mitchell going—I think he's a big fan anyway—but unfortunately he told me he cannot make it as he has a college basketball game. So why don't you ask Timmy if he wants to go."

"OK, that should be fun," replied Dominic. "I will talk to Timmy and let you know."

"Good. If he can't make it then feel free to ask your brother Jason or another friend that you would like to take with us."

"Alright, will do. Thanks for thinking of me, Father Bumbry. I appreciate it."

"I think of you all the time, my son," replied Father Bumbry smiling at Dominic. "More than you can imagine. And there's one more thing I want to share with you. Something I'm very excited about and I'm pretty sure that you will be really thrilled about as well." Father Bumbry paused.

Dominic sat back in his chair and waited a moment before asking, "Something I would be thrilled about? To be honest, Father Arnold, I can't think of anything."

Father Bumbry smiled, "Well, I haven't really given you any clues either. This is an honor that I was able to convince the powers that be to allow me to bestow upon someone who I believe is quite deserving of it. More deserving than anyone in the parish that I know."

"And who would that be?" asked Dominic.

"My son, why that would be you!" Father Bumbry responded. "You are going be a Eucharistic Minister, and after the induction ceremony, you will be able to serve communion at Mass, just like me. Because of the shortage of priests, the Archdiocese needed to come up with a plan to assist the priests in giving communion. This is quite an honor for you, and let me tell you, I had to fight hard to get a member of the youth ministry as one of the candidates. Are you pleased?"

Dominic was stunned. "I don't know what to say, Father Arnold, as I know it is a sacred duty to hold the Body and Blood of Christ. I am quite humbled and honored that you would nominate me. I know my mom will be extremely happy about this. Wow, this is really something else."

"It was my privilege to arrange it, Dominic. I know how close you are to the Lord. I only thought it right to have you serve Him in the most sacred of the holy sacraments. OK, I've told you all the good news that I have, time for you to hit the road."

Dominic got up from the chair and Father Bumbry put his arm around Dominic's shoulders as they walked toward the exit. "Just let me know as soon as possible about the concert. I gave the date and time of the concert to Mitchell and he wrote it down so he can tell you when you get home. If I told you now, you would probably just forget anyway. It's not for a while so we have some time, just wanted to give you something to look forward to down the road." They walked out into the fresh air of the parking lot and Father Bumbry continued to make small talk while keeping his arm around Dominic's shoulder.

"What's that smell?" Dominic sniffed with his nose.

"What do you mean? Oh, that must be my cologne. It's Grey Flannel. Do you like it?"

Dominic reacted with a face of indifference while Father Bumbry hid his slight disappointment. Father Bumbry raised his head up and spotted a shadow on the back porch of the rectory, its presence given away by the orange-flamed ash of a cigarette. Father Bumbry dropped his arm to his side. "OK, be safe getting home, my son. And don't forget to let me know who will be going with us. Good night."

"OK, good night, Father Bumbry. Thanks for everything! Can't wait to tell my mom!" Dominic made his way down the path between the church and the rectory lawn, and headed toward home.

Father Bumbry slowly climbed the back porch steps of the rectory.

"Good evening, Father Bumbry." The shadow blew out a stream of smoke.

"Good evening, Jimbo," replied Father Bumbry. In the darkness, Father Downey scowled at the younger priest's greeting and although Father Bumbry could not see his face, he sensed it and was glad to get the Monsignor's goat.

"Awfully chummy with the Manterra boy, no?" Father Downey let out another stream of smoke, enjoying his turn getting the goat.

"And good night, Monsignor." Father Bumbry proceeded through the back door without stopping.

Father Downey threw his spent cigarette down and rubbed it out underfoot. He contemplated having another but then thought the better of it, took a deep breath, and went inside as well.

THE BELL RANG AND the boys broke up their conversations to go sit at their respective desks.

"Anyone seen Mr. Canniston yet?" asked Van Burdick.

"Not yet," replied Timmy as Marco and Ernie shook their heads.

A fist extending from an outstretched arm covered by a black sleeve reached into the classroom from the hallway and rapped the door with a few hard knocks. The stiff extended arm then proceeded to enter the classroom, followed by a body of a short man with a mostly bald head with flat hair on the sides of it. The short man closed the classroom door behind him—under his arm he carried some books as he walked over to the teacher's desk and placed the books on them. He paused for a moment and looked out the windows, turning his gaze in a circular motion as if mentally measuring the windows before doing an abrupt left-face.

"Good morning, gentlemen. For those of you who don't know me, I am Brother Conrad Dovell." He halted his speech to let that information sink in with the students before him. "Mr. Canniston will not be in today, so I will be your substitute for the next forty-five minutes or so." Again, he stopped speaking for a moment, standing at attention while he moved his head slowly scanning the room. "This is an American history class, if I am correct?" A few heads nodded yes but he was being rhetorical.

"Well, I am a physics teacher, not that I don't believe history isn't essential, but it's not my area of expertise nor am I going to pretend that I know much more about the subject than you. Therefore, I will not waste your time or, more importantly, my time, in reviewing rises and falls, dates, events, types of government, politicians, soldiers, et cetera et cetera et cetera."

Denny, sitting behind Dominic, leaned in and whispered, "This is the crackpot with the aluminum foil on the windows in his classroom."

"Is there something you wanted to share with the class, young lad?" Brother Conrad shot a perturbed glance like a poisoned arrow at Denny. Denny sat back with his own air of defiance and stared back at Brother Conrad. "No? I didn't think so." Brother Conrad noticed an empty desk at the head of one of the rows and stepped over to it. He turned the desk around and sat down in it, facing the class. "Rumor has it this is allegedly the *brilliant scholar's* class—the best and the brightest students of ASM gathered in one room. Or so goes your reputation in the faculty lounge."

"Evidently I've underestimated the acumen of the ASM faculty,"

Denny spoke out loud. "I will have to give them some more consideration based on that assessment." Dominic rolled his eyes. Brother Conrad turned his head toward Denny and smiled. "Acumen? Now *there's* a
ten-dollar word for you, bravo! What's your name, lad?"

"Denny Massilli."

"OK, Mr. Massilli, just so we're clear, you've just used up your quota
of interruptions." Brother Conrad displayed a steely-eyed smirk. "What
to do...what to do...any suggestions?" He looked around at the blank
faces.

"How about telling us why you became a brother?" offered Dominic.

"Hmmm, now there's a thought, Mr....?"

"Manterra...Nick Manterra..." Dominic replied with his best English
accent, mimicking Sean Connery's James Bond introduction. His classmates laughed as Ernie called out, "Double oh loser!"

Brother Conrad wore a puzzled expression. "Are you English?"

Dominic wondered if he was kidding but quickly realized he wasn't
as the class grew quiet. "Uh, no, Brother Conrad, that was just a joke."
Brother Conrad shrugged his shoulders.

"Nevertheless, that is an excellent recommendation Mr. Manterra has
made and we will go with it."

For the next thirty minutes Brother Conrad shared his life story up to
the current point in time. And what a story it was. He was born in the
Midwest—outside of Davenport, Iowa. He had one sibling, a brother,
who was two years older than he was. He described their close relationship as well as that of his parents—his mother who was a school teacher
who taught chemistry and gave piano lessons, and his father who was a
physician who liked fishing and photography. When he was sixteen
years old, his parents were both tragically killed by a drunk driver in a
car accident. When he was eighteen years old, his brother, suffering from
severe depression, hanged himself in the attic of the family home—it
was Brother Conrad who found him. Brother Conrad was somewhat of a
borderline genius, excelling in mathematics and the sciences. He had
attended one of the Apostles of St. Mary high schools out in Iowa, and

through the support and guidance provided by the Order's brothers, who took him under their wing, he managed to keep himself together, focused on his studies, and eventually joined the Apostles of St. Mary, earned his doctorate in physics, and had been a teacher his whole life, dedicating himself to the education of the students of the Apostles of St. Mary schools. As the class session neared its end, Brother Conrad asked if there were any questions or comments. Dominic raised his hand.

"Yes, John Bull—what is your query?"

Dominic gave Brother Conrad a nod of his head to signal "touché" and then asked, "Brother Conrad, as you shared your life's journey with us, I couldn't help but notice there wasn't much said about God or the role faith played in your life?" The class grew quiet around Dominic as his peers watched Brother Conrad's face contort to a taut expression.

Brother Conrad took a deep breath, held it, and exhaled with some vehemence. "I believe my presence in this classroom today with all of you is a testimony to my faith. And I believe I made it very clear the role the Apostles of St. Mary played in pulling me through the tragic events of my young life. But as we are short on time, I will say this to you—and to the rest of you as well. Both as an Apostle Brother and as a scientist, I challenge you to remember that without doubt, there can be no faith. To be so sure of something as to not allow for it to not be so, is the sure path to fanaticism, blindness, and error in judgment. I would encourage all of you to cling to skepticism as a valid path to certainty. Don't believe everything you hear, don't believe everything you read, don't even believe everything you see. In the end, you will discover more often than not that the truth walks hand in hand with what is false. Therefore, the most reliable path to what is really so is best defined by the path you choose to travel on, based on your own terms."

"*Quid est veritas?*" called out Denny, sarcastically, exceeding his quota.

"Exactly!" Brother Conrad shot back, pointing his finger for emphasis and giving a scare to the students sitting closest to him.

The bell rang. As the class cleared out, Brother Conrad remained sitting at the desk, eyeing Dominic, who returned the stony glare in kind.

Dominic picked up his books and as he walked past, Brother Conrad said to him "*Quo vadis*, John Bull?"

"*Veritas vos liberabit*," responded Dominic, and the two of them exchanged sardonic smiles.

As Dominic exited the classroom, Denny and Timmy were waiting in the hallway.

"What was that all about?" asked Timmy.

"Don't know," replied Dominic.

"He's a fruit loop, that one." Denny was watching the door to make sure the subject of the conversation didn't suddenly appear.

"We better get to class," Dominic suggested.

"I will catch up with you guys later." Denny saluted them. "I have my introductory guidance counsel session now with Brother Mac. Oh, what joy." He headed off in the opposite direction of Dominic and Timmy.

"Timmy, Father Bumbry has tickets for a Bee Gees concert at the Garden. You want to go?" Dominic asked as they made their way to their next class.

Timmy made a face, "I don't know. I'm not really that big a fan. When is it?"

"It's on a Tuesday night. The date—"

"Tuesday night? No way my mom lets me go on a school night. Especially with final exams approaching."

Dominic was disappointed. "Alright, I will see if someone else wants to go."

"Maybe Denny wants to go?" suggested Timmy.

"Ha, I'd rather have sharp pencils jabbed in my ears than listen to that crap!" Denny remarked as he snuck up behind them. "Maybe Brother Conrad would like to go. But only if you spoke dirty to him in Latin while he stands behind you and moves your world with his lever."

"Don't be so gross!" Dominic snapped, punching Denny in the arm.

"You're right—the dirty Latin was crossing the line." Denny punched him back.

"What happened to your session with Brother Mac?" asked Timmy.

"He had to cancel."

"Guess your joy was short-lived?" Dominic turned serious as they walked by the watchful eye of Brother Colenza standing guard outside his classroom as students filed by. He gave Dominic a sneering grin.

"That guy is creepy," Dominic whispered.

"Brother Fluenza? A psychopath, indeed," murmured Denny.

"What else do you expect in hell," added Timmy. The three boys laughed as they entered Brother Terence's classroom.

Mr. Morris Gavin was a short man, an ASM graduate. His sandy-colored hair, which he wore long and parted on the side, showed hints of gray as did his beard and mustache. He was a modest man who had been the moderator and director of the Drama Club for a number of years, inheriting the job from one of the ASM brothers who retired and under whom Mr. Gavin had learned his initial stagecraft when he was a student. Brother Corwin assisted him with the spring musicals (handling the choreography and music) and they made a fairly good team with the exception that Mr. Gavin promoted large, inclusive casts of diverse levels of abilities and skills while Brother Corwin preferred small casts with only truly talented performers. Mr. Gavin had gathered the cast together for a pep talk before the final performance. He stood in front of the stage, leaning against it while he waited for everyone to settle down. Next to him sitting on the stage was Brother Corwin, dressed in a clingy green and brown sweat suit, a size too small, and black Capezio ballet slippers. As the choreographer for the spring musical, he had worked the dancers hard with routines that were nearly impossible. Dominic had been cast as one of the dancers as well as filling in on a few other minor parts. The leads were upper class members from both ASM and St. Mary's Academy, although there were students from other high schools in the county. Mr. Gavin motioned for attention and everyone quieted down.

"OK, you've all worked very hard and done well these past two nights.

And as tonight is our final performance—let's bring down the curtain with our best show tonight! So, for the Drama Club this year, one last time, as the saying goes—*it's show time!*"

The group broke out in cheers and clapping as Mr. Gavin and Brother Corwin exchanged smiles. Mr. Gavin continued.

"Soon the chairs will be set up, the auditorium will be filled, the curtain will go up, and we will perform our last show. But it's more than just a show. It is months of practice and sacrifice; of commitment and dedication; of doubts and fears and, yes, sometimes disappointments. But we have worked hard, we have worked as a troupe, and we have pulled together a really fantastic show that I am sure the audience will love and appreciate. My advice to all of you is to believe in yourself, to stay in character while on the stage, remember your lines, of course, remember your cues, and remember most of all to have fun and enjoy the moment. And, of course, break a leg!"

The drama club members applauded and whistled as Brother Corwin hopped off the stage and gave Mr. Gavin a hug. Mr. Gavin turned to the group and said in a loud voice, "Don't forget the show starts at 8 tonight—we need everyone back here by 6:30 p.m. sharp for makeup and to get into costume. Stage crew—I will need you here at 6 for a final sound and lighting check."

Dominic was chatting with Mike Dotson, who was also a dancer, when Brother Corwin approached them.

"You boys ready for tonight?" he asked. The two students nodded. "OK, one last pointer for you—I notice you all are counting while going through the dance numbers—I can see your lips moving—don't do that during this last performance." They nodded. "Good. What are you boys doing for dinner?"

"My mom's picking me up—she's probably waiting in the parking lot now," answered Mike.

"I was just going to go grab a sub sandwich and come back here," said Dominic.

"OK, I will do the same then," Brother Corwin replied, "if you don't mind the company, Dominic."

"Sure, no problem."

"I will see you guys later." Mike gave them the thumbs up. "Break a leg!" he said as he walked toward the exit.

"I can drive us over to the sub shop," offered Brother Corwin.

"Sounds good," replied Dominic. "I can wait here while you change your clothes."

"No need, I'll go like this. I have the car keys from running to get some last-minute supplies for Morris earlier," replied Brother Corwin, "so ready when you are."

They drove over to the sub shop in the local Rosedale shopping center. It had a number of small boutique shops, a large hardware store, a chain supermarket, and the Lan Wuh Cantonese Restaurant—a place that Dominic's father would sometimes take the boys to for a treat.

They ordered their sub sandwiches. Dominic felt a little uneasy as he sensed the stares that Brother Corwin was receiving in his ill-fitting sweat suit. As soon as Dominic's order was ready, he paid for it and headed toward the exit to wait for Brother Corwin by the car. Brother Corwin noticed Dominic's quick movements and was about to say something when the woman called out his number and drew his attention away. Dominic could hear him order a large black coffee as he pushed through the heavy glass door.

Dominic had started to eat his small bag of chips as Brother Corwin caught up to him.

"There you are, little brother. You must have been hungry the way you darted out of there." He released one of his goofy laughs. Dominic shook his head and waited for Brother Corwin to get into the car and unlock the passenger side door.

"Why don't we head over to the park by Ridgeway River and eat there?" suggested Brother Corwin.

The park was not too from the shopping center. It was about a mile away, just across the city line into Crawford, the town next to Rosedale. Brother Corwin handed Dominic his coffee and got them over to the park in about ten minutes. He found a spot with a view of the river. The park was filled with folks out fishing, joggers, dog walkers, couples out for a stroll, and people pushing baby carriages. Dominic unwrapped his sandwich and commenced eating.

"Are you nervous about tonight?" asked Brother Corwin in between bites of his sandwich.

Dominic swallowed, took a drink from his bottle of iced tea, and wiped his mouth with a paper napkin. "A little bit. My parents and some of my brothers will be coming with their friends."

"Which brothers will that be?" Brother Corwin put aside his half-eaten sandwich and now concentrated on his coffee.

"My younger brother Jason, my older brothers Mitchell and Sal, and their friend Jon Jasper, for sure." Dominic placed his half-eaten sandwich down on his lap and finished off his bag of chips, and then the pickle that came with the sandwich.

"That's good. They want to show their support."

"They want to have a good laugh at my expense and torment me is more like it," Dominic snorted.

"I remember in college, we put on a production of *Marat/Sade*. Have you ever heard of it?" Dominic shook his head without looking up. He was done with everything but the last of his sandwich and was making sure not to drop any of it on his lap or the interior of the car.

"The full title is *The Persecution and Assassination of Jean-Paul Marat as Performed by the Inmates of the Asylum of Charenton Under the Direction of the Marquis de Sade*. It takes place in an insane asylum—it's actually a play inside a play."

"Kind of like *Hamlet*?" asked Dominic.

Brother Corwin guffawed. "Not exactly, little brother." Brother Corwin was amused that Dominic could be simultaneously so knowledge-able and so naïve. Dominic knew the facts but he didn't have a clue as to the facts of life. These attributes along with his trusting nature made him so appealing. Dominic really was a freaking Boy Scout, pure and simple. Brother Corwin's thoughts broadened his grin and made him chortle as he moved his Styrofoam cup to rest on his lap.

"What's it about?"

"It's sort of a philosophical political black comedy for adults. Maybe we can go see it sometime. Anyway, I played one of the inmates and as part of my costume, I wore a rather large, let's say enormous, prop of a phallus." Brother Corwin paused. Out of the corner of his eye he took note of Dominic's facial expression. He waited as Dominic finished off the last bit of his sandwich and disposed of the various wrappers, used napkins, and empty bottle into the paper bag.

"All during rehearsals, as I played the part, there was a scene when I am basically simulating a certain act from behind with a co-ed who was playing one of the female inmates. Well, during the final dress rehearsal, she turns to me and tells me that her parents were coming to opening night, and I was not to do any simulations or come near her with my enormous phallus. What a little bitch! Of course, I made sure to be even more over the top on opening night!" Brother Corwin cackled as he remembered.

Dominic glanced at the clock on the dashboard. "Brother Corwin, don't you think we should be heading back?"

"I just want to finish my coffee, if that's OK?" Brother Corwin tersely replied.

Dominic peered out the window. "OK, I'm just going to bring my trash over to the garbage can. Do you want me to take yours as well?" Brother Corwin handed him his paper bag and Dominic got out of the car and walked it over to the trash can. He bent down to tie the laces of his sneaker. He was enjoying the fresh air as Brother Corwin's coffee breath had been killing him, especially mixed with the tuna fish sandwich the Brother had eaten. He could see Brother Corwin watching him from the car.

Dominic stood up and glanced around the river park. Trees and woods lined the river on both sides up until the point where it widened by a concrete bridge and the river disappeared under the parkway and its busy traffic lanes. They would be crossing back over that bridge to return to ASM and Dominic figured it was time to get back—and hopefully Brother Corwin was done with his coffee. Dominic climbed back into the car and gauged Brother Corwin's coffee cup—it still was about a third full.

"Beautiful day out there!" Brother Corwin sensed something was amiss.

"Yes, it is. Spring's a great time of year. Everything is coming alive. It's like nature is just bursting out everywhere—exploding all its colors all at once."

"Oh, indeed, it is." Brother Corwin grinned, dropping his head down for a moment.

"It's like nature just views the barren landscape as one big canvas of dull gray, and hurls a palette of multiple colors at it, and it transforms into a French Impressionist painting."

"I had a college roommate who always played practical jokes on me." Brother Corwin spoke up before Dominic could bring any talk of God into the picture, which he suspected was where Dominic would go.

"Huh? Oh, really?" Dominic was growing impatient to get back to ASM.

Brother Corwin continued, "But I got him back one night. It was classic."

"How?" asked Dominic.

Brother Corwin downed his remaining coffee and brought the empty cup down to his lap. "Well, one night he was out late and I was back in our dorm room. He liked to go out to drink some beers with the other guys, and on the weekends, he tended to have a few too many. As I was lying in bed I came up with this brilliant idea. I positioned the pillows on my bed along with the blanket to make it look like I was in bed sleeping, and then I crawled under his bed and waited. Sure enough, he came stumbling in from his night of drinking with the boys. From under his bed, I watched his feet as he got undressed—he liked to sleep naked. I listened as he climbed into bed and then stretched himself out. I waited a little bit of time until I thought he had entered into that realm of light sleep, right before one actually falls asleep. Then I silently slid myself out from under the bed, and slowly raised my arm around... and with my open palm—slapped it square down onto...his chest!"

Brother Corwin broke into a huge grin and looked at Dominic, who wore a puzzled look.

"What was the practical joke part? You just scaring him? It sounds like a lot of work to just say boo without using any words."

"No! Of course not! Well, I'm sure that he was startled. But no, you have to use your imagination a bit here. He wakes up from his little twilight snooze. He feels this hand on his chest but there isn't anyone in the room—not that he can see anyway. It freaked him the hell out alright. Think about it—he's lying there naked to the world and has a hand on his chest without a body attached to it!"

Dominic was unimpressed. He checked the car clock on the dashboard.

"Brother Corwin, we really should get back to school. I'm sure Mr. Gavin won't appreciate us being late, especially you."

Brother Corwin brusquely started the car and shifted it into reverse and pulled out of the parking space. He hastily slammed the brakes, put it in drive, and headed back to ASM. While he drove, Dominic contemplated the evening's performance and went over his parts in his mind to make sure he had all his duties covered. He caught a whiff of Brother Corwin's coffee breath and made a mental note to himself to get to his locker and brush his teeth before doing anything else once they got back to the school.

Brother Corwin pulled into the ASM lot and parked the car. Dominic hopped out, said a quick thanks, and jogged over to the school. Most of the cast had already gathered backstage, which was actually the hallway behind the gymnasium/auditorium. That hallway also accessed the school library and the locker rooms. Dominic was making his way toward the locker room, passing by the cast members who were busy getting their makeup on. He passed by Moira Toomey and gave her a wink. She playfully responded by sticking out her tongue at him and then smiled. Dominic smiled back, figuring her greeting was in return for his comment to her during one of the dance number practices. In the scene Dominic played a customer of the dance hall and was surrounded by all the female dancers. Moira was kneeling down next to him with her arms wrapped around his right leg. Dominic's direction was to stand there while the women danced and sang to him. He had glanced down at Moira and was served up a direct, unobstructed view of her beautiful, shapely breasts. Moira looked like a body double of Ann-Margret. She had grown up since grammar school, alright. Moira looked up and caught Dominic admiring her wares. Dominic remarked, "My, how you have grown!" Moira squinted her eyes disapprovingly and dug her nails into Dominic's thigh. Reflecting upon it as he walked by her now, Dominic thought that likely was not going to have the result she would have anticipated on a teenage boy. Hmmm, maybe he could discuss that with her at the cast party.

Dominic brushed his teeth, swooshed some mouthwash, and then returned to the backstage area. Members were starting to get a bit nervous and the voices were loud as they applied makeup while practicing their lines. Moira was putting makeup on Mike Dotson who caught Dominic's eye and gave him the thumbs up. Dominic made his way over to a table with various jars and bottles on it. He picked up one of the jars marked for base cover and went to find a mirror. There was a small square mirror posted on the wall and Dominic positioned himself in front of it.

"You want me to help you with that?"

Dominic turned his head and Brother Corwin was standing there. "I have quite a bit of experience with stage makeup. Believe me you don't want it caked on so that you look like a ghoul or have too little so that you look like a ghost under the stage lights." Dominic thought about it and then handed the applicator and jar to Brother Corwin, who accepted it and then pointed to the wall.

"Here, stand against the wall and don't move a muscle." Dominic placed his back against the wall and stared straight ahead as Brother Corwin dipped the applicator pad into the jar and then started to pat the base makeup on Dominic's face. Fortunately for Dominic, Brother Corwin had taken some mints so the coffee breath was not as potent as in the car. Dominic stood very still while Brother Corwin applied the makeup.

Brother Corwin felt like Michelangelo working on his David. Dominic's blue eyes were ebullient, heightened by the darkening of his skin by the base makeup. His skin was flawless, nary a wrinkle or blemish to speak of. His long brown hair was shiny and thick. His lips were full and gave his wide mouth a certain sensuousness. He did have a prominent Italian nose but it was well-shaped and fit his face nevertheless. Brother Corwin realized his hand was a little shaky being so close to his favorite student by far. He paused. "You need to keep very still, little brother, so the makeup goes on evenly and doesn't streak." Dominic nodded and braced himself. Brother Corwin got his hand to stop its slight quiver and resumed applying the makeup. Brother Corwin's mind raced as he deliberately and gradually and unhurriedly smoothed out the base over Dominic's forehead, on his temples, down the side of his face, on his ears, his cheekbones, his chin, down along and around his neck. Dominic did not move or say a word as he stood still and stared straight ahead. A voice disturbed Brother Corwin's process.

"I think he's, uh, all set there, Brother Corwin." Brother Corwin pulled back his hand and turned around. It was Mr. Gavin.

"He's, uh, good to go. Yes, he is. Go on, Dominic, and get ready for the opening number."

Dominic pushed himself away from the wall. "OK, Mr. Gavin. Thanks, Brother Corwin!" He hurried to get backstage with the others.

Brother Corwin glanced at Mr. Gavin, who tilted his head as to ask, "Yes, is there something you want to say?" Brother Corwin just shrugged his shoulders and raised his eyebrows at Mr. Gavin, throwing the jar and pad on a nearby table as he pushed himself past his old classmate and muttered, "Break a leg, Morris."

Mr. Gavin dropped his eyes to the floor, then looked up and around at the empty hallway filled with the tables and clothes racks hung with costume changes for the evening. He sighed, shook his head, and made his way to the backstage for a final briefing with the stage manager.

XXIV.

RUMORS

Will you be at the cast party tonight, Nicky boy?" Eddie Binder purred and waited with a faux anticipation, eyes gleaming with an eagerness of *say yes say yes say yes!*

Dominic closed his locker door, which revealed the short senior who stood standing behind it, a little too close for Dominic's comfort. "Yes, Eddie, I will be going to the cast party, if my father says it's OK."

"Oh, that's swell, Nicky boy, that's just swell. Well, if it will help sway your daddy's decision, tell him I can certainly chaperone you." Eddie winked.

"I appreciate that, Eddie, but I don't think that will be necessary. Or helpful."

Eddie made a fake pouting face. "Nicky boy, that's not nice to hear"— he changed his expression to gleeful—"but be sure to have a glass of punch with me. Or if you prefer, we can go for something stronger!" Again, Eddie winked and tramped out of the locker room. Dominic just shook his head as he hooked his Master Lock on the door of his locker and clicked it shut.

"Tell me again why you're in the drama club?" asked Timmy.

Dominic turned and standing over by the next section of lockers were Timmy and Ernie, who wore a big grin on his face.

"Yeah, Nicky boy, why *are* you in this freakin' musical? Is it for the... little perks?" Ernie mimicked Eddie's voice.

"You guys are just jealous," shot back Dominic. "What are you doing here anyway?"

"Oh, we've come to see the closing night performance," answered Timmy.

"We wouldn't want to miss this for the world. Tell us, when do you and that guy have your big scene together?" asked Ernie.

"Ernie, I believe that will be later on at the cast party. And from the looks of it, two's company!" Timmy laughed.

"Everything should be coming up daisies!" added Ernie.

"Alright, alright you two, that's enough. You'll be singing a different tune when you see the one big number when I'm surrounded by all the babes. And might I add that Terry Cartwright's assets have only gotten bigger."

"Hence the real reason we're here," Timmy smugly confided.

"There ain't nothing wrong with that." Ernie almost sounded apologetic.

"You won't be disappointed. Her top in the scene leaves little to the imagination. Hmmm, the word...*titillating*...seems the appropriate description." Dominic smacked his lips.

"Come on, Timmy, let's go find our seats," Ernie snapped as Timmy mouthed the words *"the biggest tits of them all"* at Dominic. They exited through the locker room side door. Dominic walked out to the hallway corridor that led to the backstage area, laughing to himself in between thoughts of titillating Terry.

"WELL, WHAT DID YOU THINK?" Dominic waited for a response.

"It was pretty good." David spoke first, which only made sense since he was the family's most accomplished musician. He had been playing piano for over twenty years and was already a church organist as well as playing with a local jazz band. "Things appear to have loosened up since my days here. We never put on a production like that."

"You were good, Dominic, though I could see you counting out the dance steps," added his brother Salvatore.

"All of you were, though," Jon Jasper chuckled, "and half of you looked like you were scared to death. I was almost tempted to yell out a number to see if it would throw your counting off."

"At least you got that plum part of being the customer in the "Hey! Big Spender" number. Some pretty girls working at that dance club." Mitchell winked at Dominic.

"I thought you were wonderful!" Mrs. Manterra hugged her son. "But I didn't care for the way some of the girls were dressed. Most immodest. I noticed some of the nuns from St. Mary's Academy walked out during that one particular scene." Dominic's mom shook her head in solidarity with the good sisters.

Dominic looked to his father, who hadn't said a word. He stood there with his raincoat folded over his arm, looking around. Dominic followed his father's eyes as they scanned the surrounding gymnasium filled with the cast and lingering audience members

"You're right, David, things have changed since the early days of ASM. Not so sure for the better. But your brothers are right, Dominic, you did a good job. Although I prefer drama, straight plays, this was still entertaining. There were some talented young ladies on that stage. Good singing voices." Dominic thought his father's praise was generous. "Do you want us to wait for you, to give you a ride home?" he asked.

"Actually, Dad, they're having the cast party tonight. I was hoping to go to that, if only for a little while. I won't be late." Dominic held his breath. His father grimaced but was giving it some thought.

"How long's a little while?" he finally asked.

"Just about an hour, hour and a half, tops."

"I could come by and pick him up," offered Mitchell.

"Thanks, Mitch, that won't be necessary," countered Dominic. "Andy Mackly is part of the stage crew and he will be going. I can catch a ride with him." Andy had been in Boy Scouts with Dominic, and his family lived one block over from the Manterras' house. Dominic figured this would sway his father as well.

"OK, no drinking, no drugs, and if Andy can't give you a ride, or decides to stay longer, then you give Mitchell a call and he will come get you, understood?" Mr. Manterra spoke with a no-nonsense sternness in his voice.

"Understood. Thanks, Dad. And thanks to all of you coming to the show. Hopefully it wasn't too painful." Dominic shook their hands. Mr. Manterra handed his raincoat to Dominic, who accepted it and then held it up and open for his father to slip his arms through the sleeves. Mrs. Manterra gave her son a kiss on the cheek and again offered congrats and told him to have a good time at the party. Then Mr. and Mrs. Manterra and the others headed for the exit.

Out of the corner of his eye, standing near the stage steps, Brother Corwin watched the Manterra family walk across the back of the gymnasium.

"Coming to the cast party, Brother Corwin?" Brother Corwin's observing was interrupted by Mr. Gavin.

"Yes, yes, I am, Morris. Congratulations on another successful season," and he extended his hand to Mr. Gavin, who accepted it and gave it a solid shake. "Same to you, Brother Corwin, same to you. See you over at the house."

"I APPRECIATE THE RIDE over to the party, Andy."

"No problem, Dominic. Haven't seen you much at Scouts?"

"Yeah, haven't been able to keep as active as I used to be," Dominic answered.

"Going to make Eagle or no?"

Dominic shook his head. "I think that might elude me, which I know

I will regret," Dominic replied wistfully. "I think Mark Stephens still has a shot."

Andy laughed. "I'm sure he does. It will go well on his Ivy League college application."

They drove over to Ridgeway, the town where Mr. Gavin lived. Andy parked on a nearby side street as they were arriving to the party a bit later than others and most of the closer curbside was already taken. As they walked toward the house, Dominic thought about his father's instructions.

"Hey, Andy, whenever you're ready to go home, just give me the signal, OK? I promised my dad I would catch a ride with you. But I can't stay longer than an hour or so."

"No problem. I wasn't planning on staying much longer than that. Having attended one before, they're not all that fun anyway."

Dominic smiled to himself. Andy was a member of the stage crew and not really a social person, so his assessment was not surprising.

"But this is your first cast party so it will be new to you. Based on your performance in this show, it doesn't seem like it will be your last. You'll be one of the leads in future shows for sure."

"Thanks, Andy. It was a fun experience."

"And one of the few opportunities we have to see any females in the school on a regular basis." Andy gave a knowing look to Dominic. "Funny how it always seems we were in all-male organizations—altar boys, Scouts, high school—we might as well have been in the military. It will be good to graduate and get to college so I can finally see some action. First I will have to learn how to interact with the other half of the species."

"I'm sure it's like learning to ride a bicycle," commented Dominic.

"Hey, Manterra!"

Dominic looked over by a parked car where someone had called his name. Two of the seniors from the show—Mikey Bishop and Corey Wasser—were motioning to him. He noticed Moira Toomey was coming up the sidewalk with a few of the other girls from the show as well.

"Hi, Dominic." Moira gave him a sweet smile. "You going to save a dance for me?" She kept staring him in the eyes as she brushed by him, the scent of her auburn hair giving Dominic a rush as he watched her walk up the wide wooden steps into the house. Andy gave him a punch in the arm. "Maybe one of us won't have to wait until college. See you inside, Dominic. My advice is to stay away from those two."

Dominic shook his head. "OK, see you inside, Andy." Dominic looked back to the car and Mikey was frantically waving him over. Dominic approached them with a bit of apprehension. When he drew closer to the car, he smelled something strange in the air.

"What the hell is that smell?" Dominic asked.

"Quiet, Manterra, keep your freakin' voice down!" Mikey laughed. "We're just prepping for the party with a little mary jane. I'd offer you some but I know your stance on the wacky weed." Dominic waved his hand back and forth to clear the air around him. "But we do have something else you might like." Mikey held up a pint of blackberry brandy and grinned at Dominic. "Take a couple of swigs. Loosen you up a bit for your dance with that Toomey chick."

"That's OK, Mikey. I don't need any confidence booster to dance with Moira."

"Oh crap!" Corey hissed. "Put the bottle down!" Dominic turned around to see what Corey was reacting to, and sure enough Mr. Gavin was standing on his front porch watching them. He shook his head and went back into the house. "Damnit!" snapped Dominic. And then he remembered what his mom had said to him on more than one occasion: "He that walketh with wise men shall be wise: but a companion of fools shall be destroyed." For a moment Dominic was standing on that mountain again with Mr. Wilson. Mr. Gavin had warned them about no drinking or other activities at the post–final curtain gathering.

"I will see you two inside," Dominic muttered as he walked away from the car, and then thought to himself, *Actually I won't*. Dominic climbed the steps and went into the crowded house. Most of the cast members were there and it was loud with the stereo blasting music from the popular *Bat Out of Hell* LP. He quickly noted where Andy was standing, they made contact and returned head nods, then he scanned the room for Moira, located her—she gave him an anxious glance—and his eyes met Mr. Gavin, who just shook his head. *Mom, you were so right*, Dominic thought to himself. He was feeling hungry and made his way over to the folding tables set against the wall. There was the usual buffet fare: macaroni and potato salads, a salad of mixed greens, a cheese platter, finger sandwiches, and baked ziti. He picked up a plate and filled it with a bit of everything. He mingled with some of the other cast members, every now and then noting where Moira was. Moira noticed Dominic in the corner of her eye staring at her and she smiled to herself.

Dominic was talking to some of the lighting crew guys when he felt a slight pinch on his left arm above the elbow. He turned to be face to face with Moira. She held up a plastic cup. "It appears my cup has run dry, Dominic," she smiled, "and my lips are really thirsty." Dominic stammered a bit—her eyes were sparkling—they were blue topaz gems embedded in a face he thought so beautiful it would make Beauty itself jealous!

She raised her cup to his lips. "Well, are you going to fill me up, Dominic?" She swayed her lithe and curved body back and forth with an "I'm waiting, come hither" motion. Dominic could feel her warm, fruity breath upon his cheek as the scent of her auburn hair seem to surround him.

"Um, uh, yes, uh, I will uh definitely fill you up, uh, I mean, get you another cup for your lips, uh, a cup of punch." Dominic grabbed the cup and hastily pushed his way through the crowd toward the table with the large fountain punch bowl. As Moira watched him her face beamed with the confirmation of her suspicions—no, hopes—of Dominic's feelings about her and she felt radiant inside.

Across the room, the playful exchange was witnessed by another interested party. Brother Corwin had stopped listening to the droning story of a senior female cast member as Moira's approach toward Dominic had caught his attention. He had been monitoring Dominic's whereabouts during the party, having to endure the banter of uninteresting people as cover for his making his way to an impromptu run-in with him. He was mindful of Morris Gavin's focus as well. But now this little hussy had appeared to move in on Dominic.

"What do you think of that, Brother Corwin? Brother Corwin?" the young lady speaking to him had pierced the veil of his private world with her maudlin, high-pitched voice.

"Oh, Priscilla, I'm sure whatever happens, it will be for the best!" he answered her with an air of annoyance and then scooted away. Priscilla gasped and brought her hand to her mouth. Her friend Colleen noticed and hurried over to her. "What's wrong, Priscilla?" Colleen asked. Priscilla shook her head. "I was just telling Brother Corwin about my ill grandmother in the hospital and the fact the doctors don't think she'll make it! I can't believe what he just said to me!"

Brother Corwin pushed his way through the party-goers, reaching the table just as Dominic had placed the ladle back in the bowl and was turning around to get back to Moira. Brother Corwin bumped Dominic's arm holding the plastic cup brimming with the punch, and it spilled on Dominic and the table.

"Oh shoot, sorry about that, Dominic!" Brother Corwin reached for some napkins, handing a few to Dominic, while applying one to Dominic's chest to dry off the punch that had landed on him.

"That's OK, Brother Corwin. Here, I can do that." Dominic gently pushed Brother Corwin's hand away and began to pat his own napkin on his shirt and his shirt sleeve.

"Oh, I don't mind!" Brother Corwin offered. "Gee, I'm such a klutz!" He let out one of his signature guffaws. Dominic looked back for Moira but she wasn't standing in the same spot and he figured she had given up on him to sate her thirst. His face expressed disappointment.

"Looking for someone?" inquired Brother Corwin.

"Uh, ah, no, no. I think I'm alright now, Brother Corwin." Dominic rolled the wet napkins into a ball and wrapped them with a fresh, dry napkin, extending his arms a bit to put some distance between Brother

THE TAMING OF THE ROSE

251

Corwin and himself. He glanced around for a trash pail but, not seeing one, opted to place the napkin ball on the corner of the table, behind a basket of bread.

"It was a pretty good show overall, don't you think?" Brother Corwin asked while handing Dominic a cup of punch. "Here, no hard feelings, I hope."

"Oh, that punch wasn't—" Dominic stopped himself and just accepted the cup from Brother Corwin. "Yes, I thought it was."

"Tell me what you really think about your first experience in the theater, now that you're a full-fledged thespian?" Brother Corwin gave Dominic a leering grin.

Dominic sighed thinking of his missed opportunity with Moira. "It was fun, I guess. But I'm just a neophyte at this point."

"Yes...yes...that you are," commented Brother Corwin as he raised his own cup of punch to his lips, looked directly at Dominic, and downed the glass. *If only it had some of my favorite scotch in it.* "But you won't be forever, right?"

"Yeah, right. I think I will audition for the fall play. Mr. Gavin suggested that I should do that as well. Ha, I guess he realized I can't sing." Brother Corwin grimaced. He was a student of musical theater. He did not really care for straight plays, comedy maybe, but drama no. Fortunately, Morris preferred comedies but in either case there was no role for him in the fall shows. Someone had changed the record on the stereo to the soundtrack album for *Saturday Night Fever*. The music caught Dominic's ear and broke him off his thoughts of Moira.

"Oh, Brother Corwin, are you a fan?" he asked.

"A fan? Why, do you need to be cooled off?" Dominic's forlorn look had not escaped Brother Corwin and he imagined the young vixen had marked her territory well with her scent.

"No, of the music that's playing—the Bee Gees?"

Brother Corwin listened for a moment. "Oh yes, who isn't? I remember listening to these guys before they switched to falsetto. Their earlier stuff was really good, too."

Dominic smiled. "Well, then how about going to see them?"

Brother Corwin gave him a quizzical look. "These guys? You mean live in concert?"

"Yes, I have an extra ticket. Figure I'd return the favor for the Broadway play—why don't you think about it."

"Yes, yes, sure I'll go!" Brother Corwin's reaction was ecstatic. *Hmmm,* he thought, *I guess the little tramp loses out after all.*

"I will fill you in on the details next week. My ride is signaling me." Andy was giving the thumbs up sign from across the room.

"Oh, you're leaving already?" asked Brother Corwin, disappointed.

"Yup, promised my dad I would catch a ride with Andy."

"Do you do everything your dad tells you to do?" asked Brother Corwin with a hint of sarcasm.

"Pretty much, as a matter of fact."

"How terribly boring," murmured Brother Corwin.

"One doesn't disrespect a Sicilian father, Brother Corwin. My father instilled that in us at an early age. He's often said that he'd bury us before he would ever let that happen."

"How lovingly sadistic of him." Brother Corwin flashed a broad fake smile. It quickly disappeared from his face as a thought struck him. "You know, Dominic, if you want to stay a little longer, I could give you a lift home?"

Dominic pondered the offer for a moment, and then thought better of it. "No, I better not, Brother Corwin, but thanks. I promised my dad."

"Hmmm, promises were made to be broken." Brother Corwin tipped his cup toward his mouth and threw his head back to get the last drop out of it.

"Did I mention my father was Sicilian?" Dominic laughed.

"Well, I just thought you might want a little more time for that young lady you were chatting with earlier...." Brother Corwin waited as he watched the words sink into Dominic's head. Dominic turned to take a quick look around the crowded room.

"I did sort of promise Moira a dance…" he uttered the words more to himself than to Brother Corwin.

Brother Corwin pressed his play. "Well, I'm sure you don't want to… uh…let her down, now, do you?"

Dominic's eyes found hers. Moira gave him a look that displayed annoyance but then changed to anticipation as her pout gave way to a slight smile. Then she stuck her tongue out at him for a quick second. Dominic grinned and nodded at her. She mouthed the words "Where's my punch?" and then frowned. She smiled again and mouthed the words "You promised me a dance" as she lifted her chin into the air to acknowledge the music, and her expression changed to that of, "Well?"

"You ready, Dominic?" Andy's voice broke off Dominic's trance. "Hey, Brother Corwin, congrats on a great show this year."

"Thank you, Andrew. There might be a change of plan here." Brother Corwin eyed Dominic.

"Change of plan?" Andy was puzzled.

"No, Andy, no change of plan. But give me a minute. I'll meet you by the car, OK? Excuse me, Brother Corwin." Andy nodded. "No problem, Dominic. I will be in the car. See ya around, Brother Corwin." Dominic wormed his way through the revelers, some of whom started to dance where they stood. He managed to make his way to the place where Moira was talking with some of her friends. He slid up to her, but she kept her back to him. Her friends, who were facing him, also ignored him, avoiding any eye contact with him. Dominic suddenly felt a little awkward. "Um, Moira, I have to go but I just was—"

Moira twisted her torso around—"Then go!"—and abruptly turned back to her two friends, who both made faces of disgust and shook their heads. Dominic was taken aback and, feeling kind of stupid, turned on his heels. As he walked away, he heard the loud laughter of Moira and her friends. He figured their laughter was targeted toward him. He found Mr. Gavin and thanked him for the party and for the opportunity to be in the show. At first appearing cool toward him, Mr. Gavin seemed to soften his demeanor and expressed his thanks to Dominic as well. Dominic figured that Mr. Gavin didn't smell any evidence and maybe gave him the benefit of the doubt after all. He quickly left through the front door to get to Andy before he left without him, but not without one backward glance to Moira. She did not turn to look his way, and he left.

Brother Corwin followed the unfolding of events and was pleased. He chatted with a few of the cast members, keeping an eye on the object of Dominic's infatuation. Finally, she made her move to the dessert table and Brother Corwin was ready. He came up behind her as she put a fudge brownie on her little paper plate.

"Ah, chocolate! The ideal comfort food if there ever was one," he uttered quietly.

"Huh? Oh, hello Brother Corwin, having a good time?" Moira nibbled the corner of her brownie.

"Why yes, I am, for sure. How about yourself?" he inquired.

"It's a good time," Moira responded unenthusiastically.

"I don't see you dancing? You were one of the more talented dancers in the show, too. Don't tell me your dance card isn't all full?"

Moira laughed. "It's not. But the night is young." She winked at him.

"Indeed, it is," Brother Corwin's tone was encouraging, "and I have noticed one of those upperclassmen in the group over my left shoulder studying you like he was preparing for a French exam—the tall, lean one. I think he plays baseball for Christian Brothers Academy."

Moira lifted her chin, and with a curious look stretched her neck to peer over his left shoulder. Brother Corwin smiled, thinking to himself, *Oh, vanity, you never fail me!* He helped himself to a sugar cookie, adding, "I happen to know those boys if you would like me to make an introduction." He took a bite from the cookie and sighed. Moira stepped back from him. "No thanks, Brother, I don't think I'll be staying much longer anyway. You enjoy yourself." With that, Moira slipped away and returned to her friends. Brother Corwin remained somewhat smug if not unconvinced and so thought to himself, *Now let it work. Mischief, thou art afoot.* He let out a low guffaw. *How appropriate a quote for the moment, little brother!* Out of the corner of his eye he could see the three girls huddled like a little coven as they took their measure of the upperclassmen jocks. His face formed a mischievous grin and he turned to seek out Morris.

"OK, LET ME BE CLEAR from the start here, gents. We're doing it the Ernie way tonight!"

Ernie paused to let his words sink in. Marco, Andy, Denny, and Dominic awaited further enlightenment.

"I have procured some refreshment for us to share before we head over to Trish's house for the party."

The five friends had gathered at Andy Terrolla's house, which was only a few blocks from where Trish lived and was having a small get together. Andy had managed to get Denny and Dominic invited as well despite the pool party incident. Dominic had asked if it was difficult to convince Trish to let Denny and him come to the party. Andy replied that it wasn't a problem at all—Trish insisted the two be there. Denny had winked at Dominic when he heard that.

Denny spoke up. "Alright, Ernie, enough with the theatrics, what do you have for us?"

Ernie showed the setup on the table behind him in Andy's basement.

"What we have here, gentlemen, is what real men drink. None of that tutti-frutti shit you guys drank before the Academy dance. Southern Comfort—pussy liquor."

Denny responded sarcastically, "Oh, is that what that tastes like? To paraphrase Robert Frost, one could do worse than be a licker of—

Ernie cut him off. "Alright, wise guy, very funny. With your luck it will taste like kitty litter. OK, listen up. You have a shot of whiskey. You have a glass of beer. You drink down the whiskey in one gulp, you chase it with a swig from the beer. Simple as that, one, two. In fact, in Texas it's called the two-step. Everyone got it?"

Everyone nodded yes and basically positioned themselves around the table. Dominic hesitated.

"I think I'm going to pass."

"No, you're not, Nicky boy. You'll be fine. That cough syrup you drank that night got you sick. This will actually settle your nerves. We won't be rushing the drinking like you fools did that night." Ernie handed a shot glass filled with whiskey to Dominic. "Down the hatch!" He tapped Dominic's glass and quickly threw back the whiskey. Then he slammed the shot glass down, picked up a beer, and swallowed a generous gulp. "Just like that, Nicky boy, just like that."

The others followed suit while Dominic watched. Ernie had already refilled the shot glasses.

"Come on, Nicky, just do it."

Dominic brought the shot glass up to his lips. The aroma of the whiskey kind of repulsed him but with all eyes on him, he threw back the shot and slammed it down. He started to cough a little, but Ernie thrust a beer in his hand and barked at him, "Take a swig of the beer—a big gulp now!" Dominic did just that and the boys let out a little cheer. They waited for Dominic to catch his breath and did another round.

"Just so we're clear, and we don't run into any problems, make sure you two keep your clothes on tonight!" Ernie wagged his finger at Denny and Dominic.

"With all due respect, Ernest, that will be up to the ladies to decide, not you!" Denny retorted.

"Keep the clothes on, Massilli! No one wants to see your shortcomings!"

"Jealousy makes you appear so small, Ernest! Tsk, tsk." Denny was too quick. Even Ernie laughed.

The boys walked over to Trish's house and the fresh air felt good to Dominic. He was feeling buzzed from the beers and shots, with a hint of the spins, but it was a much better feeling than when they drank the Southern Comfort. Denny even seemed to be more mellow and relaxed, with less of an edge to him.

"I hate to admit it, Nicky boy, but maybe Ernest is right about drinking like real men. Although I like the thought of a woman tasting sweet south of her border. Now that would be real southern comfort!" Yes, less of an edge, not all of it gone. Dominic just shook his head.

They arrived at Trish's house. Dominic couldn't help but notice that Denny and he received the best hello, warmly embraced by all the ladies present. Trish even held on to Denny's arm after hugging him. *I guess she wants to do the monster mash now*, he thought to himself. Some of their other classmates had arrived before them. Harry was already present as well. Greetings were exchanged and they all headed down to the finished basement.

There was a six-foot sub and chips and soda, the usual house party fare setup. There was a pool table, a ping pong table, and a dart board, along with assorted board games, and plenty of chairs and a couple of couches. With *Darkness on the Edge of Town* playing on the stereo, everyone was having a good time and all was going well.

And then Ernie decided it needed just one more thing to make it perfect.

Cigars.

"Hey, Trish, your parents smoke, right? Andy here tells us your dad likes his cigars and brandy. Think it'd be OK if we lit up a few stogies?" Ernie flashed a fistful of cigars.

"I don't see why not," Trish answered. "Please be careful with the ashes! I don't want any burns on the furniture or the rug."

"No problem. If you like, we can just hang out in the backyard and smoke them there."

Some of the boys filed out of the basement, following Ernie. He handed them each a cigar. Dominic accepted one but he wasn't sure about the idea.

"Come on, Manterra, does every pleasure and vice in life have to be a moral crisis? For Christ's sake, lighten up already!" Ernie didn't hold back.

"Or better yet, light up—the cigars!" Denny bent forward with the cigar in his mouth while Ernie struck a match and lit the cigar. Denny puffed a few times and for a moment the end of the cigar glowed a bright orange. The others followed suit. Dominic had never smoked anything in his life but shrugged and had his cigar lit. He vigorously puffed away.

"Whoa, whoa, slow down there, Nicky boy, you're not playing a saxophone. You can't be inhaling the cigar like that," warned Ernie.

The chatter among the guys centered around the usual topics—sports, school, and girls. After a short while, the boys were finishing up their smokes and getting ready to go back in the house. Ernie was closely watching Dominic. Something didn't seem right to him. Dominic had gotten awfully quiet and the coloring in his face seemed to have almost turned green. He was rocking back and forth in an unsteady motion. Ernie checked the cigar Dominic was smoking, and realized it was three quarters gone!

"Watch out!" Ernie shouted as Dominic's body began to convulse and shake. He dropped the cigar and grabbed his stomach. The vomit spewed out like an opened fire hydrant in summer. The combination of cheap whiskey and beer with the cheap cigar that he had been inhaling like a vacuum cleaner caught up to Dominic. The nasty puke went flying everywhere! He heaved a few more times and then walked over to the side of the house, leaned his back against it, slid down to the ground, and sat in a daze.

Andy ran into the house and came back with paper towels, a pitcher of water, and Trish's cologne spray. He handed the paper towels to Dominic but he couldn't even hold on to them.

"Here give me those," commanded Denny. Denny bent down and began to clean Dominic up.

"Hey, Denny and Andy stay out here with him, the rest of us are going to get back inside with the girls. We don't want them to get nervous or upset." Ernie nodded to Denny to confirm he was on board with his plan.

Denny nodded his head in agreement. "Yeah, go ahead, Ernie, that makes sense. If we can get Dominic cleaned up then we'll come back in."

"He really wreaks of vomit," commented Andy. "Let me spray some of this on his shirt." He sprayed Dominic a couple of times with the cologne, and then went to join the others inside.

"Dominic, can you hear me? How are you feeling?" Denny asked.

"Is he OK?"

Denny looked up to see who was asking. It was Harry Donaldson.

"I think the empty stomach, whiskey, beer, and cigar were not what the doctor ordered," replied Denny. "It's still early and he's in no shape to go inside or go home. Any ideas?"

Harry thought for a moment. "Yeah, let me go inside and make a phone call. I will be right back."

Denny stayed with Dominic and in a few minutes Harry returned.

"OK, he's on his way. How's he doing?"

"He's not doing too well. Probably dehydrated. Who is on his way?" Denny asked.

"Brother Corwin."

Denny reacted. "Brother Corwin? Freaking Brother Corwin? Why did you call him?"

"Because I knew he would come. He said he'll be right over and take care of Dominic."

Sure enough, within twenty minutes, a brown Ford Fairmount pulled up in front of the house. Brother Corwin hopped out of the car and hurried over to the spot where Denny and Harry stood waiting with Dominic, who was still sitting on the ground.

"Hey, Harry, got over here as fast as I could. Hello, Dennis, how are you this evening?" Brother Corwin knelt down next to Dominic. "How are you feeling, little brother, can you hear me?"

Denny bristled at being addressed as Dennis, especially since Corwin meant it to be condescending. His first impulse was to punch him in the mouth but he contained himself.

"Help me get him into the car, if you would, gentlemen." Corwin stood up. Harry and Denny each took hold of Dominic under his arms and lifted him to his feet. They guided him over to the car, where Brother Corwin had already opened the passenger side front seat door. They managed to get Dominic into the car, and Corwin closed the door.

"Thank you, gentlemen. Harry, you did the right thing calling me. Dominic owes you one." Harry just nodded.

"Where you taking him?" asked Denny, his suspicious tone barely hidden.

"Why so concerned, Massilli? If you were so concerned about your friend he wouldn't be in this condition, now would he? Or were you planning on going for a skinny dip after this?" Corwin snickered.

Harry interceded. "It's alright, Denny. Brother Corwin will get Dominic cleaned up and take him home."

"That's right, Harry, I will. I will take care of my friend. Our friend— don't you worry, *Den-knee*." Brother Corwin let out a guffaw and made his way around to the driver side of the car, jumped in, and drove away.

"That mother—"

"Come on, Denny, let's go inside and get something to eat." Harry took Denny by the arm and pulled him toward the house as Denny watched the car carrying his friend disappear into the night.

DOMINIC COULD BARELY OPEN his eyelids—they felt like they were stitched closed. Finally, with a great deal of effort he forced them open. He took a deep breath and was immediately repulsed by the combined odor of stale vomit, cheap perfume, and god-awful coffee breath. His eyes came into focus and he recognized the source of the coffee breath: Brother Corwin, who was straddled next to him in the car, stroking his forehead and hair.

"Nice nap, little brother? How you feeling?"

Dominic immediately sat up and pulled his head away from Corwin's hand.

"Wh— where are we?"

"We're in the Burger King parking lot, where you've been sleeping for a while. You passed out. Here, take this soda—it will make you feel better." Brother Corwin handed him a large fountain soda cup with a straw already in it, then reached his hand to the dashboard for his cup of coffee.

"What were you drinking tonight?"

"Just some beer."

"Just beer?"

"And a couple of shots. I don't think it was the drinking that got me sick, though." Dominic finished the soda.

"Well, from the smell of you, you were either cleaning a chimney or sucking down a stogie. Do you need another soda?"

"I'm good, I feel better. What time is it?"

"It's around 11."

"Wow, it's that late. Brother Corwin, do you think you can take me home now? I'm sure my mom is wondering where I am. I was supposed to be home at 10. I'm in enough trouble as it is."

"Sure, little brother, let's get you home." Brother Corwin finished off his coffee and tossed the empty cup out the window. He started up the car and quickly peeled out of the parking lot.

Dominic still felt ill. But he wasn't sure if it was from being sick or waking up in the car with Brother Corwin. He stared out the window, trying to avoid eye contact whether directly or indirectly with the driver of the vehicle.

"So, little brother, do you know how lucky you were tonight?" Brother Corwin had to look past his hurt feelings and redeem his good standing with Dominic.

Dominic answered, "What do you mean? I don't feel very lucky."

"Oh, but you should. You see, in your state of mind, or the condition you were in, you could have left that party, walked out into the street, and easily been hit by a car. I mean, it's a Friday night in a city, albeit a small one. You and your friends are not the only ones who are drinking to excess tonight. The only difference is you and your friends can't drive. Think about it."

Dominic slightly turned around, giving consideration to Brother Corwin's words.

"Or you could have just tripped and hit your head on the pavement and cracked your skull open. Or any number of things inside that's girl's house. Think of all the problems that would have caused for a lot of people. All because you listened to your so-called friend Denny Massilli." Brother Corwin held his breath.

"It isn't Denny's fault."

"You say that, but Denny didn't call me. Harry did. As a matter of fact, Denny tried to stop Harry from calling me. This was obvious from the hostility Denny expressed toward me when I arrived to help. You see, little brother, you have to be careful about your friends. They don't always have your best interests in mind. I'm sure your parents never found out about the stupid stunt you and Denny performed at that party at Harry's house. I know that was all Denny's doing. I can't imagine what your mother and father would have had to say about that incident. Take that time and tonight, and I'm fairly confident Salvatore Manterra the Sicilian would be extremely angry. And your mom—"disappointed" and "heartbroken" are the best words I could come up with to describe her reaction." Brother Corwin paused and kept looking straight ahead.

Dominic was thinking hard about the course of events. He didn't agree with Brother Corwin at all that Denny was to blame. Dominic chose to do the things he did—Denny didn't force him. But Dominic did agree that his parents' reaction if they knew about these two incidents would be severe and consequential. Dominic's demeanor softened. Out of the corner of his eye, Brother Corwin watched the shift and smiled.

"Brother Corwin, thanks for coming tonight and picking me up. I owe you big time. You're right, Harry really did look out for me. I'm not sure about Denny though. Denny would never do anything to hurt me, I know that for sure. I will talk to him about it. But either way, thank you very much."

"No problem, little brother. That's what I'm here for." Brother Corwin sighed. Not a total victory but definitely a major win.

The car pulled up in front of Dominic's house. Dominic again thanked Brother Corwin and quickly got out of the car and headed around to the back door of the house. His only hope was that his mom had gone to bed and he could sneak in undetected.

No such luck.

Iolanda Manterra was up and waiting, sitting in the living room, the reading light next to her on, and her Holy Bible in her lap.

"Dominic, is that you?" she asked. Dominic had tried to beeline it to the stairs but stopped cold once he heard his mother's voice.

"Oh, hi, Mom, didn't see you up. Sorry that I'm a little late. We were having so much fun, didn't realize the time. It won't happen again."

"I was worried, son. But I'm glad you're home safe."

"Me too. Again, sorry about being late. I'm really tired. I'm going to head up to bed. Good night." Dominic went to go up the stairs.

"Wait, Dominic." His mother put her Bible on the side table and stood up. She walked over to her son. "Give me a kiss good night." Dominic went to kiss his mother's cheek and she grabbed hold of him and began to breath his hair and his neck and shoulder.

"Dominic, did anything happen tonight? Were you *with* anyone?" she asked with a serious concern in her voice.

"No, Mom, I was just with the guys. We played some pool and board games, had something to eat. If you smell smoke, it's because the parents smoke in the house."

"It's not the smoke I'm worried about. Remember, Dominic, your body is the temple of the Holy Spirit. Don't ever forget that." She let go of her son.

"I won't, Mom. Sorry again. Good night." And he scurried up the stairs.

DOMINIC STOPPED AT Brother Corwin's classroom after school.

"Hey, Dominic, how are you feeling?"

"Good, Brother Corwin, thanks. I just wanted to thank you again for last Friday night and helping me out. It's much appreciated."

"No problem, little brother. Everything go alright when you got into the house?"

"Yes, I apologized to my mom for being late. She seemed OK with it. But then when I was saying good night to her, she was like sniffing me up, and then started mentioning to me that my body is the temple of the Holy Spirit. I didn't think I still had the smell of alcohol on me."

Brother Corwin guffawed. "Oh, little brother, it wasn't the liquor she smelled on you. It was the cologne she got a whiff of. It was the fact that you smelled like a New Orleans whorehouse. She suspected you had been with a girl."

Dominic thought for a moment. "I doubt very much, Brother Corwin, that my mother has ever been in a New Orleans whorehouse. Or any whorehouse for that matter. Have you?"

Brother Corwin smiled. "No, I would agree that the thought of your mother having anything to do with a house of ill repute would be impossible to fathom. That was just an expression. As for me, the last place you would ever find me is in a whorehouse. You can take that to the bank."

"OK, well thanks again. I have to get to track practice. See you around." Dominic turned and left.

So smart and yet not so smart. Quite a conundrum. Brother Corwin returned to marking papers.

XXV.

JIVE TALKIN'...IN STEREO

Mitchell walked into the room. "You ready? Or did you forget?"

"No, I didn't forget. I'm ready." Dominic closed the book he was reading and jumped up.

It was the weekly meeting with Father Bumbry for the Youth Ministry. They got into Mitchell's Plymouth Duster to drive over to St. Mary's.

"Who you going to the concert with? Besides you and Arnie," Mitchell asked.

"I asked Brother Corwin," Dominic replied.

"Brother Corwin? Why didn't you ask Timmy?"

"I did. He couldn't make it. Then I asked Brother Corwin. Why?"

"I don't know if that was a good idea. Does Arnie know?"

"Not yet. I was going to tell him tonight." Dominic thought it was kind of amusing that Mitchell called Father Bumbry by the nickname Arnie. Most of the college kids referred to Father Bumbry that way. Dominic was sort of just getting used to calling him Father Arnold. "Why isn't it a good idea?"

"I don't think the parish priests and the clergy that belong to specific Orders actually get along that much. And then when you add the priest

versus brother factor, the priests think they are somewhat superior—
the power to render sacraments and all, there's probably some degree of
rivalry."

"Maybe you're right, but they're both my friends. I don't think it will
be a problem," countered Dominic after considering his brother's words.

"I've been meaning to talk to you about Arnie anyway."

"What about him?" asked Dominic.

Mitchell sighed and his face grew serious. "I need you to be, uh, careful with him." Dominic waited for his brother to continue but several
minutes passed without a word, although he noticed Mitchell's face con-
torting into a series of anguished expressions. Finally, Dominic broke
the silence. "Is that it?"

Mitchell released a big sigh. "Not really, but I don't want to go into
too much detail."

"Mitchell, you can't just make a statement like that and then not say
anything else! What would I need to be careful about?" Dominic sounded
worried. Mitchell glanced at his brother to size up just how much he
could say to him. After some consideration, he made his decision.

"Look, I overheard Jack and David talking about Arnie. I didn't give
it much thought at the time, first because I wasn't very interested anyway, and then their worldview can be somewhat old-fashioned at times."

"Really? I always found them to be more liberal in their thinking.
Dad certainly thinks so," interjected Dominic.

"On certain things, maybe. Look, Arnie's been around for a couple of
years and we've been very involved with him not only on this committee
but on a social basis, especially you. I mean, he's practically at the house
three times a week for breakfast. Between him and Jon Jasper, it's like
Mom has two additional sons now. Although I don't mind Jon being
there. Anyway, I'm beginning to notice things that are giving me second
thoughts on what I overheard them say." Mitchell slowed down his
driving as he was close to St. Mary's and wanted to finish the conversation
first, before they arrived. Dominic had listened to what his brother had

said but wasn't sure if he was fully grasping it. He realized there were some key details missing.

"I hear you but I don't hear you. You have to tell me what you heard Jack and David talking about, because that's obviously what's driving your concerns, I'm guessing?" Dominic waited for more information.

"OK, but I don't want you to freak out or anything," Mitchell had pulled off to the side of the road by the church, letting the car idle instead of pulling directly into the schoolyard parking lot. Dominic twisted his body around and leaned back against the passenger door so he could face his brother. Mitchell was tapping the top of the steering wheel with his left hand while his right hand rested on the front seat. He turned his head and looked at his brother Dominic as he chose his next words.

"Look, it seems that when Arnie was born, his mom had wanted a girl. She already had three sons and so was really hoping for a girl." Mitchell paused. Dominic nodded to signal for him to go on. "Of course, she has Arnie and he's a boy."

"Well, she had a fifty-fifty chance," chuckled Dominic, "so back to the drawing board, as they say!"

"Just listen, OK? This isn't the time for your funny comments. I'm being serious here." Mitchell was clearly uncomfortable with what he had to say and Dominic sat up as he realized this wasn't just any information. Mitchell continued. "So instead of accepting that reality that Arnie was a boy and not a girl, she decided to treat him like a girl."

"How the hell did she do *that?*" exclaimed Dominic.

Mitchell couldn't help but grin a bit as he said his next words. "She dressed him in girl's clothes and I guess gave him dolls and tea sets to play with." Mitchell's face broke out into a broader grin as he thought of their dad and his mannerisms. Their dad was a man's man—not a feminine bone in his body. Mitchell waited for Dominic's reaction.

For his part Dominic didn't really know what to think—but his mind was quickly processing the revelation, putting it through the steps of analysis that Dominic had employed for his whole life thus far, keeping in mind what Miss Svarickova had shared with him years prior.

Mitchell spoke up. "Well, what are you thinking?"

"Huh?" answered Dominic, still entrenched in his own thoughts.

"What do you think of what I just said? About Arnie?"

"Oh, uh, um, not exactly what I expected you to say although I didn't really have much to go on. I was originally thinking more along the lines of maybe he was pocketing half the Sunday basket collection. You know the old absconding with the church funds cliché."

"I don't think he would do that," replied Mitchell.

Dominic smiled. He didn't think so either.

"That's it?" asked Mitchell. Dominic sighed, having finished processing the information.

"The way I see it is that his mother did something that wasn't right. If anything, it was unfair, really unfair to Father Arnold. He was just a kid so it wasn't like he had any choice or was the one instigating the whole thing. I mean, he was a victim of a selfish mother who only cared about what she wanted. You can't blame Father Arnold for that, not at all. Don't get me wrong, it's not an ideal experience or one that I would consider normal—eh, there's a better word than that—"

"No, it's not normal!" interjected Mitchell.

"What is normal, Mitch?"

"That ain't!"

"No, I mean, you're right but that's not a...kind way of expressing it. Wait. Let's say it wasn't healthy. That's better and more accurate." Dominic was pleased with his reasoning it out.

"Abnormal, not healthy, whatever, the bottom line is that it's screwed up and you can't tell me it doesn't have an effect on somebody." Mitchell was a little hostile in his tone.

"No argument there, Mitch, but what's this have to do with me anyway?" asked Dominic.

Mitchell sighed and gazed at his little brother with a concerned expression, "Nothing really, Dominic. It's not your issue in the overall scheme of things. I guess I just want you to be a little less book smart about things and more street smart. Not everything in life is found between the covers of a book. And sooner or later, you're going to have to get your nose out of the pages before someone shuts that book hard on your nose and draws blood while you're looking down."

Dominic nodded his head. "OK, Mitch, I will." With that, his brother pulled away from the curb, turned the corner, and entered the school-yard, parking over by the barn-house.

THE MEETING BROKE UP a little early and Mitchell was glad since he had some work to do for his college courses. As he had spent most of the weekend working at his job in Brooklyn at the residence for the adults with special needs, he hadn't had any time to complete all of his assignments. As they got ready to leave, Father Bumbry signaled to them to hold on for a moment.

"My favorite people—the Manterra brothers!" he gave Mitchell a pat on his back and reached out his other hand to Dominic, who shook it with his own. "So, how goes it, boys? Mitch, did you change your mind about the concert?"

"Sorry, Arnie, I would have really liked to go but it doesn't fit in with my game schedule."

"That's disappointing to hear. Dominic, did you ask Timmy, then?" Mitchell shot his brother a glance and then looked away.

"Yes, Father Arnold, I did ask Timmy," began Dominic who lowered his eyes as he continued, "but Timmy can't make it so I had to ask some-one else."

"Oh, that's too bad about Timmy. Who did you ask to go then—Ernie?" Father Bumbry was hoping it was not that Denny kid—he al-ways had a bad vibe around him.

"Uh, no, I, uh, asked Brother Corwin if he wanted to go," Dominic replied. Mitchell observed Father Bumbry's face and, noting the reaction, shot an "I told you so" look to Dominic and managed to slip away to go talk to another committee member.

"Brother Corwin? Uh, why, um, why didn't you ask one of your other friends?" stammered Father Bumbry.

"I did ask one of my other friends—Brother Corwin is my friend just like you're my friend," answered Dominic.

"Yes but, uh, I mean, didn't you want to take one of your school chums with you—Ernie or Marco...or even Denny?!" Father Bumbry realized he was grasping at straws.

"Well, not everyone is a fan of the Bee Gees, Father Arnold," Dominic quietly replied.

Hearing his first name again softened the news for Father Bumbry and he relented in dropping the point. "Well, OK, so Brother Corwin it is," he sighed.

Dominic smiled in relief. "Good! Brother Corwin said since you got the tickets, he will be glad to drive us into the city and cover for pizza before the concert."

"Oh, isn't that just special..." was all that Father Bumbry could muster.

ON THE DRIVE HOME, Mitchell listened to the radio and Dominic sat thinking about what they had discussed earlier and Father Arnold's reaction to him asking Brother Corwin to go. The week before, when Dominic had provided Brother Corwin the details on the concert, Dominic recalled that Brother Corwin had his own sort of reaction.

> "You mean these aren't your tickets?" asked Brother Corwin.
> "No, they aren't, but I never said they were my tickets," replied Dominic.
> "OK, so who all is going to this concert then?"
> "It will be you, me, and Father Bumbry."

"And, uh, Father Bumbry knows about this? About me going?" asked Brother Corwin.

"No, not yet. I didn't want to tell him until you decided on whether you wanted to go or not," answered Dominic.

"Yes, of course." Brother Corwin grinned.

"You two know each other, right?"

Brother Corwin's grin spread across his face as he let out a deep-bellied guffaw. "Oh yes, I know Father Bumbry, or as the saying goes, I know of him. You believe he will be alright with your choice of, uh…a friend?"

"I'm sure, why wouldn't he be? He said I could ask one of my friends. You're my friend, right?"

Brother Corwin heard the earnestness in Dominic's voice and responded, "Yes, of course, little brother, I am your friend."

"Good. So that means you'll go?"

"Yes, I will go." Thinking quickly, Brother Corwin added, "And you can tell your friend Father Bumbry that since he got the tickets, I will drive us into the city and will also splurge for pizza before the show."

"What are you thinking about?" Mitchell had lowered the volume on the radio, noticing the deep thought his younger brother was engaged in.

"Nothing really," sighed Dominic. "Hey, Mitchell, was there anything else you wanted to tell me?"

"What do you mean?"

"You said that you had noticed things about Father Arnold. Isn't that what prompted you to say something to me in the first place?"

Mitchell was approaching their house. He turned off the radio completely and then pulled up in front and parked the car. "I'd rather not go into any more detail."

"Why not?"

"Because it doesn't really matter and, you know, it's kind of speculative anyway."

"Speculative? You mean subject to different interpretations?" asked Dominic.

"Exactly. In any case, the real point is to be a little more aware of things going on around you, know what I mean?"

"You mean when Mom says 'Be wary as a serpent and harmless as a dove'?"

"Yeah, Dominic, that's a perfect way to describe it. Just promise me you'll do that, OK?"

"Will do, Mitch."

The two brothers went into the house.

"Is tonight the concert?"

Dominic was just finishing transferring items from his locker to his bookbag, when he looked up to answer the question. "Yeah, it is, Denny. Having second thoughts about not going?"

"Not in this lifetime. Though it would be of great entertainment value to be a fly on the wall," Denny sneered, "or a mouse in the corner. Just not the corner pocket, if you know what I mean."

"Ha, Denny, you are a funny son of a gun! A sick son of a gun, but funny," Dominic laughed.

"That I am. Have a good time, anyway."

"Thanks, I hope to. I've always enjoyed their music and not for nothing, they've owned the Top Ten. I mean, for how long?"

"*De gustibus non est disputandum!*" Denny quickly retorted.

"Ha, touché, old boy!" laughed Dominic. He leaned over to check the wall clock on the nearest classroom across from where they stood. "Crap, I gotta get moving here. I will see you tomorrow, Denny." Dominic closed the locker door and placed his lock in it, clicked it, twisted the face knob, and then gave it a pull. He picked up his bookbag, tossed it on his shoulder, and started off for Brother Corwin's classroom. Denny watched him go down the hallway a bit.

"Hey, Nicky boy," he called after Dominic. Dominic halted his progress and turned around. "Hey—from one mouse to another—beware *anguis in herba.*"

Dominic gave him a puzzled look, shrugged, and went on his way.

WHEN DOMINIC ARRIVED AT Brother Corwin's classroom the teacher was sitting at his desk in a suit jacket tapping his thumbs on the desk.

"Ready when you are, Brother Corwin." Dominic gave the thumbs up. Brother Corwin smirked and jumped from the desk, swinging a set of car keys, thinking to himself, *If only that were true, little brother.*

They drove over to St. Mary's rectory to pick up Father Bumbry. On the ride over, Dominic sat in the front seat but he mentioned to Brother Corwin that he would jump in the back seat when they got to the rectory.

"Hmmm, makes sense. Not sure Father Bumbry will be so comfortable back there," Brother Corwin remarked. They arrived at St. Mary's and Brother Corwin pulled the car into the schoolyard and hung a right into an open parking space near the back entrance to the rectory. Father Bumbry came right out of the back door and down the steps. He halted his steps in front of the Ford Fairmount, giving the vehicle the once over as Brother Corwin rolled down his window.

"Hallo, Father Bumbry!" called out Brother Corwin. Father Bumbry abandoned his assessment of the car and acknowledged Brother Corwin's greeting with a faint smile as he noted Dominic sitting in the front seat. Father Bumbry stretched his neck to have a peek at the back seat and thought better of the whole arrangement.

"Excuse me, Brother Corwin, would you mind terribly if I drove us in? I know you said that you would do us the honors but I'd feel a lot more comfortable if we took my car. Thanks so much." Without waiting for a response, Father Bumbry walked over to his car. Brother Corwin let go one of his low-belly guffaws as he rolled up the window. "Looks like

Father Bumbry wants to take his wheels, little brother, so out we go."
Dominic got out of the car and walked around to Father Bumbry's vehicle.

"You can get in the front seat, Dominic." Father Bumbry pointed to
make sure the instruction was clear. Brother Corwin closed his car door
and locked it while looking at Father Bumbry. The two clergymen made
eye contact, Father Bumbry with a stern and disapproving look and
Brother Corwin just looking chagrinned. "I'm sure Brother Corwin
doesn't mind riding in the back seat, do you, Brother Corwin?" Father
Bumbry sat down in the driver's seat without waiting for a response.

The ride over to the city was mostly quiet with Father Bumbry playing a cassette tape of the *Saturday Night Fever* soundtrack, which filled
the conversational void a bit. There was a certain degree of uneasiness on
Father Bumbry's part, but Dominic was basically oblivious to it while
Brother Corwin was enjoying the younger priest's discomfort. Once in
the city, Father Bumbry found a parking garage relatively close to the
Garden and they headed to Pizza Suprema for a slice. Brother Corwin
pulled out his wallet to pay.

"Are you sure you can cover this, Brother Corwin? I don't mind picking it up," offered Father Bumbry.

"That's alright, Arnold, I think I can manage it," Brother Corwin
swiped the check off the table, "and feel free to call me Willie—no need
to be so formal."

Father Bumbry winced at Brother Corwin's snideness. He was red-
faced with the combination of anxiety and frustration that he was trying
his best to hide, but his resentment of Brother Corwin's presence was
hard to control. For his part, Brother Corwin was fully aware of Father
Bumbry's sentiments—and not just towards him. The Apostle of St.
Mary was enjoying the experience of poking the rotund priest with verbal pinpricks and challenging his every opinion in front of Dominic. He
especially liked countering each of Father Bumbry's "my sons" with his
own "little brother." For Dominic, the evening had gone off without a
hitch. The ride in was met with little traffic, the pizza was very good,

and they were now heading to the Garden for his first ever concert with two close friends.

The concert was quite entertaining. The Bee Gees put on a tremendous performance with older brother Barry carrying the bulk of the showmanship. The stage, lighting, and musical numbers were spectacular and the crowd responded with adulation and applause throughout the night, joining in on the singing when the group sang a long medley of their older hits from the sixties. Dominic, sitting in between the two clergymen, noted that each of them sang along during this segment, and each one seemed to sing louder and louder. Dominic thought it amusing as both sounded fairly off-key. After the encore, they trudged along with the rest of the concert goers down the levels of the Garden, with the crowd excitedly discussing the night's performance. As for Dominic, although he felt an adrenalin rush during the actual performance, he was beginning to run out of steam.

Father Bumbry noticed the tiredness setting in. "Don't worry, my son, I'll have you home in no time. As a matter of fact," Father Bumbry glanced at Brother Corwin, "I'll drop you off first on the way back." Father Bumbry smiled thinking that he may have lost the evening's battles but he was going to win the war after all. Brother Corwin called in an airstrike, however.

"We'll still need to go back to the rectory first, Arnold. Dominic left his bookbag in my car." Brother Corwin flashed a grin at Father Bumbry.

"I don't believe that will be necessary—certainly Dominic can pick up his bag in the morning at school before his first class. Let's be serious, he's not going to do any schoolwork tonight."

Dominic spoke up. "I need to get my bookbag, Father Arnold. I have some papers in there that my mom has to sign and they are due tomorrow. And I do have some stuff to get done for tomorrow's classes anyway. It's OK though. I will take the back seat and catch some z's on the drive home."

Father Bumbry grimaced. Not only was he thwarted on the driving arrangement but he had to endure this gnome-like fiend in the front seat on the ride back. Brother Corwin simply basked in the glow of his victory over the priestly fop.

Dominic was stretched out on the back seat of the car, fast asleep before the car even left the parking garage. Brother Corwin peered over his left shoulder to look in on the sleeping youth. Father Bumbry had his eyes on the road but snuck a peek at Brother Corwin from the corner of his right eye. He could see the Apostle of St. Mary smiling and admiring Dominic as he slept. Brother Corwin became conscious of the priest's observation and, wiping the leer off his face, sat up straight in the passenger seat.

"Dominic speaks very highly of you, Arnold." Brother Corwin sought to ease the tension.

"Oh really, does he now? Funny, he never mentions you at all," countered Father Bumbry.

"Well, we probably have a different type of relationship than you two have, more like brothers." Brother Corwin maintained a cool demeanor, choosing to ignore the bait. "Obviously, you represent more of a...uh... father figure to him." Brother Corwin laced his words with just a hint of contempt for the parish priest." Although a mother figure would be a more apt role."

Father Bumbry looked in the rearview mirror and caught a partial glimpse of his own smiling face. "You're probably right about that, Br— sorry, how did you prefer to be addressed? Oh, that's right, Willie—as I was saying, *Willie*, you're probably right about that as a mother figure just wouldn't fit you at all, from what I know about your, uh, family background." Father Bumbry let out a heavy sigh. Brother Corwin bit his lower lip as he turned to look out his passenger side window as they exited the Lincoln Tunnel and headed toward the turnpike.

They pulled into the schoolyard at St. Mary's and by that time Dominic had awoken. His power nap seemed to have energized him as he was now wide-eyed and talkative. They all got out of the car and Dominic thanked Father Bumbry for the tickets and for driving. He gave Father

Bumbry a hug good night as was now their customary greeting and goodbye ritual. Father Bumbry looked over Dominic's shoulder and right at Brother Corwin during the brief embrace, giving the Apostle of St. Mary a slight smirk. Dominic walked around to the passenger side of the Ford Fairmount and gave Father Bumbry a final wave good night and got in the car. Father Bumbry stood face to face with Brother Corwin and for a moment the two men of the cloth sized each other up.

Finally, Brother Corwin spoke, "Thanks for the experience, Arnold. See you around."

Father Bumbry smirked. "Good night, Willie boy. Be sure to get Dominic home safe and sound. It's a school night, you know." Father Bumbry turned and climbed up the stairs to the rectory.

As Brother Corwin navigated the streets back to Dominic's house, he looked over at Dominic, who seemed to not be showing signs of sleepiness. "How you doing over there, little brother?" he asked.

"I'm fine. It will be good to get home though. It's late."

"Yup, have you home in no time. Watching you sleep in the back seat on the way home from the city reminded me of something that I saw returning to the residence late one night a few years ago."

"Oh, what was that?" asked Dominic as he looked out the window calculating the minutes to get back to his house. He had to go to the bathroom.

"I was living in Chicago at the time. I was walking back to the brothers' residence late one night and was walking by an alley when I thought I heard a commotion of some sort. At first, I thought I better just keep walking but then wondered if maybe someone was in trouble and might need my help." Brother Corwin paused for a moment. Dominic leaned forward a bit trying to quell the urge to go to the bathroom. "I stopped and started to quietly make my way down the alley a bit when I saw two men." Again, Brother Corwin paused. Dominic was straining at this point, coping with the urge to go, now wishing he had asked Father Bumbry if he could use the bathroom at the rectory. Brother Corwin continued.

"Well, there were two men but one of them was on the ground. At first I didn't know what was wrong with him but then I realized he wasn't conscious."

"Was he dead?" Dominic asked.

"No, no, I don't believe so. Probably just passed out, maybe drunk."

"How do you know that?"

Brother Corwin was nearing the corner of Dominic's house, and slowed down a bit. "From what the other fellow was doing. Well, doing to him."

"What do you mean?" asked Dominic, his sides now aching.

Brother Corwin made a turn at the corner. "While the first man was passed out on the ground, the second man had pulled down the first man's pants and underwear and was giving him a blow job."

Brother Corwin did a U-turn on the side street and pulled up in front of Dominic's house. Dominic was hunched over and quiet. He didn't say anything. Brother Corwin spoke softly now. "I was standing there watching while the second guy sucked the dick of the man passed out on the ground."

Dominic grabbed his bookbag with one hand, put his free hand up to the door latch, and pulled on it. It didn't work. He remembered he had to unlock the door first and put his hand back to pull up the pin. He then pulled the latch and opened the door. Without looking at Brother Corwin he said, "Thanks for the ride, Brother Corwin. Good night." Dominic climbed out and as he closed the passenger door, Brother Corwin called to him, "Good night, little brother!"

Dominic hurried toward the house. He didn't have to go to the bathroom anymore but felt like he was going to be sick.

Brother Corwin watched Dominic disappear around the side of the house. He pulled away from the curb and headed back to ASM.

Sweet dreams, little brother! he thought to himself.

XXVI

APOSTLES OF ST. MARY

Dominic stored his books inside his hall locker and secured it. He glanced at his watch and still had about five minutes to make it to the gymnasium for the school mass scheduled for 10:30. He figured he'd get a candy bar from the vending machine. He headed down the hallway flooded with bodies trying to drop off their books and make it to the gym as well. A familiar face made eye contact with him and the face immediately lit up with a big smile.

"Manterra! Hey, come over here!"

The face belonged to Mr. Phil Capparino, one of the kindest teachers and individuals Dominic had ever met in his life. Mr. Capparino was his homeroom teacher his freshman year and being part of "Capparino's Crusaders" was what made the first year at ASM so much fun. He was also the track coach and really saw his role not only as a sports leader but as mentor and role model. He was genuinely enthusiastic about life and always doing the right thing. Mr. Capparino was the shining example of being the nicest guy in the room—and it didn't matter where you finished, as long as you gave it your best and treated everyone fairly. Like his brother Jack, Mr. Capparino had been at the Novitiate in Esopus with plans to becoming a Brother of the Order but left to get married instead.

"Hey, Mr. Capparino, how's it going?" Dominic made his way over.

"Good, good, Nick. Hey, I was looking for someone to do a reading at today's mass. I remember you were in the Scholastic Olympics a couple of years ago, right? Standing up in front of an audience is no challenge for you. You can do a reading, right?"

"Sure, Mr. Capparino, I can do a reading for you if you want. Do you have a copy of the reading?"

"I have it with me here." Mr. Capparino handed him a book. "I don't know if you're familiar with that book but it shouldn't be difficult, it's a quick read. You can just take a seat with the other students and Brother Salmon will call you up to the podium. OK?"

"Yes, sir. I will do my best."

"Thanks, Nick, I wouldn't expect anything less." Mr. Capparino gave him a pat on his back and hurried off. Dominic looked at the green cover of the book with a picture of a little boy and tree and a black and white photograph of a strange looking dude on the back. He smiled and made his way to the gym.

THE GYM WAS FILLED with the entire ASM student body. Brother Salmon, who was assisting Father Guggliocello with the officiating at the mass, stood at the podium ready to call upon the next speaker.

"Now, Dominic Manterra will come up and read *The Giving Tree* for us. Dominic, please." Brother Salmon waited a moment while Dominic made his way from his seat at the back of the assembly before sitting down. As Dominic passed by his fellow students, he heard their mocking comments and snickers. Dominic reached the podium, placed the book down on it, and thought of the sage advice of Sister Margaret: he took a few deep breaths, stood up tall, looked around at all the students and faculty sitting before him—and took a pass on imagining the status of their clothing wear. He began to read.

"*The Giving Tree* by Shel Silverstein. 'Once there was a tree...'"

Four minutes and fifty-two seconds later, Dominic finished with

'...and the tree was happy.' He picked up the book and walked back to his seat. For a few moments, there was complete silence in the gymnasium. Finally, Brother Salmon stirred from his seat and stepped up to the podium to continue the proceedings...

Walking home that afternoon, Dominic explained to Timmy and Ernie how he came to do the reading that morning.

"When I returned the book to Mr. Capparino, he told me that he had never heard anyone read that story like that, he said my rendition was perfect."

Ernie conceded, "To be honest, Nicky, it was pretty damn impressive. There were definitely some tears being fought back throughout the gym."

"I would have given you a perfect score except that you *just had to* do the little shoulder wiggle when the tree stump straightened herself out. Jackass!" Timmy shook his head in disapproval.

All three friends laughed at Timmy's astute observation.

BROTHER TERENCE ST. MICHELLE was a French Canadian with a keen intellect and a keener temper. He had mellowed in his later years, or so the rumors went. This basically meant that he would use an open hand rather than a closed fist to dole out punishment to students who were not paying attention or, worse yet, disrupting his lectures. He gradually toned it down to threatening glares and sharp verbal jabs as he came to accept the changes in student dress, attitude, and intellectual curiosity—all changes for the worse from his forty years of teaching. Brother Terence was not only railing against the decline in Western educational values ("Americans do not know geography! You will know geography!") but also what he regarded as the erosion of the vocational life. Younger brothers who were joining the Order of the Apostles of St. Mary were bringing values and codes that Brother Terence believed were simply out of step with the traditions of the Order and the overall Church that he grew up in and genuinely believed in: traditions steeped in the authority of absolute principles. The new members were vain and arrogant, and much too worldly for Brother Terence's view of a spiritual life. These up and comers were of the "relativity mindset" where all positions—moral or otherwise—were subject to the perspective of anyone and no one in particular. "If it feels good, do it and feel free to do it with anyone you like" was the new Golden Rule—and accountability to anyone, no less a higher being, was not in the modern dogma. To that end, this so-called enlightened new breed of clergy touted a more accessible, universal god, made in their image and more to their liking. Tolerance triumphed over truth because everyone was entitled to a personal version of truth. Brother Terence didn't agree with it, didn't like it, and didn't accept it. Hence, he was reduced to teaching one class, world history, stripped of any and all administrative authority and policy-making. Ignoble gratitude for the years he spent as associate principal and dean of discipline in ASM's neophyte years. But he accepted it as he did derive some degree of satisfaction from identifying bright students who would benefit from his special brand of mentoring. True, they had been scarce in the waning years of his tenure, but the current class appealed to him as it contained a few hopefuls with great potential—namely, Mark Stephens, Dominic Manterra, and James Kurran. These were also the students in the Forensics Club—ASM's speech and debate club—the one student activity for which Brother Terence was permitted to be a faculty advisor. These three boys were intellectually curious, had actually looked at a globe, read maps beyond the New Jersey Turnpike and Garden State Parkway, and each had a fairly advanced wit for his age. In return for the boys' indulging his need for educated and informed dialogue, he escorted them to museums, historical sites, and other places where knowledge and learning were the motivating factors. For their part, the students appreciated and respected Brother Terence's intelligence, knowledge, and insightful stories. Yes, he was stern, but only in the sense that he never compromised propriety. He was the adult, the teacher, and they were the minors, the students. As long as that dynamic was maintained, they reaped the rewards of greater learning and Brother Terence's knack for getting tickets to sold-out exhibits that no one else seemed to get. He sincerely valued and listened to what they had to say.

For their first eligible national debate conference, only Mark Stephens qualified. But in true Brother Terence style, all three of the students were able to attend the conference in Washington, D.C. And in true Brother Terence style, the trip's itinerary was mapped out to include visits to the Smithsonian, the Library of Congress, the monuments, and various government buildings. The accommodations were at the Hyatt Regency and the three boys each had their own room. This was probably the highlight of the trip for Dominic. He had never had his own room in a hotel before, and this one was spectacular. He could practically see all of Washington, D.C. from his hotel room window and he could park a Lincoln Town Car in the bathroom.

On the third morning of the excursion, Dominic was getting ready to attend the Student Congress finals. Mark had presented well in the preliminary sessions and was picked for the final assembly. The four were hoping Mark would deliver well and obtain a trophy. He glanced at the clock on the nightstand and knew he needed to get moving so jumped into the shower. Adjusting the water temperature, he grabbed the bar of hotel soap and lathered up, quickly washing his whole body and face and then rinsed himself. Next, he applied shampoo to his thick head of hair and then leaned his head back under the streaming shower until all the shampoo was washed out. After he turned off the water and pulled back the shower curtain, He went to reach for a bath towel and suddenly stopped.

There he was.

The large mirror across from the shower showed Dominic Manterra in all his youthful glory—his naked body in full reflection before him.

When did I begin to look like this? Dominic thought.

He grabbed a towel and dried himself off. He threw the towel on the floor and ran his fingers through his hair to shape it back, then he stepped out of the bathtub and again caught his reflection in the mirror. Dominic took one last long look at himself and then hurried off to finish getting dressed.

THE SMELL OF DISINFECTANT, sprayed generously to cover the odor of mustiness and staleness that inevitably inhabits old wooden buildings, and yellowed plaster lingered in the air. Dominic strolled through the corridors of the part original, part make-shift additions of the old Featherstone Estate, or as the Apostles and their guests referred to it, Esopus, for the town where it was located. The Catholic Church had purchased the property in the late forties when the great Roman Catholic property acquisition took place in the United States, and had converted it into a Novitiate for young novices of the Order of the Apostles of St. Mary. As the years went on and the Order's recruitment seemed to dwindle, the newer breed of modern Brothers was resistant to their religious vocation and education taking place so far from the hustle and bustle of city life. The property, with its once luxurious mansion, gatehouse, boathouse, and other edifices stretched out across the sprawling Hudson River estate, had begun to show its wear and tear. Its use shifted to being the final weigh station for those Brothers too old to contribute to the cause and those sent there for "rehabilitation purposes." In addition, the Brothers hosted weekend retreats for students from the Order's network of schools, which were "all boys" institutions. In the summer, there were camp programs for disadvantaged and disabled children, for which the Order chose boys from the various high schools to be camp counselors. As an added incentive, the all-girl Catholic high schools, referred to as the sister schools, were also canvassed for female counselors. The requisite representation of nuns was included as well.

Dominic made his way through the long corridor that connected two separate buildings that originally served as living quarters for the hired help and grounds keepers of the old estate. The end of the corridor opened up to a great room that included a stone fireplace against the

back wall, and now served as the recreation room for the camps and retreats. Ping pong and pool tables were spread out across the room as well
as plenty of chairs and tables for arts and crafts and puzzles. One of the
Apostles, Brother Armand, was renowned for his storytelling. With dramatic expression and intonation, he told intriguing tales filled with
mystery and suspense, which enthralled the camp kids and permitted
some of the counselors to catch up on sleep. The occasional counselor's
snore let Brother Armand know that storytelling as an art form was losing its audience.

Dominic walked in on a couple of counselors, including his close
friend Timmy, sitting in the donated easy chairs that were set in a semi-
circle by the fireplace. Other counselors had taken the kids up to the
pool for swim time, so a few were able to catch a short break until a late
afternoon Mass and then supper. Brother Louie Ventinega from Bayonne
Catholic was sitting with the counselors. Dominic sensed a strange air
about him. Dominic noticed an empty chair next to Timmy and plopped
himself in it.

"How goes it?" he asked, with a quick glance and wink at Timmy.

"Just swimmingly," Timmy shot back. "What have you been up to?
Thought you'd be up at the pool?"

"Actually, I am heading up to the mansion to have a chat with Brother
Mac. I'm running a bit late."

"You? Late? Really?" Timmy feigned surprise.

Brother Mac was the nickname for Brother James MacDougal, resi-
dent psychologist, guidance counselor, and coordinator of the peer group
counseling sessions at ASM during the school year. These were basically
quasi group therapy sessions with students for topical discussions of issues and problems that concerned them at this "very impressionable
time" of their lives. Like with so many of the activities or committees
orchestrated by the Order, participants appeared to be carefully hand-
picked. Unlike the apparent idiosyncrasies of other brothers in the
Order, Brother Mac seemed to be legit. Or at least normal, notwithstanding the unkempt hairdo and eyebrows, the accompanying dandruff,

random nose hairs, and frumpy attire. One felt Brother Mac could be trusted.

Dominic sensed an awkward silence and sought to take full advantage of it.

"Did I miss something? Were you guys in the middle of a serious discussion?" he asked with an earnestness that annoyed his peers.

"No, you didn't miss a thing, trust me," quipped Brian Carney, one of the students from Cardinal Mallory High School in Queens, who flipped Dominic the finger from out of Brother Louie's view.

"As a matter of fact, we were heading up to the pool," added Tommy Loudon, another Mallory student. "We'll let you and Timmy continue the fascinating conversation with Brother Louie here.

"Yeah, you Jersey guys can catch-up while we see to the kids. We'll let the Ball sisters know that you guys got tied up." Brian couldn't hide his smirk.

With that, Brian, Tommy and the other Mallory boys got up and quickly made their exit. Dominic and Timmy were left sitting with Brother Louie. Dominic observed that Brother Louie hadn't stopped studying Timmy from the moment Dominic arrived.

"Those are some hairy legs." Brother Louie broke the silence. It was at that moment Dominic realized his sensing of an awkwardness was not imaginary. Timmy was wearing cut-off shorts and indeed had very hairy legs. Dominic and the guys used to kid Timmy that when he got undressed in the locker room, he was wearing a bear skin underneath his clothes. Timmy mumbled a confirmation to the statement. But Brother Louie was not through with his examination and proclamations.

"Is the rest of your body that hairy?" he inquired with a voice that was an odd mixture of innocence and lechery.

Timmy rolled his eyes at Dominic who was doing everything not to bust out laughing. He assessed Brother Louie with his greasy, patted-down red hair, cut short and neat, which contrasted so grotesquely against his pasty white skin, covered with reddish-brown freckles that appeared as if he had been doused with sparkling glitter. The horn-rimmed glasses added to Brother Louie's disturbed and creepy appearance.

"I'd be curious to find out."

The fact that the phrase was on Brother Louie's mind would not have surprised either Dominic or Timmy at this point. The fact that Brother Louie actually expressed it, startled both of them. They were clearly caught off guard, and the mischievous grin that was displayed after the comment only freaked the two friends out even more. Dominic regained his bearings and spoke right up.

"Well, I better get over to the mansion before Brother Mac thinks I've forgotten our appointment. Timmy, they probably need you up at the pool. With the day being so hot, all the kids are swimming and they need another pair of eyes to monitor their safety."

Timmy took the cue and jumped up. "Yeah, you're right. I'd better get up there and make sure the Mallory boys aren't getting overwhelmed. See you guys later." Timmy headed for the nearest exit.

Dominic stood up. "Shouldn't keep Brother Mac waiting any longer. Brother Louie, take it slow there, *hermano*. And just remember, curiosity killed the cat." Dominic bolted before Brother Louie expressed any desire to discuss the finer points of satisfaction.

Dominic made his way to the mansion, circling around the section that held the main kitchen quarters, and walked along the side to the wide portico that overlooked Mansion Hill, and the great lawn that provided a panoramic view of the Hudson River as it tiered down to the boathouse below. The Apostles of St. Mary had set up a row of Adirondack chairs that brought the culture of the Hudson Valley in stark contrast with the grand Renaissance-style architecture that the mansion was originally designed after—Dutch maple meets Italian limestone. This reflection reminded Dominic of what the Apostles of St. Mary had done to the interior of the mansion. Some of the rooms had been converted from their classic Renaissance-style to run-down New Orleans bordello décor. Obviously, some of the Brothers had discovered fluorescent paints in a spray can while drinking one night.

Brother Mac was waiting, sitting in one of the chairs and gazing out toward the river. He smiled and nodded as Dominic approached and sat in the chair next to him.

"Heck of a view. It's always been my favorite spot here, starting when I first came to the Novitiate." There was no trace of annoyance at Dominic being late for their meeting.

"Sorry about the delay. Ran into Tim and some of the Mallory guys, who were chatting with Brother Louie."

"Ah, Brother Louis." Brother Mac let out a sigh that betrayed more than he probably wanted to let on.

"Yeah, I'm thinking of referring to him as Curious George from now on." Dominic chuckled.

"How's that?" Brother Mac inquired.

"Nothing," Dominic replied. "You wanted to catch up on some things with me?"

"Ah, yes, I just wanted to follow up with our last conversation about vocations. As part of my role as the head of the Guidance Department, the consideration of the vocational life for students falls under my purview. It has been my experience, especially with your class, that there is a total lack of interest in what the Church has typically referred to as a calling. I'd be interested in your thoughts, especially in light of your own pursuit of religious and spiritual fulfillment that you have often expressed."

Dominic reflected for a moment as he surveyed the view before him. It was a gorgeous summer day and the Hudson Valley was glistening with verdant colors and a silvery sheen off the river.

"Well, Brother Mac, I can't really speak for my peers and fellow students...."

"No, of course not. I thought maybe you might share some insights just from your vantage point. Would you consider a vocation?"

Dominic paused. He stretched his arms across the broad armrests of the Adirondack chair he sat in, which in the shade of the portico were cool to the touch against his bare skin. He tilted his head to one side, giving real thought to Brother Mac's question.

"For me Brother Mac, it comes down to women. Or more to the point, sex with a woman. I think I would like the vocational life, but I can't see giving up sex. Not that I have any experience in that field but I do plan on it and look forward to it based on the advertising and marketing I have been exposed to so far." The two of them laughed. "With that being said, I know that if I were to join a religious order, even if I took the vow of celibacy, I would still intend to, plan on, and take deliberate steps to have sex with a woman I love. With that being said, there'd be no point for me to really give *the calling* any real thought because I couldn't truly live that lifestyle. If the Church permitted the clergy to marry, then I would certainly consider it. And I believe I'd be more effective at ministering to my flock if I had a female partner at my side."

Brother Mac listened attentively to Dominic without saying a word or betraying a facial expression. He stood up, walked over to a column, and leaned against it, partly to escape the glare of the sun and to collect his thoughts on what Dominic had said.

"Is that the only reason—challenge of celibacy—that is a deterrent for an interest in the clergy life?"

Dominic scratched his head and stared down at the moss and stray weeds that were poking through the cracking stonework of the once magnificent mansion. Thoughts of Brother Louie and his "curious" ways raced through his mind. Of course, Louie wasn't the only cat on the prowl. There were a few faculty—both clergy and not—that were suspected of being curious in their own unique way.

"Well, I wouldn't say that the Order has been attracting the healthiest of men—emotionally and mentally. I mean, you've got clergy who have lost both parents, siblings committed suicide or died under suspicious circumstances, or being raised like a daughter the mother never had—I mean those are some difficult issues to have to deal with no matter who you are. But combine it with the various vows one undertakes in a vocational life, the challenges are daunting, nearly impossible un-less…." Dominic paused.

"Unless?" queried Brother Mac.

Dominic sighed. "Unless one possesses the spiritual awareness and connection to God that is necessary for sustenance and endurance and fulfillment. And to be quite honest with you, Brother Mac, I don't see it in some of these clergy. I can't explain it exactly. This is how I see it perhaps. If these men weren't wearing the clergy garb, if they were just walking around in street clothes and no one knew they were a member of the clergy, would people still be able to know that they were? Is there something about their presence or behavior or speech that would make someone say that they were a brother or a priest? That's probably the best example I can come up with. I could go on but I think that identi-fies the crux of the matter, don't you think?"

Brother Mac dropped his chin to his chest and focused on his worn shoes with an expression that told Dominic that the words he expressed were more an affirmation of suspicions than a surprise. Brother Mac was no dummy—but in Dominic's mind, that only made him a silent en-abler to the hypocrisy that existed.

Brother Mac looked at his watch. "Almost time for Mass. You plan on helping out with communion?"

Dominic shook his head. Father Bumbry had nominated him to be a Eucharistic Minister and though Dominic had gone through the train-ing and induction ceremony, he didn't care for the role all that much. Possibly because he didn't believe in some of the sacraments anymore. Not because he had lost faith in God, not at all. He was just starting to believe that some rituals actually kept people from God instead of bring-ing them closer to Him.

"No, I won't be serving up any flesh and blood today. Probably get a five-mile run in before dinner."

"OK, see you at dinner. Thanks for the chat. It's been enlightening." Brother Mac gave Dominic a pat on the shoulder as he passed him to head up toward the Brothers' residence. Dominic watched Brother Mac make his way around to the front of the mansion until he was out of sight.

Dominic glanced at his shoulder and thought, *I really don't know Brother Mac's personal life story at all. Not at all.*

THE SUN HAD JUST about completed its rising up on a bright and hot August morning. The summer camp season at Esopus had officially ended the day before. Dominic, Timmy and some of the Cardinal Mallory boys had opted to stay over one more night before heading back to their respective homes. Dominic had come up to the pool for a last swim before the group would drive to New Paltz to hit the College Diner for breakfast one last time and then say their goodbyes. He removed his t-shirt and kicked off his flip flops before diving into the pool. He swam to the opposite side of the pool, touched the wall, flipped underwater, and pushed with his feet off the pool wall, swimming back to the other side. His head popped up from under the water and he took a deep breath, his nostrils smelling the chlorine combined with the clean air of the Catskills. Staying above the water, he swam back and forth the length of the pool several times, imagining himself Burt Lancaster in *The Swimmer.*

"Good morning."

The unexpected greeting came out of nowhere and startled Dominic. He glanced around the pool and standing there was a bespectacled, tall, older bearded gentleman with salt and pepper hair. He was wearing a pair of speedos and had a towel tossed over his shoulder. Dominic didn't recognize him.

"Good morning," Dominic returned the greeting.

"I didn't expect anyone up here this early. My name is Brother Leonard Vitale. I just arrived from Rome. Thought I'd get a relaxing swim in before the jet lag catches up with me. I presume you are a holdover from the camp activity. I thought that ended yesterday?"

"Hello Brother, yeah, the camp officially ended yesterday. Some of us counselors decided to stay the night and will be leaving today. I just wanted to get a last swim in before heading back to Rosedale."

"Oh, little Rosedale! Yes, I think I have been there once or twice in my travels. Mind if I join you for a swim, uh, sorry, I didn't catch your name?"

"Dominic. Sure, there's plenty of room in the pool."

"Dominic. Of the Lord. Good to make your acquaintance, Dominic. Thanks for the invite." Brother Leonard dropped his towel on the deck, placed his eyeglasses on top of it, shook off his sandals and dove into the water. He came up for air once he swam to the side of the pool where Dominic was. He stretched his arms out along the side of the pool, and spit out a stream of water like he was a fountain statue. He fixed his eyes on Dominic with an unblinking gaze that unsettled the youth. Dominic thought it best to keep a conversation going.

"Just in from Rome. How was the flight?" Dominic asked the question while swimming to the opposite end of the pool.

"Yes, flew into JFK around two this morning. It was uneventful. After a thousand flights, they all seem the same. The car service brought me up here and lo and behold, a young Adonis is my welcoming party!"

"What is it you do in Rome, Brother Leonard?" Dominic was apprehensive about the possible answer.

"Me? I'm just the Ambassador to the Holy See for the Order of the Apostles of St. Mary. I'm an attorney, an expert in Canon law, the laws of the Roman Catholic Church. You know what that is, I'm sure. Boring stuff." Brother Leonard submerged himself, kicked off the side of the pool, and swam to the spot next to where Dominic was. He rose out of the water and grabbed onto the side of the pool. "How about you? What's a young stud like yourself do for tricks?"

"I'm not a magician, Brother Leonard. Esopus seems a far way off from Rome." Dominic was wary of the stranger. "You just passing through, I guess?"

"Here on business, as the saying goes. But I always like to check in on the old stomping grounds. I used to live here in the early days of the novitiate. The glorious days of the Order I like to say. And you, do you like to swim alone? Do you do it often?"

"Like I said, just getting a last swim in before returning home to Rosedale. Such a beautiful morning in these surroundings, seemed like a shame not to enjoy it."

"I totally agree. Back at the Order's residence outside of Rome, we have a splendid property. Gorgeous grounds with an enormous flower garden, one you can walk around in with such a variety of colors and scents and shapes. It's like a patch of paradise. But the crown jewel of the place is the pool, right next to the garden. I'm talking Olympic size. It's magnificent. On mornings like this the whole house of Brothers gathers for an early swim." While Brother Leonard was speaking, he was treading the water with his outstretched legs, his eyes locked on Dominic.

"Definitely different than what I'm accustomed to. Sounds like a spectacular place, even more than here at Esopus which is pretty impressive. I'm sure the Brothers are grateful for their many blessings, owning so many awesome residences. It must really help reduce the stress from dealing with the poor and homeless." Dominic couldn't resist.

"Do you know one thing that's different when the brothers of the house in Rome gather for our group swim in the morning?" Brother Leonard asked.

Dominic thought *I guess my sarcasm is lost on this audience.* "What's that, Brother Leonard?" Dominic figured he didn't really have to ask he was going to be told anyway.

"We all swim in the nude. It's quite an exhilarating and liberating feeling. Brings one back to the days of the Roman baths, and the Graeco-Roman view of manhood and camaraderie. You know, what they say, when in Rome, do what the Romans do!" Brother Leonard submerged himself into the water than slowly rose to the surface, again spewing out water like he was on display at the Trevi Fountain. He took a deep breath. "Do you like swimming in the nude? You should try it! I can join you if you'd like. One should always be open to new adventures." Brother Leonard shot Dominic a leering smile.

"That's alright, Brother. I follow the Judeo-Christian swimming guidelines and view of manhood and camaraderie. Although if some mermaids or sea nymphs were inviting me for a swim, I might be persuaded." Dominic knew it was time to go.

"Oh, such a pity that I don't have their power of persuasion!" Brother Leonard sounded disappointed.

"Well, thanks for the chat, Brother Leonard. I'll leave the pool all to yourself now and your dreams of Rome." Dominic pushed off the side, swam to the pool ladder, and climbed out, mindful of the eyes watching him.

"I hope I didn't chase you off?" Brother Leonard called out to him.

"No, Brother, I was leaving anyway. Enjoy your swim." Dominic thought to make a wisecrack about pythons in the water but he didn't want to give Brother Leonard any false hopes.

"You went up to the pool? I didn't even hear you get up." Timmy had just finished packing up his duffle bag. "How was it? Looks like a beautiful morning in La-dee-da Estates!"

Dominic chuckled. "Yeah, it was good until Brother Leonard showed up."

"Brother Leonard? Who is he?"

"Let's just say he's the Italian cousin of Brother Louie and leave it at that." Dominic shook his head. "The Mallory boys ready for breakfast? Give me ten minutes and I will be ready to go."

"I think they're down in the breakroom already. We will wait for you there. Don't take too long."

XXVII.

JERSEY GIRL AT THE SHORE

The summer days were winding down and the boys knew it. Returning from their last week as camp counselors at Esopus would now mark the official end of summer for them. In late fall, they could look forward to a camp counselor reunion. They were hanging out near the front steps of Timmy's house, deciding whether they wanted to go to a movie or the batting cages or just hang out and play board games, maybe order a pizza. Ernie was up for the batting cages, of course. Timmy and Dominic were less than enthusiastic about that option just as Ernie had no desire to deal with bankers or generals.

"It's too nice to sit inside the house or even sit inside a movie theater. And it's not even that hot, so air conditioning doesn't even mean much." Ernie was making all solid points, as it was a milder August than usual. Timmy bounced a basketball on the step in between his knees as he sat contemplating their options. Dominic was standing on the side of the steps with his baseball mitt, tossing a hardball back and forth with Ernie, who was standing in the street. Ernie called out to Dominic, "It's coming fast and high!" and he whipped a fastball at Dominic, who caught it in the palm part of the glove.

"Damn, Ernie, what the hell do you eat? That almost broke my hand!" Ernie grinned and walked toward his two buddies.

"I got an idea. It's a great night to go down the shore. I'll ask my old man if he wants to take a ride with us, bring us down to Seaside and we can do the rides and hit the arcades. He can go over to the bar and have a few beers while catching the Yankee game. He'd be doing that at home anyway. He may like the idea to get away from the old lady." Ernie waited for a reaction. Timmy stopped bouncing the basketball.

"I'm in," said Timmy. Dominic nodded in agreement. "Me too. That's a good plan—as long as your dad is up to it."

ERNIE SAT UP FRONT with Mr. Damon, who reminded Dominic of his own father. He had the same kind of build as Mr. Manterra—thick and muscular with a ruggedly handsome face that women believed a real man should look like. Men that carried themselves with a certain style saturated in heat and that oozed raw passion. These men were tough as nails and hard as rock—and women fantasized about being nailed by these rock-hard men in a frenzy of passionate fury. These weren't the pretty boy types with smooth skin and slim stature and sweet talk. No way—these were meat and potato, rolled-up sleeves, anchor and ship tattoos on their arms, rough and tumble, scarred and sunburnt men who worked well with their hands in the shop—and even better in the bedroom. They put on no airs and didn't put up with anyone who did. To Dominic, Mr. Damon would fit right in at the table with his dad and his uncles.

"You boys gotta beautiful night for walking the boards. There should be a lotta skirts tonight for you to chase." Mr. Damon punched Ernie in the arm and gave a quick smile to Timmy and Dominic sitting in back.

"Thanks for taking us down the shore, Mr. Damon," Dominic replied.

"Yeah, thanks a lot, Mr. D.," chimed in Timmy.

"No problem, fellas. Gets me outta the house for some fresh air and some fresh inspiration, if you know what I mean. Hahaha, like the ol' lady says, 'I don't care where you work up your appetite as long as you come home to eat!' He gave a hearty laugh. To Dominic, he always

seemed to be in a good mood. And from what he could tell, he and Ernie's mom had a pretty good relationship. There was always a lot of
back-and-forth good-natured banter, especially when she pretended to
be annoyed with him and gave him a hard time. Eventually she would
break and start laughing along with him because he was too funny. "But
we can't be too late or I'll have to take care of the one-eyed snake on my
own!" he cackled and gave Ernie a backhand on the arm. Ernie laughed
along with him while Timmy and Dominic grinned, both a little embarrassed. Their dads were a little older than Mr. Damon and so not as
free-wheeling in their expression about girls and sex. Ernie was the oldest in his family whereas Dominic and Timmy were lower in age on the
family tree. They both liked Mr. Damon treating them like one of the
boys.

Mr. Damon was lucky to find a parking spot near a local watering
hole that was also across from the beach and boardwalk. The boys got
out of the car on the passenger side and waited for Mr. Damon to come
around to them.

"OK, men, go on over to the boardwalk and have yourselves a good
time. Maybe find yourselves some young honeys to have a couple of
Cokes with." He slipped Ernie a couple of twenty-dollar bills. "Here's a
few bucks to help in the effort." He slapped Dominic on the back. "No
need to be such a Boy Scout tonight, Nicky boy, loosen up a bit. I'd buy
you guys a round or two if I could! Give you guys some beer muscles!"
He laughed. Ernie tried to hand the money back to his dad. "Thanks,
Dad, but we're good..."

"Don't even think 'bout it!" Mr. Damon snapped. "Go on, have some
fun! I'm gonna be in here and have a burger and a couple of drafts, watch
Guidry pitch and see if he and the Yankee bats can beat the odds tonight," he winked, "and I'll see you men in a couple of hours." They
nodded and started to head over to the beach. He called out to them,
"And come back with some numbers, will ya?" Mr. Damon laughed and
entered the bar.

The boardwalk was a swarm of bodies in all shapes and sizes and degrees of dress. Bikini-clad breasts were bouncing and jiggling all over the place and the three boys were wide-eyed and attentive. Though it was already early evening and the sun was fast slipping away, every now and then they'd be awarded a glimpse of a shapely female still sporting only her bikini. Out on the beach itself, there were still quite a few sun-worshippers doing their best to catch every bit of the sun's rays they could. Some of the sunbathers would be making their way off the beach and would stop to rinse the sand off their bodies under the shower-head stations near the ramps leading up to the boardwalk. The three friends took turns playing spotter and being sure to bring especially hot-looking babes to the others' attention. Their heads were spinning with all the semi-clad women surrounding them on all sides. Dominic felt a tinge of sadness as some of the tanned beauties made him think of someone.

A cornucopia of smells filled the air. There was of course the smell of suntan lotions and sunburn creams; there was the competing scents of cheap cologne and perfume versus sweaty body odor; cigarette smoke for sure; sausage and peppers and pizza and burgers and seafood and fried potatoes and onions galore; and a light, refreshing late-August wind carried on itself the ocean and its saltiness so much that Dominic could taste it. The ocean waves were nearly drowned out by the cacophony and din taking place on the boardwalk: the bells and whistles and horns emanating from the rides, punctuated by the riders' screams; the hawkers trying to draw in patrons; the parents cajoling their kids; the teenagers laughing and shouting; the boyfriends and girlfriends sporadically arguing; music blasting from boardwalk bars and gaming arcades; and the vocal exchanges of orders at the food counters of the greasy spoons and ice cream shops that dotted the boardwalk.

The boys tried their hand at shooting hoops, knocking over wooden milk bottles, and tossing bean bags through small holes. They attempted to cover up a flat circle painted on the booth counter with three other smaller discs. The booth operator did it over and over again with the greatest of ease, but the three lads couldn't mimic his act. They played skittle ball and raced through a game of miniature golf. Ernie hit the punching bag and registered *future heavyweight champ* as well as rang the bell on the lumberjack sledgehammer challenge. They decided on some milkshakes and found a bench to sit on that provided the best view of the beach and the babes.

"How much time we got, Ernie?" Timmy asked. He had sucked up his strawberry shake too fast and was hit with a brain freeze.

"We got time, don't worry. I'm sure my old man has made a few friends by now and is busy exchanging war stories." Ernie was fixated on watching the passersby.

"You know, I really believe I could live on milkshakes for my whole life," Dominic commented. "Actually, it's the ice cream. I could eat ice cream for the rest of my life and be fine with that."

"I don't think that would work," disagreed Timmy. "No one can survive on just one thing. Unless of course you're talking about pizza. Pizza might be the exception."

"You're both wrong! Beef. You need beef. Whether it's roasted, grilled, barbecued, stewed, chops, steaks, burgers—gotta have it. Add chicken and pork to that." Ernie spoke authoritatively.

Dominic's straw found the last drop of milkshake, making that air-sucking sound indicating there was no more left. His lips disengaged from the straw and he sighed with satisfaction and acceptance. "Still sticking with ice cream."

"Well, well, what do we have here?" Ernie spoke with a mischievous glee and Timmy and Dominic lifted their heads to see what Ernie had discovered. They looked in his direction but nothing stuck out.

Then Dominic saw her.

Ernie was watching Dominic and realized that he had seen her. "That's right, Nicky boy, if my eyes aren't deceiving me, and by the look on your face, they ain't—I do believe that's Moira Toomey over there by the big wheel game of chance booth, next to the football toss game."

Ernie's eyes were seeing 20/20 as far as Dominic could tell. Yes, that was Moira, and Dominic could already feel the burning sensation in his cheeks. He had not seen her since the cast party fiasco and now here she was, sporting her usual golden tan; her long, gorgeous auburn locks burnished by a summer in the sun.

"You know, Timmy, we didn't see that football toss game before. I think my arm is fairly warmed up by now. I think we might get a stuffed animal out of this joint after all. What do you say?" Ernie grinned and winked as he jumped down from sitting on the back of the bench.

"You've probably got a better chance at the football toss. Anyway, life is about chances, right, Dominic?" Timmy gave Dominic a push in Moira's direction.

"I don't know about this. You know I can just wait here for you two," Dominic stammered. Ernie put his arm around Dominic's neck, drew him in close, and spoke into his ear. "Don't be a dick, that's not gonna happen. Maybe it's time you tried to get a little more of Moira. Let's go."

The three boys began to walk toward the football toss. Dominic's stomach was churning into a knot not knowing what reaction to expect if or when Moira should realize his presence. He was wondering what she was doing as he didn't see any of the usual friends with her and she appeared to be aimlessly standing there. She suddenly went into her shoulder bag as if she remembered she wanted to look for something. As her hand searched, she lifted her head as if drawn to something and looked right at them, right at Dominic. She spotted him! For a moment their eyes met and for Dominic there was no one else on that boardwalk except her and him. Her face immediately conveyed surprise—and if Ernie wasn't pushing him from behind with his strong arm—Dominic would likely have been frozen in his tracks. But then Dominic saw it— albeit for the briefest of moments—that certain flicker of sheer joy in her eyes. He was certain of it. The churning in his stomach ceased for the moment—but only for the moment. Moira's gaze was averted as a tall guy's arm circled around her shoulders and drew her in, placing a kiss on top of her head.

Dominic attempted to halt his forward progress, but Ernie kept his hand on his back and pushed him on. "Steady there, Nicky boy, don't worry, he don't mean nothing to her." Dominic wasn't so sure based on what he'd just witnessed, but Ernie saw the situation differently: Ernie saw Moira's hand go up on the guy's chest and push him away. And Moira wanted to make a quick run for it but Ernie wasn't letting that happen either.

"Well, hello, Moira!" Ernie called out as they drew near to her and her companion. "Small world seeing you down here!"

Moira was trapped and she knew it. "Hey, how are you guys doing? Having a good summer?" Dominic could see she was clearly uncomfortable but didn't know what to make of it.

"We're having a great summer, even better now that we've run into you!" Ernie sounded just like his dad to Dominic. "Ain't ya gonna introduce us?" Ernie nodded toward the guy.

"Oh, sorry, this is my...boyfriend, Trevor. He goes to Christian Brothers Academy."

"Actually, I graduated. Heading down to St. Leo's in Tampa next week. Hey, I remember you—you're on the pitching squad for ASM varsity baseball, right?" Trevor was talking to Ernie.

"Yeah, that's right. They brought me up later in the season," replied Ernie, who was stealthily pushing Dominic in Moira's direction.

"I remember you. We were beating you guys and it was pretty much over when your coach put you in for the last inning." Moira was looking down at the ground, avoiding all eye contact with Dominic. Trevor squeezed Moira's shoulder to draw her attention. "They put this guy on the mound and he strikes out the side. I'm not even sure you threw more than twelve pitches."

"It was ten," Ernie replied.

"I guess the coach should have started you," laughed Trevor.

"I thought so," Ernie shot back. "Well, we won't keep you two. Moira, have a good rest of the summer. Trevor—good luck with the Lions."

"Thanks! Take care, fellas." Trevor turned bringing Moira with him. Moira managed a weak "goodbye" and they disappeared into the crowd.

Ernie hit Dominic in the chest with a back-hand. "Man, I can see why you have the hots for that one—whew, she's a beauty! Nicky, you gotta repeat after me: going to get more of Moira to me! More of Moira to me! Get it?"

"Yeah, but I guess that doesn't really matter," Dominic replied dejectedly.

Ernie made a face. "What are you talking about? You worried about Trevor? Ha, please! Trevor, yeah, right."

Timmy weighed in. "They certainly looked awfully chummy there, Ernie."

Dominic agreed. "I thought so."

"You guys have no idea what you're talking about. No woman wants a man named *Trevor*! What does she call him—Trev? Sounds like a name you give your dog. *Here, Trevor! Come and get it, boy! That's a good Trev!* See what I mean?"

"Yeah, like Dominic is such studly name," countered Dominic.

Timmy opined, "Ernest isn't exactly up there on the manly man list, *Ernie.*"

"Hey!" snapped Ernie, playfully punching Timmy in the arm. "That's my dad's name!"

Dominic spoke up. "Speaking of which, we better head back before he sends out a search party."

"Or gets into a bar brawl, more like it," retorted Ernie. "Not a manly name, why I oughta"—and he threw an air punch at Timmy.

XXVIII.

PLAY ME

I t only seems like yesterday we were standing at this corner," said Ernie. Timmy simply nodded his head while he kept reading the paperback he was holding. "Summer went fast. OK, where is he?"

Timmy looked at his watch. "He's got five minutes. If you're gonna have a meeting time, then that's what everyone gets held to."

"He could try to be here early! He doesn't have to be on time."

"Let's just hope he's on time. That would be a victory." Timmy turned a page in the book.

"What are you reading anyway?" asked Ernie.

"*Cyrano de Bergerac*—sound familiar?"

"No, not really. Should it?"

"It was on the summer reading list. I'm guessing you didn't read it."

"Son-of-a-bitch!" Ernie said and shook his head no.

Timmy closed the book. "Here he comes now. And right on time."

Dominic ran up to his two friends, bent over for a moment to catch his breath, and then stood up and they commenced to walk.

"Nicky—did you finish the summer reading list?" Ernie inquired. "Or had you read them all already?"

"Some of them I got to. Truthfully I hadn't read any of the books on the list. *Candide, Cyrano*, the Oliver Goldsmith one—they were all new to me. I got those read but not the big one."

"*Once and Future King?*" asked Timmy. Dominic nodded.

"Son-of-a-bitch! Why didn't you guys say something?"

Dominic looked at Timmy. "We did. You said you didn't have any time. You were too busy making money," Timmy answered.

"That I did," said Ernie proudly. He worked at his dad's Tool and Die shop and made some serious spending money. "Oh well, *Cliffs Notes* here I come!" The friends laughed. "This is going to be a good year, I have a good feeling about it," Ernie continued. They were walking by Denny's home just as Denny was coming out of the house. Denny's father was in the car waiting for him.

"Hey, Denny!" Dominic called out to him. Denny gave him a wave and a half smile. "Good luck, gentlemen, in the new school year. Don't tell the Apostles I was asking for them, but you can tell them to go to hell for me if you'd like. Or better yet, tell them to go screw themselves! Oh wait, on second thought, they may take that as an invitation." Denny laughed at his own comment. "Hey, Nicky, I'll give you a call sometime, OK?"

"Yeah, Denny, definitely do that!" Dominic gave him a thumb's up and watched him disappear into his dad's car. His dad backed the car out of the driveway and waved at Dominic before pulling all the way out into the street and driving away. While Timmy and Ernie walked on ahead of him, Dominic thought about Denny. His parents had decided that he should transfer to a private school—a more prestigious school. Denny wasn't thrilled about it but he didn't have much of a choice. It was his mother who was pushing it. As a consequence, he had to attend special classes for most of the summer in order to meet certain requirements. Basically, Denny fell off the radar and that made Dominic feel sad, especially seeing his friend just now.

"Hey, Nicky boy, what are you doing back there? We're busy planning your strategy for you here, the least you could do is listen!" Ernie pointed two fingers at his own eyes and then back at Dominic's.

"What strategy is this, Einstein who didn't do any of the summer readings?" Dominic asked.

"Operation Toomey Takeover!"

"Aw, com'on, quit it already, Ernie. She's got a boyfriend. And he drives."

"He's right, Ernie. He can't compete with that," added Timmy.

"Thanks for the vote of confidence there, Timmy."

"No problem, Dominic. Just stating the obvious."

"Alright, Dominic, but that Moira's a beauty, and she ain't gonna wait for you forever. And if memory serves me well, ol' Trev is down in the Sunshine State, and believe me, he ain't just shagging flies in the outfield. The only Moira he's got on his mind is getting more-a the action on campus."

His two friends switched the discussion to the upcoming football season and Dominic returned to his thoughts. He was thinking about Denny, he was thinking about the books on the summer reading list he had left to read, and he was thinking about Moira and hoping Ernie was right.

DOMINIC CHECKED THE bulletin board in the cafeteria, which listed various announcements, upcoming events, and other items of interest. He smiled seeing that an eight-by-eleven poster from the prior year was still on the board. "God don't make no junk!" it said. It made Dominic think of Denny since he was the first one to see it and point out the double negative. He remembered Denny's observation at the time— "That confirms my suspicions all along—the earth is one big junkyard!" Maybe Denny did belong in an elite private school. Dominic found the announcement he was looking for—the audition schedule for the fall play. He wrote down the times on his pad.

"Dominic! How are you, little brother!"

Dominic turned around. He hadn't heard Brother Corwin come up from behind him. "Hey, Brother Corwin, how are you doing? Sorry I haven't had a chance to stop by your classroom to say hello. Been busy with the new classes and soccer."

"Not a problem, just was wondering how your summer went. I see you're thinking about the fall play."

"Yeah, how did you know that?" asked Dominic.

"Because you have the audition times written down on your pad." Brother Corwin grinned and guffawed. Dominic nodded his head. "Have you ever read that play?" he asked Dominic.

"Yes, of course. It's a great play!"

"That it is. I'm sure there's probably a part that Morris can find for someone of your talent."

"We'll see. I will give it my best shot. I have to get to soccer practice, Brother Corwin. I will catch up with you soon."

Brother Corwin watched Dominic walk out of the cafeteria. *I grew a mustache over the summer and Dominic didn't even notice!* He halted his thoughts. *Hmmm, what to do, what to do...I have obviously created some consternation for little brother, which I need to remedy as soon as possible...hmmm, what to do, what to do.* Looking into the bulletin board box, he noticed the poster. "God makes a lot of mistakes, too," he said out loud to himself. Then he caught his reflection in the glass window.

"There you are, Brother Corwin!"

Brother Corwin turned to see the Vice Principal, Brother Ambrose—an exasperated Brother Ambrose at that, approaching him in a harried state.

"I have been looking for you. We have a problem—a serious problem—and I hope you can be of assistance. Do you have some time now to talk?"

"Certainly, Brother Ambrose, as a fellow Apostle of the Order, it is my duty to serve." And he accompanied Brother Ambrose to the administrative offices.

"Thank you very much. I appreciate your taking time to audition and for your fine effort as well. I'll be posting the cast member list and assigned roles by Friday, end of day. I'll be sending a similar list over to St. Mary's Academy as well so it gets posted at the same time. Thanks again." The young lady picked up her things and left the stage. Morris Gavin made some notes before calling out, "Next!"

Dominic walked out on the stage holding an anthology of Shakespeare's plays. He reached the center of the stage and waited for Mr. Gavin to provide further instruction. After a few minutes of waiting, he heard Mr. Gavin address him. "Hello there, Dominic. Glad to see you coming out for the play." Dominic raised his hands to his eyes to block out the stage lights glaring down on him, barely making out Mr. Gavin's silhouette in the shadows in front of the stage.

"Hi...hi, Mr. Gavin, do you want me to start my reading now?"

Mr. Gavin sighed. "Sure, Dominic, why don't you tell me what reading you'll be doing, and what part you want to be considered for."

"OK, I will be doing a reading from *Hamlet*, from the third—"

"*Hamlet*? Why *Hamlet*? How come you're not reading from the actual play we're casting for?" asked Mr. Gavin, his tone puzzled more than annoyed.

Dominic thought for a minute and then simply responded, "I like *Hamlet*."

"OK, let's hear it." Mr. Gavin sat back in his chair. Dominic started to read: "To be or not to be..."

Three quarters of the way through the soliloquy Mr. Gavin interrupted him. "OK, Dominic, that's good enough." Dominic stood there while Mr. Gavin wrote some notes.

Finally, he lifted his head and asked Dominic a question. "What's a bodkin?"

Dominic was stumped. He didn't even know what Mr. Gavin was talking about. "A bodkin? I'm sorry, Mr. Gavin, I don't understand your question."

Mr. Gavin was tapping his pen against his lips. He put the pen down and sat back in his chair and folded his arms. "In the soliloquy you just read there's a line 'when he himself might his quietus make with a bare bodkin?' So, I am asking you what a bodkin is."

Dominic cheeks flushed with embarrassment. "Uh, I...don't know...
hmm, don't what is it. But I can look it up?"

"Yes, you should...but on your own time. Thank you, Dominic." Mr.
Gavin went back to making notes. "Next!"

Dominic exited stage left feeling dejected. The next student audition-
ing whispered to him as he walked by, "That was an excellent reading,
Dominic," but Dominic didn't even have the wherewithal to acknowledge the compliment. He made his way through the backstage area to
the exit leading out to the back hallway near the school library. Once in
the hallway he turned left to go around to the corridor that led to the
locker room.

"Dominic, you OK?"

Dominic lifted his head and in the corner of the corridor next to the
locked doors of the closed library, just a step out of the corridor light,
was Brother Corwin leaning serenely against the wall.

"Huh, oh, hey Brother Corwin, how are you doing?"

"I'm fine, but who stole your puppy, little brother?" Brother Corwin
pushed himself away from the wall and stepped toward Dominic. "You
want to talk about it?"

"It's nothing. I just had my audition. I don't think it went so well."
Dominic let out a deep sigh.

Brother Corwin put a hand on Dominic's shoulder. "You did really
well. That's a hard soliloquy to pull off. But you know your Shakespeare—maybe not the meaning of Elizabethan era words, necessarily,
but you know the poetry and emotion of his language." Brother Corwin
looked into Dominic's eyes with encouragement and gave his shoulder a
gentle squeeze.

Dominic nodded his head, and then it hit him. "Wait, you saw me
audition? You were in there too?"

"No, not officially. I watched you from the wing. You did fine. Morris
likes to challenge the students to gauge if they really understand what
they're reading. That being said, he's right, an actor should not just
memorize lines—he needs to really delve into the material and by doing

that, he can know the character and the role he's playing. Of course, it could have helped if you also did a reading from the actual play being cast. But all things considered, I wouldn't worry about it if I were you." Brother Corwin let go of Dominic's shoulder.

"Thanks, Brother Corwin, I appreciate the encouraging words."

"No need to thank me, little brother. Here, I brought this for you." He handed Dominic a thin paperback book.

"What's this?" Dominic accepted the book and then read the title aloud. *"The Little Prince.* What's this about?" asked Dominic.

"It's about actions often neglected, among other things. Dominic, I believe we were proceeding on a...let's say...a journey. We had embarked on a journey, going along the pathway of friendship and I think we hit, uh, let's say a rough patch. Over the summer, when I reflected on our relationship, I realized some missteps that may have occurred. It made me think of that book. There's a lot in there I believe you will be able to relate with, so I thought this would be a good way to....get us back together. Get us back on the right pathway."

Dominic turned the book over and read the excerpt on the back cover. "On the pathway to friendship?"

"Yes...yes, back to being friends. Sort of pick up where we left off. I think you'll understand better once you read *The Little Prince.* It will be a big help." Brother Corwin studied Dominic's body language. Dominic appeared to be mulling it over. Brother Corwin held his breath.

"Alright, Brother Corwin, that sounds good to me. I have to admit there were times over the summer I missed our conversations. I'll read the book and let you know what I think."

"Good, I'm glad. I also want to let you know that I will be taking my final vows as a Brother of the Order of the Apostles of St. Mary. This is a milestone in...my vocation...a huge step forward in my total and complete commitment to the Order. This is a special and sacred event for me. I am sharing this with you because I would be very honored if you would attend the ceremony as of one my valued friends."

"Wow, Brother Corwin, I...I...I don't know what to say...I'm very honored that you would invite me to your final vows ceremony. I mean, that's a big moment, to say the least. It's a once in a lifetime occasion. Are you sure?" Dominic was surprised by the invitation.

"I am more than sure, little brother. There is no one else that I would want there if not you. It's a very small and select group of those I consider very close to me, and you definitely should be there. I believe you will find the ceremony a spiritual event. And not just because I am designing and planning everything from the flowers to the music to the readings. I think you will be inspired as a servant of God makes his life's devotion to the Almighty a permanent and lasting relationship. I would be humbled if you, as a fellow servant to God in your own personal way, if you would accept this invitation. It would mean so much to me and make the day so much more meaningful. It will be here in the ASM Chapel. Again, a small affair with a very intimate and select audience."

"Well, if you put it that way, Brother, then of course, I will come. Thank you so much for the invite."

"Good, can't ask for anything more." Brother Corwin placed a hand on each of Dominic's shoulders, almost as a gesture of "Welcome back," then continued. "Actually, I just remembered there's one more thing." Dominic looked up while Brother Corwin brought his arms back to his side. "There's going to be an announcement tomorrow. I will need your support once the announcement's made. It directly impacts your class. I hope I can count on you."

Dominic nodded his head. "Sure, Brother Corwin. I guess you can't tell me what it is?"

"You'll find out soon enough tomorrow. It's nothing really—just a change. It's all good."

"Alright. Well, I better get going. See ya tomorrow."

"Good night, little brother."

Dominic walked toward the locker room.

"And Dominic?" called Brother Corwin behind him.

Dominic stopped and turned around. "Thanks again, little brother." Dominic gave him a head nod and continued on his way. Dominic went to his sports team locker. He wanted to grab some of his athletic clothes to take home to put in the laundry. He opened up his gym bag and put the clothes into it. He glanced down at the paperback that Brother Corwin had given him. He picked it up and opened the cover. Inside on the title page was written a note: "Dominic: Identify where you will— Brother Corwin." Dominic thought for a moment, tapping the paperback against the palm of his hand, stuck it in his bookbag, and headed out.

THE SCHOOL BELL RANG and the homeroom period was over. Dominic headed to his first class of the day, which was world literature. As he walked along the corridor, he remembered he still hadn't read *The Once and Future King*. He entered into Brother Abelard's room and went to his desk. He took out his notebook and pen and tucked his bookbag underneath. He stretched, then rested his head on one hand and started to doodle in his notebook while his classmates piled into their respective desks. The school bell rang again and everyone settled down. Hearing someone clear his throat, Dominic looked up. In front of the classroom stood the Vice Principal, Brother Ambrose, and standing behind him and to his right was Brother Corwin.

"Good morning, gentlemen. I need your attention for a few minutes and then your regularly scheduled class work will resume. I want to make this quick, so I will give you the *Reader's Digest* version. Brother Abelard, who started off teaching this class to you, unfortunately will not be here to continue this class for the remainder of the school year. Instead, Brother Corwin here has been gracious enough to add this class to his schedule of classes, and for that we are all very grateful. I am certain that the quality of the learning will be as good if not better than Brother Abelard's instruction. Your expected cooperation in assisting Brother Corwin with this transition will be greatly appreciated. Thank you for your attention, and I will let Brother Corwin take it from here. Thank you."

With that, the short, pasty-skinned man with fat fingers in the black robe turned and gave Brother Corwin a head nod and left the classroom. Brother Corwin stood up in front of the class grinning, hands clasped behind his back, like the main character in a stage musical ready to deliver his show-stopping number. Dominic thought that if Denny was there in his usual place sitting behind him, he'd have some choice commentary. Brother Corwin cleared his throat—the tenor was ready for his solo.

"Good morning, class. I am thrilled to once again be your instructor and am ready, able, and willing to make this a spectacular experience for all of you. I am a huge fan of world literature and hope to explore the sundry of literature, specifically expanding your horizons into literary forms and styles beyond traditional Western thought." Brother Corwin paused and assessed the impact of his opening statement. A sea of blank, indifferent faces stared back at him. Dominic Manterra raised his hand, and he thought, *Good going, little brother, I knew I could count on you!*

"Yes, Dominic, a query from the audience?"

"What happened to Brother Abelard, is he alright?" Dominic asked. Brother Corwin maintained his composure but inside was annoyed with the question—that was not the kind of support he was looking for. He gazed at Dominic and knew he had to respond to quell any suspicion or additional questioning.

"Brother Abelard, who you all know is French, has returned to France to the Order's principal residence to, uh, address some, uh, personal matters connected to his family who live outside of Brittany. He might come back to ASM before the next school year or perhaps he may just stay and teach in one of our French schools." As a quick afterthought, Brother Corwin added, "We should keep Brother Abelard and his family in our prayers." Brother Corwin sought to move along. "I spent last night catching up on Brother Abelard's lesson plans and I believe I am up to snuff on where he left off, so if everyone will take out your textbook, we can pick it up at chapter four." Brother Corwin went over to the teacher's podium.

Dominic glanced over at Timmy, who stared back at him, raising his left eyebrow with a "There's more to this than that" skeptical look.

THE BELL RANG ending the last class for the day and for the week. Dominic closed his folder and slipped it into his bookbag. He headed out to his locker and did a quick exchange of notebooks and textbooks that he would need for the weekend. There was a home soccer game this afternoon, so he needed to get to the field. He wanted to make it to the cafeteria to check if Mr. Gavin had posted the cast list on the bulletin board before the game. Finished with the transfer of items, he hurried down to the cafeteria. There were a few students gathered at the bulletin board. An older student passing by him remarked, "Good job, Manterra," but Dominic didn't know what he meant. He stood off to the side waiting for a chance to view the list. A space opened in front of the board and he snuck in to have a look. He went down the list of the play's characters and the names of the students next to the character roles. He found his name next to the role of Lysander. Dominic remembered the part and was surprised since it was a big role. Then his eyes opened wide when he saw the name above his and next to the part of Hermia. He looked and looked again. Then looked one more time, bringing his finger up to trace the character name to the student assigned to the role. His eyes did not deceive him. It listed Moira Toomey. Suddenly conscious of more students around him waiting to have a look at the list, Dominic backed himself away from the bulletin board and stepped to the side. The realization struck right to the heart like a thunderbolt from the little archer himself. His mind was a speedway as his thoughts raced down the straightaway and around the bank. He wasn't sure if he was anxious or excited or nervous or thrilled.

"Congratulations, Dominic," a familiar voice softly spoke. Dominic froze for a moment before turning in the direction of the speaker. Sitting at one of the cafeteria tables, a hint of a late summer tan still shading her comely face, was the damsel of his happy torment, Moira Toomey. She gave him a big smile.

"Hey, Moira, what are you doing here?" Dominic managed to ask after collecting his thoughts.

"Aren't you going to congratulate me?" she laughed.

"Congratulate you?" Dominic was puzzled for a moment as Moira raised her chin in the direction of the bulletin board and then looked at him askance, raising her eyebrows. Then it hit him. "Oh! Yeah, congratulations on getting the part!" Dominic playfully slapped himself on the side of his face to wake himself up.

"I believe we have the two best parts in the play! I know that Puck is the plum part, but we are the two best lovers." Moira paused to watch Dominic's face turn beet red. "You know, Dominic, there's even a scene or two where we will have to share a kiss. I guess we'll have to practice those a few times. I will have to keep my eye on you—you may be tempted to slip me the tongue." Moira was enjoying her teasing and Dominic's total embarrassment. "I drove over right after school. I don't know if Mr. Gavin hadn't sent the cast list over to Sister McKay or if Sister McKay just didn't get a chance to post it, so I thought I'd stop by here. And then I thought I'd stay and watch your game." She suddenly blushed. Then, looking around, she whispered, "Stop!" and pushed back long strands of her auburn hair behind her right ear and shoulder.

Dominic was staring into her eyes in a hypnotic trance not unlike Narcissus at the pool of water. Moira waved her hand in front of her and drew his attention. He returned to earth.

"Did you say you drove here?" he asked. Moira nodded her head yes. "You have a driver's license?"

"Yes, silly boy, I do." She blushed again, anticipating the follow-up questions.

"How can that be? How old are you?"

"I am a year older than you. Actually, a year and a half older than you, Dominic."

"But we were in the same grade at St. Mary's? Well, at least at one time."

"Yes, we were. But when I came to St. Mary's, my parents thought it best to have me repeat a year of school at that point since we had traveled around so much due to my father's job and my missing a considerable number of classes at the time. But the good nuns recognized my obvious brilliance, and placed me back a year ahead." She beamed. "I guess it was just fate."

"To get your driver's license?"

"No, Dominic, to play Hermia to your Lysander." Moira just shook her head and thought to herself. *What am I going to do with you, silly boy!*

Memories, scorched in Dominic's mind like relics in a catacomb, resurrected to his conscious self. Dominic smiled and asked innocently, "Your mom's not a stewardess, is she?"

"Manterra!"

The shout of his name made Dominic snap to attention. It was Coach Barilla.

"What are you doing? We gotta game or did you forget?" The coach glared at him and then his eyes noticed the focus of Dominic's attention. His disposition softened and he simply called over, "See you on the field in ten, captain!" The coach winked and left the cafeteria.

"Gotta go, Moira. I will see ya at the first play practice!" Dominic turned and took off after the coach.

Moira watched him leave and sighed. *Dominic, Dominic—you're going to have to learn to listen better*, she thought to herself. She then headed for the ladies' room before going out to the soccer field.

The game was scoreless and the ASM Tigers were giving the far superior Elizabethtown Minutemen squad a fiercely fought game. The tight match could be attributed to the defensive backbone of the team, mainly the three backs and the goalie. The Tigers went with a three-back formation—left, center, and right. These consisted of Timmy Stefano at left back; Seamus Delaney, an Irish import who towered over the other players considerably, with his shoulder-length mane and profanity-laced brogue; and Mike Kendrick, another of Dominic's close friends, who was tall, thin, and boney but fast on his feet and possessed excellent ball-handling skills. The goalie was having the game of his life and his friend Timmy suspected he knew why. At the half-time huddle, Timmy noticed Dominic's usual focus was lacking and traced the occasional glances that Dominic was stealing to a certain spectator sitting up high in the bleachers. For his part, Dominic was making phenomenal saves and subjecting his body to brutal physical play amid the cries of *"Mida aqui! Mida aqui!"* from the players on the predominantly Hispanic Minutemen team. The team captain was inspiring the troops. If they could beat the Minutemen, they really improved their chances of getting a county tournament berth as this was their toughest opponent.

The game went into overtime, scoreless. The Tigers gathered in a huddle around Coach Barilla. "Men, you have played on a whole other level today. You can do this! You can win this game! Our fans believe that, I believe that, and you must believe that! There are three kinds of people in this world—those who play to win, those who play not to lose, and those just standing on the sidelines! Now go back out there and show that we always play to win!" The team broke out into shouts and whoops. Dominic glanced up at the stands and saw Moira standing up, cheering and clapping. She spotted him and waved enthusiastically. He turned and led the team running back out on the field, slapping Mike and Timmy on their backs and egging them on as he took up his position in front of the goal.

The play was intense. The Minutemen players were incredulous that they had been taken to overtime by this small Catholic high school with no business being on the same field as them. The Minutemen were not playing not to lose, nor were they standing idly by as they assaulted the Tigers with increased trash-talking, physical play, and fancy ball-handling. The Tigers fought hard and brought their game to a level of reckless abandon, throwing their bodies and pride on the field. However, the Minutemen were relentless and were clearly demonstrating their edge on the offensive front with three shots on goal to every one attempt by the Tigers. The defensive backs and Dominic were holding the line and managed to thwart every scoring attempt with many a close call. The decisive play came on a corner kick in the ninth minute of the second overtime period. Seamus managed to cut off a shot with his foot but the soccer ball deflected to the left of the goal, setting up the Minutemen for a corner kick. Dominic checked the alignment of his defensive backs and the half-backs while assessing the setup of the Minutemen players, who had brought nearly their whole team in for the kick. Dominic positioned himself accordingly within the goal area—waiting, anticipating. The Minutemen striker raised his left arm in the air and shouted in Spanish to his Latin American compatriots. For a moment, Dominic held his breath. The striker raced quickly toward the ball and, planting his left leg, brought his right leg carved like granite forward with great power and fury. The ball seemed to be shot from a cannon as it careened from the corner and curved over the center of the penalty area in front of the goal. Dominic reacted, moving quickly toward the center of the box, timing himself to leap up and snatch the ball in mid-air before a Minutemen player could get a head on it. He noted their striker waiting and timing himself as well to jump up and head the ball toward the goal.

Dominic realized he had to time his play to intercept the ball before the striker could get a piece of it. What Dominic did not see was a Minutemen winger racing toward the spot where the striker stood waiting and where Dominic was running to himself. As Dominic and the striker both leaped up, the winger came flying in between them and the ball, swinging down overhead with his left elbow, striking Dominic square on the nose. The crack of the bone shot through Dominic's skull with a sunburst of stars circling his head like whirling, flickering lights sailing in slow motion as he hit the ground. For a moment Dominic felt suspended in time before he could hear Timmy asking him if he was alright amidst the shouting and celebrating of the Minutemen players. As Timmy pulled him up to his feet, Dominic looked about and realized the game was over—the Minutemen had scored a goal. "It was still a great game, anyhow," muttered a disappointed Mike as he walked up to the spot where Timmy stood bucking up Dominic. Seamus was bent over, his hands resting on his knees, dejectedly staring at the ground.

"Whew, Dominic, your nose is beginning to swell big time!" said Timmy, his face cringing at the sight.

"It's broken," spoke Seamus without looking up.

"How do you know?" asked Timmy.

"I know that cracking sound. That's the sound of a nose breaking," replied Seamus with almost a hint of humor seeping through his brogue. "He'll be a bloody raccoon in the morning."

In the stands, Moira's stomach had lodged in her throat as she watched her love fall to the ground like a sack of flour. She gasped and held her breath until she saw Dominic get up on his feet. It happened so quickly and she felt like she was the only one who saw Dominic go down. Everyone else had followed the ball. Harry, who was watching the game with her, assured her that Dominic was alright. The two made their way down to check on him.

DOMINIC SAT IN THE back seat of Moira's car while Harry sat up front. His head was pulsating with pain and his nose was tender to the touch. He sat feeling bad not only because of his broken nose but because they had lost the game. Coach Barilla spoke to him afterwards to congratulate him on a great game despite the loss. He shared with him that even the refs had told him that was the best goal-keeping they had ever seen in a high school soccer match. Dominic was wondering how they missed the dirty play and unsportsmanlike conduct that resulted in his broken nose. Dominic took consolation that he was now riding in the same car as Moira Toomey. Moira pulled into the parking area near the emergency room entrance for Memorial General Hospital. Harry had called Dominic's house and informed Dominic's mom what had happened and that Dominic needed to go to the emergency room. Fortunately, Mr. Manterra was in between work shifts and would head over. Moira had offered to drive Dominic to the hospital, so Harry told Dominic's mom they would meet Mr. Manterra there.

"Thanks for the ride, Moira." Dominic managed a smile through the pounding pain. Moira had turned off the engine.

"Do you want me go in with you? Wait with you until your dad gets here?" she asked.

"No, you don't have to do that, you've been a big help already," answered Dominic. "Harry will wait with me. But thanks a lot."

"Are you sure?" Her face wore an expression of genuine concern. Dominic nodded. "OK, but will you promise to call me later?" She reached in her pocketbook and found a pen and scrap of paper. "Here's my number, call me later to let me know you're OK." Dominic took the paper and said, "Yes, I promise. Thanks again."

"Take care, Moira, thanks for giving us a ride," said Harry, standing behind Dominic, who waved good bye to Moira. Moira pulled away while Dominic and Harry entered the ER door and found seats in the waiting room and watched for Mr. Manterra to arrive. After a short while, Dominic's father and his younger brother Jason walked through the sliding doors. Mr. Manterra spotted his son and Harry sitting in the waiting room.

"Whew, that's a beauty!" remarked the father. "How are you doing, Harry?"

"Hi, Mr. Manterra, I'm good," Harry responded. "Hey, Jason. Getting ready for ASM next year?"

Jason nodded at Harry and addressed Dominic. "Holy smokes, Dominic! You might want to use your hands instead of your face to stop the ball next time."

Mr. Manterra grinned. "Let's get you checked in so they can take care of this real quick. I still have to get to work. Jason, stay here with Harry while I take Dominic over to the intake desk."

Dominic was stretched on the hospital bed coping with the severe headache from the pressure emanating from his broken nose. On either side of him were the curtain walls that separated the beds in the ER area while at the foot of the bed stood his father, who quietly watched the goings-on in the rest of the ER while occasionally checking the time on the wall clock. Above and left of Dominic's head were monitors and other paraphernalia. Eventually a doctor came in and greeted Mr. Manterra.

"OK, what do we have here?" asked the doctor, examining Dominic's face while taking his pulse.

"He got tagged during the soccer match. Looks like it might be broken," commented Mr. Manterra.

The doctor touched the bridge of Dominic's nose and Dominic grimaced and groaned as pain shot through the top of his head.

"Yup, that's broken," said the doctor to no one in particular. He patted Dominic's arm. "I'll be back in a minute and we'll have you fixed up in no time." The doctor left and returned within minutes. Dominic couldn't see what it was, but the doctor was carrying something in his hand.

"OK, young man, just lie still while I adjust your nose. This will take less than thirty seconds but will hurt a bit." Dominic saw it, if only for a moment. It resembled a tuning fork except it looked like it was a foot long. The doctor slipped it into Dominic's nose with this right hand while resting his left hand on Dominic's nose, and then wiggled the instrument back and forth for a moment. Dominic winced at the intensely sharp pain and loud crackling noise. Then the doctor yanked the device out of his nose and smirked, "Alright, you're all set!" The doctor placed a nose guard on Dominic's face and fastened it in place with adhesive tape. Mr. Manterra thanked the doctor while Dominic slowly sat up and pushed himself off the bed. The doctor handed Mr. Manterra a prescription for the pain and he bid them good night. Dominic and his father walked out to the ER. Harry and Jason stood up, met them at the sliding doors, and they left.

. . .

THE NEXT MORNING the bell rang, ending the first period of class. Dominic's classmates resumed the ribbing they had started earlier. There was plenty of talk among some of the classmates who had seen the match that sounded similar to the "big fish that got away" tales. Dominic was able to shrug it off because of the chance meeting before the game and the long telephone conversation when he got home. His feeling of exhilaration wasn't going to be dampened by the loss. Not after talking with Moira on the phone for over an hour.

"Hey, Mr. Manterra, what happened to your face?"

Dominic looked up at the inquisitor, Brother Geoffrey, a tall, ghoulish-looking Apostle of St. Mary who resembled Mary Shelley's *Frankenstein* monster. Brother Geoffrey was one of the older Apostles whose time to be put out to pasture was long overdue, but he resisted the pasturing. No longer able to manage a classroom of students, he was assigned to individual tutoring tasks, sessions that had earned him the appellation of "teeter-totter tutor" from those students who had to endure his "hygiene challenges." He was renowned for his dandruff, halitosis, and liberal flatulence policy. Before Dominic could respond, his friend Ernie, walking by, did him the honors:

"Gee Brother Geoffrey, he was kissing his girlfriend goodbye last night and she crossed her legs."

Dominic wasn't sure which was funnier: Ernie's comment or the expression on Brother Geoffrey's face.

XXIX

SONGS FROM THE WOOD

The play practices for *Midsummer Night's Dream* were much different than those for the musical the prior spring. The focus was on the acting and the challenges of converting the school gymnasium and stage into a mystical forest. The coaching and directing provided by Mr. Gavin were very helpful and there was quite a bit of discussion among the actors. Commencing with the first open reading of the play by the cast members, Dominic was spending a lot of time with Moira, and that was a dream come true for him. Of course, it also served as a great distraction for him, as the more time he spent with her, the more he couldn't stop thinking about her. In class, on the field, in practice, at home, at night, in the morning, at church, in a crowd, all alone, eating, drinking, walking, talking, thinking, dreaming—she permeated Dominic's words, thoughts, actions, consciousness, and unconsciousness. For her part, Moira was still unsure what, if anything, Dominic felt for her.

As is often the case with the great story that is true love, the hero and heroine do their best to shelter their passionate feelings for the other while waiting in the shadows of doubt, tormented by whether their overtures of love would be reciprocated in kind or rejected in callous indifference. Yet, in time, the lovers dare skirt the shadows and reveal hints and snippets of their hearts' burden, not so much out of courage—though courageous it is to make oneself vulnerable to love—but rather because true love cannot be contained within the cold confines of doubt or fear. Like summer's first flower, soothingly caressed and coaxed by the warmth and assurance of the sun's gentle touch, true love must burst forth with life, with truth, and with vibrancy, sharing both its beauty and peril.

And for these two would-be lovers, the opportunity to join theirs to the annals of what is ultimately the never-ending story of true love, that moment of truth finally presented itself.

"Sorry, folks, but just got a message from the missus, we're going to have to end it early tonight." Mr. Gavin spoke with a self-deprecating tone. "Seems a certain someone forgot the significance of today's date." He smiled and pointed to his wedding ring. The cast members reacted with laughter and a few "How could you?" and "You're in the doghouse now" comments.

Dominic was getting ready to grab his things and take off for his walk home, when Moira decided to take the initiative. The timing was good as no else was within earshot of the two of them.

"Hey, Dominic, being that we're getting out a little early tonight, do you want to go to a diner, maybe grab a burger?" Moira held her breath.

Dominic looked up. "Gee, that sounds nice, Moira, but my mom usually has a dinner plate on the stove waiting for me." Dominic placed his play script into the side compartment of his gym bag and zipped it closed.

Moira persisted despite the unintended rebuff. "Why don't you just bring that for lunch tomorrow, and come to the diner with me instead?" She marveled at his thickness as by this time she felt that Dominic did indeed have feelings for her—although she was wondering if she should re-examine her own feelings about him. *Maybe he's playing hard to get?* she thought to herself, and even chuckled at her own thought. Dominic *heard* her the second time, however, and realized there had been a knock at the door of opportunity and he had unwittingly missed it. Fortunately, someone had given the door a loud kick.

"Yes, why sure, I could do that, Moira. How do you want to, uh, do this?" Dominic glanced over her shoulder and then looked behind him. He turned to look into Moira's smiling face.

"It doesn't have to be a secret rendezvous, Dominic. We're just two friends going for a bite to eat."

Dominic's cheeks flushed red as his ears caught the "just two friends" part. Moira noticed the sudden change in his complexion and thought to herself, *I hope you didn't think I was going to make this easy for you, Dominic Manterra. You are going to have to open up to me if you want to win my heart.*

Moira drove them over to the Rosedale Diner. They were seated in a corner booth by the owner, who placed two menus on the table and said a waitress would be right over. Dominic picked up a menu and handed it to Moira and then opened his for a look.

"Well, hello again! Dominic, right?"

Dominic raised his head to see who knew his name. He recognized the waitress from the time he had been at the diner with Brother Corwin. She had her order pad placed over her own name tag as she stood waiting for Dominic's acknowledgement.

"That's right, good memory, Missy, it's been a while. How are things?" Dominic grinned as Missy broke into a big smile, pleasantly surprised that he'd met the challenge. "Things are better now that I'm waiting on this table," she said as she playfully hit Dominic in the arm with her order pad. She turned to Moira. "You got a real good man here, you're a lucky girl! I'll be back with some waters and to take your order." It took a moment for Moira to catch on to what had just transpired and she gazed at Dominic as he studied the menu in front of him. She thought to herself, *I sure hope he's mine.* The waitress returned with two glasses of water, placed them on the table, and pulled her order pad out from her apron pocket. "What'll you have?"

Dominic motioned to Moira, who placed her order. "I'll have a cup of chicken noodle soup and a grilled cheese sandwich."

"Anything to drink?"

"Tab, please."

"OK, and for you, Dominic?"

"I will have a cheeseburger, please, medium."

"Non-deluxe and unsweetened iced tea?" Missy said it more as a statement than a question.

Dominic nodded. "Yes, please. Thanks!" He handed Missy the menus.

"Thank you. I'll get this order in and bring back your drinks."

Dominic took a drink from his water glass and gazed across the table at Moira.

"I take it that Missy waited on you before?" asked Moira. *Hmmm, maybe he's been here before with some other girl*, she thought to herself, *might as well find out if there's someone else competing for the heart of Dominic Manterra.*

"Yes, it was last year. I came here with Brother Corwin one night," answered Dominic. "I guess she remembered me, although I don't know why she would." Moira shuddered at hearing Brother Corwin's name, so much so that she wished Dominic had in fact mentioned another girl's name instead. She did not trust Brother Corwin and liked him even less. She didn't understand exactly why but she especially didn't trust him around Dominic.

"What do you think of Brother Corwin?" asked Moira after a long pause and observing Dominic suddenly act a little nervous picking up the salt and pepper shakers and the cheap little porcelain container with the packets of sugar and Sweet'N Low. He began flipping the song pages on the tabletop jukebox.

"Brother Corwin's alright. We're good friends, actually. We talk a lot. Well, not so much lately, but last year we did. He's been really swell to me. Takes me places and gives me books to read. We talk about a lot of things."

"Like what?" asked Moira as Missy placed their drinks on the table and dropped some straws. Dominic picked up one of the straws, peeled the paper off it, poked it through the ice in Moira's glass of Tab, and pushed it toward her.

"The books he gives me to read—I just finished reading one he gave me, *The Little Prince*. Sometimes we talk about school stuff, our past, the future, life, and things like that." Dominic placed a straw in his own drink and took a sip.

Moira sipped from the straw in her glass and sat back. "I know he's your friend, Dominic, and I hope you don't mind me saying this, but there's something about him, about Brother Corwin that gives me the heebie-jeebies."

"He's alright, Moira. He's kind of had a hard life, you know, a difficult upbringing, yeah, he's had a lot of tragedy. It's a wonder he's managed to keep his sanity."

Moira wondered to herself, *That's exactly what I mean. Has he actually managed to keep it?*

Suddenly Dominic sat back and quietly said, "Oh no!" Moira was startled and asked, "What's wrong?"

Dominic reached behind to check his back pocket: nope, it wasn't there. He had totally forgotten it. He was mortified. Moira asked him again, "Dominic, what's wrong? What's the matter?"

"Moira, we have to go back to ASM."

"Why?"

"I forgot my wallet. I left it in my locker. I don't have any money on me to pay our check."

Moira laughed with relief. "So, what you're telling me is that you're going to make me pay for our first date? Not very gentlemanly of you, Dominic Manterra, and definitely not very romantic." Dominic's eyes widened. *Did she just say date?*

Moira picked up on the possibility of his thinking and corrected herself. "Well, I guess this is technically not our first date since you didn't actually ask me out." She gave Dominic a playful kick under the table. "Don't worry, Dominic, I can pay the check tonight. Besides, I'm sure your friend Missy wouldn't appreciate us just getting up and leaving."

"Thanks, Moira. Sorry about that. Next time it's on me." The tension eased from Dominic's face as he went back to flipping the song pages on the jukebox. "Who's your favorite group?"

Moira picked up her glass with her one hand and held the straw with her other as she brought it to her lips for a drink. *Next time it's on me?* she thought. *Is this the same person who I catch sneaking lovelorn looks at me with those sad eyes? Am I reading him wrong?*

"THANKS AGAIN FOR treating tonight, Moira. I appreciate it." Dominic fastened his seat belt as Moira started up the car. Moira was thinking that she didn't want the evening to end just yet.

"Dominic, it's early yet. I mean, do you mind if we hung out a little longer?" she asked.

Dominic looked at the time on the dashboard clock. "I guess we could but I still have to walk home," he replied.

Moira paused before saying, "Well... I can give you a ride home— that would give us some extra time, right?"

"Oh yeah, but I don't want to put you out any more than I already have. I know you live close to ASM." Dominic was trying to be considerate. Moira let out a sigh, attempting to hide her disappointment with his response. Dominic took note and quickly followed up. "But if you wouldn't mind driving me, then I would definitely like to hang out with you some more."

Moira smiled. "Good. It's a beautiful autumn night, and the sky is so clear. Why don't we drive over to Warnock Park, gaze at the stars, and see how many constellations the Boy Scout can name for me?"

Dominic grinned. "You're on!"

As Moira drove, the two of them practiced their lines. They laughed as she would have to correct Dominic often and he was clearly frustrated that she not only knew her lines cold but his as well. They entered Warnock Park from the main entrance on St. Georges Avenue, and Moira slowly rode by the ice-skating rink and followed the curving route through the park. Their conversation had become quiet but it was a comfortable quiet as both were enjoying the clear night and the unusually warm late October evening, so much so, they had the windows down in the car. Dominic had spent many hours jogging in this park and coming there with his brothers to play various sports. The stars were exceptionally bright and the moon shone like a perfectly placed crystal plate.

Then he saw it. The tree. It stood out from all the other trees in the park. Its majesty and prominence were unique—it had to be the largest tree in the park. For a moment, its magnetism was drawing Dominic in, like it was personally calling out to him. He found the call irresistible. He had to respond.

"Moira, please pull over for a moment."

"Huh? Something wrong?"

"No, not at all. Just pull over, please. It will only be for a moment."

Moira quickly glanced in the rearview mirror, and then slowly pulled to the side, parking along the curb.

"I will be right back." Dominic was in a trance of some sort, Moira could tell. He opened the car door of her Pontiac Sunbird, and without looking back, he stepped out of the car, closing the door behind him. He started out slowly walking toward the tree, the unseen force of its power pulling him in with a sure but gentle siren's alluring song that only he could hear. Dominic began to remove his jacket, and dropped it to the ground as he kept going forward. He removed his sweater, then his shirt. He stopped, lifted his feet, first the right, then the left, removing his sneakers and his socks, and cast them aside. He began to walk again, as he unbuckled his pants and began to push them down along with his briefs, pausing for a moment to pull them off and leave them behind. His pace quickened and soon he was in a full-out sprint running toward the enormous tree that had some invisible power over his being. He came within a few yards of the tree and made a sudden stop. His breathing was heavy as he was overcome with a euphoric elation. Around him was utter silence, and a warm breeze enveloped his naked body as if embracing him and welcoming him to this moment of freedom. He fell to his knees. Then he fell forward, rolled on to his back and gazed up at the night sky filled with a million stars, all applauding his arrival, as if they were expecting him. The breeze trickled over his body like a thousand soft kisses from Moira's lips were glazing over him as if to awaken every sensation sleeping beneath his skin. He didn't want the moment to end. He wanted this feeling to be forever.

Then the silent song hushed, and Dominic opened his eyes. The stars twinkled as if to say it was time to go. He tilted his head back and the tree itself seemed to be in a shadow, to have pulled a sheer veil over itself, signaling it was time to go back.

He stood up and began the trek back to Moira and the car, picking up his clothing and sneakers along the way. Moira had gotten out of the car, concerned and puzzled as she stood watching the whole scene. She was quite surprised as Dominic walked right up to her, holding his clothing and sneakers in his arms, completely oblivious to the fact he was standing in front of her completely naked, and with no attempt to shield anything from her. Seeing him up close, she thought to herself, *Dominic Manterra, you are beautiful!*

"Do you see it? Did you sense it at least?" asked Dominic.

"Oh, I see it, yes, I do." Moira smiled.

Dominic smiled at her joke before taking one look back at the tree. He then quicky got dressed and they both got back in the car.

"Dominic, let's not stay here. Why don't we drive back to Ridgeway River? It will be nicer to see the sky reflecting off the water there."

"OK, Moira. Whatever you want to do. I'm just happy to be with you. Especially tonight. I feel so free. You inspire me. Moira, you are so beautiful. Your hair—I love your auburn hair. You skin is so flawless and perfect—like a petal of a rose! A precious rose! I am going to write a poem about tonight and dedicate it to you. I already have the title. I will call it My Virgin Rose of the Wood."

Moira was beyond words. Her heart was racing with so much excitement from all the love that was filling its center. She glanced over at Dominic, who was smiling and totally at ease. She didn't want this moment to end. But her mind interrupted her heart's content as the poem her Dominic was going to write weighed on her.

. . .

MOIRA PARKED THE CAR with a good view of the river and the night sky. Dominic recognized that the spot was in the vicinity of where Brother Corwin had parked when Dominic was here with him. Dominic thought it better not to make mention of that to Moira given her opinion of him. Moira unhooked her seat belt and turned her back to lean against the driver side door and be more face to face with Dominic. She noticed Dominic was still wearing his seatbelt. "Dominic, take off your seatbelt and make yourself comfortable, will you?" She wasn't sure if she should laugh or be exasperated, given what had just transpired. Dominic undid his seat belt and followed suit by turning toward Moira and leaning against the passenger side door. "It's a gorgeous night." Dominic had bent himself forward and was looking up through the front windshield.

Moira, being mindful of the time and the rarity of having this chance to be alone with Dominic, just him and her, sought to move things along. "Dominic, I'm really glad you came out tonight."

He was still looking up at the night sky. "Even though you had to pay?" he asked.

"Oh, I don't care about that. I make enough money working at the florist shop." Moira wasn't sure if Dominic was suddenly embarrassed or was really that interested in astronomy. "I was only kidding you about the constellations, Dominic." Dominic lowered his eyes, glanced at her, and then sat back. His disposition seemed to have changed to Moira. Suddenly she sensed a cloud of awkwardness lurked between them, and she became anxious.

"Dominic, is there something wrong? Do you...do you just want me to take you home?" she finally asked.

Dominic dropped his head to his chin. After a few minutes he raised his head and looked right into her eyes. "Moira, to be honest with you, there's no place else on the face of this earth where I'd rather be than anywhere with you. That's all I have thought about for the longest time, you have no idea. Sitting with you here right now, with no one else around, sitting so close to you that I can breathe in your whole presence and have the very essence that is you...fill my head....my mind, soul... fill my heart...is everything I ever dreamed of from the very first time I ever saw you. So, no, I don't want you to take me home. I don't want this night to ever end." He stopped speaking and looked down at his hands. Moira sat agape, her body slightly trembling, trying her best to not let any tears stream from her eyes. But she knew that wasn't all there was because she could feel it, she could sense it in her own heart that something was wrong—that Dominic was still holding on to something. Finally, she broke the silence: "What is it, Dominic? There's something bothering you. I know it...I feel it. Dominic, listen to me, please...what you just said was the most wonderful thing anyone has ever said to me, I don't know if I could even begin to tell you how much those words mean to me...but I feel like there's something wrong? Please—tell me."

Dominic let out a deep sigh. He spun himself around so he was facing the front of the car. He turned his head toward the passenger side window—he could see Moira's reflection like in a blackened mirror. "There is." He paused and took a deep breath before continuing, "I know that he's away at college, and naturally, you may be feeling lonely, but I have no interest in just being a fill in—you know—someone to kill time with until he comes home during semester breaks. I mean, I don't mind being friends and all, I mean I do consider you my friend....I guess what I'm trying to say is that I know how I feel about you...how I've always felt about you, and maybe over time those feelings will change but right now, it is how I feel and I've already gone through enough torment—I just don't see the wisdom of pouring the lye in my own wounds of the heart." He twisted his head around to face her. "I hope you can understand what I'm saying."

Moira could feel her body trembling. She was fighting hard to hold back the tears—she wasn't ready for that just yet. There were things that she needed to say...things that she needed to share with Dominic...and she was afraid. God, how she was afraid! She was frightened. But she knew there could be no moving forward...no future...no lasting love with him until she opened herself up...opened herself up to that risk... that risk of rejection...of having him refuse her...to refuse her his love. She had to believe...she had to believe in him...put her faith in his feelings for her...trust that all she believed about Dominic Manterra was true and real...that he was really the kind and noble and gentle and loving person she believed him to be...she wanted him to be...she needed him to be...

"I take it..." she swallowed the lump in her throat, "...you're talking about...Trevor?" Dominic looked away and nodded his head, his face displaying an anguished look at hearing the sound of his name.

"What do you want to know?" Moira asked, holding her head up, striving to balance dignity and humility.

"What do you want to tell me?" Dominic replied, not really sure what it was he wanted to know.

"No, Dominic, you tell me what it is you want to know. Tell me what is it you need to know. And I'll decide if I can...." She struggled to finish her sentence. "...if I can." She waited.

Dominic was feeling uneasy. He didn't think the conversation was going so well. He just wanted to know what was going on with the guy Trevor. To him, that was the crux of the matter here. If she was still seeing him, if she was still harboring feelings for him, well then, that was fine, just so it was clear that whatever there was between him and Moira was strictly a friendship. Then again, he certainly would feel pretty foolish about all he had just shared with her. But it was the truth—it was how he truly felt about her.

"Moira...I...I'm not asking for anything really...I just was wondering if you're...still with him...that's...that's fine...I mean, I'd be disappointed but, hey, that's how life is sometimes...but I just don't want to be...used as a temporary fix while he's away at school and you want someone to hang out with...I mean, even if you're willing to pick up the tab all the time..." He smiled, thinking a little humor would soften the sudden tension. "I just want to know...kind of...where I stand. Particularly in light of what happened before and what I just said to you a few minutes ago. Not sure what was happening or what I was thinking, to be honest with you."

Moira managed a little smile. She took a deep breath, knowing it was her turn to speak. "Trevor doesn't mean anything to me, Dominic."

"Come on now, Moira, I saw how you two were on the boardwalk this past August. I didn't need a guidebook to tell me when two people are tight."

Moira winced at the inference. "Permit me to correct myself, Dominic. Trevor *never* meant anything to me." Dominic rolled his eyes with a "Well, that's what you say now" face that didn't sit well with Moira. "Truth be told, he was just a substitute. And a poor one at that."

"A substitute? For *what?*" asked Dominic.

"Not for what, Dominic—for who! For who! Yes, he was a good-looking guy, he was an athlete, and he was popular. He had his driver's license and his own car. I thought he was nice. And at first, he was nice. He was sweet and thoughtful. Yes, he noticed me and made time for me and was not always distracted and somewhere else. A girl needs that, Dominic—a girl needs to feel like she matters, like she's important, and yes, she wants to feel like she's special. And those things can only be done if someone is paying attention to you, by spending time together and talking together and sharing themselves." She paused to see if her words were sinking in with him.

"Well, it sounds like Trevor is a dream come true," Dominic murmured quietly. "Doesn't sound like you're describing someone who doesn't mean anything to you, that's for sure."

"You're not listening to me, Dominic! True, Trevor was all those things—for the most part—but there was one thing he wasn't and never will be."

"And what was that?" asked Dominic with a hint of sarcasm.

Moira took a deep breath. *He's not going to make it easy for me,* she thought to herself. She continued, "He wasn't you, Dominic. *He wasn't you.* And no matter what we did, how we were, where we went, what we talked about, and yes, even when we were intimate—especially when we were intimate—I wanted it…I wanted it so much….so much for it," her tears began to stream down her face, "…I wanted so much….so much for you to be the one that was there. For you to be the one I spoke with, I laughed with, fought, argued, bickered with…to do everything and nothing with…I wanted you to be the one to hold me." She dropped her face into her hands and let go the tears. Dominic was very still and quiet. He felt very bad about his being so oblivious. He went to reach out his hand to her. Moira pulled back.

"No! I'm not finished!" she stifled her sniffling and tears while she quickly searched her pocketbook for tissues. She found some and patted her eyes and blew her nose. "You don't know how alone you made me feel, Dominic. I know it's not your fault. You're not a mind reader. But there were so many times I tried to let you know how I felt. You were so shy. I know you had some disappointments in your life. I realize the girls in class could be cruel. But I tried to show you that I was different—that I didn't share their opinion of you. But you were always somewhere else. It was frustrating to feel that you never noticed me—that you didn't care about me."

"But I've always cared about you, Moira. I noticed you from the very start. From that very day on the paper route…I…I…" Dominic stammered.

"And how I was to know that? Did you ever tell me? Did you even *try* to tell me? No, no, of course not. You were content with your books and your friends like Denny. And yes, with people like Father Bumbry, and now Brother Corwin. You never had time for me, Dominic. But then, last year, when we were in the musical together, I saw a different side of you. It was like you had come out of yourself a bit. And you were fun, and you were funny, and opened up a little. And I started to feel that maybe, just maybe, you might have feelings for me. We started to flirt a bit, and get comfortable around one another. Then the cast party happened and I thought that was going to be the night when we would finally break down the walls. I could not have been more flagrant in my feelings toward you. But then you were preoccupied with *your friend* Brother Corwin, and then you disappeared on me. Rejection is a horrible feeling and I felt rejected that night. So, yes, I did move on at that point. And that's where Trevor entered the picture."

Dominic sat and listened, occasionally nodding his head, other times shuddering at the realization of the accuracy of Moira's words. He wanted to repair the damage done, if he could. "Moira, I don't know what to say...I'm so sorry...I'm, I'm..."

"I know, Dominic. I know. I really believe there's not a malicious bone in your body. And that's just one of the reasons that I...I...I care so much about you. Despite everything I've said, there's no denying that the one thing I've always felt around you is...you've always made me feel safe, Dominic. You've always made me feel protected...like you would never hurt me...."

"Moira, I would never hurt you! Never! I would never ever want to hurt you!" exclaimed Dominic with vehemence.

"Are you sure, Dominic?" quietly asked Moira. "*How* can you be so sure? You shouldn't say things that you don't really mean or make promises you can't keep."

"I mean it, Moira. I promise you that."

"Because I need you to keep that promise, Dominic, I really need you to keep that promise."

Moira wept.

Dominic reached over and put his arms around Moira, and this time she did not stop him. He held her close to his chest and stroked her hair with his hand. "It's alright, Moira, everything's going to be alright... everything's alright, everything's fine...." Dominic began to softly sing the words from the song to her.

Moira buried her face in Dominic's chest. She knew that she now was reaching the point of no return. She would find out if everything she believed about Dominic was really true. She was so sure of it but...

Moira gently pulled herself away from Dominic's embrace. She wiped her tears and pushed back her auburn hair on both sides of her reddened face to behind her ears. She looked into Dominic's eyes and gave him a slight smile.

"You OK, Moira?" he asked with genuine concern.

Moira nodded. "I want to tell you everything, Dominic. I want to be totally honest with you. But I have to admit, I'm afraid. And I'm so ashamed." The tears began to stream from her eyes again, "I'm so ashamed. I don't want you to think less of me, Dominic."

"There's nothing you could ever do that would make me think anything bad about you, Moira. Nothing at all. I promise."

Moira reached over and placed the side of her hand on his cheek, and stroked it with her thumb. She then brought her hand back to her lap. "At the cast party, I was introduced to Trevor. He was there with one of his friends who was a member of the stage crew. Trevor is also the nephew of Mrs. Gavin. We talked and even danced to a few songs." She looked up at Dominic—as if to remind him that he had promised her a dance. "He asked for my number and I gave it to him. He called me—at first, I didn't feel right about it. I really wasn't that interested and figured I had only spent time with him at the party because you had left. But he was persistent, and so we started to go out and spend time together."

"To date?" interjected Dominic. It was more a statement of fact than question.

Moira sighed. "Yes, we started dating. It was fun—he really had a good sense of humor. We did cool things together. He had a car and that was nice since we were able to drive places."

Dominic thought, *Timmy was right—chicks go for the guys with cars.*

"After a while, I was even beginning to forget about my own heartache." Moira applied a tissue to her nose. "I was feeling better about myself as well. Here was someone who really wanted to be with me and wasn't afraid to talk about how he felt about me. And he was all those other things I mentioned besides."

"Yes, I heard you—the total package," Dominic sneered.

Moira softly laughed, undaunted. "So he led me to believe. He was doing and saying all the things I wanted to do and hear. He really was winning me over." She looked up at Dominic. "Are you ready to hear all this?"

"Sure, I can handle it," Dominic said confidently, although inside he was feeling much anxiety—he really wasn't sure where this was heading. Moira sensed a worrisome air about him but knew she had to get through this.

"I had...I had been sort of...holding off his advances. At first, it was just a quick good bye or good night, and I would leave it at that. At times he would try to...you know, give me a kiss, and I would pull away, push him away from me." She sniffled a bit and wiped her nose. "But eventually I got comfortable with him, and started to have feelings for him." She noticed Dominic shifted in his seat. She lowered her voice. "He was being so nice. He would bring me flowers. We went down to the beach almost every week in the summer—day trips. Of course, he liked that because he got to see me in my bikini." Again, she noticed Dominic shifting in his seat. "Things were going so well that I almost... *almost*...forgot about you." Moira paused.

Dominic cleared his throat and sort of sat up. He could feel the burning sensation in his cheeks. He may not have been so sure when she started but now, he needed to hear the rest of the story. "Go on," he murmured quietly. Moira looked up at him. "Please," he said almost as a whisper.

"We were planning to go down the shore one day, the last week of August, and Trevor suggested that we stay overnight. He had some friends who had gotten a beach house for the summer and he said we could stay there. Of course, I couldn't do that, not even if I really wanted to—my parents would never allow that. Truth be told, they weren't too thrilled about me dating Trevor anyway. My mom thought he was cute but she was concerned about his being older and the fact that he had a car. My father was not a fan at all but he has always respected me and often said to me that it was his duty to protect me, not control me. He did always ask me what happened to the Boy Scout kid." Moira touched

Dominic's arm. "My father has always liked you. Mom too, she always referred to you as that Manterra guy!" Moira smiled.

Dominic smiled. Moira's sister was in Mitchell's grade. Her younger brother was in Scouts as well but in another troop. He thought, *This must have been the night the guys and I saw Moira and Trevor on the boardwalk.*

"But my friend Kelly—you remember Kelly—her family had a shore house for the summer...and she told me...." Moira hesitated.

Dominic finished the sentence for her. "Kelly suggested that you tell your parents you would be staying with her family at their house."

Moira nodded. "The plan was for me to stay with her family that weekend, starting Friday night. Then I could go down to the shore on Thursday with Trevor, stay with him at his friend's beach house that Thursday night, and then join Kelly at her family's house for the weekend."

"And hope that nobody was the wiser for that one night," added Dominic.

"Yes, and hope that the exact time spent at Kelly's would never come up in conversation. Looking back, I don't know what I was thinking. Not just about that piece of it, either."

Dominic let out a big sigh. "What happened after that?"

Moira's gaze fell to the hands wringing in her lap. She halted her action and rubbed the top of each hand with the other to calm her nerves. It was apparent to her that Dominic was following the narrative but maybe not following the story.

"At first I resisted...I didn't think it was right. Of course, I didn't want to lie to my parents. As corny as it may sound, I had never ever lied to them. And, although I liked Trevor, and I did like him, a lot....I still cared about you more." Moira lifted her head and saw reflected in Dominic's eyes that he was pleased to hear her say that. *I hope I can convince you, my love, that I meant that then, and now so much more, even after you hear the rest*, she thought to herself.

"But Kelly kept after me, she was relentless. Maybe she thought it was what I really wanted. And Trevor for his part wasn't pushy about it at all. I realize now that was part of his whole act."

"His act?"

"You'll understand soon enough. So eventually, I gave in and agreed to the plan. That Thursday, I packed my bag for the long weekend, gave my mom a kiss goodbye, and Trevor picked me up and we went down the shore. It was a nice shore house his friends had, and I don't know if he arranged it or it just worked out that way, but most of the guys were not coming down until Friday mid-morning. We practically had the whole house to ourselves."

"That worked out well so that you didn't have to share a room with a girl you didn't know—or have to kick a guy out of his room," observed Dominic.

Moira nodded her head. She suddenly felt very sad for she knew that Dominic wasn't so much being naïve as much as he was keeping her on that pedestal—she realized he would never entertain a negative thought about her—especially her character. She braced herself for the thunderous drop of her image as it fell from that pedestal of grace and shattered at the feet of this noble soul who worshipped her like no other.

"We had a nice enough day at the beach but the whole time I was bothered by the choice I had made. Kelly had given me a pep talk on the phone the night before but instead of making me feel better, the more I remembered the conversation, the more guilt I felt. We went back to the house to get cleaned up and changed before heading over to the boardwalk."

"That's when we saw you, right? That same night?" interrupted Dominic.

"Yes, that was the night."

"You looked really beautiful that night," Dominic remembered aloud.

"Thanks, Dominic. You didn't realize it but I was so happy to see you there. I was surprised for sure but I really was happy...and I wished I could have had a chance...to...to talk...to you..." she fought hard to maintain her composure.

"It's OK, it's OK, Moira," whispered Dominic. "We can stop talking about this. You don't have to say anything more, it's OK, really."

Moira shook her head. "No, I want to finish it. After we ran into you guys, we played a round of miniature golf, and then we sat on the beach and watched the fireworks."

Dominic's feelings were hurt hearing these words for he wished it was him sitting there with his love but he managed to conceal it.

"Then Trevor wanted to head back to the house, which was OK with me because I was feeling tired. It had been a long day in the sun and I had been having second thoughts about everything and felt so torn about it all. And then seeing you—I was upset with myself." Moira paused and again raised her hand to Dominic's cheek, stroking it softly. At the feel of her touch, Dominic's body shivered with such a deep desire—a desire he had only felt in his dreams—and it shot through his whole being like a drug that combined a sense of euphoria with maddening passion. He wanted so much to take her in his arms and kiss her, like he had done a thousand times in a thousand dreams. Moira slipped her hand down to cup Dominic's chin in her palm; she brushed her thumb across his lips, and then returned her hand to her lap. She braced herself for Dominic's reaction and hoped she would not be diminished too much in his eyes.

"We went back to the house. There was another couple staying there that night but they had already gone to bed. We went up to one of the bedrooms and got ready for bed ourselves." Moira was looking down at her hands but out of the corner of her eye she could see a puzzled look on Dominic's face. "I won't pretend that I didn't know what the expectation was that night. Trevor had not arranged this simply for the sake of not driving us back north. There had been overtures made and he had been making a number of hints about it. Like I said, he wasn't pushy at all but he knew what he wanted and he was playing the part that he thought would get him what he wanted. Looking back, I was being foolish and stupid and selfish." A single teardrop rolled from her eye and over her cheek, down to her chin, where it was met by Dominic's hand.

He tenderly wiped it with his thumb before resting his hand on top of Moira's.

"On the outside, I was acting sure of myself, acting like I was the one in control of the situation. But inside, I was a bundle of nerves and I was scared, and felt so alone. Trevor had a six-pack of beer in a small cooler and offered me one thinking it would relax me because he could tell I was nervous. But I didn't want to drink. As a matter of fact, I didn't even want to be there at all. I realized I had made a terrible mistake. And I didn't know what to do. I felt so helpless. I wanted to run out of there. I had so many different emotions and thoughts and...I...I was so confused. Trevor got undressed and got into the bed—he looked at me and said for me get undressed and join him. On one hand, I was thinking that I'm a big girl now, I can do what I want, I can handle this, I'm ready for this—but inside me, in my heart, I knew that I really wasn't. And that this wasn't right. In reality, I was just a silly girl with romantic notions in my head, who was trying to act all grown-up—but who had no idea what I had gotten myself into. I was scared and yet at the same time curious. It was all so strange." Moira paused. She managed to catch a glimpse of Dominic's face but it revealed no emotion or indication of what he might be feeling or thinking. However, his hand remained on top of hers, in a comforting way, and that gave her hope. "I got undressed, except for my bra and panties, and slipped into bed next to him. He started to kiss me and...and before I knew it...it was over."

She dropped her head and began to softly cry. After a few minutes, she wiped her eyes and face with a fresh tissue. "I felt so ashamed. I felt so terribly alone. I couldn't sleep at all. After a while, I slipped out of bed and got dressed. I quietly made it down the stairs and out of the house. I crossed over to the beach and sat on it for a few hours, watching the waves and thinking about what I had done. I cried and cried. It was then I realized how horrible a mistake I had made, in so many ways, for so many reasons. I had lied to my parents, I was using Kelly's family, I had deceived myself, I had forgotten all the things we learned in school about right and wrong, and most of all...the one thing that hurt the most... the thing that frightened me the most... was the thought that I had just lost you forever." Tears were streaming down her face. "And the thought of losing you, of losing your respect, the thought that you would judge me, and rightfully so, as unworthy of you, that you would think less of me, and would not want anything to do with me...broke my heart." She bowed her head in shame, burying her face in her hands, and began sobbing. Dominic slid over on the seat and wrapped his arms around her and pulled her close to him, tucking her head under his chin, and squeezing her tight.

"Dominic, I am so sorry, I am so ashamed. Please forgive me!" her muffled pleas pierced Dominic right to the heart. She gently pushed him away and lifted her head to look into his eyes. "Please don't think less of me, Dominic. I am so sorry. Please believe me, I wish I had been like you—so strong, and good, and pure. I know that I am none of those things now. But please don't think less of me!"

Starting with the strands of hair on the right side of her face, Dominic tenderly gathered her hair, wet with tears from her cheek, and pushing it over her ear and behind her shoulder. He then did the same on the left side. He placed his right hand on the side and back of her neck, and brought her face forward and kissed her on each eye, and then on her forehead, before tucking her head back under his chin. She went to speak again but he tightened his embrace.

"Shh" he whispered. "Moira, Moira...I could never think less of you. And I would never judge you. Never. I would only want you to be safe and to be happy. Forget all this talk of guilt and shame. Let it go, it does no good."

"But I am so sad now, Dominic. I know that I have ruined everything."

"What have you ruined?"

"Your feelings toward me—they will never be the same. I realize that and it's my own fault. I remember how you were in St. Mary's, especially in religion class. You know so much about the Bible. Your mom taught you so much, you would say. I know now that I let you down. Do you think you can ever forgive me?"

Dominic kissed her forehead again. "Why do you ask me that? Forgive you for what? Forgive you for being human? Forgive you for being lonely? Forgive you for making a poor decision? The last time I checked, there's only been one perfect human being that's ever walked this earth, and He has holes in His hands and feet. Of course, I would forgive you if there was something to forgive you for. But there isn't. As for these other things—this talk of thinking less of you, and ruining my feelings toward you—nothing could be further from the truth."

Moira nuzzled herself in Dominic's arms. Despite the anxiety and anguish and tears of the conversation that had just taken place, she felt so safe and secure. Dominic had not let her down. He was just as the diner waitress described him—a real good man.

"Moira, can I ask you a question?"

Moira held her breath. "You can ask me anything you want, Dominic."

"I take it that it's over between you and...him?"

Moira wiggled herself a little and managed to wrap her arms around Dominic's waist and hugged him tight. "I knew that I never wanted to see him again and was going to tell him that. After he woke up the next morning, we went to have some breakfast. We barely spoke a word in the restaurant. When we got back to the house, I picked up my bag to go and meet Kelly at the beach. He was standing in front of the house and before I could say anything, he decided to tell me that he didn't think it was such a good idea for us to see each other anymore." She stopped speaking and Dominic could feel her whole body shaking, and she buried her face into his chest and wept.

"It's OK, Moira, it's alright, it's going to all be alright."

In between her sobs, Moira expressed her hurt. "I felt so used...so cheap...I meant nothing to him at all. He just wanted to sleep with me. He didn't care about me at all. I was so hurt. He made me feel so... worthless."

"It's alright, Moira, it's over, that's in the past. That's all behind you. Forget that it ever happened. It's done. You are with me now."

Moira let go of her embrace of him and sat up face to face with him. "Do you mean that, Dominic? Do you really mean that?"

"Of course, I do."

"What I told you doesn't change what you said before, your feelings about me and wanting to be with me?"

"Not at all. If anything, Moira, to have the courage to share with me what you did, and to be that honest with me—it only makes me...uh, it only makes me, uh..."

Dominic didn't have to worry about finishing his thoughts. Moira cupped his face in her hands and placed her mouth on top of his and passionately kissed him. It was the first time Dominic had ever kissed.

THEY SAT TOGETHER in the front seat of Moira's car, his arm around her shoulders, with her head resting on his chest, her arms wrapped around his waist. She had her eyes closed, enjoying the feel of his touch as he alternated stroking her face and her arm with his right hand while occasionally squeezing her in his embrace—like an act of assurance of his presence and affection. It was one of life's rare moments of total bliss that are all at once spectacular and fleeting, like the realization of a perfect dream before one awakes.

"What the..."

Dominic saw something in the shadows of the park—he sat up and strained to make it out more clearly in the moonlight. Moira reacted. "What's the matter?" Realizing Dominic had seen something, she added, "What is it?"

Dominic gently disengaged their mutual embrace and opened the car door. He stepped out of the car, held the door for a moment, and told Moira he'd be right back, and to lock the car doors. She watched as Dominic sprinted out toward the cinder path that circled the park—it appeared as if he was running to a certain spot. As she watched she noticed another person running—almost aimlessly, clearly not directly on the path but haphazardly through the thin woods, in and out of the shrubs and the wild flower patches that dotted the park. She could hear Dominic quietly calling to the other person as their paths were about to cross.

"Harry! Harry!" Dominic caught his friend's attention. Harry slowed down and turned to gaze at Dominic, who slowed down his pace as he drew close to Harry. Dominic managed to grab Harry by his arm and bring him to a halt. Harry was breathing hard and had a wild-eyed expression.

"Slow down, Harry, stop for a minute, will ya?" Dominic bent over to catch his breath. Harry didn't say anything but stopped running, his chest heaving a bit from his heavy breathing coupled with the tears streaming down his face. Dominic held on to Harry's arm, partly to balance himself and partly to ensure that he didn't run off. Catching his breath, he stood up and addressed his friend.

"What's going on, Harry? What are you doing out here tonight, like this?"

"Just out for a jog, just out for a jog, Dominic, just out for a jog," Harry answered. "Let me go, Dominic, let me go."

"Wait no, wait." Dominic held on to Harry's arm as he tried to pull away, "Harry, listen to me, wait a minute, what's wrong?"

Harry ceased his pulling away, dropped his head, and started to weep. Dominic wrapped his arms around Harry, hugging him close, as Harry threw his arms around Dominic, buried his face on Dominic's shoulder, his body shaking with his sobs.

"It's alright, Harry, it's alright, it's OK." Dominic patted his friend's back. "You want to tell me what's wrong? Did something happen?"

Harry calmed down and collected himself. Dominic glanced back at the car to check on Moira. He could see her watching from the car, a concerned look on her face. He waved to her and she nodded to him, while pointing at her wrist. Dominic knew it was getting late.

"Harry—you OK?"

Harry had stopped crying. He sucked in his mucous and spat on the ground. "Yeah, Dominic, I'm OK. I'm alright now."

"You want to talk about it?"

"No, no, that's alright, I'm fine. I gotta get home anyway." Harry patted Dominic on the shoulder. "I'm good, don't worry. What are you doing out here?"

Dominic scrutinized Harry's face, trying to figure out what was happening with his friend. "Seriously, Dominic, I'm fine. A little embarrassed right now, but I'm fine."

"Alright, Harry, that's good to hear. How about we drop you off at home, though?"

"We?"

"Moira is over there in her car. We had stopped in the park after going to the diner." Dominic thought about it and added, "We were just checking out the constellations."

"Perfect night for it." Harry looked up at the sky. "Thanks, but I should be able to make it home. I'm not that far from here."

"I know where you live, Harry, but it is late and I would feel better if we dropped you off. Moira's got to take me home anyway, so it's on the way. Come on, she'll be happy to see you." Dominic put his arm around Harry's shoulder and led him to the car. Harry climbed into the back seat, giving Moira a hello as Dominic got into the front seat.

"I told Harry we'd drop him off at his house on the way home, if that's not a problem." Dominic glanced at Moira and gave her a "better not to ask any questions" face.

"Sure, that's no problem. We should get going though, it's getting late." Moira started the car and drove out of the park. Moira pulled up in front of his house in no time. Harry thanked her for the ride and got out of the car, along with Dominic. They walked up the front walk of Harry's house.

"Hey, you OK, buddy?" Dominic asked, placing his hand on Harry's back.

"Yeah, yeah, hey, thanks a lot. Sorry about this. Hope I didn't spoil your night with Moira. Man, she's a good-looking woman. Really, she is."

"Thanks, yes she is, and no, you didn't spoil anything. I know it's late now, Harry, but I want to talk to you about tonight. You weren't just out for a jog—you were running aimlessly and I could tell you were very upset."

Harry took a deep breath and stood still for a moment, contemplating Dominic's words. "You're right, Dominic; probably a good thing that you were there and saw me." He looked at his friend. "God works in strange and mysterious ways."

"His wonders never to cease," responded Dominic.

"Good night."

"Good night, Harry, get some rest. We'll talk." Harry climbed the front steps and went into his house. Dominic returned to Moira's car and attempted to explain what had happened as she drove him home.

XXX.

IN MOIRA'S ROOM

As was their routine, the guys had inhaled their brown bag lunches and were discussing what to buy from the cafeteria menu—whether to go with another sandwich item or fill up on fruit pies or chocolate cakes or chocolate chip cookies. The sweet selections won out and they sat shooting the breeze with the remaining time left for lunch break before reporting for the afternoon classes.

"I don't know if any of you have heard, but there's a vicious rumor going around." Ernie leaned forward, speaking with a solemn tone while looking over each shoulder. His lunch mates huddled in closer around the table to hear what the news was.

"What is it? What have you heard?" inquired Marco.

"Yeah, I haven't heard anything, so whatta ya got?" added Timmy. Harry just sat at the end of the table with a big grin on his face.

Ernie glanced at Dominic and then lowered his voice. "Well, there's a wild rumor that a certain someone has been dating that sweet bit o' red licorice, Moira Toomey, and keeping it a secret from us."

Ernie turned and fixed his gaze on Dominic. "Yo, Nicky boy, you know anything about that?"

Dominic shrugged his shoulders and stuck the last part of a Drakes

Fruit Pie in his mouth while his classmates called out for details and particulars and made accusations that he'd been holding out on them. He washed down the pie with the last of his milk and finally made a statement in a mock news reporter voice: "Despite the rumors and the talk on the gossip mill, Mr. Manterra maintains the two are just good friends."

"We better head to class," suggested Timmy. "Lover boy here can fill us in on the details at gym class." The boys got up from the table to make their way to class. Dominic gathered up the wrappers and cartons from his lunch to toss in the trash on the way out. Harry lingered, waiting for him.

"Hey Dominic, I wanted to have a quick word with you."

"Sure, Harry. What's up?" The two friends walked toward the cafeteria exit.

"I want to thank you, and Moira, for being there for me that night. You know, over in Ridgeway River Park."

"No problem, Harry, we were just worried about you."

"And I appreciate you not mentioning it to anyone. I, uh, that night was...I really appreciate it, like I said." Dominic could tell Harry was uneasy about the incident.

"Nothing to worry about, Harry. But If you ever want to talk about it, just let me know, OK? I'm always here for you, you know that?"

"Thanks, Dominic. I'll see you later." Dominic watched his friend climbed the stairs, wondering what was really going on with him.

TIMMY APPLIED DEODORANT under his arms and then tossed the can into his gym bag. "The season seemed to go quick. The County Tournament Committee really screwed us over, not giving us a berth."

"Coach Barilla did his best to make our case for us, but let's face it, ASM has no friends on the committee. As the saying goes, we'll get 'em next year!" offered Dominic. "We can still make a statement with to-

morrow's game." They had their last game, a makeup game with Sacred
Heart High School, who did make the tournament, the next day. But
both Timmy and Dominic knew that wouldn't change anything.

"So, how long have you two been seeing each other?" Timmy asked
Dominic.

"Not too long." replied Dominic as he pulled on his pants and sat
down on the locker room bench to put on his socks and shoes.

"Typical Dominic response nowadays—vague and nebulous, no detail," chuckled Timmy. "After ten years, ya think ya know a guy!' He
zipped up his gym bag, reached into his locker for his coat, and closed
the locker door. "See you in the morning at the corner, Dominic. Have
fun at play practice." He winked at his friend.

"OK, Timmy. See you then."

Dominic finished getting dressed and headed over to the cafeteria.
Moira was sitting at one of the tables, sporting a dark-green French
beret, studying her lines, when she lifted her head at the sound of approaching footsteps.

"Hello, Hermia, is this seat taken?" Dominic asked with exaggerated
politeness and an English accent.

"Why, my darling Lysander, I expect your imitation of a love-struck
Athenian nobleman to be much better than that—unless you really
want me to marry Demetrius!" Moira sounded very convincing with a
much better English accent. Dominic sat across from her as she pushed
a brown paper bag over toward him. He reached out for it and took hold
of her hand and squeezed it. He went to pull away and she held on to his
hand for a moment; their eyes met and his body shivered with love and
desire for her.

"I made you a ham and cheese sandwich on rye, and there's an orange,
too."

He opened the bag. "Thanks, Moira. You're too good to me. Though
I could get use to this. I have something for you. But you have to promise me you won't laugh." Dominic's expression was filled with a sweet
apprehension and vulnerability that moved Moira.

"Dominic, I would never laugh at you or humiliate you. Never. You should know that by now." She said the words to reassure him. Then she flashed him a mischievous grin. "Don't forget, I have seen all of you now."

Dominic smiled back. "Yes, you have. How can I forget! This is about that night. Can't explain it, not even sure I fully understand it all, but it was a very special night and I was glad it was with you. I wrote a poem for you that you inspired. Do you want to see it?"

"Yes, of course I do!"

Dominic pulled something from his bookbag, looked around, and then slid it across the table to Moira. Moira snatched it with both hands and placed it under the table onto her lap. It was a homemade card made from red construction paper, folded in half. On top of the card was a drawing of a woman, with long hair that had been colored red, although the rest of her was just an outline. She read the words printed across the top—*My Virgin Rose of the Wood*. She glanced up at Dominic, who was sitting still with a worried face. She gave him a slight smile and then softly blew him a kiss. Looking down, she opened the card and inside, Dominic had printed his poem to her. She read the words to herself:

MY VIRGIN ROSE OF THE WOOD

Love is a lonely word
For those who've never heard
'I love you' said to them,
Like a heart condemned
To solitude so forlorn;
Such a burden borne
By an unfulfilled soul,
A half seeking its whole;
What was calling me from the trees,
What voice carrying on the breeze?
The stars sought to share their secret too—
All my feeling and thought led to you;

RJ CIVILE

Under the shadow of steadfast night I stood,
Waiting for my Virgin Rose of the Wood.

I heard a tune playing without a sound,
I felt a touch but no one was around,
I saw beauty before me though my eyes were blind,
I sensed fulfillment while I had yet set out for it to find;
My mind's thoughts are taken up with your being,
My soul seeks its completeness in your embrace
My spirit's purpose is found in your meaning,
My heart's reflection is the beauty of your face,
There is no peace in a solitary existence
Loneliness is the true curse of heartbreak,
It's your love alone that can make all the difference,
In my mind, soul, spirit and heart it does awake
All that which is true, kind, gentle, pure and good—
My love for you my Virgin Rose of the Wood.

Moira's hands were trembling and her bottom lip was quivering as the frenzied feelings inside her reacted to her melting heart. She slowly raised her head and glanced over at the anxiety-filled poet across from her.

"Do you like it?" Dominic's voice conveyed his innocence and vulnerability all at once. Moira slowly shook her head.

"No...no, Dominic. I don't. I don't like it." Moira paused to maintain her composure. "I absolutely love it. It is the most beautiful poem I have ever read. I will cherish it always."

Dominic reacted with disappointment at first but was quickly relieved when Moira revealed her true sentiment. "I'm glad. It was so easy to write. It always is when it comes straight from the heart. I mean every word of it, Moira." He looked around. "I'll be right back. You want something to drink, a Coke?"

"A Sprite would be nice." Moira just shook her head and thought, *what am I going to do with you, Dominic Manterra? How could you have this kind of power over a woman's heart, MY heart, and be so oblivious?*

Dominic walked over to the soda machine and got two cans of Sprite. He returned to the table, opened up the two cans, slid one over to Moira, then unwrapped the sandwich and started eating. "What scenes are we working on tonight, do you know?"

Moira put the card in her bag, closed her play book, and bent over the table to get closer to Dominic. "Dominic, what are you doing this Friday night?" She was almost whispering.

Dominic put down the sandwich, finished chewing his bite, and then took a drink from his can of soda. "I don't know. I mean, don't we have play practice?"

"No, we don't. I was talking to Steve Embach, the stage manager, at last night's practice and he said Mr. Gavin mentioned that he was cancelling this Friday night's practice."

"Hmmm, OK. Well, I guess I won't be doing anything." He finished the sandwich and started peeling the orange.

"No, that's not the right answer!" teased Moira. Dominic gave her a puzzled look. "I think you're coming to my house Friday night. And you're going to spend the evening with me!" Moira paused to let the suggestion sink in before adding, "Alone."

Dominic stuffed a sliver of orange into his mouth, and peeked in the paper bag for a napkin, which he found. He considered what Moira had just said and then the words hit him.

"Alone? Where's your family going to be?"

"My brother will be staying at a friend's house. My sister is away at school in Pittsburgh. My parents are going to a friend's fiftieth birthday party over in Philadelphia and then staying at a nice hotel. My dad surprised my mom with tickets to the Monet exhibit at the Philadelphia Art Museum. I have the whole house to myself." Dominic had finished the orange, so he rolled up the napkin with the orange peel and dropped it in the paper bag, rolling it up as well. "What do you think? Do you want to come over and we can hang out together, just you and me?"

Dominic sat back and gave it some thought. He knew his parents were very strict about his whereabouts. But he certainly didn't want to pass up a chance to spend some alone time with Moira, as they really never got any opportunities to just to be together without any grown-ups or other friends around.

"I will see what I can do, Moira. That sounds like fun. If I'm able to, what would you want to do?"

"We can make dinner together, make some popcorn, watch the Friday night TV shows, even practice our lines if you'd like. You could bring over some of your favorite albums, and we can listen to those, too. It would be fun, Dominic, don't you think?" She was very excited already.

"I'll find out what's happening on the home front. I'll see what I can do."

Moira tapped his shin with her foot. "OK, good. Let's practice our lines."

As LUCK WOULD HAVE IT, everything was working in Dominic's favor for Friday evening's plans. Jason was going to a sleepover at his buddy Tommy Fellin's house with another buddy of theirs. His dad was working his typical Friday double shift so he wouldn't be back to the house until Saturday late morning. His mom was headed to his sister's right after lunch. That left only Mitchell to cover his tracks with.

He waited until Friday late afternoon when he got home from school to deal with Mitchell. Jason had gone home with Tommy right from St. Mary's and his mom had already left for his sister Maria's place. Only Mitchell was at home when Dominic walked through the side door. Mitchell was at the kitchen table reading the *Daily News* having a bowl of soup. Mitchell stopped reading when he heard someone coming in from the back door as he wasn't expecting anyone.

"Hey, Mitchell," greeted Dominic.

"What's up, Dominic? What are you doing home so early—I didn't expect you until later? Skipping play practice? Morris wouldn't like that." Mitchell went back to eating his soup and reading the paper.

"Mr. Gavin cancelled it for this evening." Dominic dropped his stuff on the kitchen chair. He went into the fridge and checked out the shelves half-heartedly while contemplating his approach.

"There's some soup on the stove and I'll be picking up a pizza a little later—didn't expect you home until then." Mitchell lifted the bowl and finished off his soup.

"That's OK, I'm not really that hungry." Dominic closed the fridge and took a seat at the kitchen table.

"You've been busy. Our buddy Father Bumbry's been asking for you. I guess he feels neglected since you haven't been getting down to the barn-house too much these days." Mitchell folded over the newspaper and leaned back in his chair.

Dominic spoke up. "Mitchell, what are you doing tonight?"

"After picking up your pizza, I'll be meeting some friends in Woodridge on Route 9. We're going to hang out at Poor Willie's to have a few beers, meet up with some babes." He pushed the chair up onto its two back legs, balancing it with his body and his hands on the table. "Why, what's up in that head of yours?" Mitchell had knowledge of Dominic's latest excursion into the dating scene and suspected a scheme of some sort was in the works.

"Funny you should ask, but with Jason sleeping over at his friend Tommy's house for the night, and you not being around either, I was thinking I would just go over to my friend Moira's and hang out at her house for the evening."

"Your *friend* Moira?" challenged Mitchell. "Isn't Moira the girl you've been *dating* for some time now?"

Dominic's face turned a shade of crimson. "You could say that, though it's nothing serious."

"Of course not, why would I think that—you just spend hours on the phone with her every night and I ran into her sister Kathleen at the Guvnor Morley's Tavern one night when she was home on college break and she told me how much she talks about you." Mitchell grinned as Dominic's face turned a darker shade of red. "So, I figure her brother's not around. Will Moira's parents be home?"

Dominic frowned –his brother knew his stuff and what questions to ask. "Not exactly."

"Not exactly—as is in no?"

Dominic came clean. "No, they won't be home either. They're away for the night." Dominic waited for his brother's verdict.

"Well, you know how Mom and Dad feel about you and Jason being anywhere without adult supervision."

"But Mitchell, I'm not a kid anymore. I can handle being someplace without grown-ups looking over my shoulder or watching my every move. I'm not going do anything wrong or stupid."

"I know that, Dominic, I know that." Mitchell spoke with a supportive tone. He much preferred that Dominic was spending his time with Moira Toomey rather than the likes of Father Bumbry or Brother Corwin. Besides, he knew both the Toomey girls. He went to St. Mary's with her older sister Kathleen. Both girls were real knock-outs. His little brother did well for himself.

"Alright, here's the deal, so listen up. You can go over to Moira's house and hang out but you need to be back here by midnight. That way you'll be home before me and if Dad asks, I can say you were in bed when I got home. If no one asks about play practice being cancelled, then don't volunteer anything. And most importantly, don't do anything stupid at Moira's. No drinking, no smoking—you know the drill. And if anyone finds out—then..." Mitchell thought for a minute. "Let's just hope no one finds out."

"Thanks, Mitchell, thanks a whole lot. You have nothing to worry about, I promise."

"It's not me who needs to worry, Dominic," Mitchell gave him a serious look and then softened his countenance. "You still want me to pick up a pizza for you? Bring it with you?"

"No, that's OK. Moira said she would make dinner for us."

Mitchell was glad for his brother. He had never seen Dominic this excited about anything. Or anyone.

MOIRA WAS WAITING AT the front door of the yellow house she lived in with her parents and younger brother, leaning her head on it with one hand on the inside knob and the other resting on the side of it, near her chin. She was watching as Dominic made his way up the walkway. He stopped right before the threshold, a few albums tucked under his arm, and gave her a smile. She reached out with her hand, took hold of his and led him through the open door, closing it behind her, backing her body against it as she pulled him close to her, reaching up and giving him a kiss on his mouth. Dominic slipped his free hand around her waist and hugged her tight. She forced herself away from his lips and hugged his neck, placing her lips near his ear and whispered, "I'm so happy you're here!"

Dominic put the records down on a chair, took off his coat, and removed his shoes. He could smell the scent of cinnamon and berries competing with the aromas emanating from the kitchen.

"Hmmm, smells good in here. Like Christmassy." He looked around.

"I have some candles lit—that's what you're smelling. Fall is my favorite season, leading into my favorite holiday, which is Christmas. I love Christmas—the lights, the decorations, the tree, the anticipation— and the Christmas music! But it's all over so quickly." Moira was beaming, she could barely contain herself—so glad that Dominic was with her. She kept smiling at him, wanting so much to kiss him and hold him. She had music playing—she wanted to dance with him and lose herself in his embrace. She fought every urge to tell him how she felt— how he made her feel. "But I think I like spring just as much! Everything is so brand new—like a new beginning!"

For his part, Dominic was a mixture of nerves and excitement. This was like a dream that he could never imagine actually coming true. To

have a few hours just to themselves, to relax and talk without any pre-
tense or interruption, almost like in the car that night in the park. It
seemed so unreal to him, that Moira could feel for him the way he felt
for her. It was like a story book and he had a real-life princess. He kept
thinking someone would close the book or an alarm would ring off—
and it all would disappear.

"Is my little prince hungry?" asked Moira. Dominic nodded. "I can eat."

"I hope you can do better than that, I have made us a nice dinner for
our first meal alone together," she took his hand to lead him into the
kitchen. He hesitated. "What is it?" she asked.

"You have a fireplace? I didn't know that." Dominic was looking into
the family room, where he could see flames shooting upward.

"Yes, isn't it romantic? My dad always says a house should have three
things to make it a home. Can you guess what they are?" Moira raised
Dominic's hand to her lips and kissed it.

"Hmmm, I'm guessing a fireplace is one."

"A *wood-burning* fireplace, yes, that's one." She was still holding his
hand up and kissed it again with her lips. Dominic glanced around trying to figure out what else. Moira didn't wait.

"A wood-burning fireplace, oak wood floors, and a piano!" she continued leading him to the kitchen. "And we have all three in this
house—and I know you play piano, Dominic Manterra, and you're going
to play for me before this night is through!"

"Oh, Moira, you don't want to hear me—" She abruptly stopped and
turned around, placing her index finger on his lips, and sshh'd him.
Then reached up and gave him a kiss on the lips. Every time she kissed
him, Dominic's whole being was imbued with wild longings that made
him delirious with crazed desire for her. "You can play at least one song
for me. It can be any one you want."

Dominic stared at her and all he could think was, *My God, Moira, you
are so, so very beautiful!*

Moira had made a sumptuous dinner for them. The table was set with
simple elegance. The china and crystal—all the dishes and the serving

bowls and the silverware and the glasses and the tablecloth and the cloth napkins—they were all brand new and being used for the first time. Moira was an excellent cook and Dominic was glad he'd passed on the pizza. During the meal, they talked about anything and everything—grammar school days, the different teachers, the Sisters of St. Mary's, the classmates they remembered and forgot, their favorite things and things they didn't like so much, their dreams and aspirations, their favorite movies, songs, television shows, musicals, plays, actors, actresses, and all things in between. They laughed and took turns poking fun at each other. Both were so delighted and thrilled to permit anything to dampen their joyous mood. They were two newly-born lovers lost in the woods of their innocence and in the purity of their souls, trusting spirits who had let go of a world that couldn't possibly fathom the depth of their feelings or the singularity of their devotion to one another, if but for this moment in time when nothing else existed for them except each other.

They cleared the table and cleaned up the dishes together, Moira admonishing Dominic to show extra care with the dishes and crystal.

"After all, I need to safe keep them for that special day when we use them again, and we remember when," she said, smiling. Dominic intensified his concentration on handling the dishes and Moira sighed, knowing full well he had no idea what she meant. *What am I going to do with you, my little prince?* she thought to herself.

Dominic kept an eye on the fire as Moira looked through the record albums he'd brought. "What do you want to listen to?" she asked. "Or would you rather watch something on the television?"

"I like what you're playing now. Is that Van Morrison?"

"Yes, it's *Moondance*, my favorite record of all time. Do you really like it?"

Dominic adjusted the wood in the fireplace with the poker, his scouting skills coming back to him. "Uh-huh, I have a few favorites on that record."

"Dominic—don't put any more logs on the fire, OK?" Moira spoke softly, not looking up from the record she was holding. "You don't want to watch TV? You're not missing any programs you like?"

Dominic stood up from kneeling by the fireplace, brushing off his knees, "No, I like the fire and music. I've always enjoyed this setting. I'm going to wash my hands—I'll be back in a minute." Dominic went to walk by Moira, who was sitting on one leg on the couch while the other leg hung off the end, but she grabbed his arm and pulled him down to her. "Kiss me first!" Dominic kissed her lips, then he kissed each of her eyes and on top of her head. He pulled back, gazing into her eyes, cupped her chin, and then placed his hand on her cheek. Then he remembered he'd just handled the wood and pulled his hands back. "Oh, I forgot I need to wash—"

Moira grabbed his hand and placed it back on her cheek, she could smell the smokiness of the fire on his fingertips. She whispered, "That's alright, I don't mind" and then kissed his fingertips. "Hurry back!"

Dominic went to wash hands. When he returned, Moira had removed the back cushions from the couch and had stretched herself out. She bent her neck to look back at him. "Come here, Dominic, come lie next to me." Dominic bent over her body and maneuvered himself onto his side in between the couch back and Moira's body. She took hold of his right arm and pulled it over her body and snuggled herself against his body, resting her head under his chin, nestling her face in the crook of his arm and shoulder. She could feel his growing desire against her backside as his arousal could not contain itself being so close to her, and she was glad to have that effect on him. He attempted to move it away from her but she pressed her backside firmly against him, closing her eyes. "It's OK, Dominic," she whispered.

Dominic watched the flames lurch from the burning wood and then the sparks shoot up and disappear, expiring before they could make it up the chimney. The wood in the grate was blazing different hues of blue, orange, and red. Every now and then the fire would crack and cackle as logs intensely burned. Dominic thought of the proverb that there are three things that are never satisfied, four that will never say enough—the grave, the barren womb, land in thirst of water, and fire—which never says enough! Dominic thought the fourth—fire—was given a special place, as it's the one that is directly connected with "never says enough." And he thought of fire as symbolic for passion, for desire. Are they unquenchable? Is it the grave that brings them to their end? Or do they inevitably become barren and cold with age and the passing of time? Can they be drowned, overwhelmed by the waves of doubt and despair? Or do they burn and burn until they are consumed within themselves and all that remains is ashes?

Moira reached her hand back and up towards Dominic's face. "Are you awake?" she asked. Dominic smiled.

"No, I'm fast asleep. Don't wake me up, in case this is all a dream!" he replied.

"Just checking." She nuzzled herself closer to him.

The fire was fading out as the top of the flames sunk lower and lower. The coals were glistening in their last gasp of air. Moira pushed herself up into a sitting position,

"I love this song! Dominic, come on, stand up, dance with me!"

She jumped up and grabbed Dominic's arm to pull him up off the couch. Dominic was stirred out of his fire-induced trance and stood up, listening to the song. Moira took his hands and wrapped his arms around her waist and placed her arms around his neck, resting her head on his chest. They began to sway in rhythm with the music. Moira's hand was stroking the back of Dominic's neck, twisting the strands of his hair through her fingers. She began to sing along in a low voice...*smell the sea and feel the sky let your spirit and soul fly into the mystic and when that fog horn blows I will be coming home and when that foghorn blows, I want to hear it I don't have to fear it and I want to rock your gypsy soul just like way back in the days of old and magnificently we will flow into the mystic...*her hand guided Dominic's head down to her face and in the darkening room her lips found his. She could feel his heart racing almost as fast as hers as they squeezed each other so tight, trying to compress themselves into one being. The record ended. She raised his hand to her mouth and kissed the top of his fingers. Then she kissed her own two fingers and placed them on his lips.

"Is there an album you want to listen to, maybe one of the records you brought?" she asked.

"Do you have a cassette player? I made a cassette tape mix of some of my favorite songs I thought you might like. Actually, what time is it?" Dominic remembered his agreement with Mitchell.

"It's early yet—don't tell me you have to go already?" Moira went to the kitchen to check the clock. She returned. "It's nine o'clock."

"OK, I have to be home by midnight."

"There's still plenty of time—don't worry, I won't let you turn into a pumpkin. Do you have your cassette?"

"It's in my coat pocket."

"Get it for me." Dominic found his coat on the chair by the front door. He fished into his coat pocket and pulled out the cassette. Moira met him in the hallway after securing the ambers in the fireplace and blowing out the candles. He handed her the tape and then she took hold of his hand. "Come with me." She led him to the stairs and they climbed to the second floor. They passed some bedrooms and a bathroom until they came to her bedroom.

"My stereo system with the cassette player is in my room." She stood to the side of her doorway and stretched her arm out, "*Bienvenue à mon boudoir*, Monsieur Manterra!"

Dominic entered her chambers, lit only by a small lamp on a corner table. It was different than he would have imagined. Her bed was directly on the floor—there was no headboard or footboard or bed rails—but lots of pillows of different shapes and sizes. There was wall-to-wall carpeting and a mirror on one wall and some prints of French Impressionist art—garden scenes from Monet. There was a two-tier shelf unit comprised of two-by-six planks supported by painted cylinder blocks, upon which rested her stereo system and various books between pyramid shaped bookends. Moira went over and lit a candle and pressed some buttons. A series of lights flashed and clicking noises sounded as the stereo system turned on.

"I will be right back. Sit down and make yourself comfortable," Moira said. She picked something up that was hooked on the back of her bedroom door and left the room.

Dominic looked around for a chair, then decided to sit down on the edge of the bed. After a few minutes, Moira came back into the room and closed the bedroom door. She was wearing a silk robe. Its sheen glimmered in the candlelight. She opened the sliding closet door and threw the clothes she was carrying into a basket and slid the door shut.

Stepping over to the stereo she said, "Let's check out this tape you made." She took the tape out of its box and placed it into the cassette player and pressed the play button.

The sound of lush keyboards joined by guitar strings filled the small room as a gentle voice began to sing about a magical horse. Moira turned around to face Dominic.

"That's a sweet song. Are they all like this?"

Dominic nodded. "Yes, they're all the songs that remind me of you. All the songs that, uh, that describe, um, kind of put into words..."

"Don't be afraid to say it, Dominic. Don't be afraid to express how you feel. This night, tonight, is about opening up and letting each other in. I want you to be completely at ease. Don't worry about anything." She drew closer toward him until she was standing in front of him. "Of course, I don't want you to say or do anything you're not ready for, but I hope that you are. And I want you to know that I would never, ever hurt you..." a few tears began to stream down her face.

"Moira, what's the matter, why are you getting upset?" he went to stand up but she gently pushed him back down.

"I'm not upset, Dominic, not at all. It's just that I'm so happy. I'm so happy right now." He was holding her hand and she pulled her hand away and took a step back. "What were you going to say?"

"The songs describe how I feel about you, what I think about whenever I think about you." He smiled sheepishly.

"Dominic, do you remember that night?" she asked softly.

"That night?"

"The night in the park. And the tree? The night you wrote about in your poem to me?"

"Oh yes, *that* night." Dominic blushed.

"We never really talked about that night, Dominic. But I know it was very special to you. And it was very special to me. You shared your feelings about it in your poem to me. No one has ever written a poem to me before. You bared your heart and soul to me in that poem, my love. You bared yourself to me that night, without any sense of shame. And now I want to do the same for you."

Moira untied the belt holding her robe closed and opened it and slowly let the robe slip from her shoulders, sliding down her body, and let it drop to the floor at her feet. She wore only a pair of floral print panties and a silk camisole. She had her eyes fixed on Dominic as she spread her arms at her side as if to say, *Here I am, I hope you like what you see.*

Dominic's eyes were all at once surprised, enticed, and uncertain. He wasn't sure if he should stay or get up and leave. Moira sensed his conflict.

"Dominic, please, don't be afraid. It's alright. Trust me, my love." She lovingly stroked the side of his cheek, and brushed the hair back from his eyes.

Moira reached up and pushed aside the straps of her camisole. She gently tugged the camisole down over her ample breasts and let it slide down her torso, past her legs to drop at her feet. Dominic couldn't believe how wonderful her breasts were! They protruded from her firm and lean frame, round and full. The locks of her auburn hair reached down to rest just above them. She looked more beautiful than any woman he had ever seen in any magazine or movie–more lovely in every way than any woman he had ever seen in life or in any dream. Her skin was shimmering in the light reflecting a pinkish tone, like the sands of Bermuda beaches in pictures he had seen in a book.

"How do I look, Dominic? Am I how you imagined?" She smiled. "Are you pleased?"

Dominic stammered. He couldn't find the words. He couldn't find his voice. He was awestruck. She again stroked his cheek and brought her hand down to his chin and brushed her thumb across his lips.

She placed her hands to her sides and slipped them in between her hips and her panties and pushed them down over her thighs and let them fall to the floor. She stepped back out of the garments gathered at her feet and pushed them aside with her foot. Her nude body was on full display now for Dominic and she was happy to share her naked self with him. Dominic glanced down at the neat patch of red hair and then raised his eyes to her head of auburn hair. Moira smiled.

"Dominic, it's not polite to keep a lady waiting," she whispered. Dominic broke out of his mesmerized state to give her a puzzled look. "Allow me," she continued and reached out her hand, which he accepted, and she pulled him up from the bed. She took hold of the hem of his sweater and pulled the sweater up over his chest and over his head, as he raised his arms and pulled them out of the sleeves. She threw the sweater on top of her garment pile. She unbuttoned his collared shirt, then loosened his belt buckle, pulling his shirt tail out of his pants. She undid the buttons on his shirt cuffs. She pushed the shirt back off his shoulders and pulled on one sleeve and then the other, and let the shirt fall to the floor behind him. Dominic pulled his T-shirt out of his pants and over his head as Moira undid his belt buckle and unbuttoned his jeans. She pushed down his jeans to his thigh and then Dominic shimmied them down to his ankles and pulled one leg out of them at a time. He pushed them behind him with his foot. Moira looked into his eyes, placing her hand on his cheek, reached up and kissed him, then let her hand stroke his neck, slide down to his shoulder, over his chest, down his belly and she slipped her hands in between his hips and his briefs and pushed them down. The front part of his briefs caught and she slid her right hand along their elastic band to the front of his body, and lifted then pulled back the briefs so they could get around his hardening member. His briefs fell to the floor and he stepped out of them and pushed them behind him. Moira ran her hands up the sides of his body while taking in a complete view of him from his feet to his head.

"I have to admit that night in the park, Dominic, I was so stunned at what you did. I didn't know what to think, as I watched you run toward that tree. Then when you walked back to me, carrying your clothing, I was so surprised how comfortable you were standing naked in front of me. But I wasn't scared at all. To be honest, I felt like you were an angel, you were so natural, and sweet, and innocent. I wanted to embrace you and kiss you."

"I'm so glad you were there, Moira. I have never been like that with any girl. You're right, I did feel very at ease with you standing here. I didn't feel any shame. All I felt was peace."

She pulled him toward her and clasped her hands around his neck. Dominic's arms found their way around her waist and they pulled each other close in a passionate embrace matched by an equally passionate kiss, her tongue probing his mouth in search of his and tasting the intensity of his desire for her. She pulled away her face and placed her lips near his ear, and whispered, "Tame me!"

Dominic embraced her with all the strength in his being. He separated himself from her and stared into her eyes, then he rubbed her shoulders, and rubbed down each side of her arms with his hands until he found her hands, and clasping them, brought them up to his lips and kissed them. Her body leaned forward and sent relentless pulses of desire throughout his body. He spoke:

"Moira, I...uh...I...uh...you're so beautiful...you're the most beautiful creature on God's earth...I mean it...but...I..."

Moira felt for him. She wanted him to want this moment as much as she did. She didn't want him to have any doubts or concerns or second thoughts or torment or anguish or frustration or guilt or fear or anything like those things. Instead, she wanted Dominic to feel the love and the connection and the peace and joy and the pleasure that she was feeling. But only if that's what he truly wanted—she didn't want to force him to do anything he wasn't ready for. Or most importantly, didn't truly feel for her in his heart.

"Moira...I'm sorry...I don't even know what to do."

Moira pulled him close to her and held his face in her hands. She kissed him on his lips and then looked straight into his eyes. "Dominic, you want to do this, right? You want to make love with me? I don't want you to do anything that you don't want to do, and I don't want you to do anything unless you feel it, you mean it, from the heart. OK? You understand what I'm saying? For me, I have thought about this night, about being with you like this, and I am so happy that we are here together and I want to give myself to you in this way because...because I love you, Dominic Manterra, and I always will."

"Moira, I want to be with you, I really do. I love you so much, I have for so long. But I'm just some silly school boy, a tenderfoot scout on his first hike, not knowing how to read a compass or a map, I don't know anything, really. I don't know what or how to...to touch you...like that...I have never been with anyone like this. Not even close. This is my first time ever being like this with anyone."

Moira turned her head away. A twisting pain surged in her heart as she heard Dominic's words. A sense of shame creeped into her mind as her eyes began to well. She felt Dominic's fingertips against her cheek as he gently turned her face towards his. Looking into her eyes, he spoke in a tender voice.

"This is my first time, Moira. And this is *your* first time as well. This is the first time for both of us. You can only really give yourself to someone when your heart, soul, and spirit connect all at once. Otherwise, it isn't real. We both are new explorers in the territory of love and intimacy. And as a favorite poem of mine says, 'your slightest look easily will unclose me though I have closed myself as fingers, you open always petal by petal myself as spring opens, touching skillfully, mysteriously her first rose.' Tonight, you are my first rose, my virgin rose of the wood. Tonight, I am your first love. Your truly first love. I love you so much, Moira. I have for so long."

Moira put her fingers up to his lips and gently hushed him. Her whole body was tingling with a joyous emotion—had she really heard those words from his lips? Did he finally share with her how he felt about her? He had no idea how his innocence and lack of guile made her love him, want him even more. Now she knew he was the man she believed him to be, wanted him to be, needed him to be. The pang of regret that momentarily invaded her thoughts was immediately pushed out of her mind at hearing Dominic's words. Yes, tonight would be her first time, tonight would be her truly giving of herself to Dominic; tonight, she would be reborn and all things would be new again! She would be re-consecrated by his love for her. This night would be the consummation of their love and that's when it was real, that's when it mattered, and that's when it truly is the first time.

She stepped back from him, still holding on to his hands.

"Dominic, you make me feel so good and pure and safe and cherished. I don't how you do that but I am so happy that you do." She kissed him on his lips. "Let's sit down on the bed for a moment, across from each other."

They both turned to the bed and sat down opposite each other. Their eyes met and they both smiled and laughed as if seeing each other for the very first time. Moira held out both her hands and Dominic placed his hands into them.

"Dominic, I feel completely safe with you right now. I want you to feel safe with me as well. Don't be afraid. I won't hurt you and I won't make you feel less than. And I already know you would never hurt me or make me feel less than either. I want to be with you more than anything else. I truly believe now that you share the same feeling and desire as I do. Let's kiss and caress each other, letting our hearts lead the way. We will share with each other what feels good and what feels right, without any shame. Don't be shy and don't be scared. We will trust each other knowing that wherever we touch, the feeling should reflect what's in both our hearts and souls."

Dominic nodded his head, mesmerized by his sweet Moira's beauty and grace. Moira continued.

"We shall sit a little way apart until we are both ready to move closer to each other."

For a while, the two of them sat gazing at each other, sharing a kiss and caressing each other's hands and face. Every so often, they would lessen the space between them, as they both yearned to embrace the other. Their kissing was slow and earnest at first. But as the passion increased within both of them, they could not keep apart from each other. They stretched out on the bed next to each other, entwined in each other's arms and legs with total abandonment.

Both of their hearts were impassioned with their love and desire for each other. Moira paused to push her long, auburn hair behind her shoulder as she gazed into Dominic's eyes.

"My love, let us touch one another in a way that is slow and soft and sure, so there is no misunderstanding or doubt. Let us tell each other what we are feeling and thinking. This way, we can cherish this night like no other."

Dominic whispered, "Moira, I want to make you feel good, to please you. And I want to feel all the things I have dreamed about sharing with you. Sometimes I have thought about just laying with you and resting in the warmth of your embrace and tasting the sweetness of your kisses."

Moira kissed him and then slowly turned her back to him. She brought his arms around her waist, pulling him forward so that his body was up against hers. She could feel his member lay nicely against the small of her back. She guided him to explore her body with his trembling hands. She turned her face towards his, and looking into his eyes, whispered, "Don't worry, everything will be alright. We shall be gentle with each other. Remember, we are sharing our bodies but more importantly, we are holding each other's hearts." She raised her mouth to his and he kissed her. His hands caressed the curves and contour of her majestic body. She placed her left hand on his hip and pulled him closer to her still. She stroked the smoothness of his hip and then pulled him forward while pushing back with her hips. Her hand slipped through a passage between their bodies.

Their kissing was now relentless. Their mouths were insatiable. Their tireless lips and swirling tongues were ravenous in their pursuit of the other's desire, and in fulfilling their own.

Dominic kissed her neck. She turned her body around to face him and took both his hands and pulled his body on top of her. He hovered over her, resting on his knees and hands. He bowed his head down and kissed her on the mouth and her cheek, along her neck, then lowered himself to his elbows and kissed down to her breasts. He could hear Moira speak quiet words of assurance letting him know that she felt good with his tender caresses as he explored the essence of her beauty. She cupped his face in her hands and brought it up to hers and passionately kissed him. She pulled away and whispered, "Open your eyes, Dominic, look at me," and their eyes met.

"Wait, my love." Dominic paused. Moira gently guided him to one side as she sat up and pulled herself to the edge of the bed. She kissed Dominic on the lips and then stood up, taking hold of his hand. Moira waited as Dominic rose to his feet, then, still holding his hand, she led him out of her bedroom. He followed her as she walked down the hallway and stopped outside another bedroom. Moira extended an open hand, and Dominic crossed the threshold. There were two candles already lit in the room, the shadows of their flames dancing on the ceilings and walls.

Dominic was puzzled. "Whose bedroom is this?"

Moira pulled the heavy coverlet back, neatly folding it to the foot of the bed, then pulled back the blanket and sheet. She guided Dominic into the bed, kissing him several times as she lowered him down onto the bed. She climbed into bed next to him and wrapped her arms and legs around him, embracing him with all her might. Dominic responded in kind. They held each other for a moment and Moira eased her clasp and then sweetly spoke, answering him.

"This is my parents' bed, Dominic." She lifted her eyes to his waiting gaze. "It's a rite of passage, Dominic. This is the most sacred place in this house. It is the place of oneness and eternal unity. It is the hope of enduring love, it is the belief of trusting love, it is the heart of only love. We give ourselves to each other in this way, in a way we can give to no other. Only you and me." She kissed him. "I have written a poem for you, my love. Do you want to hear it?"

"Please tell me the poem!" Dominic had been transported back to the park, to the night of a thousand Moira kisses covering his body, heart, and soul, except this was real.

"Look at me, Dominic Manterra!"

Dominic fixed his gaze upon his love.

Moira spoke her words to him:

Carve me out of wood—
And I cannot withstand the flame
For surely, I will burn into ashes;
Carve me out of stone—
and I will not endure the wind
for surely, I will return to sand;
Cast me in bronze,
Cast me in iron,
Cast me in silver,
And it will be in vain
For surely, I will not endure,
The air and rain
Will wither me away
And I will tarnish and rust
Until I am reduced to dust;
But carve me out of your heart
And deny me your love
And I will cease to exist,
I will be a monument to non-existence.

"Moira, I love you. With all my being, I love you. With my very existence, I love you."

Moira lay back in the bed, pulling him down on top of her. She took hold of him and guided him toward her center. Their eyes were intensely locked upon each other. She accepted his full desire into her well of anticipation, both sensing the intense pleasure. Catching her breath, her womanhood, warm and waiting, joined to his emboldened manhood. Their hands clasped together as they shared the profound depth of their desire and passion for one another. They studied each other's eyes reflecting their mutual joy and gladness. Dominic moved his hips back and forth keeping his eyes fixed on Moira's, while his desire expanded and surged within him and rushed down into his central being. It was a sensation neither had ever known and one they both knew that they would never forget. But it was not just the euphoria of physical desire that was overwhelming them: they were so in love with each other, and both realized the magnitude of their passion. Looking into the other's eyes, neither wanted this moment to ever end. They could not imagine anything in life ever exceeding the joy and completeness they were feeling, coming together as one, lost in the mystery and wonder of when the spirit of true love connects two souls through the simplicity of human touch. They felt entirely lost in each other, believing for the first time that they truly understood truth and beauty all at once.

Dominic gasped, "Moira...Moira...I...I..."

"It's OK, my love, it's OK, let go...let it go...." Moira whispered as she arched her back, closing her eyes, pressing her head down against her pillow as Dominic thrust forward in quick spurts and then halted as his total desire succumbed to her relentless passion. Moira felt his release into her with his final thrust and dropped her body down from its arched position, and opened her eyes. Dominic was breathing hard, his heart racing, an intense expression screwing up his countenance. Their eyes met and she gave him a smile, and he smiled too. He dropped to his elbows, then lowered his body onto hers, the smoldering heat of her being passing through his own. He collapsed down on the bed next to her and as he did, she turned her head to face his, and reached over and they kissed. He whispered into her ear, "Moira, I love you...I love you so much, you have no idea." She caressed his cheek and softly spoke, "I know exactly how you feel, Dominic. I know just how you feel, my love." He wrapped his arms around her and pulled her in close and they kissed and kissed and kissed until the kissing was almost an inherent act of delirious pain that they pursued in fear the pain would somehow cease.

Over the next three hours or so, they explored each other's bodies and indulged each other's desires as only young lovers can. They were kind and gentle and patient with each other as they opened up their hearts and souls and spirits and bodies to the joy and pleasure of their shared intimacy. It was after the fourth round of lovemaking that Moira teased Dominic claiming that she needed to cut him off out of fear he would grow tired of her after one night.

Dominic fervently vowed, "Growing tired of you or losing my desire for you or your kiss or your touch or your beauty or your love—that will never happen!"

Moira's eyes welled up with tears. Dominic noticed when he felt the wetness on his chest. He touched her cheek and felt the tears streaming down her face.

"What's wrong, Moira? Why are you crying?" Moira shook her head and buried her face in Dominic's chest. Dominic sat up. "Come on, talk to me, Moira, tell me what's wrong?"

Moira sniffled and wiped her eyes and her nose, shaking her head. "Nothing's wrong, Dominic, nothing at all. It couldn't be any more perfect, my love. It's just...it's just..." she fought back the tears.

"Why are you so sad?" implored Dominic.

Moira laughed and smiled. "Sad? I'm not sad, Dominic. I couldn't be any happier. I love you, Dominic Manterra. I love you more than you could ever imagine in that incredibly complex mind of yours. You can know one thing for sure, Dominic, and that is that I love you. To quote your hero, Mr. Shakespeare, 'Doubt thou the stars are fire, doubt that the sun doth move, doubt truth to be a liar, but never doubt I love.'"

"Wow, that's pretty impressive," remarked Dominic.

Moira laughed, drying her tears. "What, do you think you're the only one who reads romantic poetry and memorizes quotes?"

Dominic grinned, knowing she was right. "But you're OK, right? You're not upset about anything?"

"No, Dominic, I'm not upset at all. But you know what you have done to me, don't you?"

Dominic was suddenly nervous because he did not understand her question. Moira realized his confusion and thought to herself, *What am I going to do with you, Dominic Manterra?*

"You've tamed me!" she whispered.

Dominic's expression changed. He remembered a moment as the evening began, yes, it was coming back to him now—Moira had made that reference earlier in the evening. Moira was watching his facial expressions, amused by the workings of his thought process written so clearly upon his face.

"Did you read *The Little Prince?*"

"Why, yes, I did," she said with mock pride.

"Really? How come?"

"Is Dominic Manterra the only person who owns a library card?" she smirked. "I think you forgot, Dominic, my mother was a French teacher. *Parlez-vous français?*"

"That's right, you speak French! I mean, like real French."

"*Oui, je parle couramment.* My mother wouldn't be much of a French teacher if she hadn't taught her own daughter and had me read *The Little Prince*, don't you think?"

"Yes, of course. You read *The Little Prince.*"

"*Oui, en français.* Does that impress you?"

"Without a doubt. Is there no end to what I can learn from you?" he laughed.

"Only one thing more, for tonight, anyway, but it's important: 'Vous êtes responsable de ce que vous apprivoisez,'" Moira whispered solemnly.

"I figured out responsible and a couple of you's in there," kidded Dominic.

"You are responsible for what you tame," translated Moira.

"I am responsible for what I tame," repeated Dominic. "I must remember that."

"Yes, please do," commanded Moira, and she gave him a sweet kiss.

"What time is it?" asked Dominic. He had clearly lost all track of time.

Moira reached for her watch. "Uh-oh, someone has to hurry! Dominic, you're late!"

Dominic jumped up. "How late is it?"

"Late, late! You have to hurry!"

"Damn, I promised Mitchell I wouldn't be late! I have to hurry!"

He scrambled to get dressed while Moira put on some sweats. He went downstairs and put on his shoes while she gathered his records and his tape. He put on his coat and Moira handed him his records.

"Do you mind if I keep the cassette?" she asked.

"No, of course not. Did you like it?"

"Very much so. You recorded all these songs with me in mind?"

"Definitely." He stood staring at her with those eyes of his and that gaze she knew all too well.

"Stop!" she whispered. Then she pushed her auburn hair behind her ear and over her shoulder. "On second thought, don't stop! Don't ever stop looking at me with those eyes filled with love, ever, Dominic Manterra!" and she hugged him and kissed him again and again.

At the door, Dominic gave her one last kiss and reluctantly pulled himself away to get going.

"No, wait, Dominic! Wait here a minute more. I almost forgot!" Moira turned and hurried up the stairs and quickly returned. "I want you to have this." She handed Dominic a card. "Go ahead and open it." Dominic opened the envelope and pulled out the card. He read it aloud.

To my Dominic, the love of my life,

CARVE ME OUT

Carve me out of wood—
And I cannot withstand the flame
For surely, I will burn into ashes;
Carve me out of stone—
and I will not endure the wind
for surely, I will return to sand;
Cast me in bronze,
Cast me in iron,
Cast me in silver,
And it will be in vain
For surely, I will not endure,
The air and rain
Will wither me away
And I will tarnish and rust
Until I am reduced to dust;
But carve me out of your heart
And deny me your love
And I will cease to exist,
I will be a monument to non-existence

Please seal me in your heart like I have sealed you in mine.

Loving you always,
M.

"I wanted you to have a copy to keep and to always remember what we shared here tonight, Dominic. My hope is we will have many more nights like this...for the rest of our lives."

"I will keep this forever. I will never forget how I feel for you right now. M? for Moira?" he asked.

"Yes, or could be for muse, my little poet prince," she smiled. "Now go!"

She kissed him once more, embraced him, and then reluctantly let him go. He leaped down the front steps and ran down her front walk, turning to start his trot home. As he approached the corner, he stopped in his tracks. A familiar car was parked on the side of the road. He cautiously made his way over to the car. He bent down and looked in from the passenger side window. Mitchell turned his head and, upon seeing him, waved him in. Dominic opened the door and sat down on the front seat. Mitchell started up the car.

"A wee bit late are we, don't you know, laddy?" he smirked as he pulled away.

"Mitchell, I'm so sorry, I di—"

"Don't sweat it, bro. I understand. As long as you're alright." He playfully punched Dominic in his arm. Then he spoke again. "And Moira is alright?" He glanced at his younger brother.

"We're both as fine as wine, Mitch, fine as wine." And Dominic looked out the window at the star-filled sky and thought of the many planets that were out there, both seen and unseen, and he wondered if perhaps there was a rose living on one of those unseen planets, like the rose he had here on earth.

XXXI.

MIND GAMES

Dominic sat quietly in the darkened presence of St. Mary's Church. It was Saturday afternoon and this was the typical time slot for the hearing of confessions. Growing up, Dominic went to church nearly every Saturday to enter a three-compartment wooden box near the back of the church, where he would confess his sins to a shadowy figure through a honeycomb divider while kneeling behind a closed crimson curtain made of heavy woolen cloth. The formula was fairly basic: you would enter the confessional, take your place at the kneeler; the priest would open the slider on his side of the honeycomb divider and acknowledge your presence; you would recite an act of contrition, state your last time of penance, followed by a recital of your sins for which the priest would dispense a penance; and a send-off of "Go and sin no more."

For whatever reason, Dominic always felt closer to God when he sat in St. Mary's Church on Saturday afternoons when it was dark and empty. He always admired the simple majesty of its framework done in the English Gothic style. It's columns and arches and walls were covered with ivory colored plaster that cast a serenely subdued ambience in contrast to the darkened wood of its ceiling and the arched beams of its vault. Predominantly blue and purple stained-glass windows depicting various saints and scenes from the Scriptures surrounded the height of the altar sanctuary and lined the two side walls of the church, beneath which were set the Stations of the Cross seemingly carved into and projecting from the walls themselves. All this brought a combination of illumination and mysticism to the setting that inspired those sitting in the austere wooden pews. In the back of the church was a balcony, with a tremendous organ with its tall, cylinder pipes and room for a choir to sit. The flooring was covered with large rectangular and square slates with alternating colors of gray and blue-gray. The center aisle led up to the altar and sanctuary, covered with a bright red carpeting, that matched the background behind the depiction of a risen Christ, covered in gold and white, crowned in glory, right above the tabernacle. The dancing tops of the votive candles reflecting off the walls and stained glass, casting shadows on the statues and the elegant furnishings on the altar, gave a peaceful albeit solemn air that convinced Dominic he was truly in the presence of the Almighty. His mother always spoke to him of paradise in two ways: "Eyes have not seen nor ears have heard of the glory and majesty and wonder of heaven"; and "Heaven is a place where there are no more tears, there are no fears as Jesus wipes both away." He believed both.

"Dominic!" whispered a voice that echoed through the empty church.

Dominic turned to Father Bumbry who stood at the end of the pew and waved him over. Dominic opted to exit on his side. He walked toward the back of the church parallel with Father Bumbry, who made his way up the center aisle. They met at the back and walked over to the new confessional room. As part of its evolving ministry, the Catholic Church had introduced the concept of breaking down the walls that separated the confessor and the priest. It involved meeting face to face with the priest in a well-lit room and having more of a conversational confession than just a formulaic version in the confines of a pseudo-private chamber. Although Dominic didn't really have a problem with the traditional way Father Bumbry had persuaded him to come out of the shadows and into the light of the open confessional room. It was during a conversation after Father Bumbry had noted the vigilance of Dominic's Saturday penance ritual; and had also persuaded Dominic that it would help his spiritual development to confess to one priest—Father Bumbry, naturally.

They sat down on cushioned chairs opposite each other, a statue of Mary on a side table, a crucifix on the wall, and a couple of framed prints of a beach scene and a mountain range. There was a poster of a waterfall with the words "Don't pray for an easy life, pray to be a strong person" printed down the crashing waterfalls. Father Bumbry asked Dominic if he wanted water, to which Dominic replied no. Father Bumbry was excited to see Dominic as his attendance at the Youth Ministry meetings had been waning and he hadn't been to confession in what seemed ages. Not that Dominic's confession of sins was of any real consequence: use of profanity, holding on to grudges, getting angry with his brothers, feeling sorry for himself, and impure thoughts was the typical litany of Dominic's sins. Father Bumbry had on occasion pressed the latter transgression but Dominic was rather vague on the details and no mention was ever made of masturbation. Father Bumbry wondered if perhaps Dominic didn't indulge in the act of self-pleasuring—Dominic's propensity for the pursuit of goodness and holiness made that notion a real possibility in the priest's mind. He sometimes saw the object of his affection as a modern-day St. Francis of Assisi committed to a life of pious self-denial—willing to fling himself onto the nearest thorn bush. But the realities of the pubescent male sex drive convinced him otherwise. Still, the boy was mum on that topic.

"Dominic, my son, how have you been? It's been a while. I know you are a very busy person with all your activities at ASM. I have to confess myself—heh heh—that I miss our close friendship. We did spend a lot of time together during my first few years at St. Mary's. We were best friends, very close friends—at least I like to think so."

"I'm sorry, Father Bum—Father Arnold, I know what you mean. You're right, between schoolwork, sports, and the drama club and the other clubs at ASM, my schedule has been kind of crazy. Sometimes I feel a bit overwhelmed by it all. I guess I need to just keep praying for strength." Dominic grinned.

Father Bumbry was a bit puzzled by the last remark when Dominic nodded toward the poster and the priest gave a perturbed smile. "Yes, I see. How are things otherwise? What's brought you to St. Mary's on this Saturday afternoon, my son?"

Dominic's expression turned serious and Father Bumbry noted the change. Dominic's eyes fell to the floor and he suddenly seemed uneasy. Father Bumbry's instincts told him something was amiss—this was not going to be the usual tedium of a recitation of meaningless sins that he was not even certain qualified for venial. He needed to call in all his pastoral skill to ensure that Dominic opened up.

"Dominic, it seems like something's on your mind. Call it priestly intuition but you appear to have a burden that you're bearing? What is it, my son? Has something happened?"

Dominic looked up at Father Bumbry and leaned forward, resting his two hands on the edge of the chair cushions, gazing down at his feet. Father Bumbry figured he needed a different approach.

"You know, Dominic, our Lord said that His burden was easy, His yoke was light. And He is there to help us carry our burdens. We all have our crosses to bear. And our Lord knows how heavy a cross can be—He carried His to Calvary. And like He needed Simon of Cyrene to help carry His cross, our Lord wants to help us carry ours."

Dominic let out a deep sigh. "Something has happened, Father Arnold."

"And it is bothering you, I can tell. Let me assure you, my son, there is nothing that we can do as sinners that our Lord in his infinite mercy is not willing to forgive us."

"I know that, Father Arnold. But...but that's the problem. I know what I did isn't right. Well, I know the Bible and the Church tell me it's wrong, but...but I don't feel bad about it, not really. I don't feel like it was wrong. Not in my heart. The dilemma for me is how can I ask for forgiveness for something I'm not really sorry for?" Dominic spoke with a tortured earnestness.

Father Bumbry sat back in his chair. This was a dilemma indeed. He suspected he knew what Dominic was referring to but was incredulous to think that Dominic had crossed that bridge. Well, there was only one way to find out.

"Dominic, you raise an excellent point, especially in the arena of morality and the challenges that can occur when faced with choices and decisions in everyday life. But to help me understand your, uh, dilemma, can you give me a little more detail? Did something specifically happen to bring this conflict up?"

"Yes...yes, something has happened. And I don't regret it. And I'm not sorry for it. And I wouldn't take it back even if I could. I'm happy. For the first time in my life, I can say I'm truly happy. Is that something to be sorry for? Is that wrong? Would God really consider that a sin?"

Father Bumbry wrestled with his exasperation at Dominic's avoidance of telling him specifically what had occurred but he tried again. "Dominic, I would like to answer these questions for you but it would be most beneficial to that end if you could fill me in on what has taken place in your life that has brought on this...crisis of faith?" By Dominic's facial reaction to these words, Father Bumbry was pleased with himself—he found the expression to break the impasse. Dominic let out a deep sigh.

"I...uh...was...I have...the thing is...I...I am no longer a virgin, Father Arnold." Dominic sat back in his chair and grew silent.

Father Bumbry maintained a passive, non-judgmental face although he was smiling to himself. *Well, well, Dominic, St. Dominic himself, has popped his cherry and is now in the throes of a moral crisis. The holy one himself has fallen from grace, having sampled the sweet nectar of a flower in the Garden of Eden. Welcome to the ranks of us mere mortals, Dominic Manterra. Details! We must have details! Although his noble side will resist. Hell, any of his peers would be taking out an ad in the NY Times to announce their achievement! And at this age!"*

"The first thing that comes to my mind, Dominic, is that we must remember that we are all human after all. Our Lord may not want us to sin but at the same time, He knows that we are going to sin. Hence, the power of forgiveness. And I know that you are torn, obviously, with respect to what has happened but I wonder if you shouldn't allow yourself some slack here, and celebrate the beauty of the experience and what it means to you. Based on what you've shared so far, this was not just some cheap thrill with some tramp from the drama club or something like that who didn't mean anything to you."

Dominic reacted angrily, "She's not a tramp! Not at all! How could you even say that?"

Father Bumbry responded in a quiet, comforting tone, "You're not listening to me—I didn't say she was a tramp. On the contrary, I said she wasn't one. Obviously, based on the emotion you've expressed here with me, you have serious feelings for this young lady, and you experienced an intense emotional connection along with the physical intimacy that you have shared. That makes what you did *very special*. And putting the moral ramifications aside for a moment, if you can, the fact that you were able to have your first sexual experience be one of such intense emotions really sort of mitigates the sin part, in my view. Simply put, Dominic, I don't want to see you screw up and complicate what is a natural and wonderful human experience with a boatload of guilt and angst about piety and purity. It's done either way. You enjoyed it, it made you happy, you took the necessary precautions—life goes on. Don't torture yourself over it."

Dominic looked up. "Necessary precautions?"

Father Bumbry looked at him. "You used protection, right?" Dominic's dumbfounded expression told the priest the answer. "Dominic, you didn't use a condom? A rubber?" Dominic shook his head.

Father Bumbry let out a sigh. "Dominic, you have to go to the drugstore and buy some condoms. You don't want to be sexually active, not at your age, actually not for a long time, without wearing protection. You're so concerned about moral conflict. Sex is one thing—pregnancy brings that conflict to a whole other level. Get the condoms."

Dominic's mind began to race. "Does...does that mean she's going to get pregnant?"

Father Bumbry shrugged his shoulders. "Who knows? Anything's possible. But statistically speaking, it's very unlikely. I mean, it's rare that people have sex once and there's a pregnancy—not impossible, mind you, but not likely with just one time." Father Bumbry thought his comment would provide some relief to Dominic but the expression on his face told a different story. "Dominic, have there been multiple occasions when you have had sex with...with this girl? Is it one girl?"

Dominic glared at the priest. "Yes, of course it's only one girl. It will only be one, ever, Father Bumbry."

Father Bumbry smiled at the innocence of the remark. "OK, sorry, was it more than one occasion?"

Dominic shook his head. "No, it was just one night but we did... make love a number of times."

Father Bumbry raised his eyebrows. "How many times?"

"About four times...yes, it was four times." Dominic's cheeks turned red.

"Four times! Over how long a period?"

"About three hours." Dominic's face was burning. He felt awkward providing so much detail.

Father Bumbry whistled. "Well, you better get the economy size box of condoms then."

Dominic wanted to finish his confession and Father Bumbry needed to get out to the traditional confessional box as well as he was on call for this afternoon. Dominic added his usual litany of sins but Father Bumbry noted the omission of impure thoughts this time around—and notably absent was any mention of his recent experience. He gave Dominic a few Our Fathers and a couple of Hail Mary's to say, and an appeal to spend more time doing church-related activities. As they got ready to depart from the confession room, Father Bumbry sought to relieve the young lothario of any excess guilt.

"Dominic, think about what we talked about. I'm sure as years go on, and we look back on this, you will have worked out the issues in your own mind, and we can both have a good laugh. Don't worry so much. Get the condoms." He gave Dominic a big hug and felt he was entitled to a prolonged one at that. He also took the liberty of a quick peck on Dominic's cheek. Dominic thanked him for his understanding and counsel as Father Bumbry escorted him to the church exit. The priest pushed the large, heavy wooden door open and Dominic stepped out as the sunlight flooded the church through the opened door. Father Bumbry shaded his eyes as he watched Dominic walk down the stone steps of St. Mary's. He closed the door and proceeded down the nave of the church to the confessional box. *Four times! My Dominic is quite the stud! I shouldn't be surprised!* Father Bumbry thought to himself as he opened the door to the priest's compartment in the confessional box. He sat down in the chair and push the slider over to wait for the next confessor. Sitting in the dark compartment, the conversation with Dominic ran through his mind and he imagined the events that took place the night of Dominic's sexual escapade. He dropped his hands to his lap in the quiet darkness of the confessional and closed his eyes as his imagination took over....

"Ahem, Father?"

Father Bumbry was startled. He realized he had not heard the confessor step into the box and take his place at the kneeler.

"Father, you OK in there?"

Father Bumbry was panicked as he quickly pulled himself together. "Yes...yes, my son."

"OK, Father, just checking, heh heh, I know what you were doing in there."

Father Bumbry was aghast. "You...you do?"

"Oh yeah, the heavy breathing gave it away."

Father Bumbry froze.

"But don't worry, Father, your secret is safe with me."

"It is?"

"Sure, I understand. I mean, sitting in a dark closet on a Saturday afternoon, who wouldn't doze off?

Father Bumbry breathed a sigh of relief, "You're so right! Thank you for being so understanding. Shall we begin?" And Father Bumbry knew one confessor who would be getting a light penance.

THE FIRST TWO PLAY performances had been less than a resounding success. One of the Athenian lovers, Eugene Cerrano, the ASM student who had the role of Demetrius, had violated the school code and had been suspended. The powers that be decided that included the play performances that were scheduled on school days. For the Thursday and Friday performances, the student stage manager, Steve Embach, had to stand in as Demetrius. He walked through the part on stage, carrying a script and reciting the lines.

"It's not as if the part of one of the lovers in a play about four lovers is such a big deal." Dominic was still seething.

"Tonight is the closing night, and it's Saturday so Eugene will be on stage. It will be the best night and we will make the best of it." Moira, as usual, was the voice of reason and optimism. "After all, as you know, Lysander, 'The course of true love never did run smooth.'" Dominic joined in on reciting the quote.

"I still don't understand why they couldn't let him be in the play for all three nights. Find another way to discipline him. Why punish the rest of the cast who worked so hard? Not to mention the audience." Dominic shook his head.

"Not sure the audience was actually spared by *not* seeing Eugene perform." Steve Embach commented as he came by to tell Lysander and Hermia curtain time was in fifteen minutes. All three shared a good laugh.

Dominic and Moira made an excellent Lysander and Hermia—and their natural chemistry was much noticed by the audience in the ASM auditorium. As well as by Brother Corwin, who observed the elixir of teenage love pouring out onstage.

Dominic thought the play production was so much less stressful than the musical production the prior spring. Moira insisted that it was because of the absence of a certain individual. Dominic disagreed.

"Come on, Moira, why are you so hard on Brother Corwin?" asked Dominic.

"My darling Dominic, I have told you many times that there's something not right about him. I don't trust him. And I trust him less around you. There's just something about him, I can't explain it. He's always on a stage, always putting on a show. At the same time, he has this certain look—it's there in his eyes. You can't see it?"

"Not really. I mean, I get the showman of the century bit—God knows I've seen it enough in the classroom. Very annoying, believe me, you have no idea. But he's just a goof. He spent a lot of time teaching in Brownsville, Texas—so he probably picked up a lot of that bigger-than-life persona from living in the big country—that's what they call Texas."

"No kidding, Sherlock." Moira slapped him in the arm. "You do realize I have actually traveled across the country. As well as Europe. Yes, I have been to Paris, Texas and Paris, France, thank you! " Moira enjoyed teasing Dominic. "Anyway, I don't understand why you always defend him?"

"He's my friend, Moira. No, don't shake your head. You don't know how he's helped me. He's been there for me," Dominic insisted.

"When? Go on, tell me. He was there for you when?" Moira waited for a response.

Dominic sighed. "He was there...I was able to talk about a lot of things at home. I mean, dealing with my parents and how strict they are. He came and picked me up that one night I practically passed out at that party. And in many ways, it's easy to talk to him. We do have things in common."

Moira's stomach churned. She wanted to be the one that Dominic talked to about everything and anything—which he did for the most part—but Brother Corwin always seemed to be lurking in the background. Brother Corwin's behavior at last spring's cast party still weighed on her mind. She recognized what it was about Brother Corwin in relation to Dominic that ate away at her so much: it was his possessiveness of Dominic. She sensed a certain degree of hostility from Brother Corwin aimed at her whenever their paths crossed—like at Dominic's soccer games or, more often, at the play practices when he would suddenly show up and find ways to steal Dominic away from her. Friendship was one thing, but her intuition told her something else was at play here—and she suspected it was not healthy.

"I still don't trust him," Moira stated emphatically but she wasn't sure that Dominic heard her.

The final performance was the best, and the cast received three standing ovations at the end. The cast party was going to be in the cafeteria this time, which made it easier on everyone with respect to driving and parking. Dominic's parents and brothers came to see the final performance. Mr. Manterra was really impressed, especially with the student who played Puck, who had improvised some of the best lines of the show. Chris McGill was a natural jokester and a talented artist who drew the caricatures of the students who were recognized as ASM's "Tiger of the Month." Mrs. Manterra enjoyed Dominic and Moira's parts the best, though she expressed some concern to Dominic about what she referred to as "familiarity" between the two. His parents gave him approval for the cast party and didn't even impose a specific curfew on him—"Just use your good judgment."

The cast party was smaller than the one for the musical as there were a smaller number of roles for the play and limited stage crew duties. Moira was glad the party was in the cafeteria as well because she didn't want to revisit the setting of the last party. However, one constant annoyance could not be avoided—Brother Corwin showed up for the party.

"Well hallo, Moira! Good to see Moira of you again. Excellent performance as Hermia—you really pulled off that part—even getting your Lysander in the end." Brother Corwin gave her a leering smile and she was immediately repulsed. "I don't see that boy from Christian Brothers here—I guess he wasn't interested anymore." Brother Corwin paused to put some potato chips and dip on his paper plate before looking at Moira and continuing, "In the drama club, I mean."

Moira responded, "He's in college now, but you seem so interested in him, Brother Corwin, perhaps you should look him up. I'm sure he'd love to hear from you." And she walked away.

Little bitch! he thought to himself. He scanned the cafeteria in search of someone. Over in the corner he spotted him. He chucked the paper plate in a trash can and made his way over to the corner.

"You really did a good job as Lysander, Dominic. It was like you and Moira weren't acting at all."

"Thanks, Jeff, but it was really Hermia's, I mean Moira's, performance that made our scenes work so well." Dominic took a sip from a can of soda. Jeff noticed they had company and told Dominic he was going to get some food.

"Bravo, bravo, little brother!" Brother Corwin extended his hand to Dominic. "Yes, quite the performance for such a new-comer to the stage."

Dominic shook the extended hand. "Thanks, Brother Corwin. It was a good play. I really enjoyed the experience."

"Yes, a classic of the theater with all the plots and subplots and the play within a play shenanigan. Lovers in conflict, interfering parents, and all that stuff. As you said, 'The course of true love never did run smooth.'"

"Yes, it does have all that, doesn't it?"

"Clever and witty and romantic and fun all at the same time. So, what's next on the achievement list, little brother?"

"Achievement list?"

"You seem to have set out to conquer the world with your schedule of activities between clubs, sports, church, school, and the like. It's a wonder you have time to sleep. You know, little brother, I've advised you against burning the candle on both ends. There are only so many hours in a day, and days in a year, and years in a life. One shouldn't shorten any of them by extending their respective realm beyond the possible. I believe you should give serious thought to how stretched you appear to be. You don't want an infatuation with the mundane to cause you to miss the big picture."

Dominic listened attentively and nodded his head. "Sage advice, Brother Corwin. I will keep that in mind for sure. You know, Brother Corwin, you're right. After being in this play I realize that I sometimes do miss the important things, like showing more appreciation for people who have been there for me. I just want to thank you for the time you have spent with me, the hours we spent talking about life, especially the arts and music, plays and poetry, family and stuff. I had never really been able to do that before with anyone else. So, thank you for that."

Brother Corwin placed his hand on Dominic's shoulder. "No problem, little brother. You know how I feel about you. I only want what's best for you and only have your best interest in mind. Having said that, I was wondering if you would do me a favor?"

"Sure, Brother, what is it?"

"As you might or might not know, poor Brother Abelard—*vive la France!*; heh heh—besides being your world lit teacher was also the yearbook moderator. Besides assuming his classroom duty, I have taken on the yearbook moderator role as well. I was wondering if I could make use of your considerable writing talent to help with some sections of the yearbook. It would probably only involve a Saturday or two to put some pieces together. With his sudden departure, Brother Abelard has kind of left me in a tight spot to meet deadlines with the printing company. They require drafts and outlines by certain dates in order to meet the final delivery date. What do you think?"

"Sure, Brother Corwin, I could do that, now's a good time too. I would enjoy that."

"I was hoping you would say that! We can also chat and catch up on things as well. We'll make a day of it. It will be fun!" Brother Corwin released one of his signature guffaws.

Diagonally across the cafeteria room, Moira observed the two figures talking in the corner with an uneasiness she couldn't exactly explain to herself. One person was the focus of her heart's love and desire—and the other, she loathed and distrusted. She could not figure out Brother Corwin's sinister hold on her Dominic, but she knew one thing in her heart and mind and soul: she had to break it.

"Brother Corwin, what did you think of Moira's Hermia?" Dominic asked with pride.

"Moira's Hermia? Oh, you mean the Toomey girl. Yes, uh, she did, uh, alright for herself, perhaps a little overacting here and there, but not too shabby overall. Is she here tonight? I recall at the spring cast party her being quite smitten with some athlete from Christian Brothers. I thought it a bit shameless how she was throwing herself at him. Not sure I can totally blame her. He was a tad taller than you, more of an athletic build. Although I do believe he was older. If memory serves me well, they left together—right after you went home. Anyway, let me know if next Saturday works for you?"

Brother Corwin noticed Dominic was lost in his thoughts. He traced Dominic's blank stare to the opposite corner, where Moira stood talking with Steve Embach, the stage manager and understudy for Demetrius, and Helena from the play, Regina Marie Mason McDuff. "You will let me know then?" he asked.

"Hmm...what...I'm sorry, Brother Corwin, what was that about next Saturday?" Dominic broke out of his trance.

"I said will you let me know about next Saturday—if that would work for you to assist on the yearbook writing?"

"Yeah, oh yeah, shouldn't be a problem but I will let you know for sure during the week. If you'll excuse me, Brother Corwin, I'm going to go catch up with some of the other cast members and congratulate them."

"Of course, little brother, go mingle and have some fun, you've earned it!" Brother Corwin slapped Dominic on his back as he made his way past him. Brother Corwin watched Dominic wiggle through the crowd, occasionally pausing to exchange handshakes and back slaps for mutual congrats. Sure enough, Dominic eventually reached the corner where

Moira stood. Brother Corwin wasn't sure how far little brother's infatuation with the Toomey girl had progressed but he knew one thing for
sure before it developed any further: he had to annihilate it.

He raised the can of Coke to his lips and found himself caught in the
cross-hairs of Morris Gavin's curious gaze. Brother Corwin tilted his can
toward Morris and nodded.

"I NOTICED YOU CHATTING with Brother Corwin tonight." Moira was
careful in how she brought up the subject, not wishing to put Dominic
on the defensive.

Dominic was staring out the passenger side window as Moira drove
towards his house. "Yeah, he was congratulating me on the play. He also
paid you a compliment."

Moira started to sense an uneasy tension. Her instinct was telling her
something was wrong and she needed to address it right away.

"Dominic, my love, what were—"

"Why are you so against him? Why don't you like him? What has he
ever done to you?" he snapped, cutting her off.

"Wh— who, who are you talking about?"

"You know who I'm talking about! Brother Corwin! Isn't that who
you were going to ask me about? You were going to ask me what we
were talking about, right?"

Moira was a taken back by the intensity and hostility in Dominic's
tone. "Dominic, I really don't even know Brother Corwin—"

"That's right, you don't!" he replied sharply, cutting her off again.
"You don't know him at all but you seem to have a lot to say about him,
all negative."

Moira pulled the car over and parked it.

"What are you doing?" Dominic asked.

"We're going to talk about this and we're going to talk about it like
two rational people, and we're going to talk about it right now, Dominic
Manterra!" Moira spoke with fire in her voice.

Dominic dropped his chin to his chest and grew quiet. Moira looked at him wondering to herself what poison Brother Corwin filled Dominic's head with.

"What else did your *good friend* Brother Corwin have to say?" Moira paused. "Tell me, Dominic, or so help me God you can get the hell out of this car right now and walk away and don't even think about looking back!" Moira knew she didn't really mean it but she had to jolt him somehow.

Dominic looked at her. "You really mean that, Moira? You really would do that?"

Moira was torn. She knew she had to choose her next words carefully. She couldn't surrender. Too much was at stake. But she couldn't alienate Dominic.

"Dominic, you have to know by now how much I care about you. My God, Dominic, I love you! Did you forget that night already? The night we shared ourselves—the night we gave our hearts to each other, we became one in spirit and soul? And the conversations since then? Does any of that mean anything to you? Or am I alone in believing that we have something so special, something so sacred, that only you and I can claim as our own? Am I mistaken in believing in you?"

Moira's words weighed heavily on Dominic. Her words cut right to the bone, right to his heart. He quietly answered, "No, Moira, not at all. I could never forget that night and what we shared. Never. I'm so sorry, I really am."

Moira placed her hand on Dominic's cheek and he rubbed it against her soft palm. "Dominic, I would never hurt you, trust me, I would kill myself before I would ever do anything to hurt you. But I don't trust Brother Corwin. I don't like the way he looks at you, I don't like the way he looks at me when you're talking to me. I don't like the way he plays games with people and tries to manipulate everyone and anyone with his phony act of friendship and sincerity. He's not a nice person and he may think he has everyone fooled about who and what he really is, but he doesn't fool me. But..." Moira paused.

"But what? He has me fooled, is that what you think?" asked Dominic.

Moira took a deep breath. "Dominic, I don't know what you and Brother Corwin talk about or have talked about in the past. And maybe it's none of my business, but no matter what you say, I don't think it's healthy that you have a friendship with that man. Not at all."

Dominic shook his head. "Maybe there's another reason, Moira."

"What do you mean?"

"Maybe there's another reason you don't like Brother Corwin."

"What reason is that?"

Dominic looked directly at Moira without saying anything.

"What did he tell you, Dominic? What did that sick bastard say to you?"

Dominic grimaced. He really didn't want to say anything. "Moira, I don't want to talk about this anymore."

"Tell me what he said, Dominic? Please tell me, Dominic. You owe me that much, don't you think?"

"I owe you that much?"

"You owe me the truth. You owe me your honesty. You say you love me—honesty and truth are what love is all about. So, either you tell me the truth, either you be honest with me, or you're telling me that you really don't love me." Moira knew she had to clearly lay it all on the line. "And that you took me for a complete fool that night."

Dominic wrestled with his thoughts and his emotions. He knew deep down that Moira was right—about everything. He was feeling ashamed to even bring up the conversation. But he didn't want to keep anything from Moira.

"Brother Corwin brought up the, uh, the spring, uh..."

"Cast party?" Moira's voice was ice cold. How she detested Brother Corwin!

"Yeah. He spoke about you and Trevor."

"What did he say exactly?"

Dominic hesitated for a moment. "He just said how you threw yourself at him and left with him shortly after I had gone home."

"And you believed him?"

Dominic hesitated. "I...uh...he...it's..."

"Tell me, Dominic, did you believe him?" Moira was incredulous.

"No...uh...no...I..."

"Get out. Get out right now." Her voice trembled with a combination of anger and hurt.

"Moira...no..."

"How could you, Dominic? How could you?" Moira began to cry.

"Moira, I didn't believe him. I'm telling you the truth. Why would I believe him after what you told me?"

Moira calmed herself down. "I knew he would try to get between us, Dominic. I just knew it. But I thought I could trust you to not doubt me—to not listen to his lies."

Dominic implored her. "And I didn't, Moira, believe me, I didn't."

"Then why did I feel something changed tonight? Even now, driving you home, you were quiet. You had something on your mind. You were thinking about what he told you, weren't you? Tell me the truth."

Dominic hung his head. "Moira...I...I have...to be honest with you. It did bother me...a little bit. I did start to think about that night last spring...and I..."

"But I told you everything, Dominic. I told you everything and didn't hold anything back. Why did you doubt me?"

"I don't know! Really, I can't explain it. I don't even know why Brother Corwin brought it up."

"Because he's an evil person, Dominic. He's not who you think he is. He really isn't. He's a selfish, sick man who wants you for himself, can't you see that? Please, listen to me. Believe me, he means you harm. I know it!"

"How do you know that?" Dominic was defensive. "How can you know that? Why would you even think that?"

"I can't explain it, Dominic. I can't explain it but I know I'm right. I feel it in my heart, in my soul. You have to believe me and trust me on this."

"I don't know, Moira. It's not like Brother Corwin has ever tried to hurt me. If anything, he's always tried to help me, to be there for me. I mean, he was the only person that recognized so many things about me and the only person I felt could ever talk to about so many things that…." Dominic cut himself off.

"About what, Dominic? About what? He was the only person you could talk to about anything, right? That's what he wants you to believe! That's part of his whole scheme! Well, you're wrong, Dominic, you're so wrong. You could talk to me about anything as well. You could talk to me, but you won't. You still hold back sometimes. Why? Why is that?"

Dominic fell silent. He dropped his head down into his hands. He didn't have an answer for Moira. For so long he had never shared his thoughts, his feelings, his loneliness, his hurts with anyone. But somehow, some way, Brother Corwin had managed to break through that barrier, break down those walls. He knew that Brother Corwin had sometimes said strange things and told him stories that he thought were inappropriate and not normal, crazy stuff actually, but he just attributed them to his quirky personality and trying to be funny in his own goofy, Broadway-star-wanna-be way. He just mostly ignored those times.

"Dominic…" Moira spoke softly and touched his hand. Dominic immediately raised his head and turned to her and threw his arms around her neck and held her tight. Tears started to stream down his face. "Moira, I'm sorry. I'm so sorry. You're right. I was bothered by what Brother Corwin told me. But I wasn't mad at you. I wasn't sorry about anything I've shared with you. I was just…I was just scared, that's all. I was scared that you…"

Moira stroked the back of his head, and whispered, "It's alright, Dominic, it's alright, my little prince, I promised I would never hurt you. I meant that, my love. I never would and I never will. You have to believe me. You have to trust me. You have to know that you can always turn to me." She pushed him gently back from her and took his face in her hands.

"I will always be here for you, Dominic. I would never abandon you. Do you understand?" Dominic nodded yes.

"Do you believe me?" Again, Dominic nodded yes.

"I truly love you, Dominic. You do know that, right?" Again, Dominic nodded yes.

Moira kissed him on his head, then on each of his eyes, and then on the mouth. She embraced him and held him for a little while longer.

"OK, my love, I better get you home before your family thinks you've been kidnapped by Hermia!" They both laughed as Moira started her car.

"Moira, we still have a little time left. My parents said to use my judgment for getting home. Do you think we could hang out a little longer?"

Moira was pleased to hear her love's request. "Oui, mon amour! Where would you like to go?"

"Let's go to Warnock Park! How does that sound?"

Moira smiled. "As long as Lysander is not going for another run...I don't know if I could control myself this time! Though another poem would be nice..."

"Not tonight, sweet Hermia! No such enchanted forest display planned!" Dominic touched her cheek. "You have the softest skin, Moira. Your beauty is a constant inspiration for me. I will always write poems for you, my love!" he spoke with an earnest tenderness that filled Moira's soul. Moira took his hand and kissed it.

They entered the park and drove around until Moira saw a spot that was open off the main road, with a good view of the night sky. She pulled over and parked the car.

"Is this spot, OK?"

Dominic considered the surroundings. "Hmmm, I don't know. Actually, if you wouldn't mind, why not pull up a little further and park between those two trees."

Moira saw the spot he was referring to and moved the car over, posi-
tioning it snugly between the two trees that Dominic had pointed to
and turned off the engine. She turned to Dominic and they immediately
embraced and shared a passionate kiss. Dominic gently rested her head
on his shoulder and whispered, "I am so sorry for what happened before
and for my insensitivity. I am so unworthy of you, Moira. You are so
good and kind...so wise...I...I don't know why you put up with me."

Moira pulled away from him, to gaze into her love's eyes. "Don't ever
think like that, Dominic Manterra. I am with you because I want to be
with you. I choose to be with you. You...you have touched my heart ...
in a way that no one will ever be able to make me feel. Your love for
me...makes my heart a sanctuary for joy. Do you understand that? You
have truly tamed me, my love. I am your precious rose. You prove your
worth for me with the love you have shared with me and the time you
have spent on me...never forget that, my poet prince." She threw her
arms around his neck and kissed him on his mouth. Dominic wrapped
his arms around her as well.

It happened fast, like a lightning flash before the rain falls. There was
no screeching of tires as the car did not attempt to slow down or swerve.
Instead, the car was at full speed when it made impact with the tree
behind Moira's car. It bounced off the tree and fishtailed and spun to the
side of Moira's car before sliding across the road and halting to a stop.
The loud bang startled Dominic and Moira, with Moira letting out a
short scream and Dominic reacting by hugging her closer to him.

"Are you alright? Are you OK?" Dominic quickly asked. Moira
nodded her head yes. "Alright, I'm just going to check on the other car."
Dominic gently let go of his embrace, got out of the car and ran over to
the other vehicle. Dominic looked into the car and saw only the driver
in it, who remained motionless hunched over the steering wheel. Dominic could see that he was still breathing. A police siren could be heard in
the distance. A stranger from a nearby house showed up and asked if
anyone was hurt. He said that he had called the police as well. Within
minutes, a police cruiser arrived. Dominic glanced over at Moira's car

and saw that Moira was standing at the back of her car, leaning against it. He went over to her.

"Are you hurt? Are you injured at all?" he asked her. Moira just shook her head no and then reached for him to hold her. Dominic pulled Moira in close and she buried her face in his chest and began to cry. Dominic gently caressed her back and kissed the top of her head. "Everything's alright, everything's fine, my love, we're OK, everything's alright, everything is going to be alright." Moira's crying intensified as she thought of where she had originally parked. The same thought passed through Dominic's mind as his embrace of her grew tighter and he began to softly sing to her "everything's alright, yes, everything's fine...we're both going to be well tonight..." He sang the words over and over again, holding his precious rose in his arms and gazing back at the spot they had originally parked....

XXXII.

FIRST CUT IS THE DEEPEST

Dominic was having a serious case of writer's block. He sat at a table in the ASM art and music studio room while Brother Corwin was at the instructor's desk with piles of photographs taken by members of the photography club and the yearbook staff during the first half of the school year. Brother Corwin was rummaging through the different pictures: black and white photos, color photos, photos organized by class year, club activities, sports teams, general group and individual picture categories. Dominic scrunched up another sheet of yellow pad paper and threw it at the waste basket. Brother Corwin looked up from his photos and let go one of his guffaws.

"Still searching for inspiration, little brother?"

Dominic sighed. He had questioned Brother Corwin as to why he wasn't having each section drafted by a student from the respective class year. Brother Corwin's response was that Brother Abelard had been derelict in his duties of keeping the yearbook layout on a timely calendar and there was no time for recruiting students for these tasks; that, and Brother Corwin's need for control over the content and quality of the writing. He wanted a consistency in the writing throughout the yearbook—that was best achieved by a single wordsmith. Besides, Brother Corwin's creativity was more focused when working in a one-on-one situation. Dominic had completed the write-ups for the underclassmen sections, and they had met with Brother Corwin's approval. He was struggling with the narrative for the senior class. Although he had written a number of different drafts, Brother Corwin had rejected them for being too hollow, trite, saccharin, or uninspiring—and this was the most important section.

"We need to send our graduates off with pride, pomp, and pizazz!" Brother Corwin whirled his arms in a showy display of emphasis.

Dominic sat back with his hands behind his head and looked at the ceiling. He closed his eyes and tried to think of a different angle, a different approach. He had been there for nearly five hours now, and he was worried his creative juices were drying up. He opened the pizza box on the table behind him and grabbed a cold slice of pizza with the cheese now a dried, gray, waxy glaze. Throughout the morning and early afternoon, Brother Corwin had played a variety of musicals on the cassette player, occasionally joining in on the singing. Brother Corwin flew down to Texas every June to perform summer stock. For next summer he would be staging *Man of La Mancha,* of course playing the role of the errant knight himself. From the singing he had heard from Brother Corwin, Dominic believed it may well be "the impossible dream." Dominic didn't really think Brother Corwin had a very good voice. Brother Corwin described it as a professional stage voice. Dominic's friend Denny, upon hearing Brother Corwin singing at a school mass, described it as obnoxiously off-key, lacking pitch, and tone deaf. Dominic tended to agree with Denny's assessment.

In addition to the musical entertainment, Brother Corwin sprinkled in plenty of conversation—he was making good on his vow to repair and renew his relationship with Dominic. He was feeling good about the rapport between him and his young protégé during the course of the day. Things were back on track and a full restoration of trust was definitely in sight. He just needed to be more tactical in his future approach with the impressionable and sensitive Dominic. He would achieve success in remembering that patience ruled the day and would pay the dividends that he desired. He realized he had been moving too quickly and a tad callously in his conquest of the youth. While Dominic's naïve and guileless manner were an advantage, his virtue and sanctitude were obstacles not easily overcome. The only benefit that Brother Corwin saw in them was that they would also prevent the likes of Moira Toomey to get anywhere with Dominic. He observed that Dominic was suddenly writing with intense focus, the sheets of yellow paper being turned up in quick succession. He smiled at the bolt of inspiration that had apparently struck Dominic. He went back to sorting through the ocean of photographs taken by the student shutterbug enthusiasts. Unfortunately, not one was on the plateau of his craftsmanship and he would likely have to select pictures he had personally taken.

Dominic placed his pen down, stood up, walked over to Brother Corwin, and placed the yellow pad in front of him. He returned to the table, opened a can of iced tea, and sat down. Brother Corwin picked up the pad and began to read. Dominic watched as the Apostle of St. Mary brother progressed through the pages of the pad, occasionally taking a drink from his cup of black coffee. Brother Corwin finished his reading, leaned back in his chair, and looking at Dominic, slowly released a low-bellied guffaw until the room seemed to echo with it.

"Well, little brother, we could have been done hours ago if you just started with this! It's perfect! *Instead, we offer a simple fable...*I love it. Excellent work."

"Thanks, Brother Corwin. You're right—this is the approach I should have taken from the start."

"What finally got you to this?" inquired Brother Corwin.

"The book you gave me. *The Little Prince*," answered Dominic, contemplating another slice of pizza.

"Ah, but of course. Very good, little brother. We never have had a chance to discuss that one. I take it you liked it?"

"Very much so. I would have to say it immediately became one of my favorite books."

Brother Corwin grinned. He was very pleased that Dominic was en-amored with the book. "Did you have a particular part that stuck out for you?"

"Oh yeah, definitely—the conversation with the wolf and the little prince."

Brother Corwin was puzzled. "Wolf? There's no wolf in the book."

Dominic scratched his head. "There isn't? Doesn't he talk about the hunters?"

Brother Corwin guffawed. "Oh, the fox! There's a fox."

"That's right! The fox, sorry about that. That was my favorite part." Dominic laughed at mixing up the animals.

Brother Corwin was very pleased—that chapter was the key to the book. "That's the essential part of the story."

"Uh-huh. Moira and I talked about that part. Moira had read the book before."

Brother Corwin's blood turned to ice upon hearing the words spoken out loud. Had that little vixen meddled in his affairs? What right had she to be discussing this book with Dominic? He needed to find out what damage had been done. He took a sip from his coffee and placed it gently down on the desk.

"Oh, really? What possible insights could she have provided?"

"She really knew a lot about it. I guess it helps when you've read it in the original French, right? Nothing gets lost in the translation then." Dominic smiled.

Brother Corwin bit his lower lip. "Did she now? She can read French?"

"Yup, she's fluent. Her mom was a French teacher. She's actually been to Paris. She's a really smart person. Smarter than me, that's for sure."

"It sounds like you're, uh, quite taken with the young lady, little brother."

"Yes, we've become extremely close, especially since being in the play together. We've known each other a long time before that though. We went to grammar school together. I guess you can say I've always been her secret admirer. Ever since that cold January morning when I saw her in front of her yellow house. She's beautiful. The most beautiful person in the world."

Incensed anger began to well up in Brother Corwin. He began to suspect that he had not taken this Toomey girl seriously enough. Hopefully she had not done irreparable damage. He would have to conduct an assessment. He had to think quickly about his approach.

"So, tell me, what did Moira have to say about *The Little Prince*? Did she have a favorite part as well?"

Dominic nodded. "Yes, she did, and it was the same as mine. That's how I found out that she had read it, by what she said to me."

"And what was that, little brother?" Brother Corwin asked sneeringly.

"She said that I tamed her." Dominic bit into the slice of pizza he had decided to eat, after all.

Brother Corwin's elbow knocked over the cup of coffee, it spread quickly over the desk. "Damnit!" he reacted, hurriedly moving the piles of photographs out of the spilled coffee's path and throwing the yellow pad to the floor. Dominic jumped up and grabbed the paper towels from the table next to the pizza box. He rushed over to the table and started patting dry the spill. Brother Corwin snatched the paper towels from Dominic and began wiping the desk.

"And what exactly did she mean by that?" Brother Corwin snapped at Dominic.

Dominic shrugged. "You know, Brother Corwin...I mean, you read it."

"No, I don't know what *she* meant. Why don't you explain it to me?"

Dominic felt a little uneasy sensing the hostility in Brother Corwin's voice.

"She...we...grew close. She let me in...and now I'm responsible for her."

"She let you in? *How* did she let you in?"

"We talked and she opened up to me and I opened up to her. I guess in a way, all these years we've known each other but kept our distance, you know, over time, we sort of followed our own *rites*. We were patient and actually I was always too shy to ever really speak to her. As I remember it, I was always stealing glances and staring at her when we were growing up in grammar school together. Although I had hardly ever said a word to her, I always longed for her, and secretly hoped that she had feelings for me. I guess I learned that what the, uh, fox says to the little prince is true."

"And what is that?" Brother Corwin's voice dripped with disdain.

Dominic answered dreamily, "You can only really rightly see when you look at life, at people, at love—through the eyes of the heart." He looked at Brother Corwin. "That makes sense, right? Isn't that the lesson the fox is trying to teach the little prince? We usually look at those things that matter through some kaleidoscope of our own fears and doubts and prejudices and that view really blinds us to what's important. It's funny, a thought just hit me. It's like the difference between looking at a mirror and looking through a window. The view each presents really shapes the person we are." Dominic sat down and placed his arms behind his head and looked at the ceiling. He smiled, pleased with himself. "I think I realize what Miss Svarickova was trying to tell me that night."

Brother Corwin wondered who this Miss Svarickova was—evidently another bitch from Dominic's past whose influence he would have to undo. He could hardly contain his sarcasm. "Why, aren't you the poster boy for idealistic notions and naïve visions? You disappoint me, little brother. Apparently, you have fallen prey to that most devious of life's realities."

Dominic sat up in his chair. "What do you mean? Isn't that the moral of *The Little Prince*?"

Brother Corwin frowned. "I'm not talking about that, per se. What I'm talking about is how you've been taken for a fool with your romantic notions of life and love and people. I think you need a dose of harsh reality before you're taken for more of a fool than you already have been.

Hmm, I must admit how quite surprised I am at how easily you've been fooled by it."

Dominic was confused. "I don't understand. Fooled by what?"

"By a female's deceptive skill. The art of deception is the most power-ful weapon in their box of tricks. And you, little brother, have been de-ceived in a most cruel and selfish way." Brother Corwin decided he needed to go with an all-attack. Everything was fair play now.

Dominic was even more perplexed. "What are you trying to say, Brother Corwin? How have I been deceived?"

"Obviously, by your *friend* Moira, who has convinced you of some deep level of emotional connection between the two of you."

"You're wrong about that, Brother Corwin. Believe me, Moira would never try to trick me or lie to me. I know that for sure." Dominic's tone was dismissive.

"Really? And how well do you know her?" Brother Corwin could hardly temper his accusatory tone.

"I know her very well. I know her well enough to say...*she has tamed me*," answered Dominic with a soft solemnness.

Brother Corwin stared at Dominic, gaining an immediate apprecia-tion for the full meaning behind his words. Obviously, the little vixen had wasted no time in her seduction of the idealistic youth.

"Little brother, I take it by the implication that you have been, shall we say, intimate with her?"

Dominic hesitated. He wasn't sure he wanted to discuss this with Brother Corwin as the conversation was becoming somewhat uncomfort-able. "You know, Brother Corwin, I'd rather not talk about this, if you don't mind."

Brother Corwin realized he was losing ground, and quickly. He needed to pivot and maneuver. He softened his tone. "Why is that, little brother? Are there now topics that are off limits to us? What has changed? Did you not just say last week that you recognized your lack of appreciation for the times in the past that I have been there for you?

Is this how you mean to show your appreciation for our friendship now, by treating me like an outsider?"

"No, no, Brother Corwin, of course not. I mean I just feel like..."

"Then what is it? Is it because I might be right and you're afraid of hearing the truth?"

"The truth about what? Brother Corwin, I think you're misunderstanding the situation."

"Oh, that is rich, Dominic, that is rich. You're the one being made a fool of and you're the one who is blind to the situation. You are the one not understanding what is happening and I am just trying to help you understand the reality of it. I don't want to see you make an even bigger mistake than you may already have."

"A mistake that I may already have?"

Brother Corwin gave Dominic a stern, disapproving look. "You've slept with her, right?" Brother Corwin paused for a moment to let the question sink in, and then spoke to clarify, "You've had sexual relations with Moira, am I right?"

Dominic nodded. "Yes, I have."

"And you believe that's OK? There's nothing wrong with that?"

Dominic responded, "I'm not sorry for what I have done. Nor am I ashamed—no, not at all, if that's what you're asking me."

Brother Corwin was a little caught off guard with Dominic's assured response. He couldn't let up, however.

"This Moira must be something else. *Really, something else.* No, I don't mean, of course, in terms of her sexual prowess or experience, mind you, although I'm certain she brought a considerable amount of it to the table, or should I say bed. What I marvel at is her ability to get you to so easily and readily compromise your high moral standards, your core values of purity and sanctity. What was that psalm you told me your mother use to recite to you? Oh yes, I remember it now, although you appear to have forgotten it—"Who shall ascend the hill of the Lord? He who has clean hands and a pure heart. He who is not vain in the ways of the flesh?" Something along those lines, I forget it exactly. It sounds like *you've* forgotten it entirely."

Brother Corwin's words struck at Dominic's conscience. He grimaced upon hearing the words of his childhood resound in his ears.

"So, tell me, Dominic, how do you reconcile your actions with Moira with your mother's guidance? It appears that not only do you not know Moira very well, but Moira knows so little about you and the promises you made to your mother. Or is it that Moira just has so little respect for your beliefs and in turn the beliefs of your mother? I mean, you could answer that question better than I."

Dominic's cheeks were burning. Brother Corwin was right—he, Dominic, seemed to have forgotten the words of his mother, and the promises he made to her to abide by them. But then, how could Moira be responsible for any of that? She wasn't, in his mind.

Brother Corwin pressed forward. "But I don't blame you, little brother, I really don't. As the saying goes, if you wave a red flag in front of a bull, it's going to charge. You're obviously just another victim of her deception, another notch on her bedpost. She's probably using you the way she used the boy from the spring cast party. Like I said, deception is an art form for girls like Moira. She was bored with him and then moved on to the next one. Who knows how many were before him? God knows you won't be the last."

Dominic became angry now. He didn't agree with Brother Corwin nor did he like the liberty he was taking with Moira's reputation. "You don't know that any of what you're saying has any truth in it, Brother Corwin, and I would appreciate it if you would not say these unkind things about Moira. Maybe I wasn't being clear before, but I will set the record straight now—I love Moira and she loves me and that's all that matters."

A broad grin spread across Brother Corwin's face, followed by a guffaw. "Oh, she has really put a spell on you, little brother! Bravo for Miss Toomey. It just validates my point: what better weapon to deceive the idealistic Dominic Manterra than to wrap the immoral act in the camouflage of romantic love? It would be really amusing if it weren't so pathetic! Again, I am just baffled how she was able to convince you to compromise your virtues with her own reputation being so questionable. I mean, be honest with yourself, Dominic—do you really think you were her *first love?*" Brother Corwin had no basis for the question or accusation but figured in the war for Dominic's soul, any seeds of doubt were ripe for planting.

Dominic's mind was racing. As far as he was concerned, he was Moira's first love because she didn't really love Trevor—so it didn't matter if he was Moira's first sexual experience. Not that he was necessarily thrilled by it, but it didn't change his feelings toward Moira.

"As far as I'm concerned, I am Moira's first love just as much as she is mine."

"I take it with that qualification that you were not her first sexual partner. Now comes the hard truth for you, little brother. Your boyhood delusions of romantic love aside, what makes you so sure that there haven't been others that she slept with? I mean, she is older than you and she has a car, meaning she can get around, in more ways than one. What makes you sure you're even her second? She is quite attractive, and I'm sure even among your peers she has a fair share of admirers."

"I just know it, that's all." Dominic was holding steadfast to his position. "It doesn't matter and it doesn't change how I feel about her. Period."

"And who arranged for your sexual encounter? Did you set this all up? The time, the place, the setting? I find it hard to believe based on all our conversations that Dominic Manterra has become so skilled in the practice of deceit—just the amount of lies alone must be fairly significant. All your doing and planning, I suppose?"

Dominic didn't say a word.

"Right, I didn't think so. Again, little brother, I don't hold it against you. It's difficult being your age, at this time in your life, dealing with surging hormones and sexual impulses. It strains the male capacity for self-control. That's why nature provides its own release. And then there's the option for taking matters into one's own hands. Both preferable to falling victim to the likes of someone like Moira. So, let's recap where we are at this point: one, you weren't her first sexual relationship; two, you don't know how many she actually has had; three, it's doubtful based on one and two, whether this relationship will mean you're the last; and four, how do you reconcile your act of fornication with the virtues that you have embraced your whole life up to this point, before failing to live up to those virtues because of this girl's promiscuous ways?"

Doubts were beginning to seep into Dominic's mind. Brother Corwin's points were not entirely unfounded. True, Moira had been honest with him about her experience with Trevor, and she didn't have to be; he would have been none the wiser for it. But it would also serve to appease him from suspecting any others by her being so forthcoming with one. And if there were others besides Trevor, then what did that really make him in her eyes? Was he being a fool? He didn't doubt his feelings for her, but could he really be so sure about hers for him? Finally, he had combatted his guilt about their physical intimacy by virtue of his belief in the sincerity of their love and, quite honestly, because he really enjoyed making love with Moira, he couldn't deny that. But just because he loved her and it felt good didn't necessarily make it right.

Brother Corwin observed the wrestling match going on inside Dominic's head as it was being waged on Dominic's face. He was confident the wedge was working its way in between Dominic's confidence and his conscience. Now was the time for a flank attack.

"I take it you used protection?"

Dominic did not answer, but his eyes dropped to the floor.

"Right, so no protection either. Your folly in this situation is astounding! No thought of an unwanted pregnancy, Dominic, really now? Oh wait, I could be making quite an assumption. I really don't know Moira as well as you apparently do, but is it so out of the realm of possibilities that she might want to get pregnant? God knows, I don't have any reasons that I could think of as to why she would want to but that doesn't change the biological processes of the human body. When people have unprotected sex, Dominic, there's a good chance that a baby will be conceived. Not to mention, that when you have sex with someone who may have had multiple sexual partners, there is a real chance of catching a sexually transmitted disease." Brother Corwin's voice and tone were becoming increasing louder and more severe as he spoke. "You see, little brother, life isn't a Shakespearean sonnet or a Shelley love poem. Love isn't some overflowing power of emotion to borrow from Wordsworth that doesn't have any consequence in the real world. You need to wake up from your idealistic fantasy of life as it ought to be and get a huge healthy dose of the reality of life as it is. Simply put, you screwing around like you are right now in your life has a real possibility of screwing up the rest of your life! Stop acting like a complete, pathetic lovesick fool and get a grip! Before you do irreparable damage to your life and to that of the so-called love of your life, although I don't necessarily care what happens to her as she will likely get what she deserves!" Brother Corwin's words had reached a crescendo and now he took a deep breath to see if the battle was won.

Dominic felt beaten down. As he listened, the words seared his conscience and weighed on his emotion. He did think there was much logic to what Brother Corwin was saying. He did not blame Moira or have any change of heart about how he felt about her, but the potential consequences of their actions were hitting home. Some changes were definitely in order.

"A lot of what you say, Brother Corwin, makes sense to me, there's no denying the sound reasoning. I should have given more thought to the consequences of my actions, my choices. I appreciate you taking the time to talk to me about it," Dominic's voice was quiet but steady, "and I will certainly talk it over with Moira."

Brother Corwin stiffened upon hearing those last few words come out of Dominic's mouth. Evidently, the battle wasn't over just yet. A different attack plan was warranted.

"Trust me, little brother, I don't say these things to make you feel bad. And I'm glad that you're beginning to see the light. But I would be amiss if I didn't point out that my goal here isn't about raising your awareness of consequences. I want to be clear I'm not sharing all this with you so you can take proper precautions or practical steps to avoid those consequences. I am really surprised at you, Dominic. Have you changed? Are you the same person who spoke so much about the importance of a spiritual life and being close to God? It wasn't so long ago you were sharing with me the promises you made to your mom as a young boy. Do you remember what you told me? How she explained to you that the body is the temple of the soul and the dwelling place of the Holy Spirit? Would your mom approve of your sexual relationship with Moira? What would be her reaction if she were to find out? Would our Lord give his blessing to such a relationship? And He already knows the sins you've committed. I think not. No, little brother, I do not condone your relationship with this girl and I know I stand in good company. It is clear to me that from all indications it is an unhealthy relationship—and one that must end. You have to end this relationship. It's the right thing to do."

Dominic's whole body sagged under the immense pressure brought to bear with even the thought of breaking off his relationship with Moira! Despite everything Brother Corwin had said, and most of it not wrong, none of it changed how he felt about Moira. Her face, her eyes, her voice, her smile, her laugh, her kiss, her body next to his—all these images flashed through his mind in rapid succession and he became frightened at the thought of losing her, losing her love. He couldn't possibly break off their relationship, no, not at all. He couldn't imagine breaking her heart—no less breaking his own.

"I don't think I can do that, Brother Corwin," he murmured. "I couldn't do that to Moira." Dominic looked up at him. "I wouldn't want to, anyway. I'm not saying that I disagree with most of what you say but that doesn't change how I feel about her."

Brother Corwin rubbed his face with his hand and stroked his chin. He wished he had some black coffee handy. He took a deep breath in preparation of his final assault on Dominic's last fragile stronghold.

"Dominic, I can understand how you feel, and the conflict you're struggling with here. But you must put things in proper perspective. You know what's right. You know what the right thing to do here is. However, you are overcome with guilt and remorse and the intense feelings that adolescent infatuation can bring. Believe me, those romantic feelings of love and devotion are the plague of adolescence and we all must go through them. But this is where our intellectual side must take control and harness these longings and yearnings and recognize them for what they are: the immature awakening of our emotional selves that seek out a validation of our self-image through the eyes of some other. That other becomes an object of our desire, and let's face it, lustful desire. You don't really love Moira as much as you really believe you do. Feelings don't define love as much as we like to think they do. Choices define love. Decisions define love. Love is not about holding hands and whispering sweet nothings, as pleasant as that may sound. Love is about sacrifice, self-denial, self-control."

Dominic interrupted, almost pleading. "You make love sound so cold and heartless. Why would anyone ever fall in love if it's as you say it is?"

Brother Corwin stood up and walked around the desk to sit at the table opposite Dominic. "Falling in love, being in love, all this talk of true love—these are quaint notions of love but they aren't real. You know what real love is? It's painful. It's hard. It hurts."

"But how can that be? Even the Apostle John, the closest to Jesus and the one Jesus loved the most, even he wrote that God is love..."

"Yes, and look up at that cross on that wall. Look up at that crucifix, little brother, the nails holding Jesus to that cross, the crown of thorns on His head, the wound in His side. That's love! That's real love! Do you think He was enjoying that? Do you believe He was deriving some sick pleasure out of having His body beaten and battered and lashed like that? Don't you think He felt pain and agony in expressing His love, for you? And you want to cheapen that love by your lust and fornication with this girl? Is that how you thank your God? Is that how you honor your mother's years of counsel? Alright, so you think you love this

Toomey girl. Well, then prove it. Prove that you love her. There's only one way to show that: go to her and acknowledge the terrible mistake you've made—that both of you have made. Go tell her that you both have sinned against each other and against God by disobeying His law. Say to her that you need to break off this relationship precisely because you do love her—and that you only have her best interest in mind, the best interest to save her soul as well as your own. In this way you will really prove that you love her because you are willing to sacrifice everything to do what's right. And by doing so, you will redeem yourself in the eyes of God—and in the eyes of your mother." Brother Corwin paused to let the weight of these last words sink deep into Dominic's psyche. He prepared himself for the last volley that should bring the battle to its end. "And when you cut the ties with Moira, when you finally end this with her before it becomes a real disaster, a genuine tragedy…you will have truly tamed her."

Dominic leaned forward, resting his elbows on the table, and held his head in his hands. Brother Corwin sighed, drained but pleased nonetheless, convinced that he had triumphed. In his own way, he felt sorry for Dominic—the fact that he had to go through this. *Perhaps the fault does lie in the stars, perhaps the fault lies in the fragility of the human condition. Maybe it's the fault of a God who has a twisted sense of humor that creates creatures out of flesh and blood and then extols the virtues of a spiritual realm. And to add insult to injury, brags about making man in His own image, bestows upon him free will, and then punishes him if he has the audacity to exercise it.* Brother Corwin looked up at the crucifix on the wall. *God is love? Ha, it's a sadistic love indeed if it required that kind of sacrifice.*

Then Brother Corwin heard the words that could have only been more perfect if but put to music by Sondheim himself:

"You're right, Brother Corwin."

He held his breath, anticipating, waiting for the rest.

"If I really do love Moira, I will want what's best for her. I would do my best to prevent her from doing what's wrong, even if that means hurting her…hurting myself."

"Now you are talking like someone who understands what real love is. And little brother, you must be strong, very strong. Moira is not going to understand or have a full appreciation for what you are doing for her. She will of course go through a wide range of emotional reactions—anger, crying, shouting, arguing, bargaining, accusing, denying, threatening, begging, pleading—you must be adamant and steadfast. And, of course, you must cut her off completely."

Dominic raised his head out of his hands.

"Completely? Does it...does it have to be...so final? We couldn't still remain friends?"

"Oh, if only that were a possibility! But that is the unfortunate nature of sin, little brother. Once you have tasted a piece of chocolate, you want more. It's nature at its cruelest. The only way to survive this and not to fall back into temptation is to close the candy shop. Board up the windows, lock the door, and throw away the key. That's what must be done."

As they walked down the long corridor toward the school exit, Brother Corwin noted the burden of Dominic's impending conversation literally weighing on the youth's shoulders. Brother Corwin placed his arm around Dominic's shoulders. "Don't worry, little brother, this will all soon be behind you and you will have learned a valuable life lesson. You will move on, and you will be a better man for it. Trust me. And one day we will look back on this together and smile about it."

Dominic was only half listening but managed to ask, "How can you be so sure?"

"I've always had this dream about you, more a nightmare really, where you are in some kind of trouble, serious trouble. You desperately need help, and I arrive just in time to save you. I realize this is what that dream was all about."

They reached the glass doors in front of the school building and Brother Corwin pushed open one of the doors and held it open as Dominic stepped out into the cold afternoon.

"Thanks for everything, Brother Corwin." Dominic managed a sad little smile. "I appreciate it."

"No problem, little brother, good luck." Brother Corwin watched as Dominic walked away and then called after him, "Dominic!" Dominic stopped and turned around. "Remember, you need to be strong." Dominic nodded his understanding.

Brother Corwin went back into the school building, stopping off in the men's room. He relieved himself and as he washed his hands, he glimpsed at his reflection in the mirror. *You can be despicable sometimes but it had to be done. And when it's all over, he will be all yours.* He dried off his hands and headed back to the art room.

MOIRA SAT WAITING IN the parking lot of ASM, listening to Dominic's cassette. She had to remember to ask Dominic to make another copy as she had listened to this one so much it would soon wear out. The holidays had come and gone so fast as they always seem to do, and she hadn't gotten to see Dominic very much. They had talked on the phone of course but their conversations seemed shorter and shorter, and Dominic didn't appear to be himself. She attributed it to holiday blues. She was sure that with time she would make the holidays as special for Dominic as they were for her, especially when they would be sharing them together. She had strep throat right after Christmas, so this was going to be her first-time seeing Dominic in the New Year. She was so excited when he asked if she could pick him up right after school and if they could maybe go someplace to talk if only for a little while, as it was a school night. Of course, she said yes. From her car window she watched the front entrance of ASM anticipating her love's appearance. She spotted Dominic as he came through the glass doors and searched the parking lot for her car. He found where she was parked and proceeded toward her.

"Hi!" she greeted him enthusiastically and reached over for a kiss. "It feels like forever since I've seen you. I almost forgot what you looked like! Almost." She smiled at him while starting the car.

"Hey, Moira, it's good to see you. You look beautiful as ever." He stroked her hair.

"Where do you want to go? Are you hungry?"

"No, not really. Do you think we could just go over to Ridgeway River Park?"

"To our spot, you mean?" She was so happy to see her little prince. "Of course, you'll have to promise to keep me warm!"

Dominic smiled, nodding his head.

"How are you feeling? Is your throat all better?" As Moira answered he looked out the window, with so heavy a burden on his heart, numb from the nights of anguish and torment. But he had made up his mind to do the right thing and what was best for Moira. There was no turning back now. He had wrestled with this ever since the conversation with Brother Corwin that Saturday afternoon. Brother Corwin had not really broached the topic with him since then but there were the knowing glares and stares that transmitted the unspoken message of what needed to be done. Brother Corwin had only brought it up when he mentioned that Dominic should come to him when the deed was done, for support and in case Dominic needed to talk about it.

"Dominic, are you even listening to me? Hey, you!" Moira playfully slapped his arm.

"Huh? Oh, I'm sorry. What did you say?"

"Where are you? Where did you go?"

"I'm sorry, Moira, I was just thinking, uh, about a term paper that I have to get done."

"Who are you?"

"Come on, Moira, I was distracted for a moment. What, you hear every word I say?"

"I mean it, who are you really? What have you done with my Dominic?"

"It's me, Moira. I'm sorry, alright? It won't happen again. So, what were you saying?"

"I was just asking if you know what's coming up in a few weeks?"

Dominic gave it some thought. "Hmmm, I'm stumped. It's not your birthday."

"Now I know you're an imposter! Or you better be! Dominic Manterra, I am glad we are having this conversation now because there would have been hell to pay if you were to ever forget Valentine's Day!" She gave him a gentle jab on his chin.

Dominic stiffened. The magnitude of what he was about to do hit him like a locomotive screeching by on the tracks behind his house in the middle of the night. He was suddenly racked with doubt and fear as he contemplated Moira's reaction. Moira glanced out of the corner of her eyes at Dominic. Something was definitely wrong and her intuition was telling her there was serious trouble brewing. Even now, she was sensing uneasiness, a distance between her and Dominic that she had never felt before. She didn't want to even entertain any negative thoughts. She was going to remain strong in her faith in him, in her belief in her Dominic. She pushed the negative thoughts out of her mind as she turned the car into the parking lot of the park and pulled into the same parking space as the night of their first kiss. She turned off the ignition and turned to face Dominic.

"Come here, Dominic, kiss me like you did that night we were first here!" She reached out to him and Dominic embraced her tight, kissing her with an impassioned, reckless abandon. She immediately felt relieved as his kiss told her he still loved her, instantly wiping away all her doubts and fears. He pulled back from her lips and kissed along her cheek, her ear, the back of her head as he hugged her even tighter and she rested her head on his shoulder. "How I have missed those lips, Dominic! It's been so long! Please promise me we won't ever again wait so long to share a kiss like that! Your kisses are truly wonderful! It's almost like when our lips touch, when I taste your mouth on mine, it's like your spirit fills my body and we become one. It's like I can actually feel you transfer your love into me. That's what makes your kisses so wonderful!"

Dominic began to quiver and shake, tears streaming down his cheek. Moira pulled herself away.

"What's wrong, Dominic? What's the matter? Why are you so upset? Did something happen? Are you OK? Did something happen to your family? Tell me, what's happened, Dominic?" She threw her arms around him as he collapsed into her lap. She held his head in one arm and stroked his back lovingly with the other. She became very concerned for him, worrying what had happened to make him so upset. She spoke soothing words to him, patiently waiting for him to calm down so he could explain. Dominic regained his composure and sat up as Moira reached into her pocketbook and handed him some tissues.

"Thanks." Dominic wiped his eyes and blew his nose.

Moira placed her hand on his arm. "Dominic, do you want to talk about it? Is it something you *can* talk about?" He turned to look at her and her heart ached to see his eyes looking so sad. "You know, my love, that you can trust me with anything. You can share anything with me. Don't be afraid or hold back. I want to be there for you, you know that, right? You're safe with me. Dominic, I would never hurt you."

Dominic dropped his chin to his chest. The battle raging between his heart and his head had spilled over into his soul. He didn't know what to do. Suddenly he just wanted to be invisible. He wanted to be covered by his blankets from head to toe but he wanted those blankets to be made of concrete—no, made of bronze or iron. No! No! No, he wanted it to be that Friday night in Moira's parents' bedroom. He wanted to be inside Moira, one with her once again, the both of them locked in a passionate embrace, looking into each other's eyes, to be suddenly consumed in a painless ball of fire that freed their spirits! And they would ascend into the night sky, taking their place among the constellations to be together in the eternal beauty of their youth and love.

But he knew that was, as Brother Corwin had said to him, the pathetic notions of a silly school boy infatuation.

The mind had won the battle.

"Moira," Dominic took a deep breath, "I have to tell you something."

Moira was tenderly stroking his arm. Dominic took her hand and placed it gently down on her lap. The action struck a nerve with Moira and she was slightly taken aback at the coldness of it. "I have to tell you something, and I need you to listen very carefully." He looked up at her, directly in her eyes. "OK?"

Moira nodded as her stomach churned, for the coldness in his touch had now transferred to his eyes. Those eyes were not the eyes of love. They were someone else's eyes. A stranger's gaze had fixed itself upon her being and she no longer felt safe.

"I'm listening. What is it you have to tell me, Dominic?"

Dominic looked out the window over at the gray coldness that was slowly fading into the darkness that was enveloping the setting sun. He went to speak.

"No, Dominic, look at me if you have something to tell me. Look into my eyes as you say it. I want to see your eyes as you speak the words."

Dominic turned to her and met her gaze. Her face was braced and taut as if covered with a sheen made of steel, but her eyes were merely flesh and blood, brimming with a sorrow he would have gone blind to avoid seeing. It was time.

"Moira, I can't do this anymore."

"*Do this?*" she asked, her voice cracking a little.

"I...I can't see you anymore. We have to end this. Believe me, it's not what I want but—"

"Then why would you do it, Dominic? Why would you do this?"

"Because we have to...you have to understand. It's not that I don't love you, or that I don't want to be with you...it's just that...it's not right. It's not right. Can't you see?"

Moira was stricken. "I don't believe you. I don't believe a word you're saying. I don't believe that *you* even believe anything you're saying."

"But I do. I do believe it's the right thing to do. You need to know that."

"Dominic, why are you doing this to us? Why? Why? Why would you? How could you?" Tears began to stream down Moira's face. "You don't mean this, Dominic. Please, Dominic, tell me that you don't mean what you're saying! Tell me this is just some cruel joke that you're playing! Dominic, I'm begging you, tell me you aren't serious!"

Dominic remained steadfast although inside him he was dying a twisted, painful death, a death that had started the afternoon he walked home from ASM after his conversation with Brother Corwin.

"I'm so sorry, Moira, but it's not a joke. I'm not that cruel to make that kind of joke." He looked down at his hands folded in front of him and then back at her. "Moira, I have given this a lot of thought. What we have done is wrong. I have come to that realization. And what's important here is that we get back on the right path."

"You're not cruel? How can you even say that! Look at what you're doing to me right now! To me—no, look at what you're doing to us! Dominic, you are viciously cruel. You are heartless, so heartless. Do you know why, Dominic? Do you want to know why?"

Dominic's eyes fell to his hands once again.

"Answer me, Dominic! Do you know why you are heartless? No? Do you want me to tell you? Do you?" Moira's hurt was now combining with her anger. "I will tell you why. Because you're willing to not only break my heart but you're willing to kill yours dead! You're willing to shatter your own heart and deaden it so much that it will never feel anything. It will never ever feel a damn thing for the rest of your life...if you do this to us...if you do this to me...if you do it to yourself. Please, listen to me, Dominic. You don't really want this—you don't really mean anything you're saying. I know you don't. I know! I know!"

"But I do mean it, Moira. I wouldn't be saying it to you if I didn't."

"You're wrong, Dominic, you're so wrong! You don't mean a damn word of it. You can lie to yourself. You can lie to me with the words you are saying. But you can't lie to me with those eyes! Your eyes are telling an entirely different truth, the real truth. This isn't you, Dominic, no, no, no, this isn't you at all."

"We're just very fortunate that there weren't any consequences that night. I mean, we were so stupid really. I know we were caught up in the

moment but seriously, Moira, think about what could have happened if
you were to...." Dominic's voice trailed off.

"Get pregnant? If I were to get pregnant? Is that what you are worried about? I had just had my period, Dominic. I would never have let
us get into that situation, otherwise. My period cycle has been regular
from the first time I had it. I was going to talk about what you wanted
to do for protection, Dominic. I would not have allowed us to continue
on without talking about it. And in case your next concern was about
any other *health* issues, I will save you the squirming of trying to bring
it up: I did it once with Trevor, the night I already told you about. He
wore a condom and it was over in about four minutes. And then he fell
asleep. You know the rest. Before that—there was no before that. That
was it." She turned her head away and wiped the tears rolling down her
cheek with the palm of her hand. "Remember, Dominic, when I shared
with you that night we were here, how I felt about that experience, how
I felt so cheap? I didn't think I could feel that way again but right now,
having to say what I just said to you—I feel it all over again. So, thank
you for that."

"I'm sorry, Moira, that wasn't my intention. Not at all. I...I...Listen,
Moira, I have thought this through. I know we believe that we weren't
doing anything sinful, but we did. We shouldn't have done what we did
that night—it was wrong. I am not blaming you, so don't think I am. I
was just as much at fault for our weakness. No one held a gun to my
head—I did it of my own free will. But we must end this before we really make a mess of our lives. Please, don't believe for a minute that this
is easy for me, it isn't. Not at all."

"Dominic, do you even hear what you're saying to me? Do you realize
what you're telling me is the complete opposite of everything we said to
each other, everything we felt, everything we believed? You're just dis-
missing everything? Tell me, who it is then? Tell me who is holding it?"

"Holding what?"

"Holding the gun to your head. I can see your hands are empty, and
I'm not holding one. So, who is it that has the gun to your head? Who's

making you say these things and do this to us? Damnit, Dominic, don't
you believe for a minute this is just being done to me, because it's not.
It's being done to you as well—it's being done to destroy us. Why can't
you see that?"

Dominic was torn. It wasn't like he didn't expect Moira to be very
upset with him, but he was conflicted as her words seared his heart. She
wasn't wrong about how he felt inside. But he needed to be strong.
Brother Corwin had warned him it wouldn't be easy. "Moira, I am so
sorry. I really am. But you have to understand that this is what's best for
us. I am doing this for us."

For a moment it seemed everything had suddenly halted. Moira sat
still, wide-eyed, looking out into the darkness as if she was expecting
something to appear, to occur. She didn't seem to be even breathing to
Dominic. Then she spoke: "You're not doing this for us, Dominic—not
for me, not even for you." She turned her face toward him. "You're doing
this for him, aren't you? He's the one holding the gun, isn't he?"

Dominic stared back at her. "What do you mean? Wh—who are you
talking about?"

"You know damn well who I'm referring to, Dominic. I warned you
about him. I told you he would try to get between us. Didn't I?"

Dominic shifted and turned his head away.

"Brother Corwin. *Your friend*, Dominic. He's behind all this. He's the
one who put you up to this. It all makes sense to me now—it's so obvious. That sick, jealous bastard! Dominic, can't you see what's going on
here? My love, open your eyes! He's manipulating you. I don't know
what he's told you to convince you to do this, but you have to listen to
me. You have to realize what's really going on here. Don't allow this to
happen. You don't have to do this."

Dominic replied with a voice that appeared to belong to someone
else: "I do have to do this. We've made a terrible mistake. I wish I could
take it back, not just for me, Moira, but for both of us. I never wanted
to hurt you, but I have by not being strong and stopping us from doing
what we did. I allowed myself to give in, to indulge my fleshly desire,

and by doing so have done you a great wrong. I will try to repent of that and make amends for my weakness, and I ask that you forgive me for it."

Moira's eyes grew wide with surprise, and she shook her head. "No, I won't forgive you for that night. Never. I don't regret it. Not one bit. Nor do I believe that deep down inside you, in whatever's left of your heart, that you regret it. No, I don't believe for a second that you believe anything you've said here tonight. But I will ask you one more time—please don't do this."

"Moira, I..."

"Please don't do this, Dominic. My God, Dominic, I believed in you! I trusted you! I asked you not to do this—remember what you said? You promised me. You promised me that you would never hurt me. Do you not remember what you told me that night? After I shared my poem? You pledged to love me with your very existence! You promised to never leave my side! To never let me down! But it's exactly what you're doing. And I believed you." Moira's tears were flowing as she stopped to dry her eyes with a tissue. "The funny thing is, I still believe in you. I don't know why, since you're telling me it's over and this is it, and you're breaking your promises to me. Silly me with my notions of true love and my prince, my dream-come-true romance of some stupid storybook love. You know, Dominic, it's not so far-fetched—people our age, they do fall in love. They do fall in love, they stay together, and then they get a little older, and they remain a couple, their love for each other grows, and then they make a life with each other and grow old together. My parents did it, your parents, too. At least that's how I always thought it would be. And for some silly reason, I believed you were the one. My God, Dominic, I know you're the one! And I don't care what you say, I still believe you know this and feel the same way."

Dominic brought his hands up to his face and rubbed his eyes with his fingers and his face with his hands. He felt like he had aged in the short time they'd been sitting in the car.

"Moira, I know this is hard for you—it's hard for me, believe me it is. This was so difficult a decision, you have no idea how it is has eaten away at my insides. But I can't allow us to let this go on. You're right—my heart is breaking over this, not just yours. But they say that time heals all wounds. I believe in the power of forgiveness. Maybe over time, we can still be friends—"

"I don't think so, Dominic. That won't be possible, not for me anyway. You see, I really do love you. And I know that you really do love me. I don't regret anything with you at all. Despite what you're doing, and what you've said tonight, I don't regret anything, I wouldn't change anything, I wouldn't take anything back—not anything I've said or done. And although my heart is so broken—and believe me, the pain welling inside me hurts so much, it really does, and I know it is only going to get worse—I am not angry with you about that, nor do I even feel like it's something you have to be forgiven for. No, that's not it. What I will struggle with, and I'm not sure I will ever have the strength to forgive you for it—maybe one day with the help of God, perhaps— the one thing I will never forgive you for, is that you chose him over me." Moira covered her nose and mouth with her hand as she started to cry with such vehemence that Dominic reacted as to embrace her but she put out her other hand to stop him. She regained her composure after a moment.

"Dominic, you are breaking this off and leaving me, this I know now. Before you go, I want you to know, since you brought it up, that I don't believe we have sinned, although others may hold a different view, and have used the power of that word to sway you. I don't care what others think about what we've done but as far as I believe, I don't think what we did was a sin and I don't believe God believes it was sinful. God looks at the heart, Dominic. He examines the heart, and if what God finds there is pure and true and noble and lovely, then God is pleased and blesses that heart. You know who taught me that, Dominic?"

Dominic shook his head.

"You did, Dominic. You taught me that. And you are right."

Dominic closed his eyes and dropped his chin to his chest.

"You're leaving me now, Dominic, and it makes me very, very sad.

But I knew the risk in finding true love ….and that is losing it. You see, my love, you really have tamed me."

Upon hearing those words, a shock of emotion surged through Dominic's being. He wanted to embrace and kiss Moira and tell her he loved her. That he was sorry and didn't mean a word he just said. That he could never leave her and would always protect her and keep her safe! That he wanted to make a life with her, grow old with her! That when it was their time that they would just fall asleep in each other's arms one night and wake up in heaven together!

But he did no such thing.

"Moira, it's getting late. I'm going to go. I…uh…I'm just going to walk home. I need the fresh air to clear my head."

Moira nodded her head. Dominic turned and reached for the door handle.

"Wait!" Moira whispered gently. "Dominic, look at me."

Dominic turned around to face her. Moira wiped the tears from her eyes and face, pushed her auburn hair behind her right ear and shoulder, and, looking into his eyes, gave him a smile. "I love you, Dominic Manterra. Always have and always will." Suddenly her smile beamed and her eyes sparkled, for in that moment she looked into his eyes and saw her little prince from the night they consecrated their love looking back at her. A single teardrop fell from her left eye and rolled down her cheek. Dominic reached out his hand and with his thumb caught the tear before it rolled off her chin. Moira took hold of his hand and kissed the center of his palm and then held it against her cheek for a moment. Dominic could feel how hot her skin was, how soft. She gently pulled his hand away, letting it go. He opened the door and lifted himself out of the car.

Brother Corwin gazed out the second-floor window of his classroom. The evening had settled in and the stars in the blackened sky appeared especially distant. He had watched earlier as Dominic got into Moira's car and they drove away. He glanced at his watch and figured the deed had been done by now. He drank down the last of his coffee and wiped his mouth. He let out a guffaw and turned to head over to the residence.

"LET ME GET THIS STRAIGHT. You finally get the girl you have spent almost your whole life longing for, your soulmate from all accounts that I know about, and you let her go? That doesn't make any sense, Nicky boy. No sense at all." Denny popped open a bottle of beer and handed it to Dominic. He then popped opened another one and sat back in one of the deck chairs they had set up on the flat roof over the family room of Denny's house. They were looking out over the surrounding neighbors' backyards. "Pray tell—please explain this madness to me."

Dominic took a gulp of the cold brew and rested the bottle on the top of his right knee. He looked down at it. He hadn't seen Denny except in passing in about ten months. He attempted to explain the chain of events to his old friend, who listened intently while downing the beers he had managed to procure from a local liquor store known for its loose approach to checking identification. It helped that Denny looked older than he was.

"Nicky, how many times had I warned you about Corwin. Why for the life of me you would ever listen to anything he has to say is beyond me. I had always said the guy's a freaking whack-a-doo. He doesn't know crap about women, about relationships, about love. From what you've told me, Moira called it right—the guy's an evil, sick bastard. He doesn't know a damn thing about the kind of love you and Moira experienced. I mean, he doesn't know anything about stuff like that, stuff about real men and women, about love and matters of the heart." Denny finished off the beer he was drinking and reached for another.

"This conversation isn't about him."

"It isn't? Then what's it about?" Denny chucked a bottle cap into his backyard.

"It's about Moira, and me. I miss her so much, Denny."

"I'm sure you do. She was a beauty and talented, too, as I remember. And let's face it, Nicky, she was always crazy about you all through grammar school. Everyone recognized that —except you, of course. It's funny how life can be sometimes. The two of you having these feelings for each other but keeping it hidden, and then years later, finally connecting and opening up to each other. And then, of course, you totally fuck it up and ruin the whole goddamn thing."

"Is this the part where you say things to make me feel better?"

Denny laughed. "No, this is the part where I tell you to stop being a douche bag and get off your ass and go tell her you made a huge mistake and that you're sorry and beg her forgiveness and ask for another chance. And then wait it out. And hope that she has the courage and strength to give you that second chance. Of course, it will have to be on her terms and, more importantly, her timetable. And, of course, patience being one of those virtues that you have eluded your whole life so far, it will be a real joy for you as you go through the torment of waiting for her to make up her mind."

"But what if she's changed? You know, what if her feelings have changed?"

Denny finished the beer he was drinking. "Hmmm, maybe I should have bought another six-pack. What? No, that didn't happen. She still feels the same, no matter what. This isn't about whether she still loves you, Nicky, this is about whether she could ever trust you or believe in you again. Love may be the greatest, but faith and hope are harder to recover. And remember, in the end, those three remain...fairly elusive to most of the general population. So if by chance you happen to find them within your grasp again, do yourself a favor—do a better job holding on to them."

"You're right, Denny. I totally messed up. I need to talk to Moira. If not for any reason, even if she never gives me another chance, at least to tell her she was right and I was completely wrong. Maybe I could at least regain her respect by admitting that much to her."

"Sounds like a plan, my friend. But as the saying goes, time and tide wait for no man. I would not delay—you want to act before that ship has sailed."

"Understood." Dominic sat back with his hand behind his head and took a swig from his bottle of beer.

DOMINIC CAME IN THE back door of the house, up the stairs into the kitchen. His brother Mitchell was sitting at the kitchen table. Dominic placed his bookbag down on one of the chairs. He went over to the fridge.

"Hey, Mitch, how's it going?" asked Dominic as he scanned the shelves of the fridge. A couple of minutes had passed when he realized Mitchell hadn't answered. He looked under his arm at his brother who was sitting at the table, drinking a cup of tea. He closed the fridge and turned around.

"Mitchell, what's the matter, you look so serious?" Dominic asked. Mitchell just shrugged his shoulders and sipped his tea. "Where's Jason?"

"He's upstairs, finishing his homework. Mom's at Maria's. You coming home from practice?"

"Yeah, for the spring musical. At least running track is easier than playing soccer in terms of balancing the schedule. Is the water still hot?" Dominic shook the tea kettle set on the stove.

"Should be. Tell me, does Moira have a part in the musical?" Mitchell continued to look straight ahead. Dominic finished fixing up his tea and took a seat across from his brother.

"No, I don't believe Moira even tried out for the show." Dominic blew on his tea to cool it down.

"Really, why's that?"

"I don't know, I guess her schedule didn't allow for it." Dominic lifted his cup and brought it to his lips. It was still too hot to drink.

Mitchell placed his cup down on the kitchen table a little harder than maybe he intended, but it got Dominic's attention and he jumped in his seat.

"Strange, how you could be so casual almost to the point of indifference when talking about someone who not too long ago I feel fairly confident in describing as the object of your total affection if not the love of your life? Am I wrong?" Mitchell's tone was harsh.

Dominic finally sipped his tea and placed it calmly on the table. "No, you're not wrong. Moira and I haven't been seeing other for a little while." He avoided Mitchell's gaze, although he could feel it penetrating his skull.

"And why's that? Who broke up with who?"

"It was kind of mutual." Dominic tapped each side of his cup with his fingers.

"Kind of? Like you both agreed it was best? Is that what you mean?" Dominic didn't answer. "Because I ran into her brother the other day and he mentioned that Moira hadn't been herself for a few weeks, and the family was very worried about her. He thought it might have had something to do with you. Her mother even asked Moira about you because it seemed like you had suddenly disappeared from Moira's life. They were concerned that maybe something happened between you two and that was the cause of Moira being so down and withdrawn."

Dominic's hands began to shake and his bottom lip began to quiver. Mitchell kept his eyes fixed on Dominic as he continued to speak.

"Her brother said Moira told them that no, it had nothing to do with Dominic. That Dominic was her friend, and that he was a good man, a kind and noble person...*a little prince*, I believe is how her brother said she described you." Mitchell stopped there and took a drink of his tea.

Dominic stopped tapping the cup and finally looked up. "Is that it?"

"You tell me, Dominic? Is there more to the story that anyone needs to know about? It just strikes me as awfully odd that you could be crazy mad about someone not too long ago—you do remember that Friday night—and now it's like you don't even know the person?"

"That's not true, Mitchell. I care about Moira more than anything else in this world! Alright, I did break up with her but it was a mistake, and I realize that now. I've being meaning to call and talk to her about it, I guess I have been putting it off because...I'm just trying to figure out how to go about it. I don't know if she'll even talk to me. But I need to tell her how terribly wrong I was, and how totally insensitive and selfish I was about everything. It was a huge mistake, a terrible mistake, I know that now. If anything, I just hope she'll forgive me."

"Oh, my brother...." Mitchell's expression turned to one of alarm, as he swallowed hard. "This is not good, Dominic."

Dominic reacted to the change in Mitchell's disposition. "What isn't? What is it, Mitchell? Did something happen? Did something happen to Moira? Is she OK? Talk to me, Mitchell! Tell me if something's happened to her!" Dominic jumped out of his seat and reached for the telephone on the wall.

"Put the phone down, Dominic!" Mitchell yelled at him. "Put the goddamn phone down!" He leaped up and pressed down the receiver and snatched the phone out of Dominic's hand. "Sit down! Sit the fuck down, right now!"

Dominic sat. He was quivering like a frightened rabbit snared in a hunting trap.

"Who were you thinking of calling? Moira? You can't call there right now."

"Not right now? When then?"

"I don't even know the answer to that question. But you need to listen to me and listen to me good."

"Mitchell, tell me—is Moira OK? Did something happen? I need to talk to her, Mitchell. You don't understand—I really need to talk to her!"

"That's not going to be anytime soon, Dominic." Mitchell collapsed in the chair. He suddenly looked very drained and exhausted to Dominic.

"I...I think I'm partially to blame here," muttered Mitchell. His thoughts raced back to that Friday night as he sat in his car down the street from the Toomeys' house, waiting for Dominic. Had he used poor judgment?

"Jesus Christ, Mitchell, are you going to tell me what's going on?" snapped Dominic.

Mitchell glanced at his brother, then took a deep breath as his eyes began to well up.

"Brace yourself, Dominic." He reached for a napkin and wiped his eyes and his nose. "Something has happened."

Dominic cringed as if he had been hit in the gut with a heavyweight's body blow. "To Moira?"

Mitchell nodded, "Yes, to Moira. She had been acting very different than her usual positive and upbeat self, especially these past few weeks. Her mom had been concerned enough to take her to a doctor. He said she was OK for the most part but agreed that she appeared to have a severe case of the blues. He asked if there were any recent events in her life that could have upset her—a death in the family, someone being sick, some major disappointment. Her mother couldn't think of anything out of the ordinary but then did mention that she had noticed that Moira wasn't talking on the phone with you as much as she used to or even mentioning you the way she used to. Then she had wondered why Moira didn't try out for the spring musical, especially after her big part in the play."

Dominic listened intently. He knew that Moira would never try out for the spring musical—she would never again participate in anything that even remotely involved Brother Corwin.

"What happened after the doctor's?"

"That was yesterday. This morning Moira told her mother she wasn't feeling very well and really wasn't up to going to school, and asked if she could just stay home. Her mother didn't think she looked so good and agreed to it."

As Mitchell spoke, Dominic's body was being invaded by a sickening numbness that initiated in his stomach and spread like black ink throughout his whole being, flowing through his arteries and capillaries and veins, infiltrating his nervous system, attaching to nerve endings, slowly making its way to his brain while trying to seep deeper and deeper within him, circuitous in its search for his soul.

"How is she?" Dominic's voice betrayed the vacancy that was taking up residence within him.

Mitchell sighed a sigh of a man bearing the heaviest of burdens—that of sorrowful news relentless in its means of creating endless heartache. He closed his eyes and rubbed his face with his hand as if to wake himself up from a nightmare that he could only hope was untrue. He dropped his hand to the table and opened his eyes to peer into the saddest blue eyes he had ever seen in his life.

"Dominic, I'm so sorry…"

"Mitchell…how is Moira?"

"…her mom came home at lunchtime to check on her and found her in her bed…with an empty bottle of the medication that the doctor had prescribed for her depression. Moira had taken about fifteen of them, probably not too long after her dad and mom had left for work. Her mom called 911 and they rushed her to the hospital."

"Is she…is she…" Dominic's eyes released a torrent of tears that flooded his cheeks. He dropped his head onto his hands down on the table and sobbed.

"No…she's still alive…but…."

"But what?" Dominic raised his head.

"She's in a coma, Dominic. They don't know what's going to happen yet."

Dominic pushed himself away from the table and stood up. "I've got to go see her! I've got to be with her!"

"No! Dominic, that's not a good idea!" Mitchell cried out at his brother, who was making his way to the door.

"What do you mean, Mitchell? Are you kidding me? I've got to get to the hospital! Will you take me, please, I'm begging you?" Dominic was frantic. He whirled around and looked about aimlessly, wringing his hands, tears streaming down his face. "Well, Mitch can you drive me over?"

"Dominic, you're not listening to me! You can't go there right now. It's not your place. I don't think you're seeing the clear picture here. Her family is very upset, they're very scared, and they're very angry."

"Angry? At who—me? I didn't cause this. I would never hurt Moira. They have to know that! I love Moira, I would never do anything to hurt her, I would rather—oh my God, Mitchell, what have I done? My God, what have I done?" Dominic collapsed onto the floor, crying bitterly.

Mitchell reached down and embraced his brother. "Dominic, it's not your fault, you can't blame yourself, that's not going to help Moira right now. We need to pray for Moira. We need to ask God for help and for mercy. That's all we can do right now."

Dominic lifted himself from the floor and freed himself from Mitchell's embrace. "Mitchell, I've got to get to that hospital. I've got to talk to Moira, can't you see? I've got to tell her some things, things she needs to hear from me."

Mitchell grabbed Dominic by his arms. "Dominic, damn it, Dominic, listen to me! You can't go to the hospital! You're not thinking clearly! Her family is distraught, their daughter, their sister is in a coma. They don't know why or what happened! You're the only possible link right now to anything! You're not wanted there, Dominic!"

"Mitchell, you're wrong! I can help Moira! I just need to see her! I can talk to her! She'll hear me!" Dominic lowered his voice. "Listen, listen, Mitchell, listen, I will talk to Moira. She'll hear me. She'll hear my voice. I can reach her! I know I can! You just have to drive me over to the hospital, that's all I'm asking." Dominic began to shriek, "Please, Mitchell! Take me to the hospital, I have to see her! My God, Moira, I'm so sorry, I'm so sorry! Help me, Mitchell!" Dominic pulled free from Mitchell's grasp and lunged for the door. Mitchell turned and grabbed hold of one of Dominic's arms and pulled him back and down against the chair and table, knocking the chair over and pushing the table into the counter. Dominic landed on the floor on his side, and curled up crying.

Jason came running into the kitchen. "What's going on? Did you tell him, Mitch?" Jason knelt down by Dominic and placed his hand on his brother's shoulder. "It's OK, Dominic, it's going to be OK. We're here for you, Dominic. We're here for you." Mitchell went over to the counter and filled a glass with water. He snatched a couple of sheets from the paper towel roll and handed them to Jason. He knelt down next to Dominic up near his head. He patted his brother's arm to soothe him. "Here, Dominic, drink some of this water." Mitchell looked over at Jason, who just shook his head, feeling bad for his two older brothers.

THE TELEPHONE RANG IN Father Bumbry's room. He picked up the phone.

"Hello, this is Father Arnold."

The voice on the other end was muffled and sad. "Hello, Father Arnold. It's me, Dominic."

Father Bumbry sat down in the chair next to the telephone; with genuine concern he replied, "Dominic, I'm so glad you called. I've been so worried about you. How are you feeling, my son?"

"Have...have you heard the news?"

"Yes, of course. Father Downey is over at the hospital since he's a long-time friend of the family. I was waiting here for any updates as well as hoping that you would call. I wasn't sure if you had heard or how you would find out. It all happened so quickly. As soon as I had heard what had happened, I called your brother Mitchell to let him know so that he could prepare you. Are you doing OK?"

"It's very hard, Father Arnold. Very painful, to be honest with you. I feel so powerless. And worse yet, I feel like it's all my fault."

"No, no, you mustn't think like that, Dominic. Not at all."

"But it is my fault, Father Arnold. It's all my fault. I let her down, I let Moira down. I didn't keep my promise to her. She was everything... she is everything to me, Father Arnold. I don't know what I'm going to do. I'm so scared, I feel so alone. It's the worst thing that could ever happen to me. It's something...I can never forgive myself for what I've done."

"Listen, my son, you can't think that way. You really need to understand what happened and how it happened before you can start looking to blame yourself for everything. From what I know about Moira, and from what you have shared with me, there's one thing I know for sure—Moira wouldn't want to see you like this, blaming yourself, hating yourself. That wouldn't make her happy at all." Father Bumbry could hear Dominic quietly sobbing on the other end of the phone, and he felt bad for his young friend.

Dominic blew his nose and cleared his throat. "Thanks for saying that, Father Arnold. Knowing Moira, I know you're right—that's exactly how she would feel." Dominic began to cry again.

"Listen, Dominic, do you want to come see me? Would that help?"

"Actually, it would, Father Arnold. That would help a lot. I don't really feel like I have anyone to talk to right now. Would you mind?"

"Not at all, my son. Come over as soon as you can. Press the buzzer down by the porch column and I will come down and let you in, OK?"

"Thanks, Father Arnold. I will see you in a little while."

"OK, my son."

Father Bumbry hung up the phone. He took a deep breath and bowed his head in prayer. After a few minutes, he raised his head and looked at the crucifix on his wall.

"Listen, I don't ask much from you, you know that. But for the sake of Dominic, for the sake of her family, please, I beseech you, please spare this young lady's life. I don't think that's too much to ask of the Creator of the universe. You're quite adept at taking life, I have witnessed that many a time. So, for this once, can you just give a life back? Please?" Father Bumbry closed his eyes, as if waiting for a verbal answer. He let out a deep sigh and stood up. He went over to the mini-fridge and checked inside. There were some Cokes and some cheese. He closed the fridge and then spotted a jug of red wine next to it. He decided to take a quick shower before his guest arrived.

XXXIII.

FOR CRYING OUT LOUD

Where are you going?" asked Mitchell. "It's kind of late to be going anywhere."

Dominic slipped on a light jacket. "Taking a walk over to see Father Arnold for a little bit. I just need someone to talk to. I called him—he said it was alright."

Mitchell rose from the chair in the parlor and approached Dominic in the front hallway. "Are you sure? Don't you think you should stay here and rest up? Tomorrow is going to be a tough day when you wake up and realize this isn't just a bad dream."

"I know. But it would help to talk to Father Arnold about all this. He may even have an update on Moira."

Mitchell felt sorry for his brother Dominic. He could only imagine the pain he was in and the potential agony that might lie ahead.

"Do you want me to drive you over?"

"Thanks, but I would rather walk and get some fresh air to clear my head a little." Dominic headed for the door. He paused. "Thanks for everything, Mitchell."

"Everything? I didn't do anything, Dominic."

"Thanks for telling me and being there for me. I appreciate it."

"No problem, bro. Feel better. Don't be beating yourself up about this. It's not your fault. It will be alright. Moira is going to be alright. God is merciful—He will answer our prayers, I'm sure."

"That's what I'm hoping for—a miracle. OK, see you later."

"Call me if you want me to pick you up."

"Will do. Thanks."

Although Dominic had walked these familiar streets thousands of times, tonight he felt like a traveler in a foreign country. Everything looked different—the houses, front lawns, sidewalks, trees, parked cars, street signs. It was like he had never noticed any of them before. Or was it that they were so familiar, he was so used to seeing them, that they were just overlooked props, an inanimate visual backdrop to his daily life. So many thoughts popped up in his mind like a quick succession of flash cards or a photo disc being passed through an old View-Master toy. It was all like a collage of figures and images frozen in motion seemingly busy at doing nothing. He then remembered the words of the fox to the little prince: "What's essential is invisible to the eye." He quickened his pace.

Dominic reached the rectory building and pressed the buzzer on the side of the porch column. A light went on inside the front hallway and he could hear the deadbolt being unlocked and the sucking sound of the rubber insulation around the door as it was pulled open by Father Bumbry.

"Come in, my son."

Dominic stepped in and Father Bumbry closed the door with one hand while putting his other arm immediately around Dominic's shoulders. The youth planted his face into the priest's chest and began to weep. Father Bumbry wrapped his arm around Dominic's head and patted him gently on the back. "There, there, my son, it's OK, it's going to be alright."

Dominic pulled away. "Has something changed, have you heard anything?"

With his own sad eyes, the priest looked at Dominic's down-trodden eyes and shook his head. "No, not yet, but we must be strong in our faith, Dominic. That's all we can do at this point. Let's go upstairs."

Dominic took off his jacket and sat down on the sofa. In front of him on the coffee table was set a tray of cheese and crackers. There were also two wine goblets.

"I wasn't sure if you had eaten anything, and thought you might be hungry. Unfortunately, I didn't have much on hand."

"I didn't...not really hungry, but thanks," murmured Dominic.

"Well, I'll leave it out in case you change your mind. In the meantime, I thought a little of this might take some of the edge off." Father Bumbry held up the glass jug of wine. "Just a cheap Italian table wine that I keep on hand for those times when I need a little something for the belly, as Paul advised Timothy. Sometimes it's just the right thing for what ails you." Father Bumbry poured the wine in each glass goblet, filling them. He handed one glass to Dominic and picked up the other. "To Moira and God's infinite mercy!" Dominic clinked Father Bumbry's glass and sipped a little of the wine. He then drank the whole glass down and placed the empty glass on the table.

"Whoa, my son, let's take it slow there! You don't want to drink so fast!" The priest refilled Dominic's glass.

"This is really crazy, you know that? It's like surreal to me. I still can't believe this has happened. What was Moira thinking? Why would she do this? I don't understand, Father Arnold, I just don't understand why she would do such a thing. Do you?"

Father Bumbry sipped his wine. He moved to sit down on the chair adjacent to where Dominic sat. Letting out a deep sigh, he spoke softly and tenderly. "Dominic, I really don't have the answer to that question. But perhaps if you filled me in on what happened between you and Moira, maybe we could figure out why she did what she did." Father Bumbry caught himself. "That's not to say that there's a connection at all in any way. You don't know that, I don't know that, and maybe we won't ever know until Moira tells us herself."

Dominic drank some more wine. "You really believe she will be OK? That...that she will come out...of the coma?"

"We can only hope, my son, and pray." Father Bumbry sipped his wine and helped himself to some cheese. "Dominic, if you're going to drink the wine, first, you have to slow down, and secondly, you must eat something. Please." Dominic reached for a cracker and ate it. After that confession back in November, Father Bumbry had tried to figure out who the object of Dominic's affection had been. It was when he saw the play at ASM that he put two and two together—that it was Moira who had captured Dominic's heart. The chemistry on stage was beyond the amateur acting of two young high school kids in a school play. It hit him as he sat and watched—Moira Toomey with her stunning mane of auburn hair was the most beautiful girl in the seventh-grade class when he first arrived at St. Mary's. Her beauty only increased with her development into a young woman. Even St. Dominic couldn't resist the fruit of her Garden of Eden.

"Remember when I last came to confession? And I shared with you that, uh, information?"

Father Bumbry sipped his wine. "That you had joined the ranks of the non-virgins and mere mortals?"

Dominic managed a weak smile, "Yes, that part. Well, it was...with Moira. It was Moira and me that were together that night." Father Bumbry nodded. "In looking back on that night, it was the most beautiful experience of my life. I had never felt like that, never imagined ever sharing myself with someone like that, and it was and is beyond words." Dominic emptied his glass. Father Bumbry picked up the glass gallon jug and refilled the goblet.

"So, what happened after that? Did you and Moira, uh...meet up again?"

"We started dating. And we talked every night on the telephone, went to the movies, and ice skating and fun things like that, yes."

"But...no more lovemaking?"

"There was one more time when we were together, in an intimate way, but not quite like that night." Dominic drank some more wine. "And after that second time, I did go to the drugstore, like you suggested." Father Bumbry drank his wine, smiling to himself. "Other than that time, we were affectionate with each other—holding hands, hugs, necking and stuff for sure, but never had another opportunity to be together like that."

"Then everything was OK between the two of you?"

Dominic finished off his glass of wine. It went down fast and he quivered as the first wave of intoxication rankled his body. "No, not really. We hadn't talked for a few months." Father Bumbry poured Dominic another glass of wine.

"Why was that?"

Dominic helped himself to a piece of cheese. "We had broken up."

Father Bumbry was puzzled now. "How did that happen? Did you arrive at that decision together?"

Dominic sat back and looked at the glass of wine in his hand. Tears began to stream down his face. He wiped them with his hand. "No...it was something I wanted to do."

"But why? You had told me you were never so happy in your life. Did something change?" Father Bumbry didn't expect the puppy lovesick experience to last, but he didn't think it would end so soon either. Something wasn't making sense—there was something missing here. Dominic finished the wine in his glass and placed it on the coffee table. Father Bumbry glanced at the empty goblet and hesitated. He quickly thought it through and then poured more wine into Dominic's glass.

"Well?" Father Bumbry asked. "Did something change?"

Dominic folded his hands in front of him and looked down at them. "I realized that what we had done wasn't right...that it was wrong...that we had seriously sinned. I knew that if I really did love Moira then I would have to end it so that we could stop..."

"Who told you it was wrong? Who said it was such a serious sin? I thought you and I had talked about that. You even said that you were comfortable with what had happened, that you felt no remorse. What changed your mind?"

Dominic shifted in his seat. He reached for the glass and knocked the glass over but quickly picked it back up. "Sss--sorry...I'm sorry, about th--that, Father Bumbry!" Dominic slurred his words. Father Bumbry threw some napkins on the spill and then got up and went into the bedroom. He came back with a partially wet washcloth and patted the carpet by Dominic's feet. He crumpled up the napkins and then wiped the glass table top with the dry end of the washcloth. He folded up the washcloth and placed it on the end of the table. "Really sor--sorry about that," repeated Dominic.

"No problem, my son. You should really eat some more crackers. You've been drinking a little too fast." Father Bumbry moved Dominic's glass to the side and then poured more wine, filling the glass three quarters of the way. "Tell me, what changed your mind about Moira?"

Dominic shook his head. "I really hadn't ch--changed it." Dominic closed his eyes and put his head back.

Father Bumbry contemplated the response. He restated his question. "*Who* changed your mind? Had you shared your secret with someone else?"

Dominic nodded his head.

"Who? Who else did you tell, my son?"

Dominic shook his head. The room was beginning to spin a little. He opened his eyes and leaned forward, grabbing another piece of cheese and a couple of crackers.

"Was there someone else who knew about you and Moira?" pressed Father Bumbry. "Your brother Mitchell, perhaps?"

Dominic finished chewing, swallowed, carefully picked up the goblet of wine, and washed down the cheese and crackers. "No, it wwasn't hhim," he let out a small belch, "it was Brother..." Dominic sat back and grimaced, recalling the conversation with Brother Corwin that afternoon.

Father Bumbry nodded his head, he was beginning to understand now. "Corwin? It was Brother Corwin that you told?"

Dominic nodded his head. "th--that was a mis--mistake."

Father Bumbry felt a tinge of jealousy shoot through his spine. "You told your good friend Brother Corwin about Moira? And what did he have to say?"

"Said was wrong. Th--that I had to end it." Dominic winced as he was beginning to feel a little dizzy. He suddenly felt tired. "Told...told me bad th--things about M--Moira. All lies."

Father Bumbry cringed. What he suspected about the so-called Apostle of St. Mary's designs on Dominic was confirmed. What a sonofabitch he was to manipulate the impressionable Dominic in that way for his own purposes. And because of his cruel scheming, Corwin had interfered with the natural course of the relationship between Moira and Dominic. Now it was all becoming clear to him. It was Corwin who put Dominic up to the task of ending his relationship with Moira. Moira was devastated by the abrupt change of heart in her true love and Dominic was adamant in ending the relationship because Corwin had convinced him it was the only way to prove he really loved Moira. Moira was overwhelmed by Dominic's betrayal of their youthful love, leading to the present state of affairs. Father Bumbry was filled with disdain for Corwin. He picked up his goblet of wine and drank it down. He looked over at Dominic and saw that he was beginning to doze off.

"Dominic, are you feeling OK?"

Dominic sat up and looked at Father Bumbry with glassy eyes. "Y--y--yeah, I'm OK." He suddenly reached down and picked up his glass and drank down the wine, before Father Bumbry could react. The priest stood up and took the emptied glass from Dominic's hand. "That's it for you, my son. No more vino tonight." Dominic nodded. "OK. I'm OK." He sat back and closed his eyes.

FATHER BUMBRY CLEANED OFF the coffee table. He helped himself to a few more glasses of wine as he watched Dominic come in and out of a restless sleep. No doubt Dominic was emotionally drained from the sorrowful news, combined with the burden of guilt he was feeling, left the boy in a physically weakened state. And he drank too much wine too fast. He watched and waited. Sure enough, Dominic's eyes opened wide and he began to mutter, "R--rr--room really spinning...don't feel too g--g--good...." Dominic's mouth began to drool. Father Bumbry moved quickly, picking Dominic up from the couch, placing his hands under Dominic's armpits, and hurrying him to the bathroom in the next room. They arrived at the bathroom just in time. Father Bumbry positioned Dominic down alongside the bathtub and leaned him over the edge. Dominic's body buckled and lunged forward as he spewed his vomit into the bathtub. The bathroom filled with a moldy cheese stench and the sound of him puking. Father Bumbry sat on the closed toilet seat and rubbed Dominic's back. When there was a pause in the action, Father Bumbry reached over and filled a paper cup with water from the bathroom sink and tried to get Dominic to drink some. Dominic rested his head on the ledge of the bathtub. The cool porcelain felt good against his head. Father Bumbry helped Dominic to his feet and guided him back to the couch. He went to the bathroom and returned with washcloths to wash off Dominic's hands and face. He thought to himself that it was good that Mitchell Manterra had called him after Dominic left the house to let him know what state of mind Dominic was in. Father Bumbry had let Mitchell know that if it got too late, he would just have Dominic sleep on the couch and would drive him home early the next morning. He checked the time. Had Dominic gotten here that late? It was already well past midnight, into the next morning. He glanced at Dominic sitting on the couch, his eyes half closed, drifting to sleep. He could hear the labored breathing through his partially pursed lips, the sound of dried breath being forced out. He went back to the bathroom and returned with a cup of water.

"Dominic...Dominic..." he gently nudged him. Dominic opened his eyes and closed his mouth, licking his lips with his tongue. He made a face, obviously tasting the sourness in his mouth. "Here, my son, drink some water." Father Bumbry placed his hand behind Dominic's head and tilted it forward while bringing the paper cup to his lips and pouring

water into his mouth. Dominic finished the cup of water and Father
Bumbry sat him back, then threw the paper cup in a waste basket by his
desk. He was beginning to feel the effects of the wine on himself, a
slight wooziness coming to bear in his head. He tilted his head, looked
at Dominic, and determined he looked uncomfortable sitting the way he
was on the couch. He finished his glass of wine and put the empty goblet on his desk, then went over to the sleeping youth and bent down on
his knees. He untied the laces of Dominic's sneakers and pulled them off
first, and then his socks. He paused as Dominic fidgeted in his state of
stupor and then was motionless. Bumbry continued undressing him,
opening his belt, unsnapping his jeans, and removing his pants, one leg
at time. Dominic leaned forward, mumbling, and Bumbry managed to
stop the forward motion, his hand pressed against Dominic's chest, and
pushing him back against the couch. Bumbry stood up and took hold of
the bottom of Dominic's sweatshirt and maneuvered it over his head and
arms. He folded the clothes into a neat pile on the floor by the end of the
couch. Father Bumbry stood up and slowly stepped back from the couch,
keeping his eyes on his sleeping guest. He backed into the desk, then
reached for the goblet and poured wine into it. He sipped the wine while
staring at Dominic sitting there, asleep. He put the wine glass down on
the coffee table and returned to the couch. He took hold of Dominic's
shoulders and pushed his upper torso toward one end of the couch while
reaching and picking up Dominic's legs and placing them on the opposite end of the couch. Dominic's eyes opened for a moment, then he
looked at Father Bumbry and muttered, "Need to go home" before his
eyes closed again. Father Bumbry stood himself up, placing one foot on
the floor and leaning one hand on a knee, balancing the other hand on
the arm of the couch. He hovered over the outstretched Dominic, with
his lean, muscular, athletic build, lying on his back wearing just his
underwear briefs and T-shirt. Father Bumbry picked up the wine goblet
and finished off the wine. He stepped into his bedroom and got undressed, stripping down to his boxer shorts and his T-shirt.

Father Bumbry went back to the couch and managed to kneel and

then sit down on the floor next to Dominic's body. He gently stroked
the sleeping beauty's forehead and the side of his face. The youth appeared to still be sleeping. A whiff of foul breath filled the priest's nostrils. Bumbry eyed the jar of red and white peppermint candies on the
bookshelf within arm's length. He picked one out and removed the
wrapper. He gently turned Dominic's head and froze for a moment as
Dominic's eyes opened wide and their glassy expression looked up at
him before the eyelids closed again. Bumbry waited a moment and in-
serted the mint into Dominic's mouth, pressing it down into the side of
his cheek. Father Bumbry's eyes scanned down the youth's neck, over his
chest and to his crotch. Father Bumbry shifted his weight, freeing up
the hand he had been resting on, bringing it up and placing it on the
couch cushion next to the youth's hip. He looked back at the sleeping
face, paused, held his breath, and then moved his hand onto the youth's
abdomen. He paused, quietly exhaling his breath and then inhaling and
holding it. He slipped his hand under the waistband of Dominic's
briefs....

Father Bumbry was stroking himself, but the effects of the alcohol
were taking their toll. His other hand was busy with its manual rape of
the sleeping teenager, who had slightly stirred now and then but did not
appear to awaken, who seemed almost to not even breathe at times. He
pulled his hand back out from under the boy's waistband and pushed
himself up on his knees. He pushed down his own boxers and took hold
of Dominic's arm and hand, placed the hand within his own hand and
began stroking himself with both. He gazed down on himself and his
activity, glanced at the boy, and then closed his eyes. After several minutes he stopped. He bent the boy's arm back toward his abdomen. He
paused to look at Dominic, whose head had moved side to side, and
whose lips were mumbling incoherently. He guided the boy's hand down
under the waistband of his briefs and placed them on the boy's penis.
Father Bumbry, with his own hand on top of Dominic's, rubbed the hand
and fingers over the boy's penis, pulling and stroking on the flaccid
member. After a few minutes, the penis appeared to be stimulated and

Father Bumbry began stroking himself with his other hand, incented by the physiological reaction. The boy's head turned away from its side and his mouth and tongue were moving. The priest let up on his hand movements and held his breath. The boy's head fell back to the side and the partially dissolved mint fell from his mouth onto the couch cushion. The priest withdrew the hand of the boy from under his waistband and let it rest on the boy's chest. He placed his hands on the edge of the couch and slid his knees over, further down from the boy's head. He waited a few minutes, watching the boy's chest rise and drop in steady intervals as he breathed in and out. The priest's eyes traveled down the boy's body to his crotch. He placed his hands on the waistband of the underwear, and lifted it up and pulled it down, below the scrotum. He bent over the boy's body and lowered his face over the youth's exposed member...

The lamb had wandered off from the flock. It had found its way to a grassy hill above a shallow ravine. The lamb basked in the warmth of the sun and the cool breeze caressing the hilltops and the verdant pasture land. In the tall grass near the ravine, unbeknownst to the lamb, was a predator lying low and still, hiding and anticipating. The wolf, with a lean and hungry look, patiently waited, keeping watch over the solitary lamb. The lamb smelled the water, its throat parched with thirst. It made its way toward the ravine, longing for the cool water to soothe its thirst. The wolf slowly rose from its prone position, its ears pointed, nose raised up, and its fangs bared. The unsuspecting lamb approached the narrow ravine, pausing every now and then to chew some grass. It reached the bank of the ravine and lapped up some water. The wolf quietly and slowly edged closer to the lamb. The lamb having gotten its fill of water frolicked in the grass, before lying down supine, to take a moment's rest. The wolf halted in its tracks for a brief respite—and then charged its vulnerable prey...

In the wake of his physical discomfort, Dominic heard the sounds of labored breathing. His throat was dry and sore, and he had a sweet but stale taste in his mouth. He had dreamed a strange dream. It was so in-

tensely real and shrouded in foreboding. Images of his mother and of
Moira's face had flooded his mind. They were both very frightened and
sad—calling out to him, calling out his name with an impassioned ur-
gency. He could hear and see them but he couldn't seem to get near
them or reach them. He pushed hard with all his might to get to where
they were, but the harder he pushed and struggled, the further away
they moved from him. Their faces were filling him with such dread because their calling of his name grew more and more alarming and frantic. They eventually faded from view and all went black. His skull
reverberated with a sharp pain and in his stomach, he felt queasiness as
he began to stir from sleep. His eyelids felt like shades of iron as he tried
to force them open. He managed to pry them open a sliver. Besides taste,
his other senses were all slowly awakening.

He immediately froze.

Through the splinter of his eyelids, he saw the outline of a man. He
could smell a familiar scent of cologne. He heard the sound of another's
breathing and grunts among other sounds. He felt things that filled him
with great disgust and fear. He closed his eyes tight. He lay still as if a
corpse, trying not to breathe. His mind raced with a million thoughts
and impulses ricocheting within the barrels of his skull. He had failed to
wrap himself in the cocoon of blankets! He had left himself unprotected
after all these years and the evil that had lurked in waiting had found
him exposed and vulnerable. He called upon all his powers of invisibility
to make himself disappear, but it was too late. He could do nothing. He
was frozen in complete paralysis of fright. His senses all worked but they
dwelled within a hollowed-out body. He was physically comatose but
acutely conscious of his surroundings. Fear had shocked his physical being
into a suspended state with total inertia setting in. His mind sought refuge from the ugliness about him:

*He is the king of glory/the nation rejoices/open the gates before him/lift up
your voices/who is the king of glory?/how shall we know him?/He is
Emmanuel/the promised of ages*

He is the king of glory/the nation rejoices/open the gates before him/lift up your voices/who is the king of glory?/how shall we know him?/He is Emmanuel/the promised of ages

He is the king of glory/the nation rejoices/open the gates before him/lift up your voices/who is the king of glory?/how shall we know him?/He is Emmanuel/the promised of ages

He is the king of glory/the nation rejoices/open the gates before him/lift up your voices/who is the king of glory?/how shall we know him?/He is Emmanuel/the promised of ages

He is the king of glory/the nation rejoices/open the gates before him/lift up your voices/who is the king of glory?/how shall we know him?/He is Emmanuel/the promised of ages

Over and over and over, Dominic repeated the prayer verse. It was all he could do. He lay dead on the outside while he frantically fought to stay alive within himself. The words of Emmanuel were his only hope of survival.

FATHER BUMBRY PULLED HIMSELF UP from his coarse attempts, frustrated that there were no results either way. He got himself up to his feet and pulled up his boxer shorts. He grabbed the throw blanket from behind the lounge chair and draped it over the body of the youth. He took a last look at the sleeping beauty, turned away, and dragged his feet toward his bedroom.

Dominic opened his eyes a tiny crack and watched just as the priest reached the bedroom entrance and closed the bedroom door. Dominic listened until he heard the sounds of snoring echo in the other room. He threw off the blanket and jumped up from the couch. He spotted his clothes piled on top of his sneakers and swooped them up. He quietly hurried to the door and undid the locks and stepped out into the hallway. He bolted down the stairs and through the door of the rectory. He leapt from the top of the porch to the front walk and turned down Fourth

Avenue. He raced with all his might as he began to cry hysterically. He was running aimlessly as the early morning began to lighten the overcast sky. The whole world was shrouded in a gray film. A block away from the rectory, near the stone wall of a creek, he stopped to put on his clothes and his sneakers. He grabbed his head and sobbed uncontrollably. His body was quivering and shaking and his skin was ice cold. He embraced himself, wrapping his arms around his torso, and squatted down to the ground. He was overcome with so much grief and shame and hurt. He was all alone and didn't know what to do, where to go.

"Mom, is Peter as bad as Judas?"

She pushed her sewing aside and patted the cushion next to her on the couch, beckoning Dominic to come sit beside her. Dominic went and sat next to his mother.

"Peter denied Jesus because he was afraid, and although he felt he let Jesus down, Jesus already knew Peter was going to do what he did. And Peter regretted what he did. Judas, on the other hand, betrayed Jesus, and basically helped those who wanted to harm Jesus..."

"Did Jesus love Judas?" asked Dominic.

"Yes...yes, I believe He did. Jesus as God loves all His children. But God doesn't force any of His children to love Him; that is what is called free will. And the Bible says that we must be like a child if we are to be a part of God's kingdom in heaven. And because God loves all His children, He doesn't want anyone to hurt His children. Jesus said it would be better for a man to tie a millstone around his neck and to cast himself into the ocean than to lead a child astray."

"What does it mean to lead a child astray?" asked Dominic.

"That means to lead them away from the open arms of Jesus," she said lovingly.

"I will remember that," stated Dominic in a matter-of-fact tone.

"And never lose hope, Dominic. Always hold on to hope, no matter how bad things may seem. Hope is very important. Peter loved Jesus. He faltered in his faith but he still had hope in Jesus. And it turned out alright for

him. Judas didn't love Jesus, he didn't believe in Jesus, and so in the end, he had no hope. And that is why he took his life."

Dominic nodded his head. "I will, Mommy." She embraced her young child and Dominic hugged his mother with all his might.

Dominic began muttering to himself, "Can't lose hope! Can't lose hope! Hold on! Hold on! Don't lose hope! Mom, I will keep my promises, Mom! Mom, I will keep my promise! I won't lose hope! I won't! Moira, I'm sorry! Moira, I'm so sorry! I broke my promise! I failed! You were right! I'm so sorry, Moira! God, please help me! Sweet Jesus, please help me! Please help me, Jesus! I need you now more than ever! Jesus, please help me!" Dominic buried his face in his hands.

"Dominic!"

Dominic froze. His eyes were closed and he was crouched down, leaning against the concrete wall of the bridge over the creek that flowed across Fourth Avenue.

"Dominic! What are you doing here? What's the matter, buddy?"

Dominic opened his eyes and looked up into the worried face of his friend Harry.

"Harry..." Dominic managed to whisper his friend's name before breaking down crying again.

Harry crouched down next to his friend and put his arms around Dominic's shoulders. "Dominic, what happened? Tell me."

Dominic just shook his head, "No, no—I can't. I can't tell anyone. Never. I can't."

Harry hugged his friend close and spoke soothingly. "OK, Dominic, it's OK. It's going to be alright." Harry glanced around. It was still early enough that the neighborhood had not come alive just yet but was starting to show signs of life.

Dominic attempted to collect himself. "Sorry, Harry. I'm sorry that I'm like this."

"No problem, Dominic. Don't worry about that, don't be stupid. I'm your friend."

Harry looked up the street and saw something on the sidewalk that he couldn't make out. He looked down at Dominic's feet and saw his bare left ankle. He looked back at the object on the sidewalk and realized it was Dominic's sock. Harry's eyes traced the possible path that Dominic might have taken and his eyes made their way to the top of Fourth Avenue at the intersection by St. Mary's rectory. Harry glanced down at his distraught friend.

"Come on, Dominic, we got to get out of here quick."

Harry pulled Dominic to his feet and with his arm around his shoulder and his other arm holding up Dominic by his arm, he started to walk him down the street. He thought of something and told Dominic to stand still for a second. Harry ran back up the street and grabbed Dominic's sock and quickly returned to his friend and took hold of him again and started walking briskly down the street.

THE TELEPHONE RANG. Dominic sat at the kitchen table, numb and vacant. He gazed up at the hands on the clock, which indicated it was 11:30 a.m. The time could have been 87:15 a.m. in the year 3340 for all it mattered, as far as he was from planet earth and the current time and date. The ringing of the telephone filled the kitchen and filled his head and was pounding his skull from the inside as well as the outside. He was waiting for Mitchell, who had run out to the corner to get the *Daily News* and some Kaiser rolls for their father when he got home from work. Jason was at school and Sal was at his new deli. Mom was at his sister Maria's watching the kids for the week as her husband was away on a business trip. This was the third time the telephone had rung since Mitchell left, and Dominic had to make a decision. He had to decide whether or not he wanted the ringing to stop before it shattered his skull and splattered his brains all over the kitchen table. He stood up and walked over to the wall telephone and answered.

"Hello?"

"Oh, good morning, my son..." Spoke the voice on the other end. Dominic's body stiffened in disgust upon hearing the familiar voice.

"Good morning," replied Dominic in a quiet voice after a long pause.

"It's...it's Father Arnold."

"I know."

"I...uh...was just calling to check in on you. You, uh, you left this morning before I, uh, woke up. I just want to make sure...uh...everything was alright?"

"Uh-huh."

"You were...very upset last night...and I tried to warn you about drinking too much...knowing how distraught you were...I, uh, maybe let you overdo it a bit. I don't know if you remember, but you got sick."

"Uh-huh, sorry about that."

"No, no worries, you didn't make much of a mess, so that was good." There was a pause. "But you're feeling OK now, right? You're doing OK, right?"

"Yup."

"Yeah...you...you drank a lot so you...uh...passed out after...after you got sick. You were able to sleep it off, I guess, before you, uh, left this morning."

"Seems that way."

"OK, well, I won't keep you. I figured you might have stayed home today, after the ordeal yesterday...I mean, with respect to Moira." Dominic's cheeks burned and cringed upon hearing that sacred name being spoken by the lips of such a vile human being. Anger swelled in him and the degree of hatred he felt was so intense he thought he might have a seizure. "We'll need to keep her in our prayers and hope for a miracle."

"Yeah...especially since you're so close to God, that should work." Dominic's voice was dripping with disdain.

"We are all God's children and He hears all our prayers equally, my son."

There may have been a time when Dominic believed that was true, but he didn't believe it anymore. He wasn't sure what he believed in anymore.

"Is there anything else I can help you with, Father Bumbry?" Dominic asked.

"No, no...of course not, my son, it is you who needs help and support. And you know I am here for you, right? You know I'm your friend, and that I only have your best interest in mind? But everything's good, between us, right? We'll need to get together again soon. I'm really looking forward to it. OK?"

"Goodbye, Father Bumbry."

Dominic hung up the telephone and then took it off the hook and let it hang down along the wall. He went and sat back down at the table. After about twenty seconds the dial tone transferred to a voice that advised the phone needed to be hung up and the call tried again before sounding an obnoxious alarm to indicate the phone was off the receiver. The screeching sound went on for about thirty seconds and then stopped. "We are all God's children and He hears our prayers equally, my son." The words echoed in Dominic's mind. He didn't believe in that anymore. He didn't believe in much at this point. He wasn't sure what he believed in, as every belief, every certainty, every truth was up for debate and scrutiny now. The only exception was Moira. He believed in Moira, now more than ever. But he had denied her. And for that, he knew there was no penance he could perform, no restitution he could make, that would amend that act of cowardice. Only Moira held the power to heal him, to restore his faith, to salve his scars, to take away his hurt— through her forgiveness and love. He did believe that she would give him both once again. But she had to return—she had to return from wherever she was, she had to come back to him so he could beg her forgiveness and convince her of his love. The only hope he had now was for that to happen. It was the only hope he was holding on to; if not, he would be lost forever. Moira had warned him of all this and had told him what would happen if he denied her love.

His heart was shattered, his spirit crushed, his soul emptied, his mind numbed. He wanted to cry but had no more tears to shed, for they had been drained along with his compassion and emotion. He had only three feelings that he was sure he still felt: regret, hatred, and rage. And the dominant of these was rage.

Mitchell came in the back door and up the steps into the kitchen carrying a couple of medium-sized brown paper bags and the newspapers. He placed them on the table and gave Dominic a nod of his head. He noticed the telephone hanging down. He shot Dominic a quizzical look.

"It started ringing after you left. The person kept calling back so I finally answered it. I didn't want any follow-ups."

"Motherfucker he is. I just want to go over there and beat him to death with a baseball bat." Mitchell's fury was genuine.

"Thanks, but that wouldn't be good enough."

"Here, you should eat something and we should discuss how you're going to explain this to Mom and Dad."

Dominic's head dropped. He was not looking forward to the conversation with his father. His mom could never know. It would crush her. He had no idea what to expect, or even how to go about explaining it to his father. He hadn't really given Mitchell many details either but Mitchell didn't need much to stir up his anger toward Father Bumbry. The incident was just a confirmation of suspicions that Mitchell had always harbored toward the priest through his own interactions with him. And he was angry with himself for not being more protective of his brother.

"I'm not hungry, Mitchell. But I am tired. I think I will lie down for a while. Mitch, we can never tell Mom what happened."

"You should do that, Dominic. Yeah, it's a good thing Mom is at Maria's. I agree, Mom can never know. Get some rest before Dad gets home. If you're still sleeping when he does, I'm not going to wake you though. But I will prepare him a little, if that's OK?"

Dominic nodded his agreement and pushed himself away from the table. Mitchell watched him leave the kitchen to head upstairs. Looking at the bags on the table, he realized he had no appetite either. He lit the burner on the stove for the tea kettle and sat down to wait for his father, trying to think what he was going to say to him.

Dominic climbed the steps to the second floor of the house and went to his bed. He had taken a shower as soon as he got home and thrown the clothes that he wore the night before into the trash can outside. He lay down on his bed, dressed in his clothes, and pulled the blanket over him. He tucked the sides of the blanket under his body and placed his head on the pillow. He closed his eyes. Tears began to stream down his face and he pulled the pillow out from under his head and placed it over his head and quietly sobbed.

DOMINIC HAD NOT BEEN sleeping long before he was jostled from his sleep. He opened his eyes to find his older brother Salvatore standing over him. Dominic sat up and slid onto the edge of his bed. "What's up, Sal?"

"What's up? That's all you have to say? Where the hell were you this morning?"

"Sorry, Sal, I had a very rough night and morning. I wasn't able to make it to the deli."

"Damnit, Dominic, do you know what that did to me? That's my busiest time of the day with one customer after another. I was crushed! Why the hell didn't you show up? You stuck me all alone trying to manage the store by myself. I can't believe you!"

"I'm sorry, Sal...I really am...it was a terrible night...I sent Harry to help you? Didn't he show up?"

"Yeah, Harry showed up. What good was that going to do? He never worked in a deli before. I just told him to go home because he was just getting in the way. Where the fuck were you?"

Dominic wondered how he could explain what happened. Sal was seething. "Sal, I had gone over to see Father Bumbry last night...because I needed to talk to him about something that had happened to

Moira and I fell asleep...and when I woke up...Father Bumbry was... molesting me..." Dominic choked on the last words and looked down in shame.

"What? That's what happened? That's why you didn't show up? You know what, Dominic—shit like that happens. You get over it. That's just the way things are in life. You should have been there this morning to help me. You weren't and you left me in a real bind. You probably cost me future business. I'm sure of it. People don't like to be kept waiting. Thanks a lot!" Sal glared at his younger brother and shook his head. "I got to get back to the deli. I just had to find out why you screwed me over. Be there tomorrow morning. On time. Don't leave me hanging like that again." Sal turned around and walked out.

Dominic dropped back down on the bed and stared at the ceiling. He wondered to himself, *Did that really just happen?* He closed his eyes and wondered if the pain and hurt would ever stop. He wondered if the little gnomes that had invaded his body and then taken up residence in his nervous system and by his heart, searing his nerve endings with iron pokers, would ever cease their torture of him. At times, they would provide a respite long enough to give him a sense of false hope that it was over before applying their tools of torment with a prolonged stab to remind him that the pain and hurt were still there and still very raw.

Irreparable damage had been done.

MONSIGNOR DOWNEY SAT AT the dining room table of Salvatore Manterra with the old man himself and his sons Jack, David, Mitchell, and Dominic. Salvatore Manterra carried on his face the lines and creases of a man who had weathered his fair share of life's tragedies and injustices. He was a hardened individual who had raised seven children along with his wife, Iolanda, known for her devoutness and piety. He was a man of many burdens who chose to bear those burdens on his shoulders alone, with a stoic dignity and pride. Manterra reached behind and grabbed an ashtray off the hutch and pushed it toward the parish priest.

"Go on, Monsignor, feel free to smoke."

Downey nodded his appreciation and pulled out a pack of L&M cigarettes and lit one up. He inhaled, blew out a puff of smoke away from the table and addressed no one in particular.

"I warned him about this. I had warned him and he didn't listen. I knew this would happen. It was just a matter of time. He's really left me very little choice." He tapped his cigarette on the edge of the ashtray and looked directly at Salvatore Manterra. "This isn't like the beginning days, Sal, when Roland was pastor. We had Brickley, Scalera, and myself. The old guard was rock solid, traditional men of the cloth. Times have changed. I've got one priest who no one can understand, another who spends more time at the Knights of Columbus happy hour than serving the community, a third who has the charisma of wet toast, and then Bumbry, arrogant and irreverent. How does one serve a parish with such misfits?" He stamped his cigarette out.

The Manterra men just sat emotionless and motionless. Dominic squirmed a little in his chair as he wasn't sure what to do or what was next. His father and his brothers appeared to be waiting for the pastor to lead the discussion.

"Let me understand this, Dominic, you went to the rectory that night because you had found out about the Toomey girl and you were upset? Is that right?"

Dominic nodded. "Yes, sir." Dominic remembered that Father Bumbry had told him that Monsignor Downey was with Moira's family that night. Dominic felt like the Monsignor seemed to glare at him, as though he knew something about Moira and him. He wanted to ask him how Moira was but Mitchell advised him not to bring Moira up—that Mitchell would find out on his own and let Dominic know.

"You get to the rectory, Father Bumbry lets you in, and you go upstairs to his apartment...to talk?"

"Yes, sir. Father Bumbry has a buzzer connected to his room so you can contact him without waking up the rest of the priests."

Downey frowned. He was very familiar with that buzzer and had already told the St. Mary's school custodians to come and rip it out, an order he regretted not giving sooner. "And when you got up to the apartment, there was alcohol?"

Salvatore Manterra glared at his young son. Dominic kept his eyes lowered and murmured his answer. "Yes, sir. Father Bumbry had a jug of wine, and some cheese and crackers."

"And how much did you drink?"

Dominic shrank down a little in his chair. "I don't remember, sir. Quite a few glasses, I would say. I was very, uh, upset, so I really wasn't thinking straight."

The Monsignor paused his inquisition to light another cigarette. "Have you had drinks with Father Bumbry before?"

"No, sir. That was the first and only time."

"Do you drink with your friends a lot?"

Dominic shook his head, "No, sir."

"Although you didn't have any problem drinking *that* night?"

"No, I guess I didn't. But it was just that..." Dominic paused.

"What? It was just that what?" asked Downey.

Dominic looked at Mitchell, who slightly shook his head.

"Nothing," said Dominic. "Nothing, you're right."

"What was it that you were going to say, Dominic?" The question came from Salvatore Manterra.

Dominic looked up into the serious blue eyes of his father, the eyes that matched his own. The only thing he shared with his father. His father's eyes were giving him a command, and disobedience was not an option.

"I was just going to say that I was very upset that night, very upset about my friend Moira. I had heard what had happened to her, and I felt responsible, so I was distraught and I—"

"You felt responsible? How so?" Downey put down his cigarette and leaned forward.

Dominic glanced at Mitchell, who again gave him a subtle glance not to say anything.

"She was my friend," Dominic continued. "I...I...if there was some-thing bothering her that much...I...maybe I should have noticed and... and...to see if she needed help. That's what friends do...they know when you're not in...a good place...that's all."

Downey's disposition softened. "You can't be too hard on yourself about that, Dominic. We're not mind readers, and God doesn't expect us to be. The best we can do now is to continue to keep your friend in our prayers. Her and her family. It's a very difficult time for all of them."

Dominic wanted to ask what the Monsignor meant but again Mitch-ell's eyes told him no.

"Salvatore, I don't want to take up too much of your time. I know you've other obligations to contend with. Just as we discussed on the telephone, I will be taking the matter up with the Archbishop. It's not necessary to go into detail here with the boy. The information you've provided in our phone conversation is sufficient."

"Thank you, Monsignor Downey. I appreciate you coming down to meet with us and for everything else as well."

The Monsignor gave a faint smile and went to rise from the table but then sat back down. "Oh, there's one more thing, Dominic." Dominic looked up at the priest. "I know that you and Father Bumbry were close...friends. I need to have you understand that this, uh, incident, has put us all in a very precarious situation. I'm not even sure that Father Bumbry is aware that you have brought, uh, that night to anyone's at-tention. Having said that, he will soon be confronted with that reality. I can't say, unfortunately, what substance the man is made of, how strong the foundation of his faith. But I want you to be aware that in the event he should take the...the revelation of his transgress...in a way that might overwhelm his capacity of dealing with his actions and any guilt and remorse...and should he take the coward's way out...I don't want you to be caught off guard or feel any responsibility for it. Understood?"

"Yes, sir," Dominic replied, although he was unsure what the Monsi-gnor meant.

Mr. Manterra, Jack, and David accompanied Monsignor Downey to the door and stepped outside to chat with him some more. Mitchell and Dominic stayed sitting at the table.

"What did Monsignor Downey mean by that last remark, Mitch?" Dominic asked.

"He means that when he confronts Father Bumbry about what he's done and that he's been caught, found out, that asshole may go and commit suicide. But I don't think the bastard has the balls or the good sense to do that." Mitchell stretched his neck to look out the dining room window where the four men were still talking on the front steps. He looked back at Dominic. "Would that bother you if he did? If Bumbry went and killed himself?"

Dominic looked at his brother and without hesitation answered in a cold, flat voice, "No, not at all. I hope he does." Even Mitchell was a little taken aback by the iciness and quickness of Dominic's response.

"Mitch, have you heard anything new about Moira?"

"Not yet, but I'm hoping to find out something tonight. As soon as I hear, I will let you know. But what you need to do now, Dominic, is to get your head together. You need to get back to school and back to your activities. You can't stay locked up in this house. There's bound to be speculation and talk, especially after Bumbry is dealt with. You want to be back in the swing of things so there are no connections made with any of this. OK?"

Dominic nodded. "Yup, I'm working on it, Mitchell."

Salvatore Manterra, Jack, and David came back into the house. Jack walked over to Dominic and placed a hand on Dominic's shoulder and extended his other hand to him. "Take care, brother. I will be checking in on you, and praying for you as well. I remember what Mom used to say to us kids, probably before you were even born—'This too shall pass.' I will talk to you soon." Jack gave Dominic's hand and shoulders a supportive squeeze. Jack and David said goodbyes to Mitchell and their father and left.

Mitchell stood up as well and addressed Dominic. "Alright, Dominic, I'm going to head out as well. I need to get over to Brooklyn and get to the house. The residents are probably wondering where I am."

"Take care, Mitch. I will see you soon." Mitchell nodded and then glanced at their father as he walked by the old man, who wore a grim expression and had his eyes fixed on Dominic the whole time. A part of Mitchell wanted to linger until his dad went up to take his usual nap before his next shift, but something told him that his father wasn't taking any such nap this afternoon.

"See ya later, Dad," Mitchell mumbled as he made his way past his father, who simply nodded his head.

Dominic sat and waited.

His father finally broke the tense silence. "Dominic...I don't even know where to begin..." His father spoke with a quiet and harsh tone. "I don't know how this happened. I don't know why this happened. I don't know anything about bullshit like this. All I know is that your mom and I can't be in two places at one time. Your mom...thank God she's with your sister and not here for this. Your mom does everything to raise you kids while I am at two jobs, working hard for my family, so I can put food on the table, a roof over our heads, clothes on your backs, and get all of you a Catholic school education. Things I didn't necessarily have when I was growing up. That's why it's so important that my sons realize their responsibility in not complicating their lives with bad decisions and foolish choices. And those two are best avoided by not being where one does not belong." Dominic's father walked around the table and stood across from where Dominic sat.

"What the hell were you doing at the rectory that night?"

Dominic looked up at his father with frightened eyes. "I just went there to talk to Father Bumbry."

"That late at night? To talk to him about what?"

"I was upset...because of what..." Dominic was going to say his brother Mitchell's name but quickly thought better of it. "...like I told the Monsignor, I had heard about my friend Moira...about what had happened to Moira."

Mr. Manterra stepped back from the table.

"Yes, that was most unfortunate. I could understand why you would be upset about that. The Monsignor and I were just discussing that outside. We're both wondering if there's more to that story than we know."

Mr. Manterra paused, awaiting a response from his son. Dominic looked down at Mr. Manterra's reflection in the polished dining room table top and remained motionless.

"Is there? Do you know anything more about why the Toomey girl did that?"

Dominic shook his head no.

"You don't have any involvement in that, at all?"

Dominic again shook his head no.

"You don't know anything about why she would do such a thing, nothing happened between you, nothing was ever said or anything like that?"

Again, Dominic shook his head.

Dominic figured that the grown-ups just wouldn't understand anything. They didn't believe in the things that Moira and he believed in, they didn't see life the way that Moira and he saw life. So there was no point in trying to explain anything to them, no point in trying to make them understand about matters of the heart when their hearts had grown cold. What would they know about those things that truly mattered, those things that only the heart could see? To Dominic, they are unable to see the truth and beauty of life, invisible except to those who look at life through the eyes of love. All at once, he genuinely understood what human blindness was.

"OK. So then why were you so upset?"

"She was my friend, Dad. Wouldn't you be upset if one of your friends tried to end their life?"

Mr. Manterra could feel the anger swell in his neck and Dominic could see it as well.

"Watch your tongue, Dominic. I have no tolerance for your wisecrack comments right now. What the hell were you doing drinking in that priest's apartment?" The question was shouted with a furious pounding of Mr. Manterra's fist on the dining room table that made both the centerpiece and Dominic jump.

Dominic began to shake a little. "I...I don't know. Father Bumbry said it would take the edge off...I didn't know what I was thinking...I guess I wasn't thinking...I didn't realize...."

"Right! You weren't thinking at all! You didn't use your head! You used poor judgment! You made a bad decision and a foolish choice! And now you've created this big fucking mess! That others now have to clean up!"

Dominic stopped shaking. He wasn't sure what to make of what his father had just said. What did he mean? This was his fault? He was to blame? Dominic didn't understand. Was his...was his father...angry at him? What had he done wrong?

"Do you have anything to say for yourself?"

Dominic looked up at his father, with a pleading, hurting look in his eyes. He didn't know what to say. He didn't know what his father expected him to say. He didn't know what his father wanted him to say.

"Nothing to say at all?"

Dominic shifted his eyes and stared straight ahead. He fought with all his might and strength to not break down and cry. He could not do that. His father had no patience for crying or anyone feeling sorry for himself. Any whimper or crying was a sign of weakness.

"Do you take any responsibility for what has happened?"

Dominic closed his eyes for a moment. The thought had never occurred to him that he was at fault or had responsibility or was partly to blame for what Father Bumbry had done. Did his father believe that he, Dominic, had brought this upon himself? Could he possibly mean that? Dominic opened his eyes.

"I, I don't think...I understand." Suddenly Dominic felt very weary. The intense anger he had felt toward his father a few moments ago—

anger he had to contain—drained him considerably of his strength and energy.

"If you hadn't placed yourself in that situation, if you hadn't gone to the rectory, and if you hadn't drunk the wine that night, if you hadn't... slept there...then none of this would have happened? Right?"

"Yes, sir." Dominic figured the path of least resistance would end the cross-examination and the trial quickly so they could move to the verdict, final judgment, and sentencing.

"Not to mention the ramifications of your actions to others. Your brother Sal told me about what happened at the deli that morning where you left him stranded by himself. He has a business to run, Dominic, and you were supposed to be there and you failed to show up. That's what happens when you do stupid things and neglect your responsibilities to others, Dominic."

The implication of his father's words cut Dominic to the bone. It was apparent to Dominic his father was blaming him for what had happened, and more. The discussion was now over for Dominic. He wasn't listening anymore. He was now truly on his own. He no longer had a father.

"I understand. I'm sorry. It won't happen again."

The anger and frustration subsided within Mr. Manterra. He knew deep inside that this conversation was not going well. But he didn't understand why. He didn't understand any of this. He was tired, he was weary—the burdens he carried no one could fathom or even begin to understand or have the forbearance to sustain. What about his hurt? His disappointments? His dreams unrealized? It was not in his nature or mindset to grasp what had happened to his young son because the notion of any man doing that to a boy was beyond his scope of reasoning. And because he couldn't wrap his mind around such heinous behavior, he defaulted to the thought that charged those who didn't avoid getting themselves into such situations. If Dominic had only stayed focused on his duties in life, this would never had happened. At the same time, he knew Dominic, unlike all his other sons, was not like him. Dominic was truly his mother's son. Except for those blue eyes—Salvatore Manterra could truly lay claim to those eyes.

"Son," Mr. Manterra let out a deep sigh, "we need to get all this behind us. The Monsignor is going to address this and Father Bumbry will likely be gone soon enough. You need to buck up now and be a man. Life goes on, right? There's still life to contend with, obligations to be fulfilled, the bills got to be paid. The sooner we can move on from this... this incident...the better. For you. For me. For all of us. Understood?"

"Yes, I understand. Again, I'm sorry about all this." Dominic spoke quietly with all the stoic courage he could muster.

"I know you are, son," replied Mr. Manterra. "Listen, son, I know it's...it's not...it hasn't been easy for you...and for your brothers...I'm not the easygoing type father that the television shows nowadays like to promote. And your mom isn't the happy, has-it-all-together Suzy Homemaker type either. You're the most like her. Probably the only one who really is like her, with the exception of your sister Maria."

Dominic simply nodded his head.

"I'm going to go up and get some rest before heading back to work. Think about what we talked about, OK? Tomorrow is another day."

Dominic didn't turn his head as his father walked around the table, through the hallway, and made his way up the stairs. Dominic sat staring at nothing while all the tears that he had just fought back slowly dripped down within the bowels of his being and watered the seed of rage planted there.

A NUMBER OF WEEKS had passed after the incident and Dominic, with some internal adjustments, was back into his normal routine. For the most part, he kept to himself and put on a public face that diverted inquiries to his short absence. He relied on most folks showing more concern than nosiness regarding Moira. He did not have a big part in the spring musical and so had met with Mr. Gavin to see if he could drop out. Although it may not have been a big part, it was still late in the game, and Mr. Gavin persuaded him to continue his participation. Since there was not a lot of choreography, Brother Corwin's participation was minimal, and anyway, Dominic was not in any of the dance numbers. Dominic found solace in running, which almost became an obsession.

By chance, one evening at drama practice, Dominic was in the back of the gym doing his biology homework. A shadow appeared over his textbook and he looked up from his reading.

"Hallo!"

Brother Corwin chagrined and waved his arm in a circle at Dominic. Dominic just sat expressionless, gazing up at him for a moment, and then went back to his reading.

Unfazed, Brother Corwin addressed him. "I was wondering if we might not have a chat for a few minutes."

Dominic didn't look up. "I'm kind of busy doing my biology homework."

"Well, I'm sure you could put Mr. Housen's assignment on hold for a few minutes. You're a smart enough guy you can pick up right where you left off."

Dominic wrote down some notes on his notebook, still keeping his head down. "I have to go on stage soon."

"Not for another thirty minutes by my calculation. Please, Dominic, this will take fifteen minutes, tops. And I believe it is in your best interest that we talk."

The seed within Dominic's being had quickly grown to a sapling, and a sharp branch jabbed a nerve as the sound of those last words entered Dominic's ears. "We don't have anything to talk about, Brother Corwin."

"*Au contraire*, little brother, *au contraire*, but we do. By the way, you still taking French lessons? Anyway, we need to talk about that night... at St. Mary's."

Dominic had already jumped to his feet at the crack about French lessons, but the reference to the night at St. Mary's stopped him cold. He recoiled. "Alright, so talk."

"Not here—wouldn't be prudent considering the subject matter. We can go across the hall to a classroom for some privacy."

Dominic followed Brother Corwin out the nearby gymnasium door, stepping across the hall to the first empty classroom. Brother Corwin flipped the light switch and held the door as Dominic entered. He pointed to a desk, and Dominic sat in a different one. Brother Corwin frowned and closed the classroom door. He sat in a desk across from where Dominic sat with his arms folded, wearing a look of disdain.

"How have you been, Dominic? It's been a while since we've chatted. I can't help but think you've been avoiding me?"

"You mentioned the night at St. Mary's. What are you talking about, Brother Corwin?"

"What do you think I'm talking about?" asked Brother Corwin coyly.

Dominic stood up. "I don't have time for your bullshit," he said and walked toward the door.

"I'm talking about your alleged incident with your good friend Father Bumbry," sneered Brother Corwin.

Dominic spun around. "What do you know about that?"

"I know that you were at his rectory apartment, had been drinking, and passed out. And then there were allegations of…hmmm…let's say, questionable behavior."

"How do you know that?" snapped Dominic, his arms at his side and his fists clenched.

"Harry told me all about it. How he was out for a morning run and found you by the creek all jumbled up in a ball of tears." Brother Corwin flashed a Cheshire cat smile. "You want to have a seat?"

Dominic returned to the desk he had been sitting at. *Why in the hell would Harry ever tell Brother Corwin about that morning? What the fuck was Harry thinking?*

Brother Corwin could read Dominic's thoughts by the expression on the youth's face. He guessed Dominic did not realize that Brother Corwin had several "little brothers" and was always looking to add siblings to his extensive family.

"Let me cut to the chase, little brother, you need to seek out help—serious help. And soon. I would recommend immediately. You should already be in therapy."

Dominic's eyes grew wide. "What are you talking about?"

"I'm talking about you and your need for serious, intensive therapy. You need to have a full and comprehensive psychological evaluation completed, and then an intensive schedule of therapy sessions arranged. At least three times a week to start, depending on what your insurance coverage allows but I would strongly recommend the three sessions a week even if it costs your family out of pocket."

"What the hell are you talking about? Why would I need therapy?"

"Because of what you made up." Brother Corwin spoke with a sudden dead seriousness.

"Huh? About what?"

"About that night at St. Mary's and the false accusations you made against Father Bumbry."

Dominic couldn't believe his ears. He was incredulous. "Are you out of your fucking mind?"

"No, little brother, but you might be if you don't nip this in the bud. It's obvious you have repressed feelings and emotions about your sexual orientation, and it's going to take years of therapy to work them out. Your feelings surfaced in the dream you had, so much so that your subconscious experience actually convinced you that what you dreamed about had actually happened."

"It wasn't a dream," Dominic interjected with a reserved but fierce tone.

Brother Corwin held up his hand. "Permit me to finish. It most certainly was, and here's why. You have been repressing your sexual orientation—your *true sexual orientation*—for many years now but your subconscious couldn't contain it any longer. Then you had the sexual escapade with that Toomey girl that appeased your repressed guilt and anxiety about possibly being gay—which is the abominable sin due to your strict religious upbringing, courtesy of your mother. Not to mention the reaction you would get from your father—the Sicilian. Although your sexual tryst with the Toomey girl attempted to validate your heterosexuality, it failed. You didn't feel any emotional connection with her and the sexual experience didn't overcome your homosexual tendency. The girl goes and attempts suicide and where's the one place you run to? Yes, you seek solace and comfort in the arms of a man who, by all obvious indications, is gay. The setup is perfect—your religious repression notwithstanding. You find yourself in the ideal situation. Alone with someone you obviously trust, and have great affection for, and are able to finally make yourself vulnerable to—the alcohol helps to break down the inhibitions—and voila! Your fantasy almost comes true! But that's the problem—it's just a fantasy, just a dream. You wake up from your dream, it seems so real—because you want it to be real—but it's not. And worse yet, the alcohol had worn off and you're confronted with the guilt of your religious self. Even to dream such alleged sexual deviance is an abomination! Especially since you were such a willing and able participant and were enjoying the pleasure of it all. What would God think? What would your mother think? They would not approve at all, not at all. Oh, the shame of it all! And of course, add to the mix the attempted suicide by the Toomey girl—and the guilt you're feeling over your part in that little piece of drama—well, too much for the virtuous Dominic Manterra to bear. He needs a scapegoat. And he finds one in the unsuspecting Father Bumbry, who, despite his shortcomings, was only trying to be a good friend to you that night. And how you've repaid him for all his kindnesses to you. Don't know if you've heard, but poor Father Bumbry is no longer a member of the St. Mary's family. So, you see, little brother, you need help, and a lot of it. I felt a duty and an obligation to tell you this, as hard as it is for me to do so. It's only because I care about and want what's best you. Always have."

Brother Corwin sighed deeply. He didn't believe a word he had just said but understood the tremendous power of guilt and shame—invaluable tools in the manipulation of the religious and devout. This was going to be his triumphant moment, his crowning achievement. True, he despised Father Bumbry for getting first dibs at Dominic, even more so because Bumbry was a just a horn-dog and had no appreciation for the total package that Dominic was—but at least Bumbry's exploitation of the youth provided him with this opportunity. And of course, Moira Toomey–more a nuisance than a threat—had removed herself from the equation by her act of desperation, thank God. Brother Corwin laughed to himself. *Why thank Him? Thank me—I'm doing all the work to make this happen!*

Dominic had listened to the twisted reasoning and distorted logic— lies, really—of this self-serving demonic cur. He sat motionless, sullen and brooding. The sapling within had sprouted many branches that were incessantly poking in any and every direction. He was having none of this.

Dominic stood up. His neck, chest, arms, and legs seemed to fill up and bulge with the sap of the rage dwelling inside him. He appeared to tower over the crafty coward sitting before him. He addressed Brother Corwin in a cold, solemn, and deliberate manner:

"It was not a dream. It happened in real time, in real space, and in the flesh. And I had no part in it except that I was the unsuspecting and unwilling victim. I was violated and I was betrayed. Whatever happens to Bumbry, I will leave to God to deal with him, for I know it is a dreadful thing to fall into the hands of a righteous God, especially when you have sexually violated one of His children. And that is all I have to say about him. Now let me talk about you—yes, you, the manipulative Apostle of St. Mary's, the blind guide and the false teacher that you really are. You're not a servant of God—you don't even know who God is! In the times that we had spent together, the hours upon hours talking, you never, ever spoke about the prominence Jesus played in your life. In fact, your most solemn words and devout praise were reserved for Olivier and Sondheim! You barely could contain your contempt for the devotion I expressed to our Lord, at times even mocking me with your snide remarks! Even at your final vows' ceremony, your corrupt ways were on full display! That wasn't about your commitment to serving God—it was all about you! The music, the readings, the decorations—they were all set up to focus on you, and you alone! It was as if God should have been honored that the magnificent Brother Corwin was gracing Him with his presence! All the vanity in your soul seeped into your very heart as you praised and paid tribute to Brother William Corwin! You're not a devoted servant to God—you're a circus act! All of you screwed-up clergy who hide behind the cloth and the cross to hide your truly devious and disturbed minds! How you twist the truth and prey upon the hearts and minds and innocence of the youth who trust you and believe in you! And then proudly proclaim you do it in the name of the Order, in the name of religion, in the name of God! It's the ultimate mind-fuck! But the truth is it's an Order drenched in hypocrisy! And it's your own false religion, it's a god made in your image! It's a god that serves your purposes! You pointed to that crucifix and you blasphemed its purpose and meaning to serve your own depraved desires and impulses! It is to you false-hearted clergy that Jesus will say 'Depart from me, I never knew you!' But the next thing I am going to say—you need to listen carefully, and hear me clearly, and heed the warning seriously, you sick bastard. If I ever hear you mention my Moira's name ever again, in any manner or context, I will kill you. I mean it. I will kill you dead where you stand."

Brother Corwin leaned back in his seat, aghast. Dominic seemed to be twelve feet tall and seething with an anger and rage that told Brother Corwin it would be prudent to stay silent. Dominic turned and opened the classroom door. He went into the gymnasium, gathered up his things, and walked out. He exited through the glass doors adjacent to the gymnasium and headed for the bridge that extended over the creek that ran alongside the school. As Dominic crossed the parking lot in that direction, a voice called out.

"If you can keep your head when all about you..."

Dominic stopped and his eyes followed the familiar voice to its handsome, slim owner with slicked-back hair leaning against the station wagon. Dominic responded, "Are losing theirs and blaming it on you." Dominic started to walk toward his uncle.

"If you can trust yourself...." His uncle lit a cigarette.

"When all men doubt you..."

His uncle exhaled cigarette smoke while shaking the match out. "Or being lied about..."

"Don't deal in lies."

"If you can bear to hear the truth you've spoken..."

Dominic reached the spot where his uncle was parked. "Twisted by knaves to make a trap for fools..."

"A last one, my boy—or watch the things you gave your life to, broken..."

"And stoop, and build them up with worn-out tools!"

"Excellent! How goes it, Dominic, my boy?"

"How are you, uncle! It's been a long time."

"Too long at that. I'm impressed. You can only say you truly know something when you know it from every angle and over time. I was passing through, stopped at the house, visited with my sister for a while. Your brother Jason said I would find you here. Thought I'd wait and give you a ride back, catch up a little." Uncle Tony stuck out his hand and Dominic shook it.

As they drove back, Dominic's uncle gave him an update on what he had been doing since the last time they had seen each other. They had met on a regular basis over a course of six months after their initial encounter. They both had made good on their original deal: Dominic had memorized the Kipling poem and his uncle had awarded him with a crisp twenty-dollar bill. In that period, Dominic had learned quite a bit about and from his uncle. His uncle spoke several languages and traveled extensively. He had left for Europe after that first six months but had promised Dominic he would be back to see him one day.

"What brings you around, uncle? It's so good to see you."

"Well, my boy, I'm not going to mince words with you. Your mom had called me. Wanted to see if I could pay a visit. She was concerned about you. Real concerned. So of course I said I would, especially if there was something wrong…or should I say, if you needed my help. So here I am."

Dominic grew silent. He looked out the car window. He really didn't want to talk to anyone about anything anymore. He really just wanted to run away. He wanted to pack up his books, some clothes, and some music, and move away from everything and everyone. He just wanted to be left alone and be alone. He was deeply hurt by what Father Bumbry had done. He realized what an evil bastard Brother Corwin was. He was disappointed at his father for not protecting him. He was angry at his brother Sal for being so selfish. He couldn't help but blame himself for what had happened to Moira and didn't think he could ever forgive any persons involved, including himself. But most of all he was sad, so very, very sad, because he missed Moira and nothing else mattered to him.

"I'd rather not talk about anything, really," said Dominic finally.

Uncle Tony nodded. "I can see that. May I ask a question, though?"

"Sure."

"Of all the things that I have taught you, that you and I have discussed, what do you think are the two things that *I would say* were the most important to remember in life?"

"Two things that *you would say* were most important?" Dominic gave it some thought. He and his uncle had discussed many things. It was kind of hard for him to focus anyway, so he just thought he'd give up. "I don't know."

His uncle looked at his nephew. He had immediately seen the depth of sorrow in Dominic's eyes when he first greeted him. Although his nephew had his father's eyes, it was his mother's empathy that shone through them. And that reflection stirred the thought that Uncle Tony had only seen such sorrow once before in his life, and that was in his sister's eyes.

"One—the people to most fear in life, are those who believe there is no God or worship a god made in their own image. Two—you must always be wary of those who say they only have your best interest in mind. And when the two are combined, you have a true definition of evil."

Dominic heard his uncle and nodded his head in agreement. His uncle was so right.

DOMINIC FOUND HIMSELF STANDING between the two trees where Moira and he had parked that fateful night after the cast party. The one tree still bore the markings of the car's impact. He had already walked throughout Warnock Park for a couple of hours. It was no use. He couldn't locate the tree from their special night. All along the route near where Moira had entered the park that night, he searched but to no avail. It was as if the tree had never existed. Dejected, he decided to head home.

He cut over to Candlewood Avenue and began the trek up to Second Avenue that would lead right to his house. He had just about made it to Fourth Avenue when he heard a voice calling out to him. Dominic turned around and saw someone about a block away waving at him.

"Manterra! Hey, Manterra! Wait up a minute!"

Dominic waited for the approaching caller, whom he recognized immediately as Ronnie Wenkler. Dominic knew him from playing baseball in St. Mary's little league and from summer recreation.

Ronnie bent over to catch his breath. "Thanks for stopping."

"How's it going, Ronnie? It's been a while. How's your sister Kiley doing?" Dominic remembered Ronnie's younger sister as one of the prettiest and sweetest girls in town.

"She's good, Kiley's doing really well. I will tell her that you said hi. Hey listen, Dominic, I have been meaning to talk to you. It's extremely important to me. And I need you to be honest with me." Ronnie's tone was deadly serious and it appeared to Dominic that Ronnie was distressed.

"Sure, Ronnie, what's the question? You seem upset—is everything alright?"

"Dominic, I heard something…something…about what happened…"

"Happened? What do you mean, Ronnie?"

Ronnie paused for a moment his eyes fixed on Dominic's questioning expression.

"I heard about what happened with you and Father Bumbry. I have to ask you—is it true?"

Dominic immediately tensed up. Since the incident with Father Bumbry, he had been subject to subtle and not so subtle hostility from various teachers, students, parishioners, and members of the clergy. He found their comments and innuendos vicious and flawed. He had absorbed the attacks stoically, with quiet resolve, though they seem to feed his growing inner rage. But he had no patience for any such talk today.

"What did you hear and why are you asking me about it?" Dominic coldly asked.

"You know what I heard, Dominic. He sexually molested you. Is it true? Did it happen? I need to know."

Dominic studied Ronnie's face and in an instant, he saw it—there in Ronnie's eyes. It was unmistakable. Dominic clearly glimpsed the hurt in Ronnie's eyes—and recognized his own eyes' reflection.

"Yes, it did happen. Unfortunately, what you heard is true."

Ronnie's eyes filled with tears as a sob escaped from his throat that sounded like a burden being released from his very soul.

"Thank you, Dominic, thank you."

Dominic stammered, "Did he…did…"

"Yes, the same thing happened to me. When I reported it, no one believed me. They wouldn't believe me. They just insisted that it never happened. When I heard about you, I knew I had to talk to you about it. Especially if they were going to tell you the same thing."

"I'm glad you did. I believe you, Ronnie. No matter what the bastards told you, you and I know that it did happen. The hell with everyone else, I believe you and you need to believe in yourself and not believe their lies. And most importantly, you need to hear this, you need to know this—it wasn't your fault. You're not to blame. Not at all."

Ronnie began to weep and Dominic reached out and hugged him. "It's alright, everything's going to be alright."

The two chatted for a little while longer and then quietly bid each other well.

Dominic never saw him again.

MITCHELL AND DOMINIC SAT at a booth in the Rosedale Diner waiting for a waitress to take their order. Dominic flipped the song lists on the jukebox.

"Well, if it isn't my old friend, Dominic. How are you doing, honey? It's been a while."

Dominic turned his head to see the smiling face of the waitress. "Hello, Missy. How have you been?"

"Better now that I'm seeing you." Missy handed them both menus and turned to Mitchell. "Hi, how ya doing?"

"Hello, I'm Dominic's brother Mitchell. Glad to meet you."

"Dominic, you didn't tell me you had a good-looking brother for me!" Missy winked at Mitchell, who blushed and smiled back. "Let me get you some waters and I'll be right back to take your orders."

"What are you in the mood for, Dominic?" asked Mitchell, looking at the menu.

"I'll get pork roll and cheese on a bagel, I guess."

"That sounds good. But maybe I'll get it on a Kaiser roll instead."

The waitress returned with their waters. "Hey, Dominic, how's your little sweetie doing? Moira, right? She is quite the beauty. You two make a beautiful couple. I could tell that night how much in love you two were. How's she doing?"

Mitchell shot a glance at Dominic. Dominic hesitated and then swallowed hard. "That's very nice of you to remember Moira. You're right, she is very special. I'll be sure to tell her that you were asking for her."

"Do that! And bring her around." She took out her order pad. "OK, what'll you have?"

.   .   .

MITCHELL AND DOMINIC GOT into the car. Mitchell removed the wrapper from a toothpick and stuck it in his mouth. He started up the car.

"Hey, Mitch, do you have some time? Right now? Could we take a ride, not far?"

"Sure, Dominic. What do you have in mind?"

"Just over to Ridgeway River Park. I want to sit by the river. Not for long."

"OK, not a problem, bro."

As Mitchell drove over, worried thoughts rushed through his head. He had convinced Dominic to let him take him for breakfast. Although Mitchell wanted to go to a different diner, Dominic had insisted on the Rosedale. Mitchell had sat down with him earlier that morning to have a heart-to-heart talk. Mitchell had even taken the day off from work because he wasn't sure how Dominic would react. Mitchell had found out some news from a friend the night before, and Mitchell wanted to be sure that he was the one who told Dominic before he could hear it from someone else. The news was that Moira's family had basically disappeared. They were gone. The house was sold and the family had moved away. There was not much more news than that. Except to say there was little progress on Moira's condition but she was no longer at the medical center. They seemed to have left in the middle of the night without a trace and without any hint of where they went. Mitchell thought that Dominic took the news well—and that had Mitchell worried. What worried him now was the way Dominic had responded to the waitress in the diner.

Mitchell pulled into the parking lot and found a parking space.

"Mitch, I'm just going to walk over to the bench over there and sit for about ten minutes, by myself, if you don't mind?"

Mitchell looked at his brother and then glanced over at the river. The current was moving fast and the river was deep. Images flashed in his mind and he wondered if he had to, how quickly he could run to the water and how fast he could swim if Dominic was to...

"Don't worry, Mitch, I wouldn't do anything that stupid. And that wouldn't bring Moira back to me. If it would have brought her back to me, I would have dived in long before today."

Mitchell nodded his head. "OK, I'll wait here. Don't take too long. Maybe we can grab a movie later."

Dominic walked over to the bench and sat down. He looked around him, at the trees, the flowers, the shrubs, the birds, people walking around the river, some fishing off the river bank, others fishing from the bridge. He knew Moira would have loved this beautiful morning of late spring; summer was only a week away. He stared at the river in front of him, he could see the sky and the tree branches that stretched over it and birds flying by—all reflected in it. He glanced back at the car and saw Mitchell sitting up, straining his neck to see him. He could see the worried look on his brother's face. Dominic waved and smiled to reassure him he was alright. Mitchell smiled and waved and sat back down in the front seat.

Dominic folded his hands in front of him, bowed his head, and closed his eyes. He said a little prayer first. Then he spoke to Moira: *"I hope you can hear me. I know that if I believe hard enough you can hear me. Mitchell and I went to the diner this morning. I hadn't been back since we were there. The waitress Missy asked for you and told me to tell you hi, so hi from her. I miss you every day. I wish you were here with me. Sometimes, when I'm alone I feel like you are with me. I can hear your infectious laugh. I can smell your skin. I can feel your touch. I can taste you lips. I can see your eyes looking into mine the way we looked at each other that night. And I can see you push your hair back behind your ear and smile at me. I am so sorry, Moira, I hope you know that. I am so sorry. You were right about everything and everyone. I should have listened to you. If you could ever find it in your heart to forgive me—I know I don't deserve it, but if you could—and if you could ever come back to me, I promise you I will never ever let you down again, or leave you, or hurt you. Please, Moira, believe me. I love you, Moira. Always have and always will.*

Dominic lifted his head. The morning sun was reflecting off the water into his eyes. He looked across the river to the other side and thought he saw someone, a girl all alone, walking along the riverbank. She had a familiar look. She had long, auburn hair and was wearing a yellow horse-hair ribbon hat with a flower, like a bridesmaid wears, and she seemed to be gently swaying her hips; the breeze caught her hat and it dropped down in front of her; she bent over and picked it up. She held it in her hand as the wind swept her long hair across her face. She raised her hand up and pushed her hair behind her ear, smiling, looking back at him. Dominic immediately stood up and raised his hand by his eyes to block the sun's glare. He frantically searched the other side to see who it was.

There was no one there.

Dominic dropped back down to the bench. The words of Moira's poem filled his mind, and he softly recited the words to himself:

> Carve me out of wood—
> And I cannot withstand the flame
> For surely, I will burn into ashes;
> Carve me out of stone—
> and I will not endure the wind
> for surely, I will return to sand;
> Cast me in bronze,
> Cast me in iron,
> Cast me in silver,
> And it will be in vain
> For surely, I will not endure,
> The air and rain
> Will wither me away
> And I will tarnish and rust
> Until I am reduced to dust;
> But carve me out of your heart

And deny me your love
And I will cease to exist,
I will be a monument to non-existence

He bent over and buried his face in his hands.
Dominic wept.

Made in the USA
Middletown, DE
13 May 2021